SEEN AT LAST

J.T. TIERNEY

CURTISS STREET
PRESS

For all those still wanting to be seen

1

"Grace?"

That familiar voice slammed her chest. Grace's hand went to her hair—flattened, humidity-wrecked. The coffee stain across her sleeve caught the light.

She turned. Her therapist colleague, Allie Morgan—sweat-glossed, breathing hard—stood four feet away in the Whole Foods produce aisle. A damp white cotton tank clung to her torso; overhead lights glazed her collarbones like an artist had highlighted them.

This wasn't work-version Allie. This was ... well, Christ. She'd never seen this Allie.

Her pulse kicked hard. Her reflection flashed in the cooler's glass—rumpled, stained, wilted. *Holy shit.* She pushed a hand through her hair, achieving nothing.

"Allie. Hi. You're ... grocery shopping?"

"Cooling down. Just did two loops around Fresh Pond. Needed something besides another protein bar." Allie twisted the cap off her water bottle and tipped her head back, throat long and elegant as she drank. She rolled her shoulders. The damp cotton shifted. A bead of sweat traced down her neck, disappeared beneath the tank.

Grace's scalp prickled. She looked away.

"Jesus, Allie, you make forty look ridiculous. Meanwhile—" She gestured vaguely at herself. "—I look like I've been dragged behind a bus, more disheveled with each errand."

Allie laughed. "Let me guess. Soccer gear for Mia? School supplies for Matthew?"

"You nailed it. I still have to face the Target gauntlet." She consulted her shopping list. "And pick up shallots, baby spinach, chicken. I think my family deserves something that's not pasta again."

Allie reached into Grace's still nearly empty shopping cart. Her hand came out holding a knobby yellow root vegetable that she held out at arm's length. "What is this?"

"Celeriac," Grace said.

"That's not a real word."

"Absolutely is."

Allie turned it slowly, examining it from multiple angles. "It looks like a brain that gave up."

Grace laughed. "It's celery root. Julienne it, and it's terrific on greens. Crunchy, slightly earthy."

Allie set it back in the cart with great ceremony, then stepped close enough that Grace caught the faint, salt-sweet scent of sweat drying on warm skin.

A gleam appeared in Allie's eyes. "Forget the groceries for an hour. Come walk Fresh Pond with me instead. You look like you need air. But first, I challenge you to hunt down the weirdest-looking vegetable in here. Whoever finds the winner gets to choose the smoothie we buy on our way out." She was already moving to the end of the display. "You take that side."

Grace looked at her list. Then she folded it and put it in her pocket. Nearby, kids whined for popsicles, a couple argued over the best marinade. Labor Day weekend bodies rolled carts in loose, noisy currents.

They met up at the end of the aisle. Grace had found kohlrabi—pale green, sprouting antennae, deeply unsettling. She held it out.

Allie considered it seriously. "Strong contender." She held up her own find. Yellowish-green fractal spirals, piled in unearthly regularity.

Grace took it from her. "It looks like broccoli dreamed it was a coral reef. What the hell is this?"

"Sign says it's romanesco. The obvious winner. No contest. I'm sorry, kohlrabi."

"You found it. You get to choose the smoothie."

"I was always going to choose the smoothie."

"Good Lord. Your competitive streak is off the charts."

Through her pocket, her phone buzzed again—two long vibrations. A call, not a text. Michael. She reached toward the phone, then stopped herself. "Let's get out of here," she said.

Allie ordered something green. As they walked across the street to the Pond, the sunlight made Grace squint. Wind lifted the hair at her neck. When they hit the loop path, gravel crunched beneath their shoes. Each step came easier than the last.

Walking together was one of their favorite things, escaping when their offices felt suffocating or when one of them needed a boost. Reaching for each other—in search of a gentle lift, a sympathetic ear—had become instinctive for them, especially over the past year.

But this felt different. Far away from work, on a weekend. Allie here, in the wild.

"Gracie—"

Allie was the only one who ever called her that. And it always surprised her. Not the nickname, but the way her own name sounded on Allie's voice.

Grace looked over. Sunlight threaded through Allie's shiny chestnut hair; a fine sheen of sweat glistened along her shoulders. Grace's mouth went dry.

"You look exhausted. When's the last time you did something

just because you wanted to?" She nudged her with her elbow. "Tell me this: if you could hit pause on everything for a week, what would you do? No work, no family, nothing on the list. Just you."

"Oh god." Grace let out a short laugh. "I don't know who I am without all that. I'd probably spend the first few days screaming into the void."

Allie snorted.

Grace laughed, then had to swallow hard.

They followed the path as it curved toward the water, reeds swaying along the edge. The air smelled like warm mud and algae. Sweat dampened Grace's lower back. A child's shriek came from the playground in the distance.

"Why do you ask?"

"Just thinking about all you carry," Allie said. "How heavy it must get."

Grace threw her a quick glance, trying to read her.

"Yeah, well ... everybody's got their crap," Grace said lightly. "Mine's not the worst. And you've got plenty on your plate, too. Divorced mom of two isn't exactly easy."

"Most of the time, it's fine, if you want to know the truth."

Grace hesitated. "Can I ask you something?"

Allie nodded. "Always."

"Do you ever ... miss it?" Grace kept her eyes on the gravel. "Being married. Do you ever wish you still were?"

It was the kind of question Grace had wanted to ask for months —since last spring, maybe, when Allie had mentioned her anniversary date passing with barely a notice. But she hadn't asked and still wondered about it.

Allie took a long breath, letting it out slowly. "Not the marriage, but—"

Grace's phone buzzed again. This time, she pulled it out: Michael's name on the screen, a text preview: *Where are you?*

Matthew needs— She shoved the phone back in her pocket. "You were saying?"

"Sometimes I miss the inside jokes, all the shorthand stuff that comes with living alongside someone for years. Yeah. Sometimes I miss that." Sunlight caught the curve of her cheek, the curls damp at her temples. Grace's gaze lingered before she snapped it back to the path.

Allie's arm swung close enough that Grace felt the heat of her skin.

"I have to admit, Allie, I envy you. You get little pockets of time to be yourself. Not mother or therapist. Just you. I can't remember the last time I had that."

Geese bullied the shoreline like they owned it, hissing at a toddler with a juice box. The path turned and narrowed behind a cluster of birch trees. Sunlight dappled everything.

Allie slowed, turned. Her fingers hooked Grace's, a gentle squeeze. Grace let her hand stay. She matched Allie's pace, step for step, and didn't look down at their fingers. The warmth traveled up her arm. A jogger passed them, close enough that Grace heard his breathing, saw him glance at their hands. She didn't pull away. When he was gone, Allie's thumb grazed across her knuckles once, then released.

As they resumed walking, the conversation drifted to easier things: what time Allie's ex was dropping the kids tomorrow, the to-die-for cranberry-orange scone at Darwin's.

Their knuckles brushed from time to time. Grace didn't know if she'd moved closer, or if Allie had.

The parking lot appeared too soon, before she wanted. Sun glared off windshields. She slowed, unwilling to let the moment dissolve into the banality of asphalt and errands.

Allie touched her arm lightly, her fingers warm through cotton. "The milk and eggs can wait," she said, mouth quirking. "You should take the whole afternoon off. Go home. Read. Take a nap."

Not much chance of that, but even the respite of this walk had left Grace lighter than she'd felt all week. "Maybe," she said. "In any case, this was rejuvenating. Exactly what I needed. Thanks, Allie."

Something shifted in Allie's eyes. "I'm glad," she said, then waved as she headed toward her car. "Love ya!" She called out, but she'd stopped walking, turned fully to face Grace. "I mean it, Gracie. I'm glad we did this."

Grace's throat tightened at the deliberate way Allie had swiveled, held her gaze. Something in her tone—certain, knowing—made Grace's skin tingle.

"Me too," Grace managed.

Allie held her gaze for one beat longer than necessary, then smiled and turned away.

Grace reached the crosswalk and stepped off the curb. Life reasserted itself. The dry cleaners. What she needed for dinner. The endless loop.

"Grace!"

Footsteps approached quickly. A hand grabbed her forearm, tugging her back to the sidewalk. Allie. Cheeks flushed, breath quick and warm.

A car horn blared. Grace's head snapped toward the street. A sedan, braking hard, the driver's face contorted in anger.

"Jesus." Allie's grip tightened. "You walked right out."

Adrenaline surged through her. She'd been so lost in thought she'd nearly—

"Stupid. Wasn't paying attention."

"You okay?" Allie's hand was still on her arm, thumb pressed against her pulse point. Could she feel how hard Grace's heart was racing?

"Yeah. I'm—" Grace's eyes dropped to Allie's hand, then lifted. Their faces were inches apart. "Thank you."

Allie didn't let go. "I forgot to ask: are you free two Fridays from now, the 15th? I have season tickets to Speakeasy Stage. Opening show is that night. My plus-one bailed. Would you come with me?"

Friday nights for Grace usually meant collapsing on the couch with a novel. Quiet. Predictable. Conventional. She couldn't remember the last time she'd gone out simply because she wanted to.

Allie's eyes waited, open and sure. What could Allie be thinking, inviting Grace? Why not ask one of her lesbian friends? And yet, here she was—sun-flushed, breathless, impossibly attractive—looking at Grace like spending an evening together was something she genuinely wanted.

Grace wanted to be looked at like that. Not as wife or mother. As herself.

"I'd really love that," she said.

"Good." Allie smiled, one corner of her mouth lifting higher than the other. "It's a date."

The phone rang. Grace pulled it out, Michael's name lighting the screen.

Allie glanced at it, then back at Grace. "Probably should get that." Allie waggled her fingers in a goodbye.

"Yeah." Grace stared at the phone. Four missed calls. Three texts. "I should."

She answered the call. "Hey—"

Grace watched Allie walk toward her car.

Michael's voice. "Where the hell are you? I've been calling for an hour. Matthew's coach changed practice to today and I'm in the middle of—"

"I'm at Whole Foods. I'll be home in twenty minutes."

"Whole Foods? For an hour?"

She opened her mouth. Closed it. "They were out of the roasted organic chicken. I had to wait." The lie landed easily.

She made it to her car. The leather was hot against her thighs. She picked at a hangnail. When had she started that again? She tried to steady her breathing, but her ribs felt too small.

She'd tell Michael she was going out that Friday. With a friend from work. The lie was already smoothing itself into something plausible: *Just Allie. She had an extra ticket.*

She started the car. Her wedding ring caught the light.

They had a date.

2

———

Tuesday, September 5

The copier groaned, each page sliding out reluctantly. The air conditioner rattled and wheezed, losing its fight against the heavy, wet heat that seeped into everything. Outside the tall windows, the sky over Cambridge had slipped into darkness.

Most of the other therapists had gone home to their families a couple hours ago. Grace had seen little of them today. Outside the kitchen at lunchtime, she'd overheard Claire launch into an impromptu TED Talk on building a "proper CBT practice" and veered away just in time. That meant Grace hadn't met the new guy, Travis, who was taking over Sarah's old office. Leo told her later that Travis did chakra alignment and crystal healing. She and Leo traded eye rolls. Grace had nothing against crystals in principle. She just suspected they worked better on people who hadn't spent seventeen years listening to human beings describe what they actually did to each other.

She could be home by now, too, finishing notes on the couch, while Michael queued up another video about a surgical technique or, if he was relaxing, a gory documentary about medieval surgery.

The truth was simple. Hard. She didn't want to go home to Michael's indifferent questions, his perfunctory kiss to her forehead that had become a reflexive motion detached from feeling, his nightly inventory of their life: *We're out of blueberries. Did you call about Matthew's physical?*

There was another truth, too. She didn't even mind standing in this stifling copy room, performing this clerical task. She liked the building at this hour: the hush in the hallways, the relentless chug of the old AC, the way the light took on a smoother, warmer cast.

Mostly, she liked crossing paths with Allie at this time of night, when their interactions were unhurried, free of waiting-room noise or client schedules pressing in.

Whenever she got to see Allie, even in passing, the ground under her feet felt less slippery. Allie's presence had a way of shifting her into herself, as if someone had sharpened the focus.

Without meaning to, she'd been counting the days until their theater date. Just as she thought of Allie dozens of times throughout each day, even during her sessions. It didn't mean anything other than that Allie was easy to talk to. A collegial bright spot in a long day. Nothing more.

Still ...

Footsteps in the hall. Then a familiar voice drawled from the doorway. "You're stalling."

Grace looked up. Allie leaned against the doorframe, barefoot, holding two sweating glasses of iced chamomile, her signature summer drink. She'd started making it for both of them sometime in June. Showed up one sweltering evening with two glasses and a theory about cortisol regulation. The summer had passed that way— long twilights, the building emptying around them, conversations that stretched long past when streetlights came on outside.

Now, humidity frizzed Allie's hair at the temples, giving her a slightly wild edge.

"Sorry. What?" Grace asked.

"I heard you back here abusing the copier. Thought you might need reinforcement," Allie said, handing her a glass. "Everyone else left ages ago, Gracie. And here you are, acting like you need extra copies of that form tonight." A knowing look crossed her face. "When really, you're avoiding going home."

Cold cut through the glass as Grace took it from her. "Bold move, psychoanalyzing another therapist."

"I save it for special cases," Allie said, mouth curving. "Like colleagues who glare at office equipment after hours." She pushed away from the doorframe and hopped up onto the counter, bare heels kicking lightly against the cabinet.

Grace lifted a brow. "Pot, meet kettle. Who's wandering around the building barefoot at 7:45?"

"Touché," Allie said with a guilty laugh. She tilted her head, studying Grace with the unhurried attention she usually reserved for particularly interesting clients. "Do you know your eyes go more green when you're tired?"

"I wasn't aware you'd been cataloguing my eyes."

"I'm an inveterate cataloguer." Allie shrugged, unrepentant. "And that mouth of yours." She gestured vaguely. "The lips and all that—" another gesture— "and somehow it always looks like you're about to say something."

"That is a completely unhinged observation."

"It's an accurate one."

Grace startled herself with her own laugh.

"Rough day?" Allie asked.

The copier exhaled its last page. Grace squared the stack. "Had this couple today. Six months in, still grinding the same rut. He cheated with his CrossFit instructor—"

"Ooof."

"Yeah." Grace rolled her eyes. "Naturally, she's having a hard time forgiving. And both of them want me to magic them back to happy."

"And you give them tools."

"Active listening. Empathy exercises. They nod, repeat the phrases. But when they leave—"

"They look empty," Allie supplied.

"Exactly." She sipped the chamomile. Honey-sweet, mildly bitter at the edges.

"Sometimes people just need someone to say, 'Yes, this hurts. Of course it hurts. You're allowed to feel it.'"

Grace straightened, a line of protest forming. "Maybe so, but if I don't give them something to do, they look at me like I robbed them of their copay."

Allie's lips curved, not quite a smile. "Yeah. But sometimes the most therapeutic thing is just seeing someone."

This was their familiar rhythm. Volleying ideas back and forth over lunch or coffee breaks, gentle sparring over theory until both of them were smiling.

Lately, though, that rhythm came with an extra pull. Her gaze traced the graceful curve of Allie's neck, the strong, yet delicate hands as she lifted the glass. She made herself look away.

The air conditioner rattled again—a tired, metallic cough. Allie hopped down from the counter. Their shoulders were separated by less than a foot.

Allie leaned forward a fraction, voice lowering. "Maybe they just want someone who actually *sees* them. Not what they do or provide, but who they are." A beat. "Don't we all want that? To be noticed?"

"Yeah." She held Allie's gaze longer than the conversation required, then made herself turn back to the copier. "I mean, that need is probably what keeps therapists' appointment books full."

She reached up and released her hair from its clip, letting it fall to her shoulders.

Allie watched, looked at her mouth. For a couple seconds. Then her eyes cut away, color rising in her cheeks. "How do you still look like that at almost 8 PM?"

"Like what?"

"Like it's noon and you have a one o'clock with a board of directors."

"This is just how I dress."

Allie studied her with the air of someone examining a mildly baffling artifact. "You've been here since eight this morning. It's ninety degrees. And not a wrinkle. You do it on purpose."

"What do I do on purpose?"

"The *not*-wrinkling." Allie set down her glass. "All of it. The whole—" she waved a hand at Grace. "You work very hard to look like you're not working at it."

"That is an insane thing to say about a person."

Allie smiled. "There are things in your closet you love, aren't there? Things you almost never let out because they might wrinkle."

"I have no idea what you're talking about."

"Sure you don't."

Grace looked back at the copier. "I should head home." Her voice said it. Her feet stayed where they were.

"'Should,'" Allie repeated, one eyebrow lifting. "That word usually means someone else wrote the rulebook."

Grace looked down.

"You planning another long work night tomorrow?" Allie asked.

"What?"

"This whole staying-after-hours thing. You're killing time before going home." She gave a half-shrug.

Heat prickled up Grace's neck. "That's not— I mean—" The excuse died in her throat because what could she say?

Allie had been tracking. Of course she had. The same way Grace knew if Allie was still there late, the same way she'd started scheduling her last client at six instead of five. They'd been circling each other like this since—when? Spring? That night in May when they'd both worked until nine and ended up sharing takeout in Allie's office, talking until midnight about everything except work?

"Three nights this week. Last Wednesday and Thursday, too." Allie's gaze held steady. She reached out and squeezed Grace's forearm. "When's the last time Michael noticed something about you and commented? Not some errand you ran for him or something you did for the kids. About you."

Grace opened her mouth. Closed it. The answer should have come easily. It didn't.

"That long, huh?" Allie said.

Grace looked away. "We're both busy. The kids, work—"

"Grace." Just her name. No judgment or pity. Acknowledgment.

The air conditioner clattered on, filling the silence. Her breath seized. When had anyone last noticed her patterns? Her needs?

Allie stepped back toward the doorway, giving her space. "Try not to work yourself into the ground, okay?" She rested a hand briefly on the doorframe. "See you tomorrow, Gracie."

Her silhouette slipped into the dim hall, footsteps fading toward her office.

Grace stood a moment longer in the empty copy room, the glass sweating in her hand. She should leave. Right now. Before she did something stupid like knock on Allie's door.

She forced herself toward her own office instead. She gathered her tote, her purse, a file she didn't need to bring home. She shut off the light and walked down the hallway, the old floorboards creaking under her weight.

Outside, the air was thicker than it had been in the copy room. Dense, late-summer heat pressed low over the city. Her blouse clung to her back. She crossed the parking lot, unlocked her car, and sank into the driver's seat.

She reached back and peeled the fabric away from her skin. Checked her reflection in the rearview mirror. Not wrinkled.

God.

Cambridge streets blurred into Belmont's quieter ones as she drove. But her thoughts never left the building. Allie on the counter, bare feet swinging. Seeing Grace.

At a red light, her phone buzzed on the console.

A text from Michael: *Kids and I ate. Leftovers in fridge.*

That was all. No *You okay?* No *Drive safely.* No anything.

Grace remembered their third date. Michael had asked about her dissertation, actually listened to her fumbling explanation of attachment theory, then asked three follow-up questions that proved he'd been paying attention. She'd felt seen in a way that was new, almost intoxicating. When had he stopped asking questions?

Allie's words floated back: "All any of us wants is to be noticed."

She drove the rest of the way home with the windows cracked, letting in the warm air. At a stoplight on Concord Avenue, she caught herself smiling for no reason she could name. The light turned green. She pressed the gas, and the smile faded. Her family's insistent needs and wants were sixteen minutes away.

3

———

When she reached home, Grace sat motionless in the driveway, listening to the Honda's engine tick itself quiet. Warm yellow light filled the kitchen window. Above it, Mia's bedroom window flashed the cold blue pulse of a phone screen. The whole tableau almost inviting.

Her last session of the day clung to her like smoke. "I need to understand why," the wife had said, voice cracking. "Why hurt me, why risk our marriage and the kids ... for *her?*"

Across the couch, the husband had stared into space. "I don't know. I just don't know."

Six months of therapy. The same conversation.

Grace had offered them two questions: *How do you show appreciation for each other?* And *Do you let yourselves want things? Ask for more?*

She started to form her own answers to those questions when the porch light blinked off and on, a twelve-year-old boy's insistent signal: *get in here already.*

The air outside the car smelled of cut grass and charcoal. Her feet found the old paving stones she and Michael had laid during the first summer they owned the house, when sharing garden chores was still fun, like courtship. Near the fence, the hostas she'd planted three Mother's Days ago curled yellow at the edges.

She'd barely set down her bag before Matthew barreled into the mudroom.

"The lunch you made me was gross. And did you sign my permission slip?"

"Hello to you, too." She ruffled his hair. She dug into her purse and pulled out the slip. She'd signed it that morning but forgotten to move it to his backpack in the chaos of getting everyone out the door. "Here. And next time, maybe say hello before you start with the complaints."

Matthew squinted at her signature, as if checking for forgery. "Sorry. Hi, Mom."

"Seventh grade busting your chops? Anything interesting today?"

"We're reviewing ratios. So stupid. We spent so long on them last year."

"A little review won't kill you." She kissed the top of his head, breathed in his boy-smell. Shampoo and something like dirt. "If you have more homework, go finish it. I'll be in later to say goodnight."

"Okay." He padded back toward the living room, leaving the entryway strangely still.

Grace kicked off her shoes and straightened them by the wall, wrangling Mia's and Matthew's into line, too.

In the kitchen, Michael jabbed impatiently at the dishwasher settings. The familiar scent of hospital disinfectant soap drifted from him as he latched the machine's door and started it.

He looked up. "Hey. Did you remember the dry cleaning?" His shoulders slumped, jaw tight with fatigue.

She stooped to grab Matthew's balled socks from the floor. "Forgot. Sorry. I'll get it tomorrow." Onto the mental list it went. She leaned on the counter. "Your day good?"

"Okay."

Grace waited for him to ask about her day. He reached for his water glass instead.

"I had something happen today," she tried. "A couple I've been seeing for months—"

"Did you pick up my prescription?" He leaned against the opposite counter, drying his hands on a kitchen towel.

The story about her clients died in her throat. "Not yet. I'll get it with the dry cleaning tomorrow."

He nodded.

She made herself probe, feign interest. "What was the best part of your day?"

"Telling that idiot Hendricks the new technique he's pushing is premature." He gestured at a surgical journal splayed on the counter beside her hand. "I need to get caught up on the literature."

He brushed behind her to grab the journal, fingertips touching her shoulder. Once that touch had meant something. The heat of Allie's hand on her forearm earlier that night had penetrated the cotton—and stayed.

He started out of the room, then paused, turned back. "How was yours? Your day?"

Relief bloomed in her chest. "Actually kind of interesting. I'm working with this couple—"

His phone rang. He pulled it from his pocket, frowned at the screen. "Sorry. It's Hendricks. This'll only take a second." He pressed the phone to his ear. "Yeah, I saw your email ..." He drifted toward his study, voice fading.

Grace stood in the kitchen, her half-started story hanging in the air like smoke. The kitchen gleamed from their last renovation. Quartz countertops, pendant lighting. It was beautiful and orderly, like the rest of their home.

She climbed the stairs to check on Mia, past the gallery wall of family photos with everybody smiling.

Music threaded from under Mia's closed door. Grace knocked gently. After a pause: "Yeah?"

"It's me. Can I come in?"

Another pause. "Yep."

Grace pushed the door open. Mia lay stretched across rumpled sheets, one hand clutching her phone, the other absently twisting a strand of hair. Textbooks and loose papers created islands around her. The lamplight caught the new angles of Mia's cheekbones, the way her T-shirt pulled differently than it had in June. Her eyes met Grace's for only a moment before sliding away.

"How'd your day go?" Grace sat at the edge of the bed, careful not to disturb the scattered homework.

"Fine." Mia's all-purpose answer.

"Anything surprising?"

Mia considered. "Chloe looks different this year." She picked at a frayed seam in her comforter.

"Yeah? Did she shorten her hair?"

"No, just looks ... older." Color rose in her cheeks. "She's in Chem and English with me. We've been texting about homework and stuff."

"That's good. Always helps to have a friend in your classes."

"Yeah ..." Mia's focus drifted, then zeroed in on Grace's temple. She reached out, separating strands. "You have two—wait, no, three—silver hairs."

Grace rolled her eyes. "Mm-hmm. My hair and I have been through some things. Be nice."

Mia smirked, then retreated, her attention snapping back to her phone. "I should finish. The Chem teacher is trying to show she's a hard-ass by giving us a quiz in week two."

"Okay. I'm around." No point adding, *If you want to talk.* The door was already closing.

"I know. Thanks, Mom."

By the time Grace came to bed, Michael was propped against pillows, iPad leaning against his raised knees. The white-blue glow lit his face in a way that made his features older, sharper.

He gave her a small, corridor-colleague sort of acknowledgment. "Why the late night?"

Grace gathered her pajamas. "Six-thirty appointment. Then some paperwork. Sorry."

"No need to apologize. Just that these late nights are starting to take a toll."

On you, Grace thought. The late nights took a toll on him. He'd noticed her pattern, but only because it inconvenienced his routine.

In the bathroom, she slipped into her pajamas, ran a washcloth over her face, and mechanically brushed her teeth. Her gaze in the mirror was drawn to the silver threads Mia had pointed to amidst the auburn—more of those every year, and she'd stopped fighting it, though she couldn't remember deciding to. She saw her father's balanced, slightly rounded forehead, her mother's strong jaw. And the mouth that was all her own. She leaned in closer. What was it Allie had said about her mouth? And her eyes? How did she even notice the color with all those fine lines radiating from their edges?

She slid under the covers and lay on her side, facing Michael. The iPad rose and fell with each cycle of his breathing.

"What a long day," she said, trying to create an opening.

"Mm-hmm." He didn't look up from whatever article he was reading. "You okay?"

"I— yeah. I guess I wanted to talk a little. I miss us," she said before she could swallow it back.

He gave a vague nod without looking up.

"I've just been feeling ... off," she added.

This time he did look. "You should get your thyroid checked.

Fatigue like that usually points to something hormonal." His thumb scrolled. "I can send you Morrison's info."

She waited for him to ask what she meant by *off.* By *missing us.*

He didn't.

"I didn't mean medically."

He glanced up. "Then what do you mean?"

She searched his face for genuine curiosity. Found only polite attention, the expression he probably used with surgical-supply reps.

She wanted to say: I mean I don't recognize my life. Instead, she said, "I mean us. The way we ..." She gestured between them, the space in the bed that felt wider than physics allowed. "We don't talk anymore. Not about anything that matters."

"We're talking now." He glanced at his iPad screen.

"Are we?"

He sighed. Not angry, just tired. "Grace, I don't know what you want from me. I'm here. I work. I come home. What else is there?"

"Forget it. Finish your reading."

"I should. It's a lot of data."

"I know."

Grace stared at the ceiling. For a moment, she'd thought she might reach him. But he'd already turned away. She twisted to her other side and pulled the comforter up to her chin.

Twenty minutes later, he set the iPad on his nightstand and turned out the light. The darkness dropped fast, swallowing every-thing. He rolled to his side, patted her hip once, and adjusted his pillow with the large exhale he always made before sleep. His back a solid wall.

When his breathing steadied in a slow rhythm, she slipped from bed and went downstairs.

She made a cup of tea and sat at the counter. The kitchen looked exactly as it should. Keys in the blue bowl, basket of mail waiting, whiteboard calendar full of careful notes.

"Do you let yourself want things?"

She went to the calendar and circled Friday the 15th in red.

4

Thursday morning, Grace measured loose-leaf tea in the kitchen of the old blue Victorian that housed five therapists' offices. The structure had its own tired charm: sloping floors, chipped paint on windows, wiring that buzzed when you ran the kettle and toaster at the same time. Someone had converted it into therapists' offices decades ago with good intentions and terrible execution. None of the walls were truly soundproof, so during work hours the place hummed with an orchestra of white-noise machines, each therapist's defense against the building's determination to broadcast everyone's secrets.

The kettle rattled on its base; steam curled from the spout. Footsteps approached. Brisk, confident, nothing like a client's hesitant shuffle.

A man in his mid-thirties suddenly filled the doorway. Tall, tan, a hemp blazer over a T-shirt that read YOUR LIMITING BELIEFS

ARE BORING ME. His dark hair was pulled into a strategic man-bun.

He thrust out his hand. "Travis Sinclair. Taking over Sarah Clarke's old office." His eyes swept over her. "You must be Grace Brennan. Nice to meet you."

His handshake compressed her knuckles. Grace worked her hand free. "That's me. Welcome to our little Victorian asylum."

Claire Cummings materialized in the opposite doorframe, her iced coffee held like a shield between herself and Travis. Leo Kramer loomed a half step behind Claire, his expression neutral but watchful.

"He's still here, I see," Claire muttered over her shoulder to Leo, not bothering to lower her voice. "Apparently my lecture on proper therapeutic practice wasn't deterrent enough," she said.

Travis grinned back, unfazed.

Leo inclined his head toward Travis. "The thermostat is communal property in theory only," he said. "It has very specific settings that shouldn't be fiddled with. Remember that, and we'll get along fine." At that, he turned to leave.

Grace's eyes followed his retreat down the hallway. She turned back to Travis, arranging her face into professionalism with a hint of warmth.

"What's your focus, Travis?"

"Post-traumatic growth," he said. "Helping people alchemize pain into strength." He tapped his sternum. "Phoenix rising from the ashes."

Claire's mouth flattened. "Oh, good Lord," she said. She gave Grace a curt nod, pivoted sharply, and marched back to her office.

Grace offered Travis an apologetic smile. "Don't mind her. Claire can be tough on people who have approaches different from her own."

"Hey, it's fine. Nothing I haven't dealt with before," Travis said, leaning against the counter. "Some therapists diagnose the wound; I focus on the healing. When people fall apart, they're actually falling into something better."

"The field certainly has room for different philosophies," she said, lifting her mug as a toast.

He smiled. "Agreed."

The door swung inward, and Allie stumbled through it. Hair loose, blouse untucked, skin under her eyes dark, the color of plums. "God, what a morning."

"Excuse us, Travis," Grace said. Her hand found Allie's elbow. "Come with me," she murmured. She guided Allie past Travis and out of the kitchen, not stopping until her office door clicked shut behind them.

Allie sagged against the wall, one hand bracing herself. Grace gently pushed hair away from her face.

"What happened?"

"Mark was supposed to have the kids until tonight," Allie said, words tumbling fast. "Then at seven this morning he shows up, dumps them on my porch. 'Work crisis. You can get them to school, right?'"

Grace frowned. "He didn't call first?"

"Why bother? We all know wives exist for childcare emergencies. Even ex-ones, apparently." Allie laughed once. Short, brittle. "So I'm standing there in my ratty sleep shirt, trying to conjure breakfast, when Noah mentions he has a volcano project due today. And Emma's crying because she left her special new shirt at Mark's. On picture day."

"Oh God, not picture day."

"Yeah." Allie whooshed her hand over her head. "Completely off my radar since they were at Mark's. Anyway, I threw together the volcano poster while texting apologies to my first client."

"They made it to school sort of on time?"

"Twenty minutes late." Allie's mouth twisted. "And that fucking school secretary at the front desk, lips all pursed, sliding tardy slips across the counter with her perfectly manicured fingers, giving me that pitying 'oh honey, you're clearly the incompetent parent' look."

"And Mark couldn't take them because ...?"

Allie made air quotes. "'Urgent merger' requiring his 'immediate attention.' Heaven forbid the world's most important financial analyst take his kids to school while I, who merely help people rebuild their lives, handle my schedule."

Grace's eyebrows lifted. "Did you remind him you had clients?"

"I tried. But when Mark's work is on the line, his situational hearing loss kicks in." Her fingers curled into a fist. "He actually patted my shoulder and said, 'You'll figure it out. You always do.'"

Grace ground her teeth. "God, what an a—" She stopped herself. "I'm sorry he did that."

Allie nodded. "Me, too. ... You know, Mark's fine most of the time. And the kids adore him. But sometimes ..." She trailed off, then paused, collecting her thoughts. "You know what kills me?" Allie's voice wavered. "I rearranged my entire morning for him. And then on the way to school, Noah asks why I'm mad." Her voice sharpened into mock innocence. "'Dad doesn't get mad about this stuff.'"

"Kids don't see the whole picture."

"I know that." Allie scrubbed her eyes with her sleeve. "But at eight-forty in the morning, when you're patching together everyone else's mess, rational thought is ... limited."

Grace stepped closer. Her fingers wrapped around Allie's forearm. Warmth beneath the fabric. "You handled it. You did what needed doing."

Allie exhaled, shoulders dropping. "I practically bit their heads off the entire drive to school. Some mother I am." Her eyes welled.

Grace held Allie's gaze. "Hey. You didn't fall apart. You handled Mark's mess." She stepped forward and opened her arms.

Allie stepped into them slowly, then fully, face against Grace's neck, breath beginning to steady. Grace caught the scent of Allie's shampoo, something citrus and clean. The weight of her, the warmth. Grace's hands spread across her back.

They'd hugged before—brief embraces at holiday parties, reuniting after vacations. But this was different. This was Allie's full weight against her, Allie's breath on her neck. This was the kind of holding that Grace used to do with Michael, years ago, when comfort still moved between them.

A half minute passed. Maybe longer.

Footsteps in the hallway. Heavy, deliberate. Travis's voice: "Grace, your nine-thirty is—"

Grace pulled back from the hug. She opened the door. Travis was right there. His eyes flicked from Grace to Allie, taking in Allie's disheveled state, the closed office door.

"Early," Grace finished. "I'll be right out."

Travis's expression didn't change, but something shifted behind his eyes. "Take your time." He pulled the door closed.

Allie exhaled shakily. "That probably looked—"

"He knows you had a rough morning," Grace said quickly.

Allie glanced at the clock, then looked at Grace for a moment—really looked, in that way she had—then let out a breath that was almost a laugh. "You've been holding someone who's been crying for five minutes and you still look like that."

"Like what."

"You know like what." Allie shook her head. "It's genuinely unreasonable."

Grace said nothing. But she didn't look away.

Allie smoothed her blouse. "I should make myself presentable. My ten o'clock will be here soon." She huffed out a laugh. "Another straight woman begging me to save her marriage. Fuck my life."

Grace laughed with her.

"Take your time. And Allie?" Grace caught her arm gently, her fingers wrapping around Allie's wrist. "Next time Mark pulls shit like this, don't rearrange your entire schedule to accommodate him. Let him figure out how to handle his emergency and his parenting responsibilities at the same time."

"Funny. That's exactly the advice I'd give a client in my situation." Allie managed a small smile, some light returning to her eyes. "Thanks for listening, Gracie. And for not telling me this is all part of my healing journey or whatever nonsense Travis would trot out."

Grace grinned. "He'd recommend *sacred rage*. And in this case, I'd agree with him. Female anger is the appropriate response."

Allie's fingers found Grace's, squeezed. Then she left, footsteps fading up the stairs.

Grace stood alone in her office, hands still warm from Allie's back.

Last month she'd asked Michael to pick up Matthew from practice so she could have a drink with Steph at the end of the day. He'd sighed like she'd requested he donate a kidney. "Can't you go next week?" He'd asked.

She'd canceled.

5

Friday, September 8

At 8:40 AM on Friday, Grace stood at her office window, coffee cooling in her hand.

Travis's voice ricocheted down the hallway. "You all need to see this!" He jangled keys like he'd just robbed a medieval castle.

Within seconds, offices and the kitchen emptied, everyone except Claire. Grace followed Allie and Leo to what had once been Sarah Clarke's office.

Travis stood beaming beside a tall bookshelf he'd dragged away from the wall. He gestured dramatically toward a slender door the case had concealed until now.

"I was rearranging the furniture," he said, eyes bright with discovery, "trying to make better use of the space, and boom. Hidden door."

Grace stepped closer, fingertips grazing the solid door's wood frame. Someone had painted it the same forgettable cream as the surrounding wall. Even the molding had been disguised. The brass handle looked original to the house. Solid, tarnished, with a keyhole better suited to a Victorian parlor than a therapist's office.

"None of my keys fit," Travis said, jiggling his oversized ring. "This needs a Victorian skeleton key or something."

Leo blew across the top of his tea, taking in the keyhole with narrowed eyes. "Strange that Sarah never mentioned this." He took a thoughtful sip. "Then again ... she was a sphinx. Twelve years in the next office, and I can think of maybe four real conversations."

Sarah Clarke: silver hair, cardigans in all weather, voice barely escaping her throat. In her later years, Sarah had shifted her practice to grief-counseling, scheduling mostly elderly clients in afternoon slots. A loner, she declined communal lunches with a polite but firm shake of her head.

"Probably, it's just storage. Tax records, stuff like that." Travis sighed. He clapped his hands once. "I'll get the landlord to send a locksmith." His eyes widened. "What if there's something spooky in there?"

Leo stirred his tea. "Let's proceed in order: locksmith, then ghostbuster, then exorcist. Ideally, we skip steps two and three."

Travis pressed a palm to his chest. "If I die mysteriously, I want my obituary to read: 'Beloved therapist, victim of haunted Victorian closet.'"

Leo's mouth twitched, his closest approximation of amusement. "I'll write your obit myself."

Grace's laugh burst out, sudden and loud—the kind of hoot that surprised even her. She pressed her fingers to her mouth.

Allie turned, caught her eye, and leaned in just slightly. "There it is," she murmured. "The honk."

"Stop," Grace said under her breath.

Allie's mouth curved. She said nothing else.

Grace lingered as Allie and the others drifted back toward their offices.

Her hand traced the seam of the door. A hidden space in the room where Sarah had spent decades coaxing secrets from people who'd kept them hidden. What would a woman like Sarah hide?

Back in her office, Grace checked her phone before her next client arrived. A text from her mother, sent two hours ago: *Still dizzy. But don't fuss.*

Grace texted back: *Please call Dr. Morrison. Do it for me.*

She knew her mother wouldn't.

That afternoon, Grace sat across from a young woman perched on the edge of the couch, hands clasped so tightly her knuckles blanched white.

"What brings you here today?" Grace asked, glancing at the intake form: Jessica Caldwell. Twenty-five. MIT chemistry grad student.

Jessica blinked at the question, as if she hadn't expected to be asked anything so directly. The clock ticked five seconds, then ten.

Grace offered a small, encouraging smile. "No rush."

A dust mote drifted through a beam of September sunlight between them.

"I don't know how to start," Jessica whispered.

"Start wherever feels right." Grace settled back in her chair, creating space.

Jessica drew a shaky breath. "My boyfriend, Nick—we've been together since junior year. He's ... perfect. Brilliant. Thoughtful. The kind of guy everyone says you should want." She looked down at her fingers. "My mother practically has our wedding planned."

A long pause.

Grace waited. When Jessica seemed unable to continue, Grace prodded. "Is that not what you want?"

Jessica's gaze flickered up. "There's someone at my lab. Cathryn." Her voice dropped. "When she walks in, I forget what I'm doing."

Jessica's cheeks bloomed with color that spread down her neck. "I count the days until I can see her again. I know how it sounds, but I've rearranged my schedule just to be in the lab when she's there. Last week—" She paused, eyes bright. "We had to clean the evaporator together. The chemicals smelled like rotten eggs, and I made some stupid joke. She laughed and touched my arm, just for a second. I've replayed that moment a hundred times." Jessica glowed as she said it, lit from within by the thought.

A memory flickered. Hannah's face only inches from hers, both of them breathless. Just messing around.

Then Jessica's smile crumbled. She looked down at her hands. "Last night I couldn't sleep. I kept seeing her face. The way her hair falls across her forehead when she leans over a microscope." She paused, then murmured, "I imagined brushing it back."

Grace asked, "What makes that difficult for you?"

"I've never—" Jessica pressed her fingertips against her lips. "I've only had boyfriends. Four of them since high school. I'm not into girls."

"So this is ... raising questions?"

"Yeah." She turned a silver ring on her index finger. "I mean ... I'm not wondering if I'm queer. At least, well, not most of the time. If I liked guys before, I wouldn't suddenly be into girls, right? But if what I feel about Cathryn is real, then what was I doing all those years?" Tears welled. "Nick keeps asking what's wrong. I keep saying *nothing*. But I feel like I'm lying to him every day. How do I tell him I might not be who he thinks I am?"

"There were a couple questions there. First of all, understand that sexuality is more fluid than most people realize. So, your attraction to Cathryn—to girls—is totally credible. Second, you don't have to have yourself figured out before you're honest with Nick about having feelings for Cathryn," Grace said. "Sometimes the honesty is: *I don't know what this means yet, but I need to find out.*"

Jessica looked up. "But what if I'm wrong? What if I hurt him and it turns out this was just … confusion?"

"Then you'll have hurt him by being honest about your confusion. That's different from hurting him by keeping this from him." Grace leaned forward. "You can't protect him from your uncertainty. But you can protect both of you from the fallout of how you might hurt him by keeping this inside."

Jessica wiped her eyes with her sleeve, suddenly looking about nineteen. "Yeah. Right now, I feel like I'm lying to everyone. To Nick. To myself. And I don't know what any of it means."

"When you talk about Cathryn," Grace said, "your whole expression changes. What happens inside you when you're with her?"

Jessica's voice warmed. "I feel … visible. Like I've been underwater and suddenly broke the surface. When I'm around her, even stupid things feel interesting, like cleaning that evaporator or organizing pipettes. Apparently, I hum when I'm concentrating. I never even knew that until she pointed it out." She paused. "When I'm with her, I feel like the person I want to be. It's a little terrifying, but I feel awake. Alive."

"And with Nick?"

Jessica's shoulders slumped. "Safe. Comfortable. Predictable. The path my mother wants for me."

Grace nodded. The words settled somewhere in her chest and stayed there.

"What if I'm wrong about myself?" Jessica asked.

"You don't have to resolve this overnight. It sounds like it's too soon to tell Nick you think you may be queer. Understanding yourself comes first."

Jessica breathed out. "So … I take my time."

"Yes. Think about what draws you to Cathryn. Writing about it sometimes works well for processing. See if there were moments in your past you dismissed. And spend time with her. Coffee, a walk, something low-stakes. When you're with her, pay attention to what comes alive in you, what quiets down. You're gathering information."

Jessica shifted. "Do you think I should talk to Cathryn? Tell her how I'm feeling?"

"That's something to consider carefully. May be better to think about what you need to understand about yourself first, before bringing her into it." She rested her elbows on her knees. "You're still sorting yourself out."

Jessica nodded, shoulders loosening. "Yeah."

For the rest of the session, they worked through practical steps: how Jessica might give herself space, how to talk with Nick, if and when she was ready. Grace watched tension lift from Jessica's posture bit by bit, replaced by something like cautious hope.

When their fifty minutes ended, Jessica paused at the door. "Thank you. You helped me feel less broken."

Grace offered a small, warm smile. "Nobody has it all figured out. We're all just learning as we go."

Jessica let out a breath.

"And when you know yourself better," Grace said, "you get more room to move. To shift things. To choose what fits. So, keep paying attention to what feels true for you."

Jessica nodded, eyes shining, and left.

Alone again, Grace moved to her desk. The September light had shifted, shadows lengthening across the floor. She looked at her notes: *Recognition*, circled twice. Jessica had lit up describing how Cathryn made her feel: alive, seen, like her best self.

She had one more couple to see. But for now, she stood at the window, watching Cambridge move below. She pressed her forehead to the glass.

Her phone sat on the desk. She could text Allie. Something casual.

She moved toward it, stopped.

Understand yourself before bringing her into it.

She'd just given Jessica that advice.

Her phone stayed where it was.

6

Monday, September 11

Monday morning, every therapist but Claire gathered in Travis's office to witness the Great Closet Opening.

The locksmith crouched by the narrow, once-hidden door, his tools clicking as he worked the old brass lock. Picks and tension wrench moved with patient precision.

Grace stood near the window, pretending to study the maple leaves outside. But she kept glancing toward the tiny movements of the locksmith's hands. Leo leaned in the doorway, arms folded. Allie stood next to him, shoulder almost brushing his.

"Got it," the locksmith said at last.

The lock gave with a metallic sigh. The door swung outward on creaking hinges.

Everyone leaned in.

The space behind it was small. A shallow closet, barely deeper than an arm's reach. Gray horsehair plaster walls from the house's original bones. From a hook, a blue cardigan dangled in its dry-cleaning plastic, ticket stapled crookedly near the top. On the floor: a plastic bag stuffed with paper decorations: crumpled Halloween pumpkins, faded Christmas garlands, all brittle with time.

And on the shelf, a wooden box with a tiny brass clasp. On the lid, block letters in black marker: SARAH C.

Travis blinked twice. "Seriously? That's it? No skeleton? No case files of doom?"

"Just some old storage," the locksmith said, already packing his tools.

"Stuff she shut away and forgot about," Allie murmured, then turned to leave.

Grace's gaze followed Allie's retreating back. "We shouldn't just toss the box," she said, nodding toward the shelf. "We don't know what's in it."

Leo studied the label. "Sarah had a sister. I'll ask Claire if she still has contact info. We'll see if the family wants it."

The locksmith shut his kit with a click. The door, now open, had revealed its ordinary secrets. The house seemed to exhale.

Grace wandered back to her own office. Its two neutral chairs angled toward each other at the precise forty-five degrees she'd read was optimal for client comfort. The unobtrusive print above the desk—a coastal scene, blues and grays, chosen because nothing in it could mean anything to anyone. A box of tissues on the side table in a cover meant to make them invisible. She'd made the room into a container. Useful, featureless, designed to hold other people's things.

It was nearly eight that night when Grace wandered back to the communal kitchen to make tea.

The old Victorian had emptied hours earlier. Leo had left at precisely five-thirty, as always. Claire had drifted out around six with a distracted wave. Travis had bounced off at seven, humming some pop anthem as he went.

Now the September heat clung to the house, trapped in the old wood and plaster. The air conditioner had given up. Night pressed against the dark windowpanes.

Grace stopped short at the kitchen doorway. Allie stood at the counter, spooning vanilla ice cream into two ceramic bowls. A jar of chocolate sauce waited open beside them, lid abandoned.

A floorboard creaked under Grace's foot. Allie turned, a strand of chestnut hair slipping loose and falling across her cheek.

"Good. You're still here." Allie held up the chocolate sauce. "I was afraid you'd sneak out before I could corrupt you."

"You've been trying to corrupt me for years."

"And I've made so little progress." Allie shook her head mournfully and scooped generous mounds of ice cream into the bowls. "The woman who eats half a granola bar for lunch and calls it fine."

"I had a full lunch."

"You had twelve almonds and an optimistic attitude." Allie began a slow drizzle of chocolate over each bowl. As she poured, her eyes lifted to meet Grace's and stayed there a beat too long, causing a thin ribbon of chocolate to miss the bowl and land on the white countertop.

"Oops." Allie glanced down, then back up at Grace. "Go ahead."

"What?"

"The look. You're doing the look."

"I don't have a look."

"You have a very specific look. It's the one where you're judging something but you've decided to be evolved about it."

"I'm not judging. I'm observing. Clinically."

"Mm-hmm. Eight years, Grace."

Grace's mouth twitched despite herself. "Some of us would like our ice cream before another eight years pass."

"Can't rush perfection." Allie dragged her index finger through the chocolate spill. Then, before Grace could step back, she reached out and drew a warm, sticky brown stripe across Grace's forearm.

"You did not just—" Grace lunged for the jar.

Allie pivoted, shielding it with her body, and Grace followed, one hand reaching over Allie's shoulder, the other at her hip. Their bodies pressed together.

Allie's laugh vibrated through Grace's chest. Her hip bumped Grace's thigh as she twisted away. Grace laughed too. When Allie straightened, they were close. Too close. Their faces hovered inches apart. Grace could hear her own breathing, sharper than it should be.

She should step back. She didn't. She bumped Allie's hip with her own. "You're trouble."

Allie's eyes sparked. "Trouble? Hardly. I add excitement to your life."

The chocolate cooled on Grace's skin in a tacky stripe. "You planning to clean this up?"

Allie reached for a paper towel with her right hand. With her left, she circled Grace's wrist, drawing her arm closer. "Hold still," she said.

She wiped the chocolate away in slow, gentle strokes, her thumb tracing the inside of Grace's forearm. Grace's skin prickled warm in the wake of Allie's fingers.

"If we don't eat that soon, we're going to be drinking it," Grace managed.

"Do you want this clean or not?" Allie inspected her work, then let Grace's arm go.

Grace touched her forearm where Allie's fingers had been.

Allie slid the ice cream back into the freezer. "My office?" she said lightly. "The couch actually has some give. Unlike that medieval torture rack you call furniture."

"After you."

Allie's office sat just above Grace's, tucked under the eaves. The ceiling sloped low in places, making the room feel like a secret attic.

The dove-gray sectional sofa curved along one wall, pastel throw pillows scattered across it. Books spilled along mismatched shelves: clinical texts pressed against worn poetry collections. Grace's eyes landed on a battered Adrienne Rich with a spray of sticky flags.

Allie curled into one corner of the sectional. Grace took the other. Two cushions of neutral fabric stretched between them, more a suggestion of distance than actual space.

"Your office actually has a personality," Grace said. "Mine's just a room where therapy happens."

Allie smiled. "You made it that way."

"It's a therapy office."

"So is this," Allie said. "You chose every single thing in that room of yours, Grace. The chairs, the print, the tissue box cover. You just chose things that don't give anything away." She let that sit for a second. "That's a choice, too."

Grace said nothing. It was, she supposed, exactly that.

Allie smiled. "Besides, this room is my second home. When the kids are with Mark, my house feels like a hotel lobby at 3:00 AM. So, I end up here." She scooped up a spoonful of melting vanilla and chocolate. "Living my best life in a Victorian with shitty acoustics."

Grace watched her, too aware of the way Allie's lips closed around the spoon, lingered a second, then released it. A small sound escaped Allie as she chased a smear of chocolate from her lip.

She looked down quickly, stirring her ice cream. "What do you do when they're gone?" she asked. "On those nights."

Allie groaned. "Oh God, I've tried everything. Yoga classes? Lots of couples in matching outfits. Book clubs? Apparently, for old people. Dating apps?" She rolled her eyes. "My last date spent thirty straight minutes explaining her moon water ritual. Thirty minutes, Grace."

Grace's spoon paused midair. Her last date.

"What is it?" Allie asked.

"Nothing." Grace shook her head comically. "Brain freeze."

They sat in silence for a while.

Grace said, "What about friends? Don't you have anyone you can grab a drink with?"

Allie set down her bowl. "I have two good friends from grad school. But one's in Portland, the other in Chicago. And Mark got most of our local couple friends in the divorce." Her voice went flat. "Turns out they were his friends who tolerated me." A pause, then her eyes brightened. "But I've made a few women friends since the divorce. I hope you'll meet one of them Friday night at the theater. ... What about you?"

Grace thought of Stephanie. "I have a best friend from college. I'm lucky she's here in Boston, too. We see each other pretty often, but not as much as we'd like." She shrugged. "Busy lives."

Grace traced the edge of her bowl. "And I never made mom friends. Everyone else was doing playgroups and school pickup while I was here seeing clients."

"Same." Allie leaned forward. "And we're in this weird profession where our daily social exposure is having intimate conversations with people we can't actually be friends with."

Grace exhaled without realizing she'd been holding her breath. "It's definitely bizarre."

"So we end up here." Allie gestured at the office. "Where at least there are other adults who understand the work. Even if Leo won't stop talking about his bran muffins."

Grace laughed. "And Travis wants to cleanse your aura."

"Small price to pay for a bit of human contact." Allie's smile faded. "But it's not enough, is it? I mean, it's not the same as having someone to just ... be with. Without having to be 'on' all the time, competent and professional."

She leaned back against the cushions, barefoot, ankles crossed. "I keep telling myself I should be fine alone," she said. "Independent feminist icon, right? But when the kids leave, the quiet feels like ... missing oxygen." She stirred the melted ice cream. "So I come here. First car in, last car out." She canted her head. "Remind you of anyone?"

Grace studied a loose thread on her sleeve. "My schedule's packed," she said. "The paperwork alone—"

"Don't bullshit me." Allie shifted, their knees almost touching now. "We all have full caseloads. But you and I are the only ones who linger like this place has something home doesn't." Her gaze turned curious, but still gentle. "What's missing at home, Grace?"

The question snagged inside Grace. Last night: Michael on the couch, eyes on some surgery video. She'd said hello, stood in the doorway for a full minute. He never looked up.

"Nothing. I—" she started, then stopped. The lie tasted flat.

Allie waited.

"Do you and Michael ever just ... talk?" Allie asked quietly. "About anything that actually matters?"

Grace set her bowl aside. Her fingertip traced the rim. "We ..." She searched for a specific memory and came up empty. "Maybe last spring?" It sounded flimsy even to her.

"What did you talk about?"

Grace tried to remember. "I think ... I was worried about Mia. About her math grade slipping." She paused. "He suggested a tutor. Problem solved."

"That's not conversation," Allie said. "That's triage."

"I know." The admission came out smaller than she intended. "Sometimes I try. I'll start to tell him about my day, about a client who reminded me of something, or just ... I don't know, a thought I had. And he—" She stopped.

"He what?"

"He doesn't look up. Or his phone rings. Or he's already thinking about the next thing." She threw her hands up. "It's like I'm talking to air."

Silence settled between them. Not awkward, more like a held breath.

"Look at us," Allie said at last, a wry smile tugging at her mouth. "Different lives, same lonely."

Grace looked up. This close, in the dim lamplight, she noticed things she hadn't before: the faint white scar above Allie's eyebrow, the way her left dimple appeared a fraction of a second before the right when she smiled. She'd been noticing these details for months now. The scar—from a childhood bike accident, Allie had told her in June. The asymmetrical dimples—Grace had first caught them in May, during that lunch when Leo had made his terrible pun about "Freudian slippers."

She'd catalogued Allie without meaning to: the small mole on her collarbone, visible when she wore V-necks. The way she twisted her hair when she was thinking. The exact cadence of her laugh when something genuinely surprised her. When had observation become memorization?

Allie collected their bowls and nested them on the coffee table with a quiet clink. She glanced at Grace, then leaned forward without quite announcing it, and touched her index finger to the corner of Grace's mouth. Drew it away. A small smear of chocolate.

She held Grace's gaze for a moment, finger still raised. She licked the chocolate off. Then she sat back and angled her body slightly more toward Grace. "Okay. Give me one thing nobody else knows about you."

One honest answer and everything would shift. "That's dangerous territory."

"I'm not wearing my therapist hat," Allie said.

Grace took a breath. "Sometimes," she said slowly, "I sit in my car in my own driveway when I get home. For twenty minutes. Half an hour. I just ... sit there."

Allie's expression didn't change, except for a mild sharpening at the edges. Listening.

"I picture putting the car back in gear," Grace continued, "and just ... driving. Not toward anything specific. Just away." She gave a short, brittle laugh. "And then I imagine getting to I-95 and realizing I have no idea where to go. So, I stay parked like an idiot in my own driveway."

"Very dramatic," Allie said. "I approve. Deeply on-brand."

"I'm not dramatic."

"Sure. You're contemplative." Her lips twitched. "Where does the road lead, in your head?"

"That's the problem," Grace said. "I can't see it. Just ... blank."

Allie was quiet for a moment. "That's not nothing, you know. The blank." She picked at a loose thread on the cushion. "Most people can't even get that far. They just sit in the driveway and never admit they want to drive away."

She pulled her knees up. "I got so good at being Mark's wife," she said quietly, "I stopped existing as a separate person. After a while, I couldn't tell where he stopped and I began. So, when the marriage ended ..." She shrugged. "There was no one left to go back to."

"Was that part of why it ended?"

"One piece." Allie's fingers laced loosely around her shins. "I spent years contorting myself to fit what he wanted. And then—" She hesitated. "Then I was also starting to realize I'm gay."

"Did you know, when you married him?" She wasn't sure who she was asking about, Allie or herself.

"I don't know," Allie said. "There were ... intense friendships in college. Some kissing. Dreams I'd wake up from and pretend I hadn't had." She exhaled slowly. "I told myself I wanted the normal thing. Husband, kids. It was easier to believe that when I had the marriage to point to."

"And afterward?"

"After the divorce," Allie said, "the marriage wasn't there to hide behind." She gave a small, humorless laugh. "Terrifying doesn't begin to cover it. Also liberating, on a good day. But mostly terrifying." She shook her head. "There's no manual for this: gay mom, divorced, starting over near forty."

Grace remembered the afternoon Allie had told her, almost five years ago, *Turns out I'm gay.* Grace had smiled, hugged her, said all the right supportive things.

Without thinking, Grace reached for her again now. Her thumb landed on the inside of Allie's wrist, where the skin was thin and warm. A strong thump. Whether it was Allie's pulse or her own nerves, she couldn't tell.

She flattened her other palm against the couch cushion to keep from doing something even more revealing.

Her phone screen lit up on the table: 9:23.

"I had no idea it was so late," she said.

"No rush here." Allie stretched, arms lifting over her head. Her sweater rode up. A line of bare skin above her waistband. "Mark has the kids. What about you? Do you need to head back?"

"Michael had an emergency surgery," Grace said. "We have a sitter. But I should go relieve her." She didn't move.

"Right," Allie said. She stood, smoothing her sweater. "I should let you go."

"You're not keeping me," Grace said. "I just ... don't want to go." She looked at the door. Looked back at Allie. "But I should," she said at last.

"Okay." Allie walked her to the top of the stairs. "Drive safely, Gracie."

Grace nodded, slipped past her, and headed down the creaking steps.

When the light turned green at the Alewife intersection, traffic surged toward the Route 2 rotary in a series of jerky advances, brake lights blooming in front of her.

Grace rested her forehead briefly against the steering wheel. The churn of the engine thrummed through her bones.

A horn tapped behind her. She eased forward. The road opened up in front of her.

7

Wednesday, September 13

Grace waited. The clock ticked. Across from her, Nicole Fiori was methodically shredding the tissue in her lap, turning it into a small pile of damp confetti.

At forty-six, nine months into her divorce, Nicole had moved past sobbing into something harder: resignation.

"Why would I try again?" Her voice was flat, scraped-out. "Dating sounds awful. What if I end up with someone worse than Anthony?"

Grace settled deeper into her chair, crossing one leg over the other. Nicole had been coming since the husband left for his dental hygienist: younger, enthusiastic, everything Anthony said he needed. Nicole's progression had been textbook. Rage, bargaining, depression. Now, paralysis.

"Makes sense that you'd be scared," Grace said. "You got burned pretty badly. Your mind's trying to protect you from more hurt."

Nicole's laugh was sharp as broken glass. "So I should just stay home forever with Netflix and my judgmental cat?"

"That's one option," Grace said, mouth tipping. "Question is, does that actually give you what you want?"

"No," Nicole said. "I want ... someone to talk to over dinner. Who laughs at my dumb jokes." Her voice cracked. "I just want to not feel so damn alone."

"Wanting that is normal," Grace said. "People aren't built for isolation. But connection always involves risk. So, the question becomes—" She paused. "Is the chance of finding that worth the fear?"

Nicole studied her with tired eyes. "You make it sound simple."

"Not simple," Grace said. "More like getting back on a bike after a crash. You don't start on a hill during rush hour. You start in an empty parking lot. Short rides. Tiny experiments."

"Experiments," Nicole repeated, as if trying the word on.

"Yes. What if, instead of protecting yourself from hurt, you focused on staying open?" She hesitated, hearing her own earlier phrasing. "Not naïve, just ... available to surprise."

Allie's bare feet in the kitchen flashed in her mind—not just last Tuesday, but other nights too. The afternoon in July when Allie had shown up at her office door with popsicles, laughing about the heat. The stripe of chocolate on her forearm Monday night. Small moments that had accumulated like sediment, building something she hadn't wanted to name.

"Available sounds better than 'vulnerable,'" Nicole said. "That word makes my skin crawl."

"I know. We therapists overuse it." Grace smiled faintly. "Think of openness instead. Letting someone see you without all the performing. That's how intimacy starts."

Nicole went quiet, the look crossing her face one that Grace recognized from hundreds of sessions: an idea taking root.

"My coworker Jake asked me to grab coffee next week," she said. "I haven't answered."

"What's stopping you?"

"Fear," Nicole said simply. "That he'll see how broken I am. That I'll like him and he won't like me back. Or that I'm just ... not ready."

"All possible," she said. "Or maybe you'll have a decent conversation. Maybe he'll get to know you better and like what he sees." She leaned in slightly. "Trust yourself to handle whatever happens. Even if it goes badly." She lifted a brow "You've survived worse."

Nicole sat a little straighter, some essential shift settling into place. "True. I'll text Jake tonight. Say yes."

"Good." Grace meant it. "And notice how it feels, being open to it."

They spent the last minutes on logistics: neutral locations, exit strategies, what to do with first-date nerves. When Nicole left, Grace sat in the silence. The afternoon light had turned more gold, slanting low, the kind of light that made you nostalgic for things that hadn't even happened yet.

"Be available to surprise," she'd said to Nicole.

The words came back at her now, uncomfortably close to a dare.

Darkness pressed against the windows by the time the workday ended. The building had gone mostly silent, save for the muted drone of the cleaning crew's vacuum on the first floor.

Grace's phone lit up her dim office. A voicemail from David Castellano. Again. The fourth message since their last appointment.

She could practically hear it already: mundane details about his day, a memory of Elena, another earnest line about how talking to Grace was the only thing that brought him comfort. Nothing clinically urgent. Just the sound of a man reaching across the boundary line, because grief had blurred his sense of where it was.

She set the phone face-down on her desk and put her head in her hands.

A rap on her doorframe made her flinch. Allie leaned against it, coat buttoned, bag slung from one shoulder. "You okay?"

The automatic *I'm fine* died on her tongue when she met Allie's eyes.

"Just ..." She gestured vaguely at nothing.

Without asking, Allie stepped in and closed the door behind her. She crossed to the couch, dropped her bag to the floor, and patted the cushion beside her. "Come sit. Whatever this is, it looks heavy."

Every instinct reached for deflection. *Nothing, long day, I'm fine.* But the steady invitation in Allie's gaze loosened something.

Grace exhaled and crossed the room, sinking onto the couch at a slight angle toward her.

"There's this widower. David," she began. "I counseled him and his wife, Elena, through her cancer. She died in July." Her hands wove together in her lap. "I've been seeing him alone since then, and things are getting ... complicated."

"Complicated how?" Allie shifted back slightly, making room.

"At first it was small stuff." Grace looked down at her thumbs, moving against each other. "He'd linger after sessions. Find reasons to stay. Then he started bringing coffee. Last week, flowers. 'Just something from the farmer's market that made me think of you.'"

Allie's brows rose. "Did you take them?"

"No." Grace pressed her fingers to her temples. "I gave them back. Did the whole boundaries speech." She closed her eyes briefly. "His face just crumpled. He mumbled about gratitude, about how I was the only one who'd 'walked through the darkness' with him."

"Bit melodramatic," Allie said.

"You think?"

"Did you hold the line?"

"Yeah." She sighed. "But now he leaves voicemails after midnight. Three this week. And one a few minutes ago. Nothing urgent. Just ...

his voice, telling me what he had for dinner or some story about Elena, and how I'm the only one who understands."

Allie didn't answer right away. She just watched her.

"What's going through your mind when you hear those messages?" she asked.

Grace almost laughed. That classic therapist question, turned on her. "I don't know," she said, and heard the lie. "Part of me gets it. Elena was his whole world. Every conversation, every decision orbited her. When the meds made her confused, he'd remind her where she was, who he was. They were so ... tethered."

When was the last time Michael reached for her hand? Her gaze dropped to her fingers, knotted tight.

"Grace," Allie said quietly. "Tell me."

"I keep picturing him in that house now," she said. "Sitting in her chair, not his. Everyone around him pushing him to move on, to join a hiking group or a bowling league. And I'm the one person saying, *It's okay to be sad. Stay with it as long as you need.* She traced a small circle on her knee. "Intellectually, I know it's transference. I've become his safe harbor." She met Allie's eyes. "I should refer him out. But if I do, am I abandoning him? And if I don't ..."

"If you don't ...?" Allie prompted.

Grace picked at an invisible thread on her skirt. "If I don't, am I letting something cross a line because I like the attention?" The admission came out in a rush. "Because it feels good to matter to someone? To be ... important to them?"

She stared at her hands.

"You're human," Allie said gently. "It feels good to matter. Especially when that fills a space that's been pretty empty."

Grace went still. Allie's eyes held clear knowing. Her breath caught.

"I should refer him out," she said quickly, straightening a little. "Transfer his case to someone who can keep cleaner boundaries than I apparently can."

Allie's hand landed lightly on hers. "Maybe not yet. Cut yourself some slack."

"Really?" Grace's laugh was thin. "My consulting therapist would have a field day with this."

"Look at me," Allie said.

Grace hesitated, then did.

"The fact that you're sitting here naming this instead of brushing it off?" Allie said. "That awareness is the boundary. That's you doing your job."

Grace blinked hard. "Yeah. Maybe. It just ... God. Seventeen years in this field and I can't even—"

"Stop." Allie's fingers brushed Grace's wrist, then retreated, leaving a tingling trail. "You think the rest of us don't struggle with this?" She huffed a quiet laugh. "Last month I caught myself scheduling a client at the end of the day in the hope she might stay a little longer." She held Grace's gaze. "We all have feelings."

She hesitated, then added quietly, "And sometimes we stay late at the office because home feels empty, and work feels ... less empty."

All those nights claiming they had paperwork, emails, notes to finish—when really, they were just finding excuses to stay. To talk. To sit in the same room, breathing the same air. Grace thought of every evening in July and August she'd told Michael she'd be home late. Most of those nights, she'd sat in Allie's office doing nothing that couldn't have waited until morning. Nothing but enjoying Allie's company.

Their eyes met.

The first sob surprised her, a hiccup that became a shudder, that became tears spilling hot down her cheeks.

"God, I'm—" She tried to wave it away, her hand fluttering uselessly in the air.

Allie moved in one fluid motion, sliding off the couch to kneel in front of her. Her arms came around Grace's shoulders, drawing her in. At first, Grace's muscles locked; then, slowly, she let herself lean, forehead finding the warm hollow of Allie's shoulder.

"Let it come," Allie murmured into her hair. "You take care of everyone else. Let me do it for you."

Grace's fingers curled into the knit of Allie's sweater, soothed by her arms, the warmth of her, the lemony-clean scent of her. But eventually she pulled back, reaching for a tissue.

"Thanks," she managed.

For a moment neither of them moved. Allie's eyes searched hers. She couldn't look away. Bit her lower lip.

"I should—" Allie started, then stopped. She rose, her palm lingering on Grace's shoulder. "Mark's dropping the kids off soon." Her voice was careful now. "You okay?"

Grace nodded.

Allie's fingers found hers and squeezed once, warm and sure. "Looking forward to Friday night." Then she was gone, the door clicking shut behind her.

In the silence, Grace stayed frozen on the couch. Her phone lit up: a text from Michael. *Running late. Don't wait up.* She stared at it. Then deleted it without reading it again.

Friday night. Almost here.

She gathered her things and left, still feeling the exact pressure of Allie's arms, the warmth of her breath against Grace's hair.

8

———————

Thursday, September 14

Grace sat in the leather chair across from Therese Hansen, studying the framed Matisse print on the wall above her therapist's head, bold blue figures dancing in a circle. Grace had sat in this same chair for three years now, monthly sessions that had become a kind of anchor. She still couldn't decide if the dancers looked joyful or desperate.

Therese settled into her seat, notepad balanced on her knee. Her curly light-brown hair caught the afternoon light streaming through the window. "How have things been?"

Grace was quiet for a moment. "I think my marriage might be over."

Therese's pen stilled. "That's the first time you've said it that directly."

"I know." Grace twisted her wedding ring. "I've been dancing around it for months. Years, maybe. But I can't pretend anymore."

"What shifted?"

"I'm not sure. That's the problem." Grace looked out the window at the September afternoon. "But it all just feels ... more and more wrong. Like something needs to change. I feel so alone and I just can't keep on that way."

"Have you tried talking to him?"

"Last week. I told him I was feeling off, that I missed us." Grace's laugh was hollow. "He suggested I get my thyroid checked."

Therese's expression flickered—not surprise, but recognition. They both knew this pattern well.

"And when you explained what you actually meant?"

"He said, 'I'm here. I work. I come home. What else is there?'" Grace went quiet, met Therese's eyes.

"You feel he just isn't seeing there's a problem?"

The question landed hard. Grace considered it. "Right. I think he believes this is just a rough patch. That we'll white-knuckle through it like we have everything else. So, no, he doesn't see it. To be fair, I'm not sure I do either, fully. But something is fundamentally wrong."

"How so?"

"I've spent so long trying to make it work, trying to be patient, trying to understand what's standing between us. But I'm exhausted. Trying to breathe life into something that might have been dead for years."

Therese was quiet for a moment. Then: "Can I push back on something?"

Grace looked up.

"You're describing a lot of patience. A lot of effort. But I'm wondering—and I want you to sit with this before you answer—how much of that effort has Michael actually been able to see? Have you told him directly what you need? Not hints, not hoping he'd notice. But plainly, clearly."

Grace opened her mouth, then didn't say anything for a moment. "I've tried."

"I know you have. But trying and saying it directly aren't always the same thing." Therese's voice stayed neutral, unhurried. "Sometimes we protect ourselves from a hard conversation by having a softer version of it and then feeling frustrated when it doesn't land."

The words settled over Grace. She'd said almost exactly that to clients. Dozens of times.

"Maybe," she said finally. "Maybe I've been waiting for him to meet me halfway without ever showing him where halfway is."

Grace looked at her hands. The admission didn't absolve Michael. It didn't absolve her either.

"That's worth sitting with," Therese said. "Because if you're going to make any decisions about this marriage—in either direction—you'll want to be honest with yourself about what you've actually put in front of him. And what you haven't."

Therese paused, as if hesitant. "Do you think you're clear in your own mind about what you want, what you need?"

The comment hit with a jolt. What was Therese seeing?

She started to speak, then stopped, looked away.

Therese waited a while, then said, "Do you think it might be time to consider couples therapy?" She said carefully. "A structured space where you're both accountable to showing up, physically and emotionally."

Grace looked back. Shook her head. "I don't think he'd go."

"Have you asked?"

"Not directly."

Therese didn't move on. "There it is again. Why not directly?"

Grace opened her mouth, then closed it. The honest answer was sitting right there, and she didn't want to say it. "Because—" She stopped. Started again. "Because I'm not sure I want him to say yes."

Therese waited.

"If he agrees—" Grace looked at her hands. "Then I have to sit in a room with him and a therapist and try to explain what's wrong. And I'm not sure I can do that honestly. Because I'm not sure the problem in this marriage is fixable. I'm not sure I want it to be."

Grace was quiet for a moment.

"What do you mean it might not be fixable?"

"I mean—" Grace stopped. Outside, someone laughed on the sidewalk. The ordinary world, carrying on. "I mean that even if Michael became everything I've been asking for—present, attentive, connected—I'm not sure it would be enough."

A long pause. "Go on," Therese encouraged.

"I'm not sure I know how to want him." She said it carefully, like testing weight on a frozen surface. "I don't know if I ever did."

Therese looked at her, made a note. Said nothing.

"That's a terrible thing to say after seventeen years," Grace said.

"It's an honest thing," Therese said. "And important." She paused. "But I still think you should ask him. About therapy. Not to save the marriage necessarily—but because you need to know you tried. And because he deserves the chance to show up, or not. That's his choice to make, not yours to make for him."

Grace nodded slowly. "You're right. I know you're right."

"You don't have to figure out what you want from the marriage before you ask. You just have to ask." Therese then shifted gears. "How are the kids?"

"Good. Mia's doing well in school. Matthew's in his seventh-grade chaos phase." Grace smiled. "They're the best part of my life."

"And work?"

"Busy. Same as always." Grace hesitated. "Though, actually, I have this colleague. Allie. We've worked together for years, but over the past six months or so, we've been spending more time together. Late nights at the office, lunches, walks, just talking. It's ..." She searched for the word. "Easy. Comfortable."

Therese made a note. "Tell me about her."

"She's smart. Funny. We have this rhythm. We'll debate theory, argue about cases. She actually listens when I talk. Remembers things." Grace caught herself. "I mean, it's just nice to have someone to connect with at work. It makes the long days better."

"It sounds like it's more than just collegial."

"What do you mean?"

"I mean the way you talk about her. The way your whole affect changes." Therese's voice stayed neutral. "I'm not suggesting anything inappropriate. Just noticing that this person brings you something you're not getting elsewhere."

"She's a friend. A good friend." The words came out defensive. "We're going to the theater together tomorrow night."

"Okay." Therese didn't push. "I'm glad you have that." Her pen paused. "We might come back to this."

They were quiet for a moment.

"Grace, when you think about your future, what do you want?"

The question sat between them, too large to answer quickly.

"I want to stop being the person everyone needs and who's lost track of what she needs herself," Grace said. "I want to feel alive." She looked down at her hand, then back up. "Is that selfish?"

"Not at all."

Grace wiped her eyes. "Then why does it feel awful to admit?"

"Because admitting it means something has to change. And change is frightening, even when staying still is worse."

Grace nodded.

"Think about the couples therapy," Therese said. "I think you'll need to know you tried before you make any bigger decisions about your marriage."

Grace was quiet for a moment. "I'll think about it." She gathered her bag and stood.

"Same time next month?" Therese asked.

Grace hesitated. "Can we do two weeks? I think ... I might need that right now."

"Of course. Two weeks."

Grace walked to the door, then turned back. "Therese? Do you think I'm making too much of this? The loneliness?"

"No," Therese said simply. "I don't."

Grace nodded and stepped out to the waiting room.

Outside, the September air felt crisp, almost autumn. A bench in the small park across the street from Therese's building sat in bright sunlight, beckoning to Grace. She crossed the street, dropped her purse on the seat beside her, and tilted her face toward the light.

She listened to two chickadees calling back and forth from distant trees. Something about the steadiness of it—call, answer, call, answer—loosened the tightness in her chest.

Her phone buzzed with a text from Michael: *Late surgery. Home when I can.*

She set the phone down without responding.

Then it buzzed again. Allie this time: *Coffee run. Want anything?*

Grace stared at the text. At the simple question. The small gesture of someone thinking of her.

She typed: *Skim latte would be amazing. Thank you.*

Allie replied, *You got it. See you in 20.*

9

———

Friday, September 15

Late Friday afternoon, Grace hustled Matthew out of his friend's house and into the car, her mind already three steps ahead, worrying about clothes and hair. What would Allie notice first? By the time she reached her bedroom, her stomach was fluttering.

She stripped, tried on a blouse, then another. Nothing felt right. Too professional. Too buttoned-up. She tossed them onto the bed. The camel cashmere twinset stopped her. Sensuous to the touch and with a low neckline she knew was alluring on her. She chose it, not entirely sure what invitation she was making. She paired it with chocolate-brown corduroys, the good pair, the ones that made her feel like she still had a body under all the responsibility.

In the bathroom, she studied her face. Makeup wasn't her habit, but she reached for the eyeliner anyway. A thin line. A little mascara. Lipstick made her mouth look fuller, almost hopeful. She hesitated, then added the gold teardrop pendant necklace Michael had given her years ago. It caught the light at the hollow of her throat.

What are you doing? she asked the woman in the mirror. *It's not a date.*

The woman in the mirror looked skeptical.

She checked her reflection one more time, adjusted the necklace, checked again.

Allie was waiting at the bottom of the old Victorian's porch steps when Grace pulled back into the lot. Gone were Allie's sensible work slacks and cardigan. Tonight, slim black pants traced the curve of her hips, a sky-blue silk top catching the light. Her hair was loose, brushing her shoulders.

"Wow," Grace said out loud, stopping short. "You look gorgeous."

Allie's smile deepened. "Right back at you." Her gaze traced down and back up. "We clean up pretty well for therapists, huh?"

"Speak for yourself. I'm wearing emotional-support Spanx under this."

"You are not."

Grace grinned. "No, but I should be. I wasn't sure—" Her hand went instinctively to her collarbone. "If this was too much."

"It's not," Allie said, voice low, almost conspiratorial. "Trust me."

The evening unfolded with precision. Dinner reservation perfectly timed, parking close enough to walk to the theater. With Michael, there had always been chaos, last-minute scrambles, the frustration of always being late. This felt ... deliberate. Considered. Like Allie had built the night around Grace instead of squeezing her into the gaps.

The Beehive buzzed with voices and clinking glassware. Amber light pooled on tabletops. Their corner booth wrapped around them, building a small world where their hips touched along the cushion. The leather was worn smooth, warm beneath her thighs.

The wine arrived first, a Sancerre that caught the light like liquid gold. Allie raised her glass.

"To us," she said.

They drank. Conversation slid easily into grooves.

"So, book recommendations," Allie said, leaning back. "Hit me with something that'll wreck me emotionally."

Grace laughed. "You want to suffer?"

"I want to feel something. My last three books were about self-actualization and they left me numb."

"Okay. *The Year of Magical Thinking*. Joan Didion. But fair warning—"

"Okay. I won't read it on a plane." Allie finished. "Unless I decide to give my fellow travelers something to worry about."

The server arrived with their food. Allie tapped her wine glass, signaling the server for a refill. She lit into her salmon, then looked up at Grace, fork in mid-air. "How's your mother doing this week?"

Grace blinked. She hadn't expected that. "Still dizzy," she said. "Refuses to call her doctor. Keeps insisting she's fine."

Allie frowned. "Well, she hates waiting rooms. And she still doesn't trust that new cardiologist since her old one retired."

Grace stared at her. "You remember all that?"

"Of course I remember." Allie's tone was matter-of-fact. "You told me back in March, the day she fell in her kitchen. You were wearing that navy sweater, trying to pretend you weren't crying."

The sweater. The specific day. The tears she'd tried to hide. That day had been the first time Grace realized Allie paid attention in ways no one else did. She'd mentioned her mother's fall offhandedly—one sentence in a longer conversation about difficult clients—and Allie had followed up the next day. Asked how her mom was doing. Noticed Grace's exhaustion. Since then, Allie had asked about her mother a dozen times. Remembered her name. Knew she lived alone, hated doctors, made the best lemon bars Grace had ever tasted. Michael was a surgeon and still couldn't remember which medication Grace's mother took for her heart.

"I wasn't crying," Grace protested weakly.

"Tears were making a break for your chin," Allie said, mouth quirking. "But sure."

Grace laughed despite herself. "Okay. Maybe a little." The server arrived with Allie's second glass of wine; Grace's finger traced the rim of her own, still half full. "My mother's like that. Stoic, never complains. Even after my dad died, she just ... carried on. Did everything alone and never said a word about being lonely."

"Sounds familiar," Allie said quietly.

Grace met her eyes. "I'm trying not to be like that anymore."

"I know." Allie reached across the table, her long fingers finding Grace's. "That's one of the things I—" She stopped. They'd been dancing around this for months—these almost-confessions, these sentences that started and died. Back in August, Allie had started to say something after Grace had mentioned feeling invisible at home, then changed the subject. In July, Grace had nearly told Allie she was the only person who made her feel seen, then chickened out. Every conversation lately felt like walking up to an edge and stepping back.

Allie looked down at their hands. "I remember everything you tell me."

She should look away. She couldn't.

Around them, silverware clattered and voices rose and fell, but the sound blurred. There was only Allie's face in the amber light, the way she looked at Grace like she was the only person in the room.

Later, wet pavement slick underfoot, they walked the block toward the theater. At the crosswalk, Allie's palm found the small of Grace's back, guiding her forward.

The lobby funneled them inside. They squeezed past knees to their center-row seats. The theater smelled like old velvet and perfume. Around them, programs rustled, voices murmured in anticipation.

"I'm so glad you're here," Allie whispered, breath warm against Grace's ear.

A moment later Allie leaned in again, playbill open. "Look, there's Sadie." She pointed to a small photo beside a paragraph of text. "My friend. She adapted all the French lyrics. She's brilliant. I'm hoping she'll be in the lobby later so I can introduce you."

The orchestra swelled. The show began. *Les Chansons d'Amour.* All moody harmonies and messy hearts. Grace tried to sink into it, but her attention circled back to the woman beside her. Their arms brushed. Their knees aligned. At one point, she felt fingertips very near hers.

She didn't know whose hand had moved first, but suddenly their fingers were threaded. Not quite fully clasped, but undeniably joined.

Oh God. We're holding hands. In public. At a play.

She should pull away. Make it casual. But Allie's thumb moved in a small circle against her palm.

When the house lights came up for intermission, their hands drifted apart automatically, as if they'd only been resting there by chance.

Allie stretched. "Want to brave the lobby?"

"Sure. Especially if your friend might be out there."

"Probably will. Fair warning: she's going to embarrass me."

"Good. Can't wait."

In the lobby, a woman with copper curls threw her arms around Allie, then turned immediately to Grace. "You're Grace." She took Grace's hands between hers. "I've heard so much about you."

Grace ducked her head. Allie had talked about her. Enough that this woman recognized her on sight.

Sadie kept hold of her hands, studying her openly. "So you're the one."

"Sadie," Allie warned, color rising in her cheeks.

"What? I'm just saying—" Sadie grinned at Grace. "She doesn't shut up about you. 'Grace wore the prettiest skirt today.' 'Grace thinks I should—'"

"Okay, that's enough," Allie cut in, laughing but clearly mortified.

Grace leaned toward Sadie, conspiratorial. "Does she tell you I'm funny? Or is she just being nice when she says that to me?"

"Oh, she thinks you're funny," Sadie said. "Then again, she's completely—"

"Sadie!" Allie snapped, cutting her off.

Sadie looped an arm around Allie's shoulders and squeezed. To Grace, she said, "You know what this one did when my husband left me? Showed up at my door every night for ten days straight. I was in bed by three most days, barely functioning. She'd text at six: *Put pants on and unlock your door in five minutes.*"

"I wasn't that bossy," Allie muttered.

"You absolutely were." Sadie's eyes were tender when she turned to Grace. "She brought food and terrible rom-coms I pretended to hate, and she just ... stayed. When I cried. When I rage-cleaned my kitchen." Her voice thickened. "She didn't try to fix me. She just showed up."

Just as Allie had been doing for her. She looked at Allie; she looked away.

"She's got this whole competent-professional thing going," Sadie said, waving toward Allie, "but underneath? Pure heart. Don't let her fool you."

"Stop," Allie said, but she was smiling, her hand finding Sadie's and squeezing.

Sadie leaned closer to Grace and dropped her voice. "She doesn't let many people in. But when she does? She's all in, too." Her gaze held Grace's for a beat. "I hope you know that."

Grace flushed and nodded.

Allie put her hand on Sadie's shoulder and said, "That second verse in 'Midnight in Paris.' Pure genius. The way you captured being lost and found at the same time. So proud of you."

A cluster of well-wishers descended on Sadie, turning her away. Sadie squeezed Allie's hand once more before letting the crowd absorb her.

The lights flickered, signaling the end of intermission. Allie's fingers brushed Grace's elbow.

"Sorry about that," she said. "Sadie has no filter."

"Don't apologize. She's wonderful." Grace smiled. "I learned you're a secret softie who watches terrible rom-coms."

"I watch them ironically."

"Sure you do." Grace's smile deepened. "What else don't I know about you?"

Allie caught her hand. "Stick around. I'll tell you."

They slid back into their row just as the house went dark. This time their hands laced together almost immediately, no pretense of accident.

The second act swept her along. Onstage, the lovers finally said the thing they'd been circling. Applause built, music swelled. Grace kept stealing glances at Allie in the glow from the stage. The way her eyes shuttered at certain lines, the way her fingers gripped harder at a moment of confession.

They didn't let go of each other until they needed to clap during the curtain call.

∼

Back in Cambridge, Allie eased her car into the lot, sliding into the space beside Grace's Honda. The harsh security lights made the evening feel suddenly smaller, too bright.

"Tonight was wonderful," Grace said, turning in her seat to face Allie fully.

"It was." Allie smiled back.

Their eyes held, neither of them looking away.

Grace leaned in for a simple goodnight kiss—a quick, polite *thank-you* on the cheek. Somewhere in that small movement across the console, her trajectory shifted. Her lips found the warm hollow just beneath Allie's earlobe.

Skin. Heat. A subdued trace of perfume. She kept her lips there. The pulse in Allie's neck fluttered against Grace's mouth. When Allie turned her head, their faces hovered inches apart. For a second Grace thought she might—

A car horn blared on the street behind them.

Grace jerked back. She gripped the center console like it might keep her from falling.

Allie's eyes were wide, pupils blown.

For a second, neither spoke. Then they both laughed, too quickly.

Grace fumbled for the door handle, then dropped her keys when she climbed out.

"You okay?" Allie called through the half-open window.

"Fine!" She snatched the keys off the pavement. "Great. Tonight was—"

"Grace."

She stopped. "Yeah?"

Allie's smile went supple. "Good night."

Grace watched her taillights disappear at the end of the drive. The lot fell quiet.

She pressed her fingertips to her lips. They still felt the warmth of Allie's skin, the tap-tap of that pulse.

Oh.

Oh, God.

She'd kissed Allie's neck. Not her cheek. Her neck. She'd lingered there, breathing her in.

The handholding, the remembered navy sweater from March, Sadie's *you're-the-one* look.

What had she done? The question rose just as quickly as another, louder one: *What did she want to do next?*

10

Saturday, September 16

Grace woke to silence, disoriented in the early morning light. Then memory slid in: their fingertips brushing in the theater's darkness, her lips lowering to the warm hollow beneath Allie's ear.

She rolled onto her back. Gray light seeped through the curtains, thin as tissue.

What was she doing?

She hadn't stumbled into that moment or misread the angle. She'd wanted to kiss Allie's neck. Wanted it so badly she'd lingered, breathing her in. And the worst part? The wanting hadn't faded overnight. It had sharpened.

Beside her, Michael faced the opposite direction, back rigid. She remembered mornings when they'd woken tangled together, when the first touch of the day had been his hand finding hers under the covers. Now, even in sleep they maintained their separate territories. She couldn't remember the last time they'd woken facing each other. And she no longer wanted that.

But something from last night snagged at her. Coming in late, still electric with Allie's presence, she'd found the kitchen light on and Michael at the table—not with his iPad or his laptop, as usual, but with a battered paperback she didn't recognize. He'd looked up when she came in, and there was a moment before either of them spoke.

"Good book?" she'd asked, because it was easier than saying anything true about the evening she'd just had.

He'd held it up so she could see the cover. *The Remains of the Day.* "Found it in a box in the basement. I read it in my third year of med school." He paused. "Forgot how good it is. Ishiguro's got this thing where his characters spend the whole book lying to themselves about what they want. And you can see it from the outside, but they can't see it at all."

She'd stood there in her coat, keys still in her hand, and said only, "I know. Excellent book." Then she'd laid down the keys, hung her coat. "Coming up?"

"Not yet. Hope you had a good evening. Sleep well."

Now, in the gray morning light, she mulled it over. Had he been talking about himself—about the life he'd built around work and habit and absence, the feelings he'd learned to skirt around? Or had he been talking about her? Had he seen something, sensed something, and reached for the only language available to him? She didn't know. She wasn't sure she wanted to.

Grace slid out of bed before he could stir.

In the kitchen, as the coffeemaker hissed, she pressed her forehead to the cool window. Outside, a man in his bathrobe padded down the sidewalk, walking his corgi. A woman in yoga pants fished the *Globe* out from under a hydrangea. Saturday morning, the neighborhood carrying on with its ordinary rituals.

She carried her coffee to the couch and scrolled the *Times* without absorbing a word. She picked up her phone and texted Allie: *Thanks again. Best time I've had in ages.*

Next to Allie's name, three dots appeared, vanished, then returned: *So much fun. You're lovely in every way.*

She read it twice, then a third time. She couldn't stop smiling. She'd kissed Allie's neck last night.

Matthew thundered down the stairs, hair sticking out in improbable directions. He slapped a wrinkled worksheet onto the counter.

"I need a digestive system. By Monday."

She sipped coffee. "Yours seems to be working fine. I heard you ate four slices of pizza last night."

He gave her the flat stare reserved for parents being purposefully dense.

"A *model*, Mom. For science. We're supposed to build it. Out of stuff."

Mia followed, hand trailing the banister. "Hey."

"Morning, honey. Dinner with Dad go okay?"

"Fine. He complained about the cut of my shorts." She studied a split end. "Can we go to the bookstore after soccer? You promised."

"Of course."

An hour later, flour dust coated the kitchen like snowfall. A pink-painted paper-towel tube labeled ESOPHAGUS lay across the counter. A balloon stomach sagged sadly in the corner. Food coloring streaked their hands—Matthew's a violent red, Grace's a nebulous rose.

Michael came into the kitchen, rubbing sleep from his eyes. "Good morning. What have we here?"

Matthew grinned. "The human digestive system. For science class."

Michael bent low, peering at the model like he was looking in the windows of a doll house—intent, curious. "Damn good job, buddy." He pulled Matthew into a hug. "You make your surgeon dad proud."

Matthew peeled glue from his fingers, beaming at the compliment. "Thanks," he said, surveying their creation. "Yeah, I think this one is actually not terrible."

"High praise," Grace said.

"I mean it. This one's good."

Matthew bumped his head against her shoulder in rhythmic little taps, the kind of spontaneous affection he offered less often these days. "Thanks for helping, Mom."

Michael kissed her on the forehead, poured himself coffee, and went into the living room.

Matthew took several pictures of the model from different angles. Grace picked up her own phone and snapped one, too: the ruin of flour, the lopsided stomach, the chaos that felt like weekend parenting.

On impulse, she sent it to Allie with a text. *Behold: the artisanal intestines of Belmont.*

It had started innocuously—a funny client story back in May, a photo of the therapy house's repainted front steps in July. By August, she was texting Allie pictures of sunsets from her backyard, links to articles she thought Allie would like, random observations about nothing. Michael never asked who she was texting. And she'd stopped offering.

A moment later, Grace laughed as she read Allie's reply: *Please tell me you charged at least $250 an hour for that session*

Another text from her came through on its heels: *BTW, does lunch this Wednesday at noon work? Oak Bistro?*

Grace replied: *YES! It's a date!*

"Okay," she said to Matthew, voice steadier than she felt. "Let's clean this up. We've got Mia's soccer in an hour."

"Do I have to go?"

"Yes. We're all going to the bookstore from there."

∿

A little before noon, she was steering Michael's Volvo toward Lexington. The car smelled of citrus from orange slices. Mia sat beside her, firing anxious observations about midfield formations and number twelve's footwork. Grace murmured encouragements, her mind unspooling somewhere else.

"Mom! The exit!"

She jerked the wheel. The sign blurred past.

"Sorry. Thinking about a client situation."

Mia's stare landed hard. "Happening a lot lately."

On the sidelines, cold wind cut through Grace's jacket, finding every gap. Parents lined up shoulder-to-shoulder, coffee steaming, voices rising in cheerful chatter. She whooped when Mia intercepted a pass, nodded when another mother commented on strategy, but her mind kept slipping away.

On a red plaid blanket nearby, a woman nestled against her husband's chest, his arm wrapped around her shoulders. He kissed the top of her head without looking down. The easy intimacy made Grace look away.

Her fingers kept sliding to her pocket, tapping the shape of her phone like she could summon a text from Allie by wanting it hard enough. She pulled it out. Checked. Nothing. Put it back. Two minutes later, she checked again.

"Mom! Did you see that?" Mia was waving from the field.

Grace hadn't seen anything—her mind filled only with the warmth of Allie's neck under her lips, the sound Allie made.

Mia's team won 3–1. Back at the car, victory flushed her daughter's cheeks.

At the bookstore, Matthew vanished into the graphic novel section, while Grace trailed behind Mia, who methodically prowled the young-adult shelves.

"Chloe's reading this one." Mia held up a book with two girls on the cover, heads tilted toward each other. "She says it's really good. She's been reading a lot of books like this lately."

"What kind of books?"

"Girls falling for girls." Mia's tone stayed casual, but her eyes flicked up. "She told me last weekend she thinks she's gay. She's not sure."

Grace kept her voice even. "That must be confusing for her."

"Yeah. She likes this girl in math class. *Gets butterflies,* she said." Mia traced the book's spine. "But Ryan asked her out and she went, and ..." She shrugged. "She said it was like kissing her brother."

Had she ever gotten butterflies with Michael? Even in the beginning? She couldn't remember. Or didn't want to.

Grace waited for Mia to continue.

"She's scared to tell her parents. Her dad says stuff, like, *There goes the neighborhood,* when he sees guys holding hands."

"God, that's awful. Is she okay?"

"I told her I'd be her friend no matter what. That she could tell me anything."

"Chloe's lucky to have you."

Mia frowned. "I wish I could do something. Like, stop her dad from being such an asshole. But I can't."

"No," she said. "You can't. But being there for her matters more than you think."

Mia looked at her mother.

"Can I get these?" Mia asked, lifting her stack of books, the one with the two girls on the cover balanced carefully on top.

"All of them," she said, her voice steadier than she felt.

At home, the afternoon settled around them. Books scattered across the counter, tomato soup simmering, the smell of grilled cheese filling the kitchen. Her phone sat on the counter like a magnet. When it buzzed, she reached for it immediately, but it was only a text from Michael: *Be home soon.*

"Who was that?" Mia asked, not looking up.

"Your father."

"You sound disappointed. Were you hoping it was someone else?"

"No. Just waiting to hear from a client I'm trying to reschedule." The lie came easily, too easily.

Mia's eyebrow went up. "Okay, Mom." The tone was carefully neutral, the tone Mia used when she knew Grace was full of shit but was choosing not to push.

A moment later, Mia leaned in close. "Did you get more tampons?"

Grace nodded and whispered back, "Under the sink in my bathroom. I bought a different kind, too, if you want to try it."

"Thanks."

"You okay?"

"Yeah." Mia rolled her eyes. "Mom, I've been doing this for almost four years."

"I know, I know."

Mia headed upstairs. Grace watched her go, remembering the mortification of having to tell her mother her first period had come. Margaret Brennan had handed her a box of pads without meeting her eyes and said only, *You know what to do with these.* That was the whole conversation. Grace had sworn she'd do better with her own daughter. At least she'd managed that.

Twenty minutes later, the back door squeaked open. Michael appeared in the kitchen doorway in his running clothes, cheeks flushed.

"Good run?" Grace asked.

"Ten miles. New route." He filled a glass with water, drained half of it. "Kids around?"

"Upstairs."

He nodded, scrolling his phone with his free hand. "I'm going to shower." He started out of the room, then turned back. "Want to watch something tonight? After the kids are in bed? I was thinking we could watch the film version of *Remains of the Day*. Anthony Hopkins and Emma Thompson. Supposed to be fabulous."

"Uh, yeah. That would be great." Her stomach clenched at the thought of sitting beside him through that story.

He snapped his fingers. "Damn. You know? I'd better not. I have charts to review. Big case Monday and may not have time to get them done tomorrow. Rain check?"

"Absolutely." She squeezed his arm.

Something moved across his face—not quite a smile. "Good." He kissed her forehead and headed for the stairs.

She stood in the kitchen, listening to his footsteps overhead, the sound of pipes as the shower started. She picked up her phone. No new messages.

She opened her thread with Allie and reread her text from that morning: *You're lovely in every way.*

The house grew still, sunlight slanting through half-drawn blinds. Grace scrubbed a coffee ring from the counter until her fingertips blanched.

She picked up Michael's half-drunk tea mug from the counter—one of three he'd abandoned around the house today while they were out. He never finished anything: drinks, conversations, plans. Work always pulled him away mid-sip. There'd been a time when she'd found it endearing—his obliviousness to his own trail of inattention. Had he gotten worse or had she changed?

Her wedding ring caught the light. A thin rainbow flashed across the quartz countertop. She twisted the band once, twice. It felt loose. *When had that happened?*

Seventeen years of marriage. Two children upstairs. And Wednesday at noon, she'd go with Allie to Oak Bistro.

Grace set the mug in the sink and let herself think about what outfit she might wear.

11

———————

Wednesday, September 20

Early that morning, all the therapists happened to be in the kitchen at the same time. Making tea, getting coffee. Gabbing.

Travis asked, "Claire, any luck finding Sarah's sister?"

"I heard back from the attorney." Claire stirred her tea without looking up. "The sister died last year. Cancer. So, there's no one to give the box to."

Silence settled in, broken only by the whir of the microwave warming Leo's bran muffin.

"So what do we do with it?" Travis asked. "Just ... keep it in my office forever?"

"We could dispose of it," Leo suggested gently. "If there's no family to claim it."

"Seems disrespectful," Allie said. "Sarah kept it for a reason."

"But we don't know what that reason was," Leo countered. "Maybe she'd want it disposed of. Maybe keeping it would be the disrespectful thing."

"She didn't throw it away," Allie said. "She kept it. Here, not at her home. That means something."

"It does," Grace agreed.

"So we open it?" Leo asked.

"I'll get it," Travis said, already halfway out the door.

He returned with the box. Mahogany, with brass hinges and a small clasp. The lock so insubstantial it was nearly ornamental. He set the box on the table. They gathered around it. Travis pried off the clasp with a butter knife; the flimsy lock snapped free. They all leaned over.

Inside lay four bundles of letters, each tied with faded blue ribbon. The top envelope bore no address. Just a single word in elegant, masculine handwriting: *SARAH*.

"Love letters," Claire whispered.

"We don't know that," Leo insisted, but half-heartedly.

"Come on. They're tied with ribbon and hidden in a locked closet," Claire said.

Grace smiled at the unspoken *duh*.

"From her husband?" Travis asked.

"I'd guess not," Allie said, a sly note in her voice.

"So what now?" Travis asked.

"Throw them out," Leo said. "This is too private. She wouldn't want us reading them."

"But she's gone," Travis said. "And whoever wrote these probably is, too."

"Wonder why she kept them," Claire murmured.

"Maybe she couldn't let go," Allie said.

Everyone turned to look at her. Grace studied the grain of the kitchen table and said nothing.

"Of someone who mattered," Allie explained. "Maybe these were all she had left."

"Why leave them here?" Leo asked.

"Maybe she didn't want them at home where family could find

them," Allie said.

Claire nodded. "Or maybe she forgot they were in there. She'd started to lose her mental sharpness in the months before she finally let this office go."

"Someone should keep them," Grace said. "In case there's something in them that matters. Something someone should know someday."

"Who?" Leo asked.

"I'll do it," Claire said.

"You sure?"

"Yes."

Travis carefully placed all four bundles back in the box. Claire took it, held it against her chest.

"Thank you," she said, though it wasn't clear who she was thanking or for what.

A few minutes before noon, Grace waited outside, at the foot of the building's front stairs. Allie appeared, the light on her sweater accenting the curve of her breasts. Grace bit her lower lip.

They fell into step down Prospect Street, words flowing without effort. Allie told a story about a client who'd worn mismatched shoes to three consecutive appointments; Grace shared about a teenager who'd stormed out mid-breakthrough. When they dodged a crack in the sidewalk, Allie's arm brushed hers.

The hostess at Oak Bistro seated them on the patio, under the broad eponymous oak shedding its first yellow leaves. Sunlight dappled across Allie's freckles, along the sweep of her lashes. Grace couldn't move her eyes away as she unfolded her napkin, smoothed it across her lap.

The server appeared with pen poised. They ordered an autumn flatbread to share—caramelized onions, pancetta, and goat cheese—

and individual salads. Roasted squash for her, pears and candied pecans for Allie.

"And to drink?" the server asked.

"Sparkling water with lemon," Grace said automatically.

"I'll have a Sauvignon Blanc," Allie said, fingers tapping once against the table.

Grace raised an eyebrow. "Wine? You have appointments this afternoon."

"So? You don't think the occasion warrants it?"

"What's the occasion?"

"It's Wednesday." Allie grinned. A pause. "Come on. One glass won't kill you."

Grace hesitated, then waved to the server. "Actually, make that two, please."

The wine arrived quickly, pale gold in the afternoon light, condensation already beading on the glasses.

Allie clinked her glass to Grace's. "Cheers."

Grace took a generous swallow. Cool, crisp. A small rebellion on her tongue. She took another sip.

Allie drank, too, then leaned back. "Did you always want to do this? Be a therapist?"

"God, no. I wanted to be a travel writer. You know, passport full of stamps, filing stories from Bali or Morocco. Sand in my cuffs." She swirled her wine. "Instead, I sit in an office listening to people talk about their regrets."

"What happened to the travel-writer plan?"

Grace traced the rim of her glass. "My grandmother, actually. Nini, my dad's mom. She was this warm, nurturing woman. After my dad died, she basically kept me afloat." Grace smiled at the memory. "But when I told her I wanted to be a travel writer, she said, 'Don't you want a career with more meaning? Something that makes a difference in people's lives?'"

"Ouch."

"She didn't mean it as a criticism. She thought she was steering me toward something better." Grace took another sip. "And I heard it the way she intended it. As wisdom. So, I chose psychology, became a therapist. Did the sensible thing."

"Like you were supposed to."

"Exactly. My older brother was the screwup of the family. I was the good girl who always pleased everyone." She looked down at her wine. "I'm still doing it, apparently."

"And the travel writer?"

Grace hesitated. "She's in here somewhere, I guess." She met Allie's eyes. "You ever wake up and think: wait, whose life is this? Like, you made all these choices that seemed fine at the time, but now ..." She shrugged.

Allie leaned forward, wine glass cradled between her palms. "God, yes. Like: when did I agree to this? Can I have a do-over?"

"Exactly."

Their food arrived, the flatbread fragrant with the sweet scent of onions that had surrendered to slow heat. Between bites, Allie leaned back in her chair. "Okay, important question. Guilty-pleasure rom-com. Go."

"*When Harry Met Sally*," Grace said instantly.

"Really? That's your go-to? The one where they take, like, ten years to figure it out?"

Grace laughed. "Hey. Slow and steady wins the race. There's this scene at the end. New Year's Eve. Harry finally, really sees her—not as his friend's ex, just as Sally. And he runs across the city to tell her." She traced the rim of her wine glass. "I've been waiting my whole life for someone to look at me like that."

Silence. Then Allie asked, quietly, "Has anyone?"

Grace lifted her eyes. "Not until recently."

Allie looked down, a flush rising at her throat.

"What about you?" Grace asked quickly. "What's yours?"

"Imagine Me & You," Allie said. "It's this small British film. Woman falls for someone at her own wedding."

"Her wedding?"

"Yep. To someone else." Allie's voice dropped. "It's about realizing you've been living the wrong life. That you made all these choices because you thought you were supposed to. And then someone walks in and you just ... know."

Grace went still. "Does she leave?"

"Eventually. Takes her a while."

Their fingers met over the same slice of flatbread. Held there a beat too long. Allie's thumb brushed the side of her hand. Those fingers. Grace's breath caught.

Allie pulled back, took a sip of wine. "You think people actually get happy endings?"

Grace steadied herself. "I tell my clients to appreciate what they have. Stop waiting for perfect." She looked at her plate. "Then I go home and resent everything I have."

"What did you want? Your ending?"

Grace met her eyes. "I'm just starting to figure that out."

A fork clattered at a nearby table. Grace startled, reached for her wine. By the time the server cleared their plates, the wine had sanded the world's edges.

They wandered back toward the office, shoulders repeatedly bumping in a way that felt less accidental each time. Neither seemed in a hurry.

How many times had they done this walk back to the office the past few months? Grace had lost count. The coffee shop on Mass Ave., the bookstore in Central Square, the Harvard Art Museum in August when the heat had been unbearable. Each time, they'd walked a little slower on the way back. Found more reasons to stop, to look at something, to extend the time before they had to return to their separate offices and pretend they were just colleagues.

Allie stopped at a small construction site, crouched down, and collected a handful of rocks—five for herself, five for Grace. She challenged her to a contest to see how many times each of them could hit a nearby stop sign.

"Did you play sports?" Grace asked, as she threw artlessly, missing entirely.

"Lacrosse. Four years. Why?"

"Just wondering where it comes from."

Allie smiled without looking at her. "Where what comes from?"

Grace didn't answer. She already knew Allie knew exactly what she meant.

At the building steps, Allie brushed a tiny yellow leaf from Grace's shoulder. The afternoon had gone warm. Grace caught the fresh scent of Allie's perfume.

"We should do this every week," Allie said. "Wednesday lunches. I'll block off the time."

Every Wednesday. A standing date.

"Yes. I'd like that." Too quick. Too eager. She didn't care.

Back in her office, Grace shut the door and leaned against it. Allie's eyes across the table. The way she'd said *eventually*. The warmth of their fingers touching over the flatbread.

She pulled out her phone and opened her calendar. Scrolled forward. Wednesday, September 27. Blocked. Wednesday, October 4th. Blocked. Wednesday, October 11. Blocked. She kept going. Through the rest of October, November, December, into spring. Every Wednesday at noon, claimed.

What was she doing?

She knew exactly what she was doing.

12

At five-thirty that afternoon, the knock came. Grace closed the Cohen file. She knew their patterns by heart after three months. Mindy entered first, as she always did, posture defensive and alert. Ethan followed, already preparing for another hour of being the villain in his own story. They took their usual places on the sofa. Mindy perched forward, arms crossed; Ethan sagged back, phone visible in his pocket, though he wasn't touching it.

"How was your week?" Grace asked.

"Fine," Ethan muttered.

Mindy inhaled sharply. "He had dinner with his parents Wednesday and didn't mention it until Friday," she said. "And he told them everything was 'getting better.'"

"It *is* getting better," Ethan said, voice thinning.

"For whom?" Mindy shot back. "Because I'm still having nightmares. I'm still wondering every day if you're actually sorry or just sorry you got caught."

Ethan's face flattened into the usual I-can't-win mask.

Grace didn't let him hide behind it. Not today.

"Ethan," she said, her voice sharp. "Mindy just told you she's having nightmares, and your response is to deny her reality. Can you imagine how that feels to her?"

He shifted. "I just ... I don't know what she wants me to say."

"I've let you get by with 'I don't know' for a long time," Grace said, leaning forward. "But I can tell that Mindy's frustrated by it, and she's right to be. Frankly, I think you owe her more. So, let's try to unpack it."

Mindy sat taller. Ethan glanced toward the door as if hoping it might swing open. "What do you mean?"

"There are always reasons. Not excuses. Reasons. What were yours? Excitement? Attention? Feeling noticed? Feeling ... alive?"

Mindy's eyebrows rose.

Ethan rubbed the back of his neck. He shifted in his seat. "I don't —" He stopped, catching himself.

Grace pressed. "Ethan, you're a successful ad executive. Your job is understanding what motivates people. I think you can do better here than 'I don't know,' even if the answer is uncomfortable."

Silence stretched.

Ethan eventually spoke. "I don't know why I did it. I love Mindy. I love our kids. It didn't make sense."

Outside, a siren wailed past, then faded. Grace waited through the silence.

"Think back," Grace probed. "Before the affair. What were you feeling?"

He shook his head. Said nothing.

"Sometimes it's not the person; it's the escape," she said. "A way to step outside your own life for a while."

Ethan looked up at her. "Maybe. Yeah, being with ... her ... just felt easier. No hassles."

"What kind of hassles?"

"The daily stuff. Dishes. Dirty kitchen floor." He paused. "With her ... everything was easy. There were no chores, nothing was ever messy, noisy. No fighting, no requests or demands."

Mindy stared at him, her nose slightly pinched.

Grace said, "Okay. Good. Stay with this, Ethan. At home, you felt ..." Her tone prompting.

Ethan seemed lost in thought, then he said, "Worn down. And like the hired hand of the house. It felt like the central family unit was Mindy and the kids, and I was ... I don't know, staff. And like Mindy and I had completely lost the connection we had."

He stopped and looked at his hands. He glanced up at Grace. She nodded, encouraging him to keep going.

"But when I was with ... her ... well, the hard parts of home life fell away, and I was with someone who needed nothing from me. I felt lighter. Appreciated and valued for being myself not the performer of tasks."

Mindy's face had sharpened into hard angles. When she spoke, her voice dripped with sarcasm. "Yeah. I bet life feels pretty light and easy when you're having afternoon sex in a hotel room."

Ethan flinched. His hands opened, helpless. "I— I know what I did was wrong, I'm trying to ..." He trailed off. He crossed his arms.

Grace tried to keep him from shutting down. "That was very helpful, Ethan. Honest. Hard, but honest. I knew you could get there." She turned to the other end of the couch. "Mindy, what happens in you, hearing all that?"

Mindy wiped her eyes. "I hate it. But it's the first thing that makes sense. Better than *I don't know.*"

Grace nodded. "Honesty is the ground you can rebuild from. Or choose not to. But it's real."

She waited. Let the silence sit.

Ethan looked at his hands, then at Mindy. "I didn't know how to get back to what we had. And I missed you. That's what I don't understand. How could I miss you so much and still ..." He seemed unable to find the words to finish.

"Still seek connection somewhere else?" Grace supplied quietly.

He nodded.

She said, "Sometimes when we feel overwhelmed or depleted, we make choices that surprise us. And the need for connection is extremely powerful."

Allie's fingers, the way Allie said her name.

"I miss you," Mindy whispered, turning toward her husband. "I miss talking to you."

He reached over and gripped her hand, the first time in three months Grace had seen them touch.

They spent the rest of the session developing strategies for reconnection: daily check-ins, weekly dates without discussing logistics, ways to rebuild intimacy slowly. The words came easily. She'd given this advice a hundred times, could do this part in her sleep.

When the session ended, Mindy thanked her. Ethan gave a small, exhausted nod. Mindy's hand brushed Ethan's arm as they stood. He didn't pull away.

Grace sat alone in her office after they left. She closed the file and set it on the stack with the others, then sat back and stared at the ceiling, pulled out of her thoughts only when the light in the room dimmed.

On the drive home, the afternoon replayed itself: sunlight on Allie's face at the bistro, the way Allie had said *eventually,* the brush of their fingers over the flatbread.

"Jesus," she whispered, shaking her head. "Get a grip."

As she waited at a traffic light, her phone buzzed. A text from Michael: *Emergency surgery. Will be late. Arranged for Sofie to be with the kids.*

His absences, his late nights. They'd begun to feel like freedom.

He wouldn't be home for hours. Sofie would handle bedtime with the kids. She didn't have to go right home. But she should. She should give Sofie her evening back. She could check Matthew's math homework. He'd texted her that morning about a problem he didn't understand, and she'd told him to ask her tonight, then forgotten about it entirely until this moment. She could make herself a cup of tea, help him, read her novel. That's what she should do.

She sat with that for a moment. Matthew waiting for her to come home and explain the problem. Sofie putting him to bed instead, telling him his mom was working late again.

She was a good mother. She had always been a good mother. It was one of the things she knew about herself without question.

She texted back to Michael: *Thanks. Hope it goes well.*

She paused about ten seconds. Then she pulled a U-Turn. Back toward the office. Back toward Allie.

The building had fallen silent, white-noise machines switched off for the night. At the bottom of the staircase, her fingers curled around the smooth wood of the banister.

She could still leave. Go home to her good-girl life.

She knew she wasn't going to.

She climbed the stairs.

13

———

She reached the top of the staircase. Light glowed under Allie's door. The shuffle of paper, the scrape of a chair leg. Definitely here.

She could still go home. Text Allie tomorrow. Pretend she never came back.

She knocked anyway. "It's me." She pushed the door open.

Allie looked up from a stack of papers, surprised. "Hey, you. Thought you were heading home after your five-thirty."

"That was the plan." Grace went in and closed the door behind her. "Halfway home I got a text from Michael. Emergency surgery. He got a sitter. So ... I came back."

Allie grinned. "A nice surprise. Wine?"

"God, yes. You have some? Here?"

Allie crossed to the corner cupboard and pulled out a bottle of red. "Don't tell the licensing board," she said, smiling as she worked the cork. "For special occasions. Or emergencies. Not sure which this is."

She poured into two mismatched coffee mugs and handed one over.

"Classy," Grace said.

"Only the best for you." Allie kicked off her heels and dropped onto one end of the couch, tucking her feet under her.

Grace sat on the other end. They drank in silence, inching inward without acknowledging it. The office was chilly; the radiator ticked.

"God. This place is freezing," Allie said. "Landlord's going to get an earful tomorrow." She studied Grace. "You okay? Why'd you come back?"

"I mean—" She wrapped both hands around her mug. Lie? Say she forgot something? She couldn't. Not tonight. "Actually, I'm not okay ... I'm a bit of a mess, honestly." She exhaled. "I came back because you're here."

There. Said it.

Allie went still. "Grace."

"Yeah. I know." She had to stop, breathe. "The fact is— I'd rather be wherever you are. I'm— I don't—" She shook her head. "I can't stop thinking about you. I keep trying to talk myself out of it, but it just ... doesn't work."

She set down her mug. "I came back because I don't know how to stay away from you anymore. I think I'm— God, I *know* I'm—" She stood, looked at the door, sat back down. "I'm in love with you."

The words hung in the air. No taking them back. Allie was quiet for a moment. She, too, set down her mug and moved closer on the couch. She asked, "Grace, do you know what you're saying?"

"I do. And I know how it sounds. Believe me, I know." She looked up at Allie. "I'm married. I have kids. I'm forty-two years old and I've never felt this way about anyone in my entire life, and I don't know what to do with it except—" She paused. "I had to tell you."

Allie was quiet for a moment. She reached for Grace's hand. Then she let out a long, unsteady breath.

"I—" She stopped. Started again. "God, Grace." She looked down at their hands. "I've been trying not to say this for months. Telling myself it was just— that I was lonely, or that I admired you, or—" She shook her head. "I kept waiting for it to go away."

A beat.

"It didn't."

She looked up. "I'm in love with you, too. I am. I just—" Her voice caught. "I didn't know if you could possibly—"

She stopped again. Squeezed Grace's hand instead of finishing.

"Love a woman?"

Allie nodded.

"Well, I do. I didn't know I could feel this strongly about anyone. But I do." She laughed, a short, disbelieving sound. "I keep waiting for it to feel wrong. It doesn't." Her thumb traced slow circles over Allie's knuckles, a small, steadying rhythm. She looked up. "What am I supposed to do with all this?"

"You don't have to do anything," she said, voice low. "Just ... sit with it. See how it feels."

They sat there, hands joined, the weight of what they'd just said settling around them. Allie broke away to draw a tissue from the box on the coffee table. She wiped a tear from Grace's cheek, tucked the tissue in her sleeve.

Allie reached up again, this time brushing her fingertips along Grace's jaw. "I want to kiss you. Okay?"

Grace nodded. "Please."

Allie leaned in. Their lips met. Then again. Short, testing kisses at first, then one that lasted. Their lips parted and the kiss deepened. She slid her hand up to Allie's wrist, where the pulse jumped beneath her thumb.

They shifted closer, holding on. Allie's free hand moved to Grace's cheek. Grace closed her eyes. When she opened them, Allie was watching her.

"Oh, God, Allie. What are we going to do?"

"I have no idea." Allie leaned still closer. "But right now I want to touch you so badly it's almost embarrassing."

Grace snorted. "Then touch me. Now. Or I swear I'm going to take your hands and move them around myself."

Allie laughed, breathless, and slid her hand down to cup Grace's breast through her sweater, thumb moving slowly across it.

Grace gasped. Or moaned. She wasn't sure which.

Their next kiss deepened. *Oh, god.*

When they finally broke apart, Grace couldn't catch her breath.

She pressed her fingers to her mouth and started to laugh. "Oh, shit."

"Yeah."

"I don't— I've never—"

"I know," Allie said.

"How are you so calm?"

Allie let out a shaky laugh. "What makes you think I'm calm?" She took Grace's hand. Pressed it against her chest.

And then Grace wasn't thinking at all; she was kissing Allie again, harder this time. Allie's hands were in her hair, at her back, sliding under the hem of her sweater. Warm fingers on bare skin. Grace gasped.

She didn't want to stop. She wanted more.

They ended up horizontal somehow, Grace half on top of her, the couch too narrow, one of them knocking a mug to the floor. Wine spread across the rug in a dark bloom. Neither of them cared.

Allie's hands moved up and down Grace's sides, thumbs brushing the underside of her breasts through her bra. Grace's hips pressed down before she could stop herself. Allie made a low sound from somewhere deep inside. "Is this—" Grace began.

"Don't," Allie said. "Don't think. Not yet."

She didn't. She kissed Allie's mouth, her jaw, the buttery smooth place at her neck. Allie's fingers dug into her back. Everything narrowed to heat and pressure and the way Allie said her name—

"Grace ... god, Grace."

When they eventually stilled, Grace became aware of everything at once: the press of the couch arm against her hip, her sweater twisted around her ribs, the wine-dark stain on the rug below them.

She rolled onto her side, wedged between Allie and the back of the couch. Allie looked just as wrecked. Lipstick smeared, breathing uneven.

"Oh my god," Grace said.

"Yeah."

"I'm married."

"I know."

"I have kids."

"I know."

"I'm freaking out."

Allie looked at her. "You want to leave?"

Grace thought about Michael barely looking at her anymore. The life she kept sleepwalking through. Her world set on autopilot.

"No," she said. "I don't."

Allie's arms tightened around her. Grace buried her face in Allie's neck, breathing her in.

She lay there listening to the radiator tick and the city sounds outside. She couldn't think about looking into Michael's face when she got home, or what Mia and Matthew would think. She couldn't look past this moment. The warmth of Allie's body, the taste of her lips. She held on and let herself stay.

14

―――――

Thursday, September 21

Grace woke to the familiar gray square of dawn on the curtain. Kids' footsteps. Grumpy voices from the hallway.

She lay there replaying last night. Allie's mouth on hers. The weight of Allie's body. How utterly right it felt.

When her feet hit the floor, guilt arrived with them. She'd kissed a woman. More than kissed. While her husband worked late and her children slept.

The strangest part was how little she wanted to take it back.

She showered and stood in front of the fogged mirror longer than usual, waiting for it to clear. Early in their marriage, Michael used to leave notes for her on this mirror—small observations, inside jokes, nothing profound but enough to make her smile. She couldn't remember when those stopped. Somewhere between Matthew's birth and Michael's promotion to chief resident, the notes had disappeared like they'd never existed

Now, when the fog cleared, she looked the same. Auburn hair

dark with water, the jaw that always looked like it meant something she didn't intend. She felt completely different and couldn't decide if that was visible.

In the kitchen, Grace laid out breakfast options that her children would mostly ignore.

"Mom, why are you smiling at the toaster?" Mia asked from the counter, spooning yogurt.

Grace hadn't realized she was smiling. She looked away quickly.

The coffee maker gurgled. Morning light caught the dust motes above the table.

"Just thinking about something at work," she said.

"Sure." Mia studied her over the yogurt container. "Where are the glue sticks?"

"Same place they always are. Drawer by the stove."

Matthew hunched over his iPad, barely looking up. "Can I stay after school to shoot? Diego said the gym is open."

"Not today. Homework first."

"But—"

"We can shoot in the driveway tonight if you finish early."

Matthew shrugged. "Okay."

She was pulling her coat on when Michael came into the kitchen. He reached out and tucked a strand of hair behind her ear, something he used to do years ago, before everything between them went quiet.

"You look tired," he said. Not a criticism. Concern, quiet and unpracticed. "You okay?"

She almost said *fine* before catching herself. He was looking at her — actually looking, the way he almost never did anymore.

"Long week," she managed.

"You've got appointments all day?"

"Mm-hm."

"Hope they go well." He held her gaze longer than usual. Last night she'd been in Allie's arms. Now Michael was looking at her like he'd lost something and wasn't sure what.

She should tell him.

"Thanks," she managed.

He reached past her for his coffee, and the moment closed. His eyes went to the clock and he was gone.

She parked in her usual space, surprised not to see Allie's car there yet. She sat motionless behind the wheel.

Michael had said she looked tired. His voice neither cold nor clinical. Something gentler underneath it that she didn't have a name for. She'd spent so many years cataloguing his absences that she'd almost missed it when he showed up.

She didn't know what to do with that. She went inside.

She opened her laptop, staring at the same sentences without reading them. She heard every footstep in the hallway, hoping each would be Allie's. First, Leo's measured pace. Then Claire's quick steps. And Travis's drum-major clomp that always sounded like a performance.

Finally, at 8:50, she heard it. Allie's footsteps. Past her door, toward the stairs. The pause. Key in lock. The squeak. The careful shut.

Grace stared at her closed door. She stayed seated, pretending she was a professional person doing professional things.

Twenty minutes later, she couldn't stand it anymore. She needed coffee. Just coffee. People went to the kitchen for coffee, didn't they?

Leo was at the table reading the *Globe*, tea steeping beside him.

"Morning," he said without looking up.

"Hi, Leo." Grace started to pour coffee. Before half the mug was full, the door swung open and Allie stepped into the room. Scarf looped at her throat. Hair in a loose knot. Like at the start of last night. Grace's grip tightened on her mug.

"Morning," Allie said, her voice carefully casual.

"Hi."

Leo glanced up from his paper, then back down. Allie moved to the tea cupboard. Just feet away. Grace caught a hint of her perfume, the same citrus scent from last night.

"Cold out there," Grace managed.

"I like it," Allie said, not looking at her. "Makes you want to stay inside."

The silence stretched. *Say something. Make this normal.* She set down her mug before she spilled the coffee.

"I should prep for my ten," Grace said, too quickly. She left before Allie could respond.

In the hallway outside the kitchen, she leaned against the cool plaster wall, listening to Leo's chair scrape across the floor.

Back in her office, she tried to concentrate on her upcoming session at ten with Valerie Clemmons, who struggled with her daughter's college search and her own anxiety about letting go.

She heard a knock at the door. Allie came in. Grace closed the door behind her. They stood there, a few feet apart.

"Hi," Allie said with a grin.

"Hi."

"Last night—"

"I know."

Allie stepped closer. "I've been thinking about you all morning."

"Me too," Grace said quietly.

"When can I see you? Actually see you, not like this."

A knock at the door made them both jump.

Grace called, "Come in."

Claire opened the door and stepped in. When she saw Allie there, she said, "Oh, sorry. I didn't know anyone was here with you. I'll come back."

Grace said, "No, no. Come in, Claire. We were just chatting. What's up?" She motioned for Claire to sit.

Claire perched on the end of the couch. "I— I read a few of the letters in Sarah's box." A pause. She glanced between Allie and Grace. "We were right. They're love letters. Sarah had an affair."

Grace leaned in. "Do you know who he is? Was?"

"No. They're all signed with just an initial. P. Unless there are more somewhere else, they appear to have stopped coming in 1993. I want to read them. All of them. How wrong would that be?"

Grace looked to Allie, then back to Claire. "Sarah's been dead for about six months now. And this was her lover from three decades ago. We have no idea if he's still alive."

Claire nodded.

Grace said, "I think it's okay to read them, Claire. You were the only one of us close to Sarah. And it's been thirty years. What harm could it do now?"

Claire looked to Allie and raised her brows.

"Yeah," Allie said. "I agree with that. I think it's okay, too, Claire"

"Thank you. I just ... I needed someone to tell me it wouldn't be ghoulish or creepy."

"It wouldn't be," Grace said. "Not at all."

Allie nodded in agreement. "As I said the day we opened the box, Sarah kept those letters for a reason. Maybe she'd want someone to know."

Claire stood, gripping her mug tight. "Thanks, you guys. I'll let you know what I find. If there's anything worth knowing."

"Only if you want to share," Grace said.

Allie stood, too, saying, "Better go prep my ten o'clock. Talk with you later, Gracie."

When they'd left, Grace looked out her office window, thinking about Sarah Clarke keeping love letters for thirty years. Letters from someone who'd signed with just an initial. All those years of holding onto something that had ended.

Grace wondered who "P" was, and whether Sarah had ever considered leaving her marriage. Or if she'd simply chosen to live with both. Husband and hidden love, present and secret.

15

Friday, September 22

Grace smoothed the tablecloth for the third time. The invitation had escaped her lips yesterday morning in the office hallway. She'd been so eager for more time with Allie, she hadn't thought through what it would mean: Allie walking through that door into seventeen years of Grace's carefully constructed normalcy.

The doorbell chimed at exactly six-thirty. Grace opened the door.

Allie stood on the porch shifting her weight, a wine bottle in one hand and autumn flowers in the other: golds and rusts against the deep blue of her sweater. Allie's mouth lifted in that crooked way.

"Hi," Allie said, looking a bit sheepish. "I brought these." Allie extended the bouquet. "And wine. Couldn't decide which was more appropriate."

Their fingers brushed over the wine bottle. She pulled back too quickly. But then she took both, inhaling the flowers' scent to steady herself. "Perfect. Come in." Light slanted into the foyer from the living-room doorway, which framed the worn leather couch and photos lining the mantel.

She watched Allie's gaze gather impressions, moving from Matthew's backpack slumped against the stairs to Mia's mud-crusted cleats by the door.

Michael descended the staircase, his hair still damp from a shower. His face broke into an easy smile as he extended his arms. "Allie Morgan. In the flesh." He pulled her into a brief hug. "Has it been since that terrible Christmas party two years ago?"

"Yep. The one with the undrinkable egg nog. Good to see you, Michael."

"How are Emma and Noah doing?"

"Both great, thanks. Constantly rolling their eyes at me."

"We get the same treatment." He tilted his head toward the electronic beeps and explosions coming from the living room. "Matthew," he called, "please pause that and come in here."

The game sounds abruptly stopped. Matthew shuffled into the foyer, shoulders slouched, controller dangling from one hand.

"Hey."

Allie crouched slightly to meet Matthew's eye level. "You may not remember me. I have the office above your mom's. She mentioned you've been creating something pretty incredible in Minecraft lately?"

Matthew straightened. "Yeah. I've got this whole city going. With working redstone circuits and everything."

"Noah, my son, tried explaining redstone to me last week. I nodded like I understood, but ..." She made a whooshing sound over her head. "Completely went past me."

"It's just like electrical circuits, but virtual." His controller hung forgotten. "With red dust lines you can place anywhere."

"I'd love to see what you've built sometime," Allie said.

Matthew grinned. "Really?"

"Sure."

"Okay. Cool."

Grace said, "Matty, go wash up for dinner, please."

As Matthew left, Michael took the wine and flowers from Grace's arms and disappeared toward the kitchen.

Grace called up the stairs. "Mia! Come down and say hi to Allie."

A figure shifted at the top of the staircase. Mia emerged, one hand sliding along the banister, the other tugging at the hem of her oversized sweatshirt. Her dark hair was piled into a loose bun that bobbed as she descended. Mia looked Allie over.

"Mia, this is Allie from my office," Grace said. "You've met before. But quite a while ago."

Allie grinned. "Good to see you, Mia. Your mom talks about you a lot. How's soccer going?"

"Good." Mia paused on the third step, looking between them. "Mom says your daughter plays, too."

"Yep. Emma. Has a game tomorrow at Payson Field."

Mia studied Allie with frank curiosity. "You have pretty eyes. Really blue."

Allie laughed, flustered. "Oh, I— thank you."

"Mom talks about you a lot."

Grace busied herself adjusting a picture frame on the wall. "I talk about all my colleagues."

"Not really," Mia said matter-of-factly. "Except the new guy and his crystals." She dropped her voice an octave, mimicking Grace's tone and cadence perfectly: "'It's all bullshit, but his heart's in the right place.'"

Grace and Allie laughed. "Poor Travis," Allie said.

"We'll be in the living room," Grace said, squeezing Mia's shoulder. "I'll call you when dinner's ready."

"OK." Mia turned and trotted back up the stairs.

"She's wonderful. Has your gift for playing a part."

"She's something," Grace murmured, guiding Allie to the couch.

Michael returned with a cheese board, three wine glasses hooked between his fingers, the bottle tucked under his arm. He arranged everything with practiced efficiency, filled the glasses generously, and lifted his. "To good company."

Grace watched him play host. Charming, attentive, the way he was at hospital fundraisers. The way he used to be with her.

Michael swirled his wine, studying Allie. "So how's life? You seeing anyone?"

Grace set her glass down too hard.

Allie glanced her way. "Not at the moment. Dating apps are …" She made a small explosion gesture.

"I can't imagine dating now. I'd be hopeless," Michael said with a laugh. "What do you look for? When you're considering someone?"

"Michael," Grace said. "A bit personal."

"It's fine." Allie's fingers traced her wine glass stem. She looked at Grace. "Well, the first pass, of course, is whether I find the person's face appealing. And whether their profile shows a sense of humor. But then, when I meet them, it's about whether the person is curious enough to want to see me underneath my exterior. Someone who'll join me in trying to make everyday things fun."

Grace cleared her throat and looked away, her thoughts landing on the romanesco at Whole Foods, the stop sign.

"Interesting. And nicely put." Michael raised his glass. "Here's hoping the right person comes along for you."

"I'm optimistic," Allie murmured.

Grace reached for her wine glass and drank longer than necessary.

Michael launched into something about a breakthrough surgical procedure. Words Grace didn't hear. Allie's voice resonated in her head: someone who wants to see what's underneath; someone who wants to make things fun.

When the meal was ready, they gathered at the dining table. Grace claimed the seat directly across from Allie, guaranteeing their eyes would meet over the candles throughout dinner.

"Everything looks amazing," Allie said, watching Grace set down the roast chicken. "You shouldn't have gone to such trouble."

"Are you kidding? Always good to have an excuse to use actual dishes." Grace's fingers grazed Allie's as she passed her a plate. "Besides, I couldn't exactly serve you fish sticks. You'd never come back."

Allie grinned.

Michael asked her about her practice. She told a story about a therapy session where a husband had brought puppets as visual aids. Grace laughed with the others, and felt, for a strange moment, completely herself—the specific self that responded by calling couples therapy "the world's most expensive improv class" and meant it with equal parts affection and exhaustion. She'd forgotten that self existed at this table.

Mia watched her mother and Allie, like someone working out a puzzle. When the laughter faded, she said, "So, you guys work together, right?"

"Yes," Grace said. "Both cognitive behavioral therapists."

Mia canted her head.

"It operates on the principle that thoughts, feelings, and behaviors are interconnected. This approach—"

"TMI, Mom. I just meant you see a lot of each other."

Grace blushed, "Right."

Allie jumped in. "Your mom is very good at the job. She has this gift for knowing what people need and seeing that they get it."

Mia's eyes widened for just a moment. Then the look vanished.

"Mom's good at lots of things," Matthew mumbled around a mouthful of chicken. "Last Saturday she helped me make this model of the human digestive system." He turned to Grace. "It was awesome."

Grace smiled and ruffled his hair. "We had fun, didn't we, kiddo?"

"We did."

Michael said, "Don't talk with your mouth full, Matthew."

Allie smiled across the table at Grace, then looked at both kids. "Your mother can be a lot of fun when she allows herself the freedom."

Grace inhaled wine instead of air. She coughed—once, then ten times. Michael reached over to pat her back while Mia watched, fork suspended in midair, a small smirk playing at her lips.

"Wrong pipe," Grace managed, still coughing. "I'm fine."

Allie bit her lip, trying not to laugh.

Grace wanted to throw her napkin at her. Or kiss her. Both.

When her cough reflex had subsided, Grace pointed to her glass of wine and said, "This is lovely, if a bit deceptive."

"From that shop on Huron," Allie said. She reached for the bottle and refilled her glass.

More questions about Allie's kids. Matthew's talk about digital dragons. Mia's complaints about the asshole coach who made them do extra laps.

Grace nodded at appropriate moments, but her attention kept returning to Allie. The glossy hair tucked behind her ear. The way she laughed at Matthew's jokes. How easily she belonged here.

Grace stood to clear plates. Allie was on her feet instantly.

"Please sit," Grace murmured. "You're our guest."

"I insist." Their fingers brushed as Allie took Michael's plate and followed Grace to the kitchen.

The sounds from the dining room faded. Every time they passed each other—Grace reaching for Tupperware, Allie opening the dishwasher—Grace swallowed.

"They're lovely, your family," Allie murmured, rinsing a glass.

"They like you. Matthew never talks to adults about his games. You made him comfortable."

"He's a great kid. They both are." Allie turned, hip against the counter, inches away. "That's your doing. A testament to you."

Grace looked up.

Allie's hand lifted, fingertips almost touching Grace's cheek. "Gracie—" Their faces now only a couple inches apart.

"Everything under control in here?" Michael asked from the doorway.

They froze, too close. Grace jerked away. Her elbow bumped the edge of a serving bowl. It tilted, almost slipped over the counter's edge. Allie caught it, steadied it.

Michael's smile faltered. His eyes moved between them. Grace flushed, Allie's hand still on the bowl.

"You okay?" Something in his voice had shifted.

"Fine," Grace said, not looking up. "Just ... slippery."

"Kids want dessert if you're interested."

"We'll be right there."

His footsteps retreated. Grace pressed her hand over her mouth, but a laugh escaped anyway. Muffled, slightly hysterical. The absurdity of it: trying not to laugh, while her husband was twenty feet away. This was her life now.

Allie covered her face with both hands. They leaned forward until their foreheads touched, both trying desperately not to make noise, laughing into the silence.

"Jesus Christ," Grace said.

"Yeah. That was close," Allie breathed.

"Too close."

In the dining room, they served apple tart and coffee. The conversation turned lighter. Shows available to stream that no one had time to watch, political crap everyone was disgusted by.

Just after nine, Allie stood. "I should head home. Thanks for including me tonight."

"Let me walk you to your car," Grace said, already moving.

Outside, Grace's shoulder bumped Allie's with each step, neither adjusting their path.

At the car, Allie turned, her face inches away. "I'm grateful to you," she murmured, "for letting me see this part of your life."

"Having you here ..." Grace searched for words. "It felt right."

They stood inches apart. She should step back, say goodnight, go inside. Instead, her hand found Allie's. Their fingers intertwined. Grace moved even closer. Their foreheads touched. She could feel Allie's breath.

"Grace, where is this going?"

"I don't know. But I don't want to stop."

Allie's palm found Grace's cheek. "Me neither."

She kissed Grace quickly. Too quickly. Then she was in her car, and Grace was alone on the curb, where she remained long after the taillights vanished.

Inside, she found Mia starting up the staircase with a glass of water.

"She's nice," Mia said, her tone carefully neutral.

"She is." Grace smiled.

Mia studied her mother's face in the dim light. "You were happy tonight."

Grace went still. "What?"

"At dinner. You seemed ..." She shrugged. "I don't know. Different."

All Grace could manage to say was, "It's late. You should get to bed."

Mia disappeared upstairs.

Grace stood alone in her kitchen. She gripped the counter. Mia had noticed. And once Mia noticed something, she didn't let it go.

16

Saturday, September 23

Around 5:30 the next night, Michael came through the back door with his hospital badge still clipped to his coat. He kissed the air near her cheek and set his bag on the bench.

"Sorry I had to go in. Emergency appendectomy. Saturday afternoon surgeries are a bitch."

"No need to apologize. Dinner will be ready about 6:15," Grace said, stirring the risotto on the stove. The kitchen smelled of garlic.

Grace had put out two glasses, a bottle of wine, and a small cheese plate on the counter. Michael gestured toward the setup. "What's all this for?"

"I thought maybe we could sit and talk for a few minutes before the kids come down."

Michael smiled and squeezed her upper arm. "You're sweet. But that surgery set me back and I have a ton of email to answer."

He was gone before she could respond, the door to the den

clicking shut. Then, muffled sounds of him typing. Rapid, purposeful.

Grace had tried, done everything she could to make it easy for him to say yes. Deflated, she put his glass back in the cupboard and poured a glass just for herself.

She used to tell herself he worked so hard because he cared about them. She still tried to believe that. It didn't make the empty glass any easier to put away.

By 10:30 that night, the kids' bedroom lights were out. Grace and Michael were both upstairs, and Grace knew she had to do it. Now. She couldn't take another day of this.

Michael was in bed, laptop still open.

"Michael, I need to talk to you about something."

"I'm swamped here. Can we do this tomorrow?"

"No. Please put that away."

He looked up and set the laptop aside. "Okay."

Grace lowered herself to the edge of the bed. She took a breath, let it out slowly. "I need to tell you something. Just ... can you listen? Don't try to fix it or explain it away. Just listen."

His expression changed. Careful, neutral. The look he gave patients. "Okay."

Grace gripped her hands together. "Something's been happening with me. I've been spending time with Allie. Some evenings, lunches. We've gotten close." She looked away, then back. "I've developed feelings for her."

"Feelings. What kind of feelings?"

Grace held his gaze. "Strong ones. I'm attracted to her; I can't stop thinking about her."

She waited. Nothing.

"When I'm with her, I feel more alive than I have in years."

He was quiet for a long moment. Then: "I don't understand. I thought we were okay. Not perfect, but ..." He trailed off, looking at her, genuinely bewildered. Then, after a brief silence, his mouth twisted, and he said, "Wait— so, you've got a girl crush on your colleague?"

She sat straighter. "It's not a crush, Michael. It's—"

"What would you call it, then? Some kind of midlife infatuation?"

Heat flooded her cheeks. "I don't know what to call it." But she did know. She just couldn't say it yet. Not to him. "That's why I'm trying to talk to you," she said.

He exhaled sharply. "Look, I get it. Allie's smart, funny, charming. And, yeah, beautiful. But, Grace, as a psychologist, you know what this is: you're getting attention from someone you're around a lot. See every day. Attention from her you're not getting at home. It feels good to be noticed. That's all this is." He leaned forward. "People get crushes. They pass."

"Stop making this small."

"I'm not—" He nodded, taking a deep breath. "But really, this is no big deal. We can fix this. We'll do date nights. Reconnect. I'll pay more attention. We can work on this." He reached out, rubbed her shoulder.

Grace pulled back. "Dinner at Oleana won't fix this, Michael. You're not hearing me." He was doing it again. Turning her into a problem to be solved.

"That's not—"

"Yes, it is. You're treating this like a phase. It's not. It matters."

He exhaled slowly. "Fine. It matters to you. What do you want me to hear?"

"That my feelings for Allie are real. There's desire, Michael."

His face went flat. "Jesus Christ. You're having sexual thoughts about her?"

She paused. Lifted her chin. "Yes. Sensual, romantic. This isn't just, *oh, she's nice.*" Saying it out loud made it real.

He rubbed his face. "Okay. Okay. Let's just— Are you doing anything about these feelings?"

"Doing anything?" She didn't look away. "We've kissed. And not just a friendly peck. We made out." There. She'd said it.

His face went pale. "When? Where?"

"Wednesday night. In her office."

Silence. He looked down. Then he nodded, as if he'd suddenly figured all this out. His voice took on a bitter edge. "Okay, so Allie made a move. She saw an opening—a vulnerable colleague—and went for it. That's—"

"No!" Grace said. "Michael, I wanted it. We kissed each other. This wasn't something Allie did to me. It was mutual."

He paused, thinking. "Okay. A gay woman wants you; you're responding to being wanted. Understandable. That's all this is." He raked his hand through his hair. "Hell, I'd like to be wanted by her, too."

"Michael, please—"

He held up both hands, as if calming a patient. Infuriating. "Look, I understand it feels good to be wanted. But come on, Grace. You're not gay. You're not bisexual."

The words hung in the air.

"I didn't say I am. All I said is I'm drawn to her."

"People want things," he said, his voice taking on that doctor cadence. "This'll pass."

He headed for the bathroom. Grace followed him in. He reached for the door. She pushed it back open. In the mirror above the sink, his face was flushed, hers pale.

"I don't want to be alone with this anymore. I've been carrying something enormous and you had no idea. I thought if I told you, you'd finally have to see me. Not the version of me that keeps everything running. Me."

He looked at her in the mirror. "Okay." He nodded. "You're right. We need to spend more time together. We can have sex more—"

"'Have sex more'?" Grace stood. "That's your solution? Date nights and more sex?"

"I'm trying to—"

"That's ridiculous. Besides, we don't have sex, Michael. We have a routine. You kiss me for thirty seconds, you push inside me, you finish, it's over."

He cut her off, stung. "That's not fair. I try—"

"You don't try. There's no foreplay. No attention to what I actually need. No—" She stopped, then made herself say it. "Michael, I haven't come in years."

He jerked back. For a moment she saw it. Actual pain crossing his face. Not the doctor-neutral expression or the fixing mode. Pain.

But she didn't want to take it back.

"I'm not trying to attack you." Grace gentled her tone. "I'm trying to tell you: I'm lonely. Even when you're right next to me. Even when you're inside me."

He put his face in his hands and dropped to the edge of the bathtub. He said, "I can't ... can't do this right now."

Grace stayed where she was. A minute passed. He didn't look up even once.

He said, "I don't know what you want me to do. I can't forbid you from seeing a colleague who works alongside you."

"I wanted to tell you the truth, because it feels awful to be hiding this. And I thought if I told you—"

"That what? You'd feel better by confessing? Rid yourself of guilt?" He stood, now looking at her, his voice bitter. "Or what? That you'd somehow improve our marriage by confessing you want to fuck someone else? ... Look, Grace. This is some sort of midlife crisis. You should talk to your therapist about this. Or I can write you a prescription for something short-term—"

"Stop turning this into a diagnosis," Grace said, her voice breaking. "I'm trying to be open with you, and you're looking for ways to put this on a shelf and ignore it. Make it go away."

He spoke with weary kindness. "Grace, whatever this is you're going through ... it isn't real. You're confused. This will pass."

It wasn't as if the thought hadn't occurred to her. Christ. It *was* confusing. But not real? Sure as hell felt real.

He turned on the sink faucet and washed his face as if the conversation were already over.

Grace went into the bedroom, grabbing her phone from the bedside table before walking into the darkened hallway. She leaned against the wall. Heard the water shut off. A dog barked somewhere in the neighborhood.

This will pass.

She stepped into the guest room and sat on the bed. She opened her phone and texted Allie: *Told Michael about us.*

Within a minute, Allie's reply came: *Wow! How'd that go?*

Grace typed, *He said it's a girl crush. That I'll get over it.*

Allie's response was succinct: *Fuck that.*

Right, Grace replied. *This is real. He can deal with it or not.*

She set down her phone. The window reflected her face. Older, tired. Upstairs, Michael was probably already in bed, convinced this would blow over.

17

Sunday, September 24

Grace hadn't slept more than two hours. Every time she'd drifted off, she'd jolted awake, the conversation replaying in fragments. When she went downstairs around 7:00 AM, he was already in his coat, getting ready to leave. They hadn't spoken since she'd left the bathroom last night. She'd slept in the guest room, claiming a headache. He looked exhausted. Eyes red-rimmed, hair uncombed.

"They need me at the hospital," he said, his gaze fixed somewhere past her shoulder. "Probably won't be back until dinner." He grabbed his keys from the bowl. "We can talk more then, if needed," he added as he closed the door.

If needed. As if her feelings for Allie were an illness he could monitor between rounds. Nothing acute. Just something to keep an eye on. Take two aspirin and see if you feel better.

Christ.

Mia came downstairs around ten, took one look at Grace's face, and asked, "Are you okay, Mom?"

"Couldn't sleep."

"Where's Dad?"

"Hospital."

Mia studied her, then nodded and poured herself cereal. She didn't ask more questions, but twice during breakfast Grace caught her daughter watching her, assessing. Mia knew something was wrong. But she didn't push, and Grace was grateful.

Matthew spent the morning on his video game, only emerging to ask for snacks and complain that Jake from school had beaten his high score.

At 11:30, Grace tied the laces of her sneakers by the door. "I'm meeting someone for lunch at Amarin. Then to Wilson Farm. Back around three or four."

Mia looked up from her phone. "Who you meeting?"

"Steph," Grace said.

"Hmm." Mia's thumbs paused over her screen. "I thought maybe Allie."

Grace went still. How much had Mia pieced together? "Just Steph," she said, keeping her voice light.

The door to Amarin swung open, releasing the aroma of lemongrass and chili. She breathed it in, letting the warmth of the restaurant envelop her like a hug. Gentle Thai music played beneath the hum of conversation. An orchid bent its delicate neck over the corner table, where Steph was already seated.

Steph stood when she saw her. "Hey, you."

When they embraced, Grace held on tight.

"Whoa," Steph said holding Grace at arm's length. "What's going on?"

"Can we order first?" The words came out uneven. "I need a minute."

"Of course."

Their server materialized with water and menus. Grace requested pad thai without glancing down. Steph asked for chicken yellow curry, then leaned across the table. "Talk to me. Your text this morning was … intense."

Grace had texted at 6 AM: *Free for lunch today? I need to talk to someone who might understand. Please.*

"Sorry to pull you away. It's Sunday, and I know you have things to do."

Steph waved this away, reaching across the table, her fingers warm against Grace's cold ones. "I want to be here. Spill."

Grace looked at her oldest friend's face. Twenty-three years of friendship history there. "I'm in love with someone. A woman. I don't— I don't know what to do."

Steph's gaze remained steady. She nodded once, slowly. "Okay," she said carefully. "Tell me more."

"You remember that colleague I told you about back in June? The one I went with to Canobie Lake amusement park?"

Steph nodded.

"Her name's Allie. Her office is upstairs from mine. We've—" Grace pressed her napkin against her mouth. "We've known each other for years, but these past few months—" She hated rambling. "God, Steph, I can't focus on anything but her. I kissed her last week. I told Michael yesterday. My life's a hot mess."

Steph went very still. "Wait. You told Michael?" Her water glass hovered. "What'd he say?"

"He called it a girl crush and a passing phase."

"A girl crush?" Steph leaned back. "Jesus, Grace. It's obviously more than that to you. I can see it in your eyes."

"God, yes." Words poured out. She couldn't stop. She spoke of the conversations that stretched into hours. Allie's attentiveness, Allie's lips against hers. Michael's dismissive smirk last night as she tried to tell him.

Steph listened without interrupting. When Grace ran out of words, Steph sat with the silence.

"When did you first know?" Steph asked gently.

"That I love her?"

"No. That you're into women."

"That's just it. I'm not sure it's about women. It might just be about her."

Steph tilted her head. "Yeah, okay. But she's a woman. So—"

"I know." Grace twisted her napkin. "What I mean is, it's not like I'm gay. It's about her."

Steph studied her. "Grace, have you thought about that?"

"Thought about what?"

"Whether you might be gay."

"Not ... in a serious way."

"Don't you think maybe you should?" Steph paused. "Wasn't there a while in college when you thought you had a thing for that— What was her name? Jordan? Jamie?"

"Jennifer," Grace said quietly. "And I didn't have a 'thing' for her. We were just—"

"Grace." Steph's voice was gentle but firm. "You talked about her constantly. You got weirdly jealous when she went out with that guy from BU. And that night at her apartment, you both fell asleep watching a movie, her head on your shoulder—"

Grace had forgotten she'd told Steph about that. Or maybe she'd wanted to forget. "I was confused."

"Yeah, well, you said you almost kissed her when she woke up. You didn't stop talking about it for a week."

"It didn't mean anything."

"Or maybe it meant something and you couldn't let yourself see it." Steph leaned forward. "If it were true—if you are gay—would that totally freak you out?"

Grace didn't answer immediately.

"How could it not?" Grace said. "I'd have to rethink my entire life. Everything I thought I knew about myself. And, I mean— what would people say? Michael, the kids. My mom."

"I've known you longer than all of them except your mom," Steph said. "And it wouldn't change anything for me."

"Yeah. I know." Grace exhaled. "It's just ... with Michael and the kids, it's different. It would actually affect them."

"True." Steph set her water glass down carefully. "My colleague Lisa left her husband last year for a woman. She has two kids and was terrified they'd hate her. Six months later her daughter looked at her and said, 'Mom, why do you smile more now?'"

Grace's eyes widened.

The restaurant had swelled with people. Couples leaned close across tables, a server dropped a tray with a crash that made everyone look up.

Their food arrived in a cloud of fragrant steam. Grace picked up her fork, then set it down again, appetite gone. She watched as Steph pushed a piece of pineapple through her curry.

"So you might leave Michael?" Steph asked, her voice low.

Grace looked down at her hands, twisting in her lap. "I keep trying not to let my thoughts go there. But I can already see that this is dangerous. That if I let it go on, pursue it, there's potential for it to blow things sky high."

Steph took this in. Nodded.

Grace continued. "Then I try to calm myself down. Tell myself I'm just confused. That Michael's right, and it's nothing but some pathetic midlife cliché that will burn itself out."

Steph leaned forward, elbows on the table. "And when you stop overthinking it, what does your gut say?"

Grace looked up at the ceiling, blinking. "That this isn't confusion." Grace looked back at Steph. "That when she looks at me, everything else falls away. And all I want is her."

Steph studied Grace. "I guess what matters is whether you like who you are when you're with her. Whether that version of yourself feels right. If it does, then fuck the labels."

Grace let the words settle. "Yeah. And I know I don't have to figure everything out right now."

"I'm happy for you, Grace." Steph reached across the table again. "I am."

"But what if I lose everything? My marriage, my family."

"You might lose the marriage. But remember who you're talking to here. I know your marriage is shit. So, really, it's just the kids you have to worry about. And you'll still have the kids. Sure, it'll be different. But maybe different is good. Better." Steph leaned forward. "You'll never know if you keep trying to think your way out of it."

They finished their meal slowly, talking about other things. Steph's kids, her work at the nonprofit, the new restaurant opening in Harvard Square.

Outside in the parking lot, they hugged, then turned toward their separate cars.

Grace navigated her Honda into Wilson Farm's crowded parking lot, joining the weekend parade of suburbanites. Between pumpkin pyramids and regimented rows of burgundy and yellow mums, families drifted in their annual ritual. Toddlers in fleece jackets touched everything within reach, while their parents juggled coffee cups and wrestled with elaborate strollers.

A woman with four children behind her said, "Excuse me." Grace realized she was blocking traffic. The woman herded her children past like she was leading a very small, very loud marching band.

Grace loaded her cart with pumpkins and cornstalks, moving on autopilot. Muscle memory of previous Octobers.

Near the cider stand, a small line had formed. Grace joined it, deciding on candied apples for the kids and hot cider for herself. The air smelled like cinnamon and wood smoke. Around her, families laughed and jostled, kids pulling parents toward the pumpkin displays.

"Medium cider, please," Grace said when she reached the front. "And two candied apples."

The man behind the table—short, with a weathered, flannel shirt—nodded and reached for a cup.

"Grace?"

She turned. David Castellano stood beside her, hands in his jacket pockets. She jolted with surprise. Her client. The widower she'd been seeing for grief counseling, the one whose boundary issues she'd mentioned to Allie.

"David. Hi." Her therapist voice kicked in automatically, warm but professional. "What a coincidence."

"I didn't expect to see you here." He smiled, sheepish. "Well, I guess everyone comes to Wilson Farm this time of year."

"You here by yourself?"

"My daughter and her kids are around somewhere. Probably lost in the corn maze by now." He gestured vaguely toward the back fields. "You?"

"Here alone. Stocking up on pumpkins and ..." She held up the bag of candied apples. "Bribes."

He laughed. "The universal parenting currency."

They stood there for a moment, the awkwardness of a therapist-client encounter in the wild. Grace was aware of the line behind her, people waiting for cider.

"Well," she said. "Enjoy the rest of your afternoon."

"You, too. See you Monday."

Grace nodded and moved away, the cup of cider hot in her hand.

In the flower bulb aisle, she stood holding a mesh bag of tulips and couldn't remember whether the back yard got real sun in April. She couldn't picture April. Couldn't see that far ahead.

A little girl in a puffer coat pointed at the bulbs and announced to her mother, "These are the flower eggs." Grace wanted to hug her. Flower eggs. Of course they were.

At the register, the teenager scanning her items asked if she'd found everything she needed. Grace looked down at her cart. Forty pounds of decorative squash and a hundred dollars worth of other things she didn't need.

"Yes," she said. "Thank you."

Back in her car, Grace sat with both hands on the steering wheel, watching families in coordinated flannels shuttle across the parking lot. The farm bag tilted, and apples rolled into the footwell. Grace let them be.

When she looked back up, she noticed David Castellano walking toward a silver Ford three rows over. Alone. No daughter. No grandkids. Had he lied? To her face? Manufactured a scenario where running into her would seem accidental, coincidental?

She put her car in gear and left, checking her rearview mirror twice before pulling onto the road.

By 6:00 PM, Grace had transformed the front porch into something worthy of Pottery Barn's fall catalog. Corn husks flanked the front door, their pale gold catching the porch light. Inside, garlands of burnished maple leaves draped the mantelpiece, and the dining table bore a precise arrangement of gourds in graduated sizes.

She stood in the doorway, surveying her work. Everything looked exactly as it should. Seasonal, appropriate. And all she felt was hollow.

The garage door rumbled open. Michael was home. She had nothing to say to him.

Grace glanced back at her perfect fall display. She headed upstairs, leaving it all behind.

18

Monday, September 25

The old Victorian had never been a comfortable office building when the weather turned chilly. The windows leaked, and the furnace wheezed through every winter like a chain smoker on a treadmill. But that unseasonably cold Monday, it let out a bone-rattling *clank-thud-wheeze* that caused the entire building to shudder.

For the first hour, everyone pretended nothing had happened. But by eleven, real chill crept in. Scarves stayed knotted, sweaters appeared under blazers. Grace tucked her hands under her arms between sessions.

By noon, the kitchen had become a refuge. Grace and Allie arrived there at the same time, finding Leo and Claire clustered around the stove, its red coils radiating heat. They joined in, so now four therapists huddled around an electric burner like it was a campfire. Grace had seen sadder things in her time in this building, but not many.

"Anyone know what the hell's going on around here?" Allie asked.

"The house is clearly having an existential crisis about the onset of winter," Leo said. He wore a thick cardigan over his usual flannel button-down, and his nose had taken on a decidedly pink hue.

"More like a mechanical crisis," Grace said, opening the cabinet where she remembered having once seen a space heater someone had stashed. "That sound this morning—"

"Was the death rattle of our heating system," Travis announced, sweeping through the door with his usual dramatic entrance. "Had to be. I'll go down and check."

Nobody attempted to dissuade him. The basement was a dim warren of cracked concrete floors and dangling bulbs. If Travis wanted to brave it, more power to him.

The sound of his footsteps clattering down the wooden stairs was followed by muffled exclamations and a few creative curse words. Five minutes later, he reappeared, his neat appearance now adorned with cobwebs and a streak of soot across his cheek.

"Travis, you look like you fought the furnace and lost," Grace said.

"Diagnosis?" Claire asked.

"Terminal," Travis announced grimly. "Our furnace has departed this mortal coil."

Grace laughed.

"I'll call Brenda," Travis offered.

Their landlord, Brenda Davidson, was a no-nonsense woman in her sixties who treated the Victorian like a beloved but troublesome grandchild.

Her voice carried into the kitchen through the speaker on Travis's phone. "Oh, for Pete's sake," Brenda said with a resigned sigh. "I've been nursing that old beast along for three years. Knew I should've replaced it two winters ago, but I'm an optimist. Or a cheapskate. My accountant says I'm both. I suppose the damn thing decided to spite me."

"It chose its moment dramatically," Travis said. "Right at the start of cold season."

"Isn't that always the way? I'll get my HVAC guy out there this afternoon for the official pronouncement, but I'm guessing it's toast. I'll try to get them to put in a new unit ASAP."

"Until then?" Travis asked.

"Until then, I guess you all get to practice gratitude for modern heating by temporarily not having it. Could you do me a favor and put notices on the doors, so your clients know what's going on?"

After ending the call, Travis rubbed his hands together with obvious relish. "Who wants to help me craft a death notice for our dear departed furnace?"

"Do you think you're the right person for the job?" Claire asked. "It should be professional, not buffoonish."

"You wound me," Travis said. He left the room. Soon, Leo followed.

The laughter died. Claire's face had gone serious. In a low voice, she said to Grace and Allie, "I finished reading them. All of Sarah's letters."

Grace and Allie glanced at each other.

"Turns out P was widowed," Claire began. "His wife died after a long illness. Sarah and her husband had been friends with them for years. Decades, probably. The friendship turned into something else after his wife passed. The letters span about two years, 1991 to 1993."

"A love affair," Grace said.

"Yeah. And not a casual one. Not just sex. It was wholehearted. A life. These letters—" Claire stopped, swallowed. "They're beautiful and terrible. He was completely in love with her. And she with him, based on what he writes back to things she must've said or written."

"What happened?" Allie asked.

"Sarah was going to leave her husband. P was waiting for her, ready. He writes about the apartment he was looking at for them, about how he'd take her to Italy like she'd always wanted. He was patient, supportive. But she kept postponing, making excuses."

Grace set down her mug carefully, as though the table might not hold it.

Claire blinked rapidly. "The last letter is dated August 1993. It's devastating."

"What did it say?" Grace asked.

Claire pulled in a breath. "He wrote that he had come to understand that waiting for her to be ready meant waiting forever. That he loved her enough to let her go, though leaving her behind would be the hardest thing he'd ever done." She wiped at her eyes. "But he said he couldn't be the person she loved in secret anymore. That he needed to be someone's whole life, not their hidden one."

Allie sat very still, jaw tight. When she looked up at Grace, their eyes met.

"She kept those letters for thirty-one years," Claire continued. "Never threw them away, never moved on. Just held onto them like —" She gestured helplessly. "Like proof of the life she didn't choose."

Grace heard a bus outside hiss at the curb, then move on. But all she could think about was Sarah Clarke spending three decades carrying that choice. About what regret would look like after thirty years.

"Thank you for telling us," Allie said. "That couldn't have been easy to read."

Claire nodded, standing. "All that love, all those years." She shook her head. "And she kept his words in a box."

Silence hung in the room.

"I promised I'd let you know the story." Claire smoothed her skirt. She looked from Allie to Grace. "You two take care."

"Thanks, Claire," Grace said.

When they were alone, Grace and Allie sat still, not looking at each other. Silence. Grace stared at her hands.

An hour later, Grace laughed as she read an email Travis sent to all of them:

"Colleagues: Here's the notice I drafted for the outside doors. Think this is okay?"

IN MEMORIAM: HEATING SYSTEM (1985-2023)

9/25/23

Dear Clients and Visitors,

It is with mixed emotions (mostly cold ones) that we announce the passing of our heating system this morning. After 35 years of faithful service, our furnace has joined the great HVAC system in the sky.

Cause of death: Natural causes, possibly complicated by old age and what the basement suggests was a complete loss of will to live.

A replacement system will be installed ASAP. Until then, we recommend layers, hot beverages, and the therapeutic value of shared adversity.

In lieu of flowers, please bring warm thoughts (or warm socks; we need those more).

Yours in solidarity,

The Management

Claire wrote back a reply-to-all: "This is exactly the kind of self-satisfied piffle I feared from you, Travis. I will put up an appropriate notice."

By late afternoon, the house had taken on an oddly festive atmosphere. Clients were offered tea upon arrival, therapists had shed their usual professional distance in favor of practical cooperation, and the kitchen buzzed with constant activity as people rotated through, warming hands around mugs and sharing weather predictions.

Grace found herself lingering longer than usual between appointments. She was refilling her tea when Allie appeared in the doorway, wrapped in a burgundy cape that made her look like she'd stepped out of a Victorian novel.

"Is this where the refugees gather?" Allie crossed to the kettle and reached for a mug.

"Refugees and survivors," Grace confirmed. "How are your clients taking it?"

"Surprisingly well. Mrs. Patterson said it reminded her of her childhood. No central heating, everyone gathering in the kitchen for warmth. She was almost nostalgic about it."

They stood in comfortable silence, steam rising from their mugs. Outside, the wind rattled the old windows.

"I should get back," Grace said eventually. "My four o'clock will be here soon."

"Right. Me too."

But neither of them moved.

❧

As evening approached and the last clients departed, the house settled into an unusual quiet. The absence of the heating system's familiar rumbles and hisses made every other sound more noticeable. Footsteps on stairs, doors closing, the old building's creaks and sighs.

Grace was gathering her things when she heard voices in the hallway. Leo and Claire, discussing dinner plans with the camaraderie of disaster survivors.

Allie appeared in the hallway, pulling on her coat. "Heading out soon?"

Grace smiled. "Yeah, it's been a day." She knotted her scarf more tightly around her neck.

"Well," Allie said, keys already in hand. "I hope the new heating system has more stamina than the old one."

"Here's hoping," Grace agreed.

"Goodnight," Allie said, heading toward her car.

Grace stood in the cold parking lot, watching her go.

Sarah Clarke had waited. Had kept letters in a box for thirty-one years instead of living the life she wanted.

19

Thursday, September 28

The next morning, Grace tried to focus on her notes for her ten o'clock session, but her mind kept drifting to Allie. At 9:52, she typed: *Need to see you. When are you free?*

The reply was immediate: *Between 11 and 12.*

Grace typed quickly, before she could change her mind: *Meet me at 11:15. Basement. We can pretend we're checking out the new furnace.*

She grinned at Allie's reply: *Very convincing cover story.*

At 10:34, she glanced at the clock for the sixth time. Her client was mid-sentence about perfectionism. Grace nodded, said something about self-compassion, and checked the clock again. 10:35.

At 11:13 she went to the kitchen. Nobody there. She opened the door to the basement and descended. Dim light filtered from ground-level windows. The new furnace droned among ancient pipes and flaking concrete, the air sharp with cut metal and dust.

She stood by the new machine, listening to footsteps descend the wooden stairs. Allie appeared at the bottom, paused when she saw Grace.

"Hi," Grace said, the word inadequate.

Allie's mouth lifted. "Hi."

They didn't move for a beat and then they did, closing the space between them. Grace reached first, her fingers sliding along the line of Allie's jaw. The kiss was urgent, desperate.

Allie's embrace pressed Grace's back against the cool rough-stone wall of the foundation. A creak overhead. Footsteps crossing the floor above them. They froze, listening. The footsteps moved away.

She pulled her head back a few inches to look at Allie. "This is insane."

"I know." Allie's forehead rested against hers. "But I can't think of anything else."

"Neither can I." Grace touched Allie's face.

"When can I see you again?" Allie asked. "Really be with you?"

Grace scanned her mental calendar. "Michael has a conference all day on Saturday."

"Damn. I have the kids all weekend."

"Well, we could still get together. You and me. And all the kids. Maybe the Science Museum? Matthew's been bugging me to go."

"It's a plan," Allie said.

Grace closed her eyes, already anticipating it. "We should go back up. Separately," she said. "You first, I'll wait three minutes." Allie kissed her once more, quick and sweet, then pulled away.

Grace checked her reflection in her phone's camera. Lord. She fixed her hair and straightened her clothes. She pressed on the swollen lips, trying to will the flush away. Good enough to fool Leo, Claire, Travis. Good enough to hide what she'd just been doing. She smiled, embarrassed. Then climbed the stairs, practicing her neutral face.

Professional development, she'd joke, if anyone asked why she was down there. *Learning about HVAC systems.*

Grace sat in her own therapist's office, hands wrapped around a cup of tea she wasn't drinking. Rain lashed against the windows. She'd been staring at those Matisse dancers for five minutes, unable to find words. The room was too warm, Therese's space heater purring in the corner.

"You look exhausted," Therese said. "What's been happening since we last met?"

Grace took a breath. "A lot. Remember I told you about my colleague Allie?"

Therese said, "Yes. I planned to ask you about her. You were going to the theater with her the day following our last appointment."

"Yeah. Well—" Grace paused. "I kissed her neck that night. Then last week, we made out in her office. And a few days ago, I told Michael and —"

Therese set down her pen. "Whoa. Slow down. All this is important. You made out?"

"Last Wednesday night. After a session. I went back to the office and—" Grace shook her head. "I couldn't stop myself."

Therese nodded. "And then you told Michael. When?"

"A few days later. Saturday night. I couldn't—" Grace ran her fingers through her hair. "I couldn't keep lying to him. Every time he looked at me, every time he asked how my day was, I was carrying this enormous thing and he had no idea. It felt unbearable."

"That's one reason," Therese said carefully. "Was there another?"

Grace was quiet for a moment. "Maybe. Yeah. I think something's been shifting in me—something I don't have a name for yet. And I wanted him to know the changing person. The real Grace, whoever she is." She looked at her hands. "We've been married seventeen years. He deserves to know who I am. And I thought— maybe if I told him this, he'd finally see me, the way Allie does. He'd have to look at me and understand that something fundamental is happening to me. That I'm not the person he married. Or maybe I am, finally, and that's the problem."

"What did you tell him?"

Grace laid out the conversation. Her confession, his dismissal.

Therese listened without interrupting, then asked, "How did that land?"

"Like confirmation of everything I already knew. I told him I have strong feelings for another woman. That we'd kissed. He reacted, but not the way I needed. He went straight into fix-it mode. Date nights. More sex. As if I'd told him we were out of milk, and he realized we needed to restock. He suggested it was a phase. That I needed help." She let out a short, humorless laugh. "Seventeen years, and that's what he came up with."

"You sound angry."

"I *am* angry. I'm furious." Grace pressed her palms against her thighs. "Not just because he dismissed it. Because even then—even when I handed him the most vulnerable thing I've ever said out loud —he couldn't see me. He just couldn't do it."

Grace stood, unable to sit still. She moved to the window, watching rain slide down the glass. "I keep replaying it. Thinking maybe I wasn't clear enough, maybe I should have said it differently. But I was clear, Therese. I told him I have feelings for someone else. I told him we've kissed. And he just ..." She turned back, returned to her chair, sank into it, and sighed. "He doesn't care. Or he can't let himself care. I don't know which is worse."

Therese allowed a silent beat. Then she leaned forward, elbows on her knees. "How does it feel to be with her that way? Kissing her?"

"Terrifying. Exhilarating. Like I've been numb for years and suddenly I can feel everything. I've never felt this before, Therese. This kind of wanting. Not with Michael. Anyone."

"What do you mean?"

"I mean— with Michael, sex was always just something I did because married people do that. But I never felt this ... hunger. This need to touch someone, to be close to them. With Allie, I can't think straight. My whole body feels like it's on fire."

"That must be confusing."

"It's not confusing. That's the problem." Grace held her gaze. "It's the clearest I've felt in years. When I'm with her, everything makes sense. And when I'm not—when I'm home with Michael—I feel like I'm suffocating."

"Grace, I need to ask you something."

Grace waited.

"Do you think you're gay?"

The question hung in the air.

"I don't know," she said, her mind skipping back to Stephanie asking her the same question. "I've been trying to figure that out. I keep going back through my marriage, trying to remember if I ever really wanted Michael. Sexually. And I honestly can't tell if I convinced myself I did or if I actually did at some point."

"And with Allie?"

"With Allie, I know." Grace's voice was steady. "I want her. In a way I've never wanted anyone. But I don't know if that means I'm gay or if it just means I'm attracted to her specifically. What matters is that I can't keep pretending. I can't keep living a life that feels like a lie."

"What feels like a lie?"

"All of it. The marriage. The house. The family dinners where we all sit around pretending everything's fine." Grace's hands moved as she talked. "I look at Michael and I feel nothing. Worse than nothing. I feel trapped. And then I think about Allie and I feel—" She stopped. "I feel alive."

They sat in silence for a moment. Rain continued its steady beat against the windows.

"I don't want to hurt my kids," Grace said. "I don't want to blow up their lives." Tears formed. "But I also can't keep living like this."

"I understand."

Grace wiped her eyes. "So what do I do?"

"Nothing until you sit with this a while longer. Then, eventually, you'll have to make a choice. And then live with it." Therese leaned back. Straightened her shoulders. "There's no perfect answer here, Grace. No path that doesn't hurt someone. You just have to decide what you can live with."

Grace nodded, unable to speak.

"What do you want to happen with Allie?"

"I want more. I want to know what it's like to actually be with her. Not just kissing in her office, terrified someone will catch us. I want—" She stopped, but Therese's steady gaze pulled it out of her. "I want to sleep with her. I want to wake up next to her. I want to stop hiding."

"And your marriage?"

Grace was quiet for a long moment. "I think it's over. I think it's been over for a long time, and I was just too scared to admit it."

"What do you think you'll do?"

"Last time I was here, you suggested I try to get Michael into couples therapy."

"Yes. I think that's a good idea."

"But you suggested it as a way to save the marriage. Or, at least, to assure myself I've done everything I can to save it. But that's not why I want to do it."

"Why then?"

"Because I want a professional to help Michael see the marriage is unsalvageable. That I can't keep living like this. That he needs to let me go."

Therese was quiet for a moment. "So you've already decided."

"Yes."

Therese nodded. "Okay. You've been forming that decision for a long time. And what about Allie? What happens there?"

"I don't know. We haven't talked about it. About what this is or where it's going. We're just ..." Grace searched for the word. "Existing in this moment. Stolen kisses in her office. Texts that make my heart race. I don't know how to stop it."

"That sounds exhausting."

Grace started to say *it's not*—and then stopped herself. "Actually, can I say something that's going to sound like I'm arguing against my own happiness?"

Therese waited.

"Like you, I'm sure, I've explained the concept of limerence to clients countless times. Laid out for them the neurochemistry of new attachment—the obsessive thinking, the euphoria, the way everything else flattens out by comparison." She pressed her lips together. "And I keep wondering ... what if that's what this is? What if I'm considering blowing up my marriage and my kids' lives for something that has a half-life of two years?"

"That's an important question," Therese said. "What does your answer tell you?"

"That's the thing." Grace was quiet for a moment. "When I try to argue myself out of my feelings for Allie—when I tell myself it's just neurochemistry, just novelty—it doesn't hold. Because it's not just that I want her. It's that when I'm with her I feel like a person I recognize. Like I've been living slightly outside myself for years and I finally stepped back in." She shook her head. "Limerence doesn't explain that. Does it?"

"What do you think?"

"I think—" Grace stopped. "I think I'm afraid to trust my own answer. Because I want it to be real so badly." A pause. "But also—this is the best I've felt in years. Even with all the guilt and fear and confusion, when I'm with her I feel like myself. Like I'm finally allowed to be real." She gave a small, tired smile. "So if that's limerence, fuck it. I'm signing on anyway."

"Hold onto that," Therese said. "Whatever happens next, hold onto knowing what feeling real feels like. You're going to need it."

Grace gathered her things: coat, bag, the crumpled tissues she'd pulled from the box on Therese's side table.

"Do you want to schedule our next session?" Therese asked.

"Let's leave it for now. I'll be in touch. Thanks, Therese." She turned to go.

"Grace?"

She turned back.

"You've spent a long time taking care of everyone else's happiness. It's not wrong to include your own."

Grace nodded, not trusting her voice.

In the building's foyer, she stopped to check for any messages. Nothing from Michael. One from Allie: *Thinking about you. Hope your day is okay.*

Grace stared at the simple acknowledgment of her existence. At the heart emoji following it.

She typed back: *It's better now.* And appended a heart emoji of her own.

She stepped out into the rain to go home and be who everyone needed her to be.

20

Saturday, September 30

Saturday morning, Grace woke at 5:52 to the sound of Michael's car pulling away, heading to his conference in Hartford. She rolled onto her back and exhaled.

In the kitchen, she found Michael's handwriting on an index card by the coffeemaker: "Back tonight around 7:00. Enjoy your museum thing."

He'd reduced her whole day—Allie, the carefully planned outing, the risk of bringing their worlds together—into two dismissive words scrawled on an index card. *Museum thing.*

An hour later, Grace whisked pancake batter in a large blue bowl, watching the lumps slowly disappear. Matthew wandered in from the living room, his game controller dangling from one hand, his hair still rumpled from sleep.

"Mom? We still going to the Science Museum today?" he asked, leaning against the counter.

Grace nodded, pouring the first circle of batter onto the griddle. "Yes. And not just us. We're meeting Allie and her kids there."

Mia slouched in the kitchen doorway, still in pajamas. "Allie's daughter—" She crossed her arms. "What's she like?"

Grace hesitated, unsure how to answer. She knew Emma only from Allie's scattered anecdotes: Emma, brilliant one moment, sullen the next, slamming doors after friend drama. Fragments that didn't quite assemble into a whole person Grace could describe to her daughter.

"I'm sure she's great. You'll meet her soon enough. Breakfast is coming in a few minutes." She poured more batter, this time into the elongated, snakelike shape that always made Matthew smile.

They ate, then each of them trailed off to their own activities. After an hour, Matthew reappeared, bounding down the stairs, fully dressed, his sneakers already double-knotted. He bounced on his toes, hands gripping the kitchen doorframe.

"Is it time yet? Can we go? I've got a whole plan: first the dinosaurs, then the lightning generator, then—" His words tumbled out faster than his breath could keep up.

"It doesn't open until nine, sweetie. We'll leave in about half an hour." How fun to have him this excited.

In the car, Matthew narrated every red light as if Cambridge's traffic system was a personal affront, while Mia concentrated on the screen of her phone like she was defusing a bomb.

They pulled into the museum's parking lot at 9:12, finding it already crowded with minivans and SUVs. Grace spotted Allie's car three rows over. In minutes, Mia and Matthew would be face-to-face with Emma and Noah, four children who had no idea they were part of something larger than a casual museum outing.

Inside, morning light flooded the atrium. Grace spotted Allie immediately, standing near the ticket counter with two children beside her, all three of them searching the crowd. Allie saw her and smiled.

Allie held a paper cup of coffee while Emma leaned against her shoulder. A willowy girl with her mother's coloring but her own sharp features and catlike alertness. Noah hung back half a pace, determined not to look like a little kid, but he fidgeted with his jacket zipper, his restless energy barely contained.

When they reached each other, Allie closed the distance with a one-armed hug. Grace's fingertips found the curve of her waist, lingering. "Matty's been counting down the minutes."

The kids shuffled into a semicircle, eyes darting, mouths twitching. Mia hung back, assessing Emma with teenage caution. Emma offered a small, waist-level wave. Noah and Matthew sized each other up like dogs deciding whether to play or fight.

Emma glanced at Mia, then pointed to the suspended T-Rex skeleton. "Do you think its arms could actually reach its mouth?"

Mia's eyebrows lifted slightly. "That's ... random."

Emma looked down. "I just meant, like ... oh, I don't know. My brain just goes to weird places sometimes."

"No, I mean— it's a good question," Mia said quickly. "I never thought about it." She smiled at Emma. "My brain does that, too."

Grace could hug her daughter in that moment for smoothing over the hurt.

"Well, they didn't use utensils," Noah announced.

"But could it pick up food?" Matthew said, and suddenly the boys were arguing about whether a T-Rex could hold a foot-long sandwich with those short arms.

The four of them drifted toward the exhibit, the girls a bit behind the boys. Grace and Allie fell into step behind them all.

An hour passed as the kids disappeared into one exhibit after another. When they emerged from a mock-up of a wind tunnel,

Matthew's hair pointed in seven directions, which made Emma laugh so hard she had to sit down.

Matthew's arm shot up. "The lightning show starts in five minutes!" He was already three steps ahead, beckoning them toward the Theater of Electricity.

In the darkened theater, the Van de Graaff generator cracked and whistled, producing bolts of purple artificial lightning. Matthew leaned forward, transfixed. Noah shifted in his seat. Emma watched while pretending not to. Mia filmed on her phone. Grace sat with Allie in the back row, holding hands in the dark below the shared armrest.

After the lightning demonstration, they worked through other exhibits. In the insect room, Allie explained to Matthew how butterflies taste with their feet, her long, slender fingers mimicking the motion.

In the planetarium, the dome went dark, stars appearing one by one overhead, the narrator's voice low and reverent. The kids sat in the row in front of them—Mia and Emma shoulder to shoulder, Noah and Matthew on the outsides, all four tilting back when Orion flared.

The narrator asked for everyone to imagine a place they loved at night, and Mia whispered something to Emma, who nodded. Grace watched them.

Outside in the bright lobby, Grace checked her watch. 12:30. They'd been here three hours. Mia's phone buzzed and she glanced at it and smiled, a blush hitting her cheeks. She typed something back, and pocketed it.

Grace watched the blush spread. *Chloe?* "Who was that?" She asked, keeping her tone mild.

"Just a friend from school." Mia's tone said *drop it,* and Grace did.

"We should probably get lunch," Allie said.

"There's the cafeteria here," Grace started, then stopped. The cafeteria would be safe. Neutral territory, contained. But the kids were getting along now, and the day felt unfinished. "Or ..." She looked at Allie, took a breath. "You could all come back to our house. I could make pasta."

Grace felt Mia's eyes on her. When she glanced over, Mia was watching with that assessing look, the one that saw too much.

Allie's eyes searched hers. "Are you sure?"

She nodded. "Yes. If you want to."

"I'd like that," Allie said.

Back at the house, shoes piled up by the door as they all spilled into the kitchen. Noah knelt before Matthew's Lego collection in the living room, spreading pieces across the worn oak floor. Emma and Mia settled on the window seat with Mia's laptop, scrolling through playlists. The boys' excited voices competed with each other.

"What can I do to help?" Allie asked.

"You could start water boiling. Big pot in that cabinet."

They moved around each other carefully at first, then with more ease. Allie got the pasta going while Grace started on garlic bread, both of them working side by side at the counter. Their shoulders bumped as they reached for the same cutting board. Allie's hand brushed Grace's passing the butter.

Allie patted cherry tomatoes dry with a dish towel. "This is nice. Being here with you."

The boys' voices rose from the living room, some debate about Minecraft versus Roblox escalating.

The pasta timer went off. Grace drained the pot into a colander while Allie called the kids to the table. They came in a herd, still arguing, taking seats with easy chaos.

Grace served pasta into bowls, Allie poured milk, and for a few minutes it was just the work of feeding six hungry people. Then

Noah twirled a fork of spaghetti and lifted it, the strand dangling precariously.

"I bet mine's longer than yours," he challenged Matthew.

"No way." Matthew immediately began measuring his own spaghetti, and the meal dissolved into adolescent male competition: who could get the longest strand, who could slurp the loudest, who could wear the most sauce on their face.

Grace smiled. Noah: just like his mother. Well, he came by that competitive spirit honestly.

Emma wrinkled her nose. "You guys are disgusting," she said, even as she laughed.

"Boys are gross," Mia agreed, but she was laughing too.

After lunch, everybody moved back to the living room. Some TV, idle chat. The kids drifted upstairs, back down.

After a while, Grace and Allie migrated back to the kitchen and cleaned up together. At the sink, both stared out the window at the gray November afternoon. Allie's hand found Grace's, squeezed once, let go.

"I should probably get them home."

Grace nodded. Her eyes fell to Allie's lips, the desire to lean in and kiss them almost painful.

The goodbyes spilled into the hallway. Matthew was already making plans with Noah about Minecraft.

Emma pulled out her phone. "What's your number?" she asked Mia.

Mia rattled it off, and Emma typed it in. "I'll send you that playlist we were talking about."

"Cool."

Emma paused at the door, turned back to Grace. "Thanks for inviting us. This was fun."

"You're welcome," Grace said. "You're welcome here anytime."

Emma smiled—quick, genuine—then followed her brother out to the car.

Mia and Matthew remained in the doorway while Grace walked halfway to the curb. Allie got the kids settled in the car, then walked back to where Grace stood, stopping just at the edge of appropriate distance.

"Thank you," Allie said. "For today. For all of it."

Grace was aware of Mia and Matthew watching from behind her. She couldn't hug Allie the way she wanted to. Couldn't touch her face or let her fingers linger. Instead she reached for Allie's coat belt, which hung loose, and looped it without thinking, pulled it snug, tied a quick knot. A gesture she could explain away as practical if anyone commented.

Grace glanced over her shoulder. Mia and Matthew were still in the doorway. Mia's eyes narrowed slightly, then she turned and pulled Matthew back inside.

Allie held Grace's eyes a second longer than necessary. "I'll text you."

"Okay."

Grace watched until the car turned the corner, then went back inside where Mia and Matthew had already scattered, Mia to her room, Matthew to his video game. She started picking up the remaining mess: Lego pieces on the floor, empty milk glasses on the coffee table, the small debris of six people having occupied space together.

Ten minutes later, her phone buzzed with a text from Allie: *Thank you again. The kids had a great time. So did I.*

Grace sat on the couch, staring at the message. She thought about the six of them in her kitchen. Allie at her stove, Emma and Mia laughing. Matthew and Noah making plans.

She typed back: *Me too. And let's get them together again soon.*

She set her phone down and let her eye move across the room: the photos on the mantel, the familiar furniture, the life she'd built here. Suddenly none of it looked the same. Everything felt different now.

Michael's car pulled into the driveway at about 7:30 that evening. Grace heard the garage door grind open, then the engine cut. She was at the kitchen sink, hands in soapy water. The kids were upstairs, their movements a low thrum through the ceiling.

The door from the garage into the mudroom opened. Michael came into the kitchen, conference lanyard still around his neck, shirt untucked.

Grace's hands stilled in the soapy water.

"How was it?" she asked.

"Fine. Long. The keynote was actually interesting, but the breakout sessions were mostly people rehashing the same studies." He opened the fridge, pulled out leftover chicken, ate a piece cold while standing there, scrolling his phone. "Kids okay?"

"They're good. Matty's been building all evening. Mia's on the phone."

He nodded, chewed while scrolling.

Grace dried the last dish and set it in the cabinet, wondering if he'd ask anything else.

"I'm going to change," he said, heading for the stairs. "Be down in a bit."

She wiped the counter in slow circles, listening to his footsteps overhead, the creak of their bedroom floor.

Twenty minutes later, Michael appeared in sweats and a t-shirt from a 5K they'd run together six years ago. Grace settled on the living-room couch with a book she didn't read, while Michael tapped at his laptop. Same room. Different worlds.

Matthew whipped down the stairs around 8:30, hair wild, face bright. "Dad! We went to the Science Museum today with Mom's friend Allie and her kids and it was so cool. Way better than when you took me that time because we stayed longer today and got to see everything and then they came here and we had spaghetti and it was so funny and Mia said—"

"That sounds great, Matthew." Michael didn't look up from his screen. "I need to catch up on work, okay?"

"Oh, and Allie's son Noah knows about Minecraft mods that I didn't even know existed and Emma is older but she's actually pretty cool for a girl and we're going to play online sometime this week—"

"Mm-hmm."

"—and her kids are going to come over again maybe next weekend if their dad doesn't have them and Mom said we could probably go—"

"Matthew." Michael glanced up. "That's nice. I'm glad you had fun. But I've got a lot of work to catch up on, so maybe tell me more tomorrow?"

Matthew's shoulders dropped, his face fell. "Okay. Night, Dad."

Grace watched him retreat. If she defended Matthew, she'd have to explain why today mattered. And then she'd have to say Allie's name again. Watch him not care again.

"Night, bud." Michael's attention returned to his laptop without pause, as if the conversation had never happened.

Grace put her finger in the book, holding a place that didn't matter. "They really did have a great time," she said.

"Good." He typed something, frowned at the screen.

"Allie's kids are lovely. Emma's thirteen, very bright. Noah's eleven, funny, good with Matt."

"Mm-hmm."

"We all came back here for lunch. Spent the afternoon here. The kids got along so well they're already planning to do it again."

"That's nice." He highlighted something on his screen, copied it into another document.

She laid the book down harder than necessary. "Michael."

"Hmm?"

"Can you look at me for a second?"

He glanced up, eyebrows raised. "What?"

She hadn't planned what to say. "I brought Allie and her children into our house today. Into our kids' lives. And you seem completely uninterested in that. Haven't asked a single question about it."

"You said it went well. What else do I need to know?"

"Maybe you could want to know. Be curious about it. Or, I don't know— be bothered. Or upset. Something."

His eyes narrowed slightly. "Grace, it's eight-thirty on a Saturday night. I just got back from a conference. I'm behind on notes. Can we not do this right now?"

"Do what?"

"Whatever fight you're trying to start."

"I'm not trying to start a fight. I'm trying to have a conversation."

"About what? You took the kids to a museum with a colleague and her kids. You had lunch. It sounds perfectly fine. What am I missing?"

Maybe he wasn't missing anything. Maybe he'd chosen not to know.

"Nothing," Grace said. "You're not missing anything."

She wanted to ask: Do you remember what I told you about Allie? Do you remember me saying I have feelings for her? Do you understand that something is happening here that you're choosing not to see?

But she didn't.

She picked up her book. Michael returned to his laptop. In the silence between them, Grace could still hear Matthew and Noah's laughter from this afternoon, still feel Allie's hand in hers in the planetarium.

She knew which world she wanted to live in. She just didn't know how to get there yet.

21

Saturday, October 6

The following Saturday afternoon, both kids had gone off to sleepovers—Mia to Chloe's, Matt to Jake's. This didn't happen very often, and Grace had said yes to both, grateful for the break. It was almost too silent for a Saturday afternoon. Unsettling. But at least she had the afternoon to herself, time to catch up on a bit of work and on laundry before the kids came back with more.

She pulled two case files from her tote and spread them on the kitchen table. Jerry McCaffrey, struggling with his wife's emotional withdrawal after her heart attack. Jennifer Hayden, distraught because her boyfriend wouldn't discuss moving in together after three years.

She lingered on Jennifer's, recalling the twenty-eight year old's voice—exhausted, defeated: *He only sees me when he needs something. The rest of the time, it's like I'm not there.*

She had given her the usual lines at their last appointment about communication patterns and attachment styles. All the calibrated language she was trained to offer. Now, looking at the file again, it felt thin, too clean.

She picked up her pen and wrote in Jennifer's plan: *Name what you want. Say it out loud. Don't justify it. Let it exist before you decide what to do about it.*

Her hand stilled. She tilted her head back and said it aloud into the empty kitchen: "I want her."

There. Spoken. No crash of guilt. Just the truth.

An hour later, she closed her laptop and went to switch the laundry. In Mia's room, Grace folded t-shirts and jeans with the efficient precision that came from years of doing.

She opened the dresser to put away underwear and socks. She noticed something tucked behind the neat rows: a folded piece of notebook paper, the edges worn from repeated handling. Grace hesitated. She wasn't the kind of mother who snooped. But the paper was right there, and something about the way it was hidden—carefully, deliberately—demanded her attention.

She opened it slowly. The handwriting was round, loopy, distinctly teenage female.

M—I can't stop thinking about yesterday. Do you feel it too? —C

Grace read it twice, then refolded the note and held it against her chest for a moment before carefully replacing it exactly where she'd found it. She closed the dresser drawer.

It might be nothing. Girls were intense at this age. Dramatic friendships that meant everything and nothing. Grace remembered her own teenage letters, the friendships that felt like falling in love because you didn't yet know the difference.

The afternoon had morphed into an evening that dragged on too long. Grace was now in sleep clothes—cotton pants, old t-shirt—putting away more laundry when Michael came in, hair damp from the shower. He wore only boxers. She set down the shirt she was holding.

"Hey," he said, closing the door behind him, his voice warmer than usual.

He'd been different since their conversation about Allie. Quieter, more careful. Trying, she thought, to prove something.

"Hi," she answered, warily.

He sat on the bed, next to where she stood. He rested his hand on her hip. Gentle, a little tentative. "We have the whole place to ourselves," he said, the words almost careful.

She looked down at his hand. They hadn't touched like this in months, maybe longer. She'd stopped keeping track a long time ago.

"Michael—"

He hesitated, then said, "I miss you. I miss ... us."

She looked away. This was Michael. Her husband.

"Okay."

He stood and kissed her, his hand moving to her face. Grace closed her eyes, trying to feel something besides obligation. Outside, a car passed. The bedroom window rattled slightly in its frame.

His lips were dry, his touch careful. She let him pull her shirt over her head, shivering as the air hit her bare skin.

"Cold?" Michael asked.

"A little," she said.

He pulled her down onto the bed, his body covering hers with a familiar weight.

Michael tried this time; she could tell. He kissed her ears, her neck, and his hands were gentler than usual.

He propped himself up, searching her face. "Tell me what you want."

She opened her mouth. Nothing came. Not because she didn't know—she knew exactly, had known for years what she needed and never said it. She'd told clients a hundred times: *Say it plainly, your partner cannot read silence.* And here, with Michael looking at her with genuine effort on his face, she couldn't say a single word that was true.

"Just— keep going," she said.

His hand lingered at her breasts, his thumb brushing her. She forced a small sound. "Mmm." Her body remained cold, distant.

He moved lower, pausing before sliding off her pajama bottoms. She nodded.

"You're beautiful," he said quietly. His hand slipped between her legs, fingers tentative, then more insistent. He circled her clit, slow and steady, glancing up for a reaction.

"Yes," she said, though her body wouldn't respond.

Grace's mind drifted to Allie's touch, Allie's breath at her ear. The way she'd felt alive.

"Grace?" Michael's voice broke her reverie. "Are you ...?"

She opened her eyes. He was looking at her with hope. "I don't think ..." she started, trailing off. "Maybe you should just—"

His eyes changed. He looked at her for a moment—not angry, something closer to resigned—and she saw it: he knew. Not about Allie—but about this, about them. What it meant that she was lying here unable to want him. What it meant about their marriage, their life together. He withdrew his hand and she thought he was stopping.

Instead, he reached for the lube without a word. He didn't ask again. He positioned himself between her legs and pushed inside her. He tried at first, his rhythm careful, his eyes on hers. But soon he shifted, his rhythm faster, less careful. His eyes closed.

Grace stared past his shoulder at the ceiling, silent, unmoving.

She let her arms fall at her sides, let her mind go blank, waiting for it to end.

When he came, he collapsed onto her with a grunt, then rolled away.

They lay side by side, neither speaking. Grace turned her face to the wall, blinking hard.

"I tried," Michael said.

Grace shifted her stare to the ceiling. "I know."

He was quiet for a moment. "Have I ever known? What you want?" His voice wasn't accusatory. It sounded like a question he'd been carrying for a long time and had finally run out of reasons not to ask.

She didn't answer. What could she say? That she didn't know either—not with him, not ever? That the truth was more complicated than fault, that some of the silence between them had been her own?

After a while, Michael turned away and slipped into sleep, his breathing slow and even.

Grace lay perfectly still, feeling hollow. She no longer wanted him. Maybe she never had, not the way she wanted Allie.

Grace slipped out of bed and went to the bathroom. She sat on the toilet, cleaning herself, feeling the soreness, the wetness he'd left in her. When she finished, she washed her hands and looked in the mirror. The light was harsh. Her face unchanged, just older, a few more lines, hair tousled.

Something inside her shut down, like a door closing. She leaned on the sink.

Is this the life I want for the next forty years?

No.

She didn't want this. Not anymore.

Her marriage was over.

Grace switched off the light and slid back into bed. Michael snored beside her, oblivious. She lay wide awake, staring into the dark.

∾

The next morning, Grace found Michael in the kitchen, already dressed for his run. He was tying his shoes by the back door.

"Morning," he said, not quite meeting her eyes.

"Morning."

He grabbed his phone and earbuds from the counter. "I'll be back in an hour or so."

She nodded. The door closed behind him, and she stood in the kitchen, listening to his footsteps fade down the driveway.

A couple hours later, Grace found him in the den, still in his running clothes, typing notes into his laptop. The room smelled of sweat and coffee.

"Hey," she said from the doorway.

He glanced up. "Good run. Did seven miles."

"That's great." She lingered. "Do you have a minute?"

Her tone got his attention. He saved his document and looked up at her. "What's up?"

Grace stepped in and closed the door. She sat in the old leather chair, her legs restless, a knee bouncing.

"I've been thinking. About us. About everything." She drew in a deep breath. "I think— I think we need to see someone. A couples therapist."

He blinked. "Marriage counseling?"

"Yes."

"Because ...?"

"Because we're not okay. You have to know that." Her voice

stayed level. Her hands curled in her lap. "We don't know how to reach each other."

He leaned back, rubbing his neck. "I'm not sure what you're getting at. Things seem ... fine."

She repeated the word. "'Fine.' Michael, nothing's fine. We can't communicate. And there's no real connection between us. Emotional or physical. Last night in bed— you felt it too. I know you did. That's not the way it's supposed to be."

"Grace—"

"But that's the least of it. Last Saturday, I tried to tell you about our day with Allie and her kids. Matthew tried to tell you, too. He was so excited he could barely get the words out. And you couldn't bother to look up at him."

"I'd just gotten back from a conference. I was exhausted. I had work—"

"You told Matt you were too busy to talk. *Tell me tomorrow,* you said. But then you were at the hospital all the next day. Did you ever have that conversation with him? Did you ask him?"

"I don't remember."

"You didn't. Because it doesn't register for you. Not what Matthew did or what he cares about. Christ, you didn't even seem to care that I brought Allie and her children into our kids' lives. The woman I told you I have feelings for."

"So what do you want, Grace? You want me to be jealous? Grill you about your crush? Make a scene every time you bring up this woman?"

She almost said yes—yes, that's exactly what I want. But she stopped herself. Was that fair? She'd handed him an impossible situation and then faulted him for not reacting the right way.

Grace's voice rose. "I want you to care. Connect the dots. Pay attention to what's going on around you. But you keep ignoring what's right in front of you while our marriage falls apart."

When Michael spoke, his tone was careful, clinical. "Fine. I hear you. You've got a thing for a woman at work; you're hanging out with her and her kids. What do you want me to say?"

"All I want you to say right now is that you'll go to couples therapy," she said again. "I want us to talk to someone who can help us figure out how we got here."

"And you think a therapist is going to fix what? Your crush on someone else?"

"I think a therapist could help us figure out how our marriage turned into ... whatever this is."

He studied her. "You really think it's that bad?"

"I do. Don't you?"

He looked away. "I think we're busy and overworked. I don't think we're ..." He trailed off.

"Not what?"

He shrugged. "Broken. Whatever it is you think we are."

He didn't see it. Or he chose not to.

"Will you go?" she asked.

He exhaled hard. "If that's what you want, then yes. I'll go."

"I'll find someone. And I'll find appointment times that work with both our schedules."

Michael pushed his chair back and headed to the door. "Fine."

"Michael—"

He paused. "Yeah?"

"Nothing," she said. "Go ahead."

He left. Grace stared at the empty doorway. She'd asked for couples therapy. He'd said *fine.*

She said it aloud again into the empty room: "I want her."

22

———

Friday, *October 13, 2023*

By 6:00 pm the following Friday, the therapy house had emptied. One by one, the white-noise machines had fallen silent, their week's work of guarding secrets completed. Amber light poured through the windows.

Grace appeared at Allie's doorway. Peered in. Allie stood at her desk, sliding folders into her tote.

"Heading out?" Grace asked.

"Not for a few minutes. Come in." Grace stepped inside and eased the door shut behind her, the latch catching with barely a sound.

Allie leaned against the desk. "Tomorrow. We're still on for the afternoon?"

"One o'clock. I'll be there."

"What excuse did you come up with to get away?"

"Michael thinks I'll be at this." She pulled up a screen on her phone and held it out to Allie: a webpage with Tufts University's logo prominent at the top.

"There's a symposium on attachment theory and trauma. From one to five, followed by the obligatory dinner and drinks with colleagues." Grace's finger scrolled through the program schedule. "I've memorized enough of the speakers and topics that I can discuss it convincingly if he asks later. Which he won't."

Allie's eyebrow arched. "You've thought of everything."

"No, but enough."

Grace slipped her phone back into her bag. God, how easily all of that had come out of her—dates, times, speakers, dinner plans, the imaginary colleagues. A whole scaffolding of lies built without effort. Surprising—and a little upsetting—how easy it had been, how natural it had felt, when something she truly wanted waited on the other side of deception.

Allie stood, her hand reached for Grace's. "Sorry. I know lying doesn't feel good."

"No, it doesn't." Grace's gaze dropped to where their skin connected. "It sucks. I hate how easy it's getting. I've never lied to him before, Allie. Not about anything important like this."

Allie's thumb stroked her knuckles.

Grace straightened her back and managed a smile. "But I'm so excited to have real time with you tomorrow. Seven or eight hours instead of a few stolen moments." She inhaled, steadying herself. "I'll take Mia to soccer in the morning; her game starts at eleven. Then I'll come to you around one?"

Allie smiled. "Hours alone. Just us." She reached up and touched Grace's lips with her fingertip.

Grace looked away, then back. "Allie, you should know: I'm not sure I'll be able to do—"

"Shhh." Allie pressed her finger harder. "We'll talk it all out tomorrow, when the clock isn't ticking against us."

Allie leaned in, about to kiss her.

"We said we wouldn't—" Grace whispered. "Not here."

"I know we did," Allie said, closing the remaining distance. "But I'm kissing you anyway."

The first kiss was careful. The second was not.

A door slammed somewhere below them. They jerked apart. Footsteps faded away.

Grace groaned, then leaned back in and grabbed Allie, kissing her harder, before making herself step back.

Allie smoothed her hair. Grace adjusted her coat and waited for Allie to gather her things and lock up. They exited the building through the doorway at the bottom of the staircase. In the parking lot, they allowed themselves one look across the roofs of their cars.

On her drive home, Grace kept thinking about the discipline it took to pull apart when they could've kept going.

Grace arrived home to find the kitchen counter covered by the Halloween costumes she'd bought for the kids—Harry Potter glasses, wand, and cape; a black Wednesday Addams dress. At the kitchen table, Mia and Matthew had the three carving pumpkins lined up like orange soldiers awaiting surgery, as they spread newspaper across the table.

"Why so soon?" Grace asked. "Halloween's still almost two weeks away."

"Nobody cares about Halloween decorations once the day is past. Better to have them out early," Mia said, unfolding the logic like she was explaining it to a child.

"Dad's not coming home for dinner," Mia announced. "He texted that he's staying late for a consult."

Matthew, with a twelve-year-old's pragmatism, said, "That's okay. Mom's better at doing the scary face than Dad is." Such a small thing, being preferred for pumpkin carving. When did *Dad's not coming home* become normal?

These moments—unhurried, easy. This was what home should feel like.

Matthew looked up at Grace. "Will you do it? Help us with the faces?"

Grace grinned and nodded.

She changed her clothes then came back downstairs and carved careful faces while her children chattered about costume plans and candy strategies, the three of them close around the kitchen table, Matthew's elbow bumping hers as he worked. Michael's empty chair felt like a pattern now, not an exception. How many dinners had it been? How long since she'd stopped noticing?

When Mia finished a jack-o-lantern, she shifted her attention to the Wednesday Addams costume. She picked up the dress and held it out by her finger tips, her face pinched like the thing smelled bad. "I changed my mind. I want to be a sexy French witch."

"What does that mean, exactly?"

"Black dress, red lipstick, fishnets. Something that doesn't look like a kid costume."

Grace paused, mid-carve, knife suspended. "Trying to impress someone at school?"

Mia's jaw set. Defensive. "No. I just— Can I or not?"

Grace studied her daughter—almost sixteen, testing limits, searching for herself. Figuring out who she wanted to be, what drew her attention. Grace recognized the restlessness, the hunger to become someone new. She knew that feeling.

"OK. Not your good black dress. But you can rework this costume dress. Aim for cool, not sexy. There's a difference."

"I know, Mom." Mia rolled her eyes, grabbing the costume and fleeing upstairs.

Grace watched her daughter disappear, then returned to the pumpkin in front of her. She carved a triangle eye, then another.

Matthew focused on his own design, humming as he worked. Some K-pop tune she'd heard in the background a hundred times.

This—her son beside her, the scratch of knife on pumpkin shell, the kitchen warm around them—this was real. So was what she felt for Allie. Both things were true. She didn't know how to hold both of them at the same time.

23

—————

Saturday, October 14

The next morning at 8:30, her kids were still in bed when Grace's phone buzzed against the kitchen table, interrupting her scrolling through the *Times*. Michael had left for the hospital before she got up. She glanced at the notification, expecting this to be his usual update on when he'd return from doing his rounds.

Her coffee paused halfway to her lips as Allie's name appeared instead. The message stopped her: *I'm sick. Can't stop throwing up. Can barely stand. Have to cancel.*

Grace stared at the screen, her stomach dropping. She typed quickly: *Oh no! Do you need anything?*

Several minutes passed before a reply came: *Just need to sleep. So sorry about this. I'd been counting the hours.*

Grace tapped: *Don't apologize. Focus on feeling better. Text me if you need anything.*

Then her mind conjured Allie collapsed on cold bathroom tile, too weak to get up, alone and hurting. Grace scribbled a note to

Matthew and Mia, who were still asleep. *Ran to check on a friend who's sick. Back in time for soccer.* She left it on the counter.

Nine minutes later—the traffic mercifully light this early on a Saturday—Grace practically jogged from the curb to Allie's porch and jabbed at the doorbell.

After a long moment, the door swung open. Allie leaned heavily against the frame, one arm supporting her weight. Damp strands of hair clung to her temples, framing a face drained of color except for redness rimming her eyes. She wore only an oversized, faded T-shirt that barely reached mid-thigh. Allie—always so composed, so together—reduced to this.

Allie blinked slowly, as though trying to determine if the figure before her was real or hallucinated. "Grace? What are you—"

"I had to come." Her hand reached forward and hovered near Allie's elbow.

"Please go home." Allie swallowed with visible effort. "Whatever this is, you don't want it."

"Too late." Grace slipped past her into the foyer, the scent of sickness hanging in the air. "I'm already here."

Allie's protest died on her lips as her face drained of what little color remained. Her hand flew to cover her mouth. Her eyes widened in panic. She staggered backward. Bare feet slapped toward the bathroom.

Grace was at her heels without thinking about it.

Allie hunched over the toilet, her body shuddering with each heave. The oversized t-shirt rode up with each convulsion, exposing bare skin, too much bare skin.

She knelt beside Allie on the cold tile, forcing her gaze up, one hand gathering damp strands of hair away from Allie's face. The other traced slow, steady circles across her back, each convulsion rippling beneath her palm.

When the heaving finally subsided, Allie collapsed against the wall, her skin ashen and gleaming with sweat. Her mouth twitched as she glanced at Grace. "Not exactly how I wanted you to see me."

Grace smiled and cupped her cheek. She stood and dampened a washcloth with cool water. Pressed it to Allie's temples, then offered a glass with just enough water to rinse her mouth.

Grace led Allie back to the bedroom. She drew the comforter up, her fingertips grazing Allie's shoulder, then her collarbone, as she settled the fabric in place. The bed dipped as Grace perched beside her, dabbing the cool cloth against Allie's hot skin.

Grace pressed the back of her hand to Allie's forehead. "How long have you been feeling like this?"

"Started around four." Allie's face suddenly tensed, her complexion going from pale to gray-green. She inhaled sharply through her nose, held it, then slowly released the breath. "Every time I think it's over ..." The thought hung there, unfinished.

Grace rummaged through the bathroom cabinet until she found a thermometer, one of those digital ones with a cartoon frog at the end. The display blinked: 99.9—not dangerous, but enough to explain the glassy sheen in Allie's eyes.

"Stay put," Grace said, brushing a damp strand of hair from Allie's face. "I'm going to see what I can find downstairs."

Allie managed a weak smile. "Trust me, I'm not going anywhere."

Grace scanned Allie's kitchen. She found a half-full bottle of Canada Dry ginger ale in the refrigerator door and a half-empty sleeve of saltines pushed to the back of the pantry. Tylenol tucked beside coffee filters above the stove. She arranged everything on a wooden tray alongside a glass of water and carried it upstairs.

"Think you can manage to sit up?" she asked.

Grace steadied her with a hand at her back, feeling each vertebra through the thin cotton of her shirt. She pressed two pills into Allie's palm and held the water glass to her lips.

"Tiny sips," Grace instructed. "Just enough to wet your mouth."

Allie sank back against the pillows. Her eyelids fluttered closed. Grace pressed her lips to Allie's forehead, lingering for a moment before pulling away.

"You sleep," she whispered. "Mia has soccer at eleven. But I can come back after. Around one?"

"You shouldn't—"

"I'm coming back," Grace said. "Just get some rest."

"Thank you," Allie murmured, the words barely audible.

Grace lingered in the doorway, one hand still on the frame, watching Allie's breathing slow into sleep. She slipped out, easing the door shut.

When Grace arrived home, each family member was busy in their own familiar way. Mia was on FaceTime with Chloe. Matthew hunched over his Switch at the kitchen counter, thumbs flying across the controllers. She found Michael in the den, surrounded by manila folders, his glasses perched at the end of his nose.

"Who's sick?" he asked, eyes fixed on the page before him.

"Allie."

He glanced up for barely a heartbeat. His pen resumed its neat little march across the page.

She started to go, when his voice stopped her. "Want to talk?"

It was such a small gesture. She could see what it cost him—the reaching toward her, however clumsy. She was suddenly aware of her sorrow for what they'd never managed to be for each other.

"I'm in a hurry. Have to get Mia to soccer."

His eyes showed relief. He hadn't really wanted to talk. He just knew he was supposed to try. He asked: "Was Allie planning to attend that Tufts thing, too?"

"Yeah. She's definitely not making it to that."

He nodded. No follow up. That appeared to be the extent of his engagement on the topic of Allie. He disappeared again back into his paperwork, his pen scratching away.

At her closet, she dressed in layers fit for both lives—leggings and a tank top first, then conference-appropriate wide pants and a cashmere sweater over them. Easy to peel away at Allie's, then to put back on before stepping into this house again.

She managed the soccer drop-off, arranged a ride home for Mia with Olivia's mother, and within an hour was pushing a cart through Star Market's fluorescent aisles. Real ginger ale, the water crackers Allie liked, ingredients for home-made chicken soup.

Grace let herself in with Allie's key at 1:15, pausing in the entryway to listen. Silent. She placed the grocery bags on the kitchen counter before climbing the stairs, each footstep absorbed by the thick carpet.

She found Allie propped against her pillows, awake now, the bedroom curtains drawn against afternoon sun. A glass of water sat untouched on the nightstand beside that cartoon frog thermometer. Allie's sickly pallor had receded somewhat, her cheeks now almost back to their normal color, her gaze more focused.

"You came back," Allie said, her voice scratchy but steadier than before.

Grace crossed to the bed. "Did you think I wouldn't?" She laid her palm on Allie's forehead. "Fever's down. That's something."

"Tylenol helped. And look—" She held up a glass half-full of ginger ale. "All that's still inside me." Allie put down the glass, shifted against the pillows, and grabbed Grace's hand. "But, Gracie, I feel terrible about ruining our plans and—"

"Stop." Grace covered Allie's hand with her own. "We're together, and I want to be here." Her thumb traced small circles on

Allie's palm. The corner of her mouth lifted. "Not the afternoon I'd pictured, but I wouldn't be anywhere else." She squeezed Allie's hand. "Think you could try some soup?"

"Maybe in a bit." Allie sank deeper into her pillows and patted the empty space beside her. "Just ... be with me for a while?"

Grace slid off her shoes, peeled away her outer layers until only leggings and the thin tank top remained. She drew a deep breath and eased onto the bed, sliding below the comforter but deliberately above the blanket and top sheet.

Allie folded against her, tucking her forehead into the curve where Grace's neck met shoulder. Grace exhaled, then breathed in the warmth of Allie's hair. She placed her lips against the crown of Allie's head.

Allie's arm slid across her waist, grazing bare skin on Grace's stomach where her tank top had ridden up. Grace startled, but only for a breath, then covered Allie's hand with her own, holding it there.

Time dissolved as they lay entwined, Allie's breath growing steady in sleep, then quickening when she'd surface, only to drift under again. Grace scrolled through her phone, half-listening to the suburban symphony outside—the whine of leaf blowers, the rhythmic thump of a basketball hitting concrete.

When the bedside clock blinked 3:00, she eased away from Allie's warmth, untangling their limbs with care, and padded downstairs to transform her grocery haul into something healing.

The aroma of simmering chicken broth and herbs eventually reached upstairs, and Allie's voice drifted down. "Whatever you're making smells like heaven."

"The question is whether heaven wants to stay put in your stomach," Grace called back. "Only one way to know."

Grace carried a steaming bowl up on a tray. She watched as Allie's spoon made slow, deliberate progress through half the soup. When thirty minutes passed without a dash to the bathroom, they exchanged a triumphant look. Thumbs up.

As the afternoon wore on, words flowed freely between them, unhurried by the usual ticking clock of their brief encounters. Allie recited fragments of a poem she loved. They traced the fault lines in their marriages. Their voices mere murmurs, though no one else was around.

When Grace admitted how terrified she felt of wanting this so badly despite what it would cost her if she left her marriage, Allie's fingers gripped hers in silent understanding.

"When I left Mark, I was terrified, too. The kids were so young. Noah was only five. But you know what? They adjusted faster than I did. Kids are resilient when they see their parents become happier."

Grace was quiet for a moment. Then: "Are you happy? Now, I mean. Not in the abstract."

Allie smiled. "I'm getting there."

It was a therapist's answer. Warm, deflecting, pointed outward. Grace recognized it, had used versions of it herself when she didn't want to get too close to something revealing. She waited, giving Allie the silence that was supposed to pull more out.

Allie didn't fill it. She reached over and tucked a strand of hair behind Grace's ear instead. "You ask good questions," she said softly.

Grace let it go. But she'd noticed. And she wondered why Allie, who could see Grace so clearly, resisted letting herself be seen in return.

The afternoon light faded around them as they lay side by side, talking in low voices about fear and desire, and all the complicated ways those two things intertwined.

Around five, Grace got up to use the bathroom. She gathered the empty soup bowl and water glass on her way. "I'll take these down and clean things up in the kitchen. Back in a bit."

"Grace?" Allie's voice was quiet, almost tentative. "You don't have to. But—when you come back—I'd love it if you got in with me. Properly. Under the covers." A pause. "I just need to feel your skin next to mine."

Grace turned toward the window briefly before answering.

"Sure," she managed.

In the kitchen, she dried each bowl, wiped down counters twice, her hands busy while her mind replayed Allie's request: *Properly. Under the covers.*

When she finally returned upstairs, the bedroom had fallen into shadow. Allie lay curled on her side, features softened by sleep, breathing deep and even. Grace lingered in the doorway, caught between relief and disappointment, the weight of desire pulling her toward the empty space beside Allie's sleeping form.

But instead of slipping under the covers, Grace stood at the side of the bed. She reached out, tucking the blanket higher around Allie's shoulders, fingers gently sweeping a wayward strand of hair from her forehead.

She gathered her things in silence—outer clothing layers pulled back on, phone and keys collected. She scribbled a note on the bedside pad: *Didn't want to wake you. Sleep is the best medicine. Text me when you wake.*

Driving home, Grace kept seeing Allie's face—not composed and clever as at work, but flushed and vulnerable, hair tangled against the pillow. The intimacy of it clung to her. She hadn't expected that—to feel closer to Allie asleep and unguarded than when Allie was fully present, fully herself, seeing everything.

24

Monday, October 23

When she heard her client knock at 2:00 PM, Grace smoothed the front of her sweater and opened the door to David Castellano. In his early fifties, David had the compact, well-kept look of a man who believed in routines—hair trimmed, clothes chosen to avoid attention, posture polite but pitched forward as if he belonged in the threshold.

He smiled, that same grateful expression she'd grown used to. "Grace, hi. Got stuck in traffic. Glad I'm not late. Wouldn't want to miss any minutes here." The phrasing landed differently than he'd intended it. Or maybe exactly as he'd intended it.

When they were seated—David on the couch, Grace in her chair across from him—she pulled out her notepad and asked, "How was your week?"

"Better, actually. I had dinner with my brother and his family on Sunday. First time in months that I didn't feel like I was just ... going through the motions, you know?"

"That's great, David. I'm happy to hear it."

His hands clasped loosely in his lap. "I laughed. Really laughed, at something my nephew said. And for a minute I didn't feel guilty about it. Like maybe Elena wouldn't want me to be miserable forever."

Grace nodded. Laughter would have been impossible for him back when Elena was dying and every session they came to together had been about their fears and regrets and the logistics of dying. So this was progress. The guilt was easing. "What do you think Elena would want for you?"

"She'd want me to be happy." His voice was steady. "She used to worry about what would happen to me after she died. She made me promise I wouldn't just ... give up."

"And how are you doing with that promise?"

David's expression grew thoughtful. "Some days better than others. But sitting here, talking with you— It always helps."

Autumn light slanted through her tall window. Outside, a landscaper's leaf blower roared to life, then faded. He moved forward in his chair, leaning toward Grace. "You knew Elena. You saw how much we loved each other. When I tell you about missing her, you understand in a way that feels ... safe."

She straightened in her chair, creating distance. "David, what you're doing here—learning to live with grief, finding ways forward —it's important. But it's also important that you build connections outside this office. Therapy isn't meant to be your primary source of emotional support."

"I know that," he said quickly. He looked down at his hands, his wedding ring gleaming. He'd mentioned once that he couldn't bring himself to take it off. "Of course I know that. It's just ..." He leaned forward slightly. "I look forward to these sessions. Sometimes I find myself thinking about things I want to tell you, or wondering what you'd think about something. I know that probably sounds strange."

Textbook transference. But his earnestness complicated it. And wasn't she doing something similar? Replaying every moment of Saturday with Allie in obsessive detail, manufacturing reasons to be in touch with her.

"Not strange at all. It's normal to develop strong feelings in therapy," she said gently. "You're doing vulnerable work here. Of course that creates a connection. But part of my job is to help you build those connections outside this office, in your real life."

David nodded, his smile fading. "Right. Of course. I'm sorry, I didn't mean to imply anything else."

"You don't need to apologize. These feelings are part of the process. But let's use them productively." Grace glanced at the clock. They still had thirty-five minutes. "Why do you think it feels safer here than with your friends? Your family?"

For the rest of the session, they explored his isolation. She asked about his fear of burdening friends with his grief, his sense that no one else could understand what he'd lost. David leaned forward, watching her face intently as he spoke.

As their time ended, he paused at the door.

"Grace, what you're doing for me means a lot. Elena would be glad I'm still seeing you. That's all. Thank you."

After he left, Grace sat at her desk, staring at David's file. He was looking to her for something she couldn't give him.

Her phone buzzed with a text from Allie: *Feeling almost human again. Coffee tomorrow before work? I need to see you.*

Grace's fingers hovered over the screen. She should say no. Should suggest they take some space, reestablish their own professional boundaries. Should remember she was married, that Allie was her colleague, that Saturday had been—

She typed: *Yes. Early? 7:30?*

The response came immediately: *Perfect.*

Grace set down her phone and looked at David's file again.

Professional boundaries. Appropriate limits. All the things she'd just counseled him about. All the things she was about to ignore again tomorrow morning.

25

Halloween — Tuesday, October 31

Mia swept into the kitchen at 7:15 AM, her witch's hat tilting sideways. Purple glitter streaked her cheek as she frowned at her reflection in the microwave door. "This looks like a growth on my head."

Grace was already reaching for bobby pins. "Doing your hair differently might help."

From the living room: "Mom! The glasses! The Harry Potter ones! They're missing."

"Check the den," Grace called back, wrestling Mia's hair into something that might support the hat. "I saw them on the little table in there."

Mia squinted at her distorted reflection in the toaster. "Oh my god, Mom, no." She tugged at the strands Grace had just pinned, tearing them loose.

Grace plucked the bobby pins from between her teeth. "I thought a sexy French witch would wear her hair up."

"This is so stupid. I hate everything." Mia snatched the hat and thundered upstairs, leaving a trail of purple glitter.

The familiar choreography swept around her: lunch boxes, backpacks, someone always yelling for something. Adding costumes to the morning chaos was a step too far. When had wearing costumes to school become a thing?

A buzz from her phone cut through the noise. A text from Allie: *Noah just did a flying kick and nearly decapitated my grandmother's lamp. I'm rethinking ninjas as a concept.*

She smiled and typed: *At least ninjas are quiet. My French witch had a noisy meltdown over hat and hair structure.*

A photo appeared: Emma transformed into a cat—painted whiskers, a pink nose, a rhinestone tiara perched on her head.

Grace commented: *Perfect! Feline royalty!*

She set her phone screen-down. Matthew had materialized beside her, tipping the syrup bottle at an alarming angle, amber liquid flooding his plate.

"Whoa there," she said, catching his wrist. "Leave some dry land for the poor waffle to stand on."

His eyes sparkled with mischief.

Her phone chimed. Allie calling.

"So, my daughter the cat queen is now grooming herself, licking her 'paws' with her tongue," Allie said without hello.

"Authentic feline behavior, I suppose."

"Exactly what she said. I told her to limit the method acting because real cats also lick their asses and puke up hairballs on pillows."

Grace laughed. "You're such a buzzkill."

"Damn it, Noah! ... Shit. Sorry, Gracie. Gotta run. My ninja almost knocked me out with his nunchucks. Have to disarm him."

~

That evening, she stepped onto the porch into air thick with woodsmoke and the sweetness of decaying leaves. The house looked fully committed to Halloween: jack-o'-lanterns glowing along the railing, fake cobwebs stretched between columns, dried cornstalks framing the steps. A hay bale leaned against the lamppost like a tired farmer.

No messages from Michael. Of course. He'd be at the hospital well past midnight, elbow-deep in whatever injuries Halloween delivered to the ER. This night always landed on her.

Her own mother had done this alone, too, after Grace's father died. Years of handing out candy by herself, never complaining.

Mia appeared at the bottom of the stairs. The witch's hat stood tall now, stuffed with gift tissue. The modest costume had become something else entirely, skimming mid-thigh, neckline plunging into unmistakable cleavage. Sheer black tights. Bat-wing eyeliner sweeping from her lids, smaller bats taking flight down her cheek toward her throat.

"That's ... wow," Grace sputtered. "How did you—"

"YouTube," Mia cut her off with a shrug that couldn't quite hide her pride.

Grace tried to draw a breath. Fifteen was too young for this much skin, this much confidence. But wasn't this what teenage girls did? Test boundaries, push limits?

Matthew bounded into the room, his Harry Potter robe billowing behind him. The round glasses slid down his nose as he waved his glow-light wand in an elaborate figure eight.

"Am I magical enough?" he asked, eyes wide behind the lenses.

"You're practically Dumbledore," Grace said.

He pushed up his bangs, revealing a precise lightning bolt Mia had drawn. "Pretty cool, eh?"

"The Boy Who Lived," she said.

She snapped photos of them posed beside the glowing jack-o'-lanterns, capturing Mia's dramatic bearing and Matthew's exuberant wand-waving. The Henderson children from next door waited at the sidewalk, their costumes adding to the growing spectacle.

She switched on the porch light, set out the candy bowl, and braced herself for the nightly challenge: right-sizing the candy hand-out. Two pieces for little kids, one for teenagers who hadn't bothered with costumes.

She texted Allie a selfie of her with Mia. *French witch pleased with herself. Crisis averted.*

Allie's reply made her swallow: *Damn! 15? Look at your face in that photo. You're trying so hard not to show it.*

She turned the phone face-down on the counter.

The doorbell chimed every few minutes. Dragons, pirates, miniature surgeons, creatures wearing plastic masks that fogged with their breath. She settled into the rhythm of treats and compliments.

October air nipped at her neck. Down the street, parents laughed, kids shrieked. Porch lights blazed up and down the block.

The littlest kids arrived first: a parade of wobbling superheroes with masks askew and princesses trailing glitter. Grace dropped extra Snickers into their bags.

All of it so familiar. Yet this year felt so different with her marriage in active dissolution. And instead of complete loneliness, she had this zing of connection with Allie, their back-and-forth texts threading through the gaps between trick-or-treaters.

Allie wrote: *I have what I think is a baked potato and the world's smallest unicorn sizing-up each other on my porch. Tense standoff.*

Grace replied: *Here, a tiny Spider-Man just tripped over his own web-shooter.*

Half an hour later, Grace kept an eye on the sidewalk through the living-room window when Allie called.

"You need to hear this one live," she said, breathless with laughter. "This dad showed up carrying his toddler, who had his security blanket pressed to his ear. When I asked what he was dressed as, the kid froze like the matter had never occurred to him. After the longest pause, he murmured, 'I'm a bed.'"

Grace laughed. "That child is a genius."

"Right? And the dad nodded at me, dead serious, and said, 'It's conceptual art.'"

Grace pressed her forehead to the window, laughing.

A kid with a dachshund in a hot-dog-bun costume trotted past the window. Behind them, a woman dressed as a wine bottle.

"Oh my god," she said. "You have to see this." She snapped a photo.

"Send it," Allie said.

A ding on Allie's end, then a laugh. "That woman is doing the Lord's work."

"Incidentally," Grace said, "I'm conducting a preemptive strike on the remaining candy. All Reese's Cups will mysteriously vanish into safekeeping for you before my kids get back."

"You must want something," Allie said.

"You bet I do," Grace sighed.

By 8:30, only clusters of minimally costumed teenagers wandered the streets. Matthew and Mia trudged up the walk, silhouettes backlit by the streetlamp. They spilled into the foyer, candy bags sagging.

"Look at that haul," Grace said. "You must've hit every house in the neighborhood."

She poured Matthew some milk, drew an imaginary UN line down the dining table to separate the candy piles, let them barter like seasoned diplomats.

Her phone buzzed. She picked it up, smiling.

Mia glanced at her mother's face for a beat. "Is Allie funny or something?"

"What?" Grace looked up.

"You laugh every time she texts." Mia picked through her Skittles, not looking up. "Like, a lot. And that's like the tenth time tonight."

Grace's smile faded slightly. "We're both doing Halloween with our kids. Just comparing notes."

Mia's eyes held hers for a beat too long, then returned to her candy pile. "Mm-hmm." Grace's phone buzzed again in her hand. She didn't look at it.

After five minutes, Grace invoked her usual rule: "Three more pieces tonight. Choose wisely."

When they headed upstairs to brush sugar off their teeth, Grace sank onto the couch and picked up her phone and sent Allie yet another text: *Halloween candy inventory results: 90% of Reese's Cups successfully diverted to secure location.*

Her phone lit up seconds later: *Your sacrifice for the greater good has been noted. Four premium KitKats await delivery to their deserving recipient.*

She typed back: *What will this delivery cost me?*

Grace's stomach fluttered at the reply: *You already know the price.*

She started to type a response when footsteps creaked on the stairs above her. She looked up.

Mia stood on the landing in her pajamas, witch hat in hand, watching her mother on the couch with the phone.

"Who are you texting?" Mia asked.

Grace's thumb hovered over the screen. "Just Allie. Comparing your candy hauls."

"Right." Mia turned back toward her room. "Night, Mom."

Grace watched her daughter disappear down the hallway, then looked back at the glowing message on her screen.

You already know the price.

26

———

Wednesday, November 1

Grace arrived at Elisa Hamilton's office fifteen minutes early for the noon appointment, her hands folded tightly in her lap as she waited. She'd been to the therapist building in Wellesley, a restored brick mansion, years ago for a case consult. It looked unchanged inside: cream walls, a white noise machine droning in the corner of the waiting room.

She forced herself to take deep breaths. This should've felt routine; she led these sessions herself, after all. But sitting in the client's chair was its own disorientation.

The door opened. Michael entered in scrubs, a jacket thrown over one arm. He stowed his phone, sat across from her, not beside her.

"Hey," he said.

"Hi." Her voice felt strange in her own mouth.

They sat in silence, two people waiting for a stranger to help them speak.

At noon on the dot, Elisa Hamilton appeared—tall, early sixties, light brown skin, black-and-silver hair pulled back. Dark slacks, a burgundy sweater. She moved without hurry, the calm stillness of someone who had learned to fill a room by taking up less of it. Grace had spent years trying to cultivate the same quality.

"Grace, Michael. Come on in."

They followed Elisa down a short hallway to her office. The room was larger than she expected: two chairs angled toward a small couch, windows overlooking a courtyard, a ficus in the corner. Certificates lined one wall: Washington University, post-doc, various trainings.

Elisa gestured to the couch. Grace and Michael sat at opposite ends, leaving a careful gulf of space.

Elisa settled into a chair, legal pad on her knee. "I appreciate you both being here." She glanced between them. "Why don't we start with why you're here. What brings you to therapy?"

Grace waited, but Michael didn't speak; he just studied the ficus, his jaw tight. She filled the silence. "I feel ... lonely. Like we're going through the motions, not really connected anymore." She searched for the right words. "It's not unusual, I know. Two kids, busy careers, married seventeen and a half years. But lately, the disconnection feels sharper. Like I woke up and realized how far apart we've drifted."

Elisa nodded, making a note. "Michael?"

Michael shifted, staring at the floor. "We're in a rough patch. Communication, stress, the usual stuff after this long together." He glanced at Grace. "We just need to reconnect. Make more time for each other."

Elisa looked at them both. "Okay. So, we have work to do. First —" She asked about their history: how they'd met, when things had shifted. They traded off the facts like depositions.

"Do you both want to work on the marriage?" Elisa asked.

"Yes," Michael said quickly.

Grace hesitated, the silence stretching. "I want us both to understand what's happening to us." Even as she said it, she knew she was hedging. Understanding wasn't the same as fixing.

Elisa's eyes lingered on Grace. She wondered what Elisa had just heard in that.

"Let me ask," Elisa said, "was there a recent event or change in circumstances that made therapy feel urgent?"

Grace stared at her hands. "My loneliness in the marriage has become more acute lately. I'm more aware of how little emotional intimacy we have."

Elisa nodded and turned to Michael. "When was the last time you and Grace had a conversation about something that mattered to one of you?"

Michael frowned, thinking. "We talk every day. About the kids, schedules—"

"Not logistics. A real conversation. About feelings, fears, hopes."

Michael's face went blank. Grace watched him search his memory, coming up empty.

"I guess ... I don't know," he said finally. He looked at Grace, genuinely bewildered. "Do you remember?"

She hesitated, then said, "I think the closest we've come was the conversation we had about starting this couples therapy."

"Let me ask it slightly differently." Elisa said after a pause. "Michael, can you tell me about a recent time you felt close to Grace? Really connected?"

Michael thought for a moment. "We had sex weekend before last. First time in a long while. So, that was good."

Grace wanted to scream at the answer.

Elisa nodded, then turned to Grace. "What about you, Grace? When was the last time you felt close to Michael?"

Grace's mind went blank. There were pleasant-enough moments. Family dinners, private jokes, helping Matthew with homework. But close? "I can't think of one," she said.

Neither of them spoke.

Elisa turned to Michael. "Does that surprise you?"

He shifted. "I guess I didn't realize it was that bad for Grace."

"Grace, can you help Michael understand what 'close' or 'connected' means to you? What would that actually look like?"

Grace searched for words. "It would mean being curious about each other. Actually listening. Being present." She paused. "Feeling like I matter to him for more than just keeping the household running. Like he wants to understand me as a person."

Michael's face flickered—hurt, maybe, or just fatigue. "I know you're unhappy. I know you think I don't pay enough attention. But, Grace, I'm working sixty, seventy hours a week. I come home wiped out. I'm doing my best."

"I know you are," Grace said. And she did know it—that was the complicated part. He wasn't lazy or indifferent by nature. He was a man who had poured everything into his work because that was the shape his love took, the only shape he knew. She'd understood that once. Maybe even admired it.

"This isn't about blame. I just—" How to say it without saying it? "I think we've lost each other somewhere. And I don't know if we can find our way back."

Michael's tone sharpened. "But do you ever try? When's the last time you tried to be vulnerable with me? When's the last time you were even home in the evening? It feels like half the time the kids are in bed before you walk through the door."

His last comments landed hard. She felt her face go still.

"Maybe I don't try as often as I should to make it easy for you to reach me, to help you see and understand me," she said carefully. "But I have tried."

"When? Tell me one time."

Grace let her mind scan. And the honest answer—the one that surfaced first and wouldn't go away—was that she couldn't remember. Not because she'd never tried, but because the trying had been so tentative, so hedged, so easy to abandon when he didn't immediately respond.

Then, without thinking, she said, "A month ago, when I told you about—" She caught herself.

"Ah." Michael's lips curled, not quite a smile. "I wondered how long it would be before that topic came up."

Elisa looked between them. "Sounds like there's something we need to discuss."

Grace nodded. She'd been intending to talk about Allie at some point during these sessions, though not this soon. But she'd accidentally kicked the door open; there was no closing it now.

She steeled herself. "I've developed feelings for someone," she said, her voice steady but low. "It's made me realize how much is missing in our marriage. How long it's been since I felt seen, understood."

"How long has this been going on?" Elisa's tone was neutral.

She hesitated. "A few months. Since summer. Late spring."

"Is this person aware of your feelings?"

"Yes. We've ... spent time together. Talked."

Elisa jotted a note, then turned to Michael. "Michael, were you aware of this?"

"Not until a few weeks ago, when Grace told me she had strong feelings for this person."

Elisa looked back at her. "May I ask: is this person male or female?"

She felt her face flush. "Female."

Elisa gave a small, professional nod. Michael didn't look up.

"And how did that conversation go?"

Her agitation broke through. "Not well. Michael dismissed my feelings as just *a girl crush*. Said I needed help. Suggested I'm having some sort of mental breakdown."

Michael sighed, voice clipped. "Well, come on. It's absurd, Grace.

You're not gay. You've never been attracted to women. This'll pass if you stop feeding it."

And there it was again: his certainty that she was malfunctioning rather than changing. That she didn't know her own feelings, her own truths.

Elisa turned to Grace. "Have you been attracted to women before?"

"I don't know," she hedged, shifting on the cushion. "I guess I never thought about it, not really."

"So this is new territory for you."

Grace nodded. "Yes." Her hands twisted in her lap. "But I'm not sure it's accurate to say I'm attracted to women. I'm attracted to one woman."

Elisa made another note and looked to Grace. "For the sake of our conversations, let's give this person a name for privacy. Let's call her Ruth. Would that be all right?"

Grace and Michael both nodded. She registered the strangeness of it: Allie reduced to 'Ruth,' a placeholder, a variable in an equation. But maybe that was safer. Ruth was abstract, theoretical. Allie was real, too real to discuss in this clinical space.

Elisa let the silence build, then returned to her. "You said the time you spend with Ruth makes you more aware of what's missing in your marriage. Can you say more?"

Michael sat forward.

Grace said, "Ruth pays attention. When we talk, she's present. She asks questions, remembers what I say. She cares." Grace knew this would hurt, but she couldn't lighten it. "She makes me feel ... interesting. Like I matter."

"And you don't feel that way with Michael," Elisa clarified gently.

"No. Not for a long time."

Elisa looked at Michael. "What's it like hearing that?"

His jaw muscles working, he said, "I don't think that's fair. I listen to her." He turned to Grace, his face tight. "I listened when you told me about her."

"You heard the words. You didn't listen."

Michael dropped into silence.

After a moment, Elisa leaned forward on her elbows. "Michael, what do you love about Grace?"

He looked startled by the question. "What do I—" He paused. "She's a good mother. She's smart. She keeps everything running."

The therapist waited.

"She's ... reliable. Steady."

Something inside Grace went very still. He was describing an employee. A business partner. Not a wife he desired.

Elisa turned to Grace. "Let me ask you the same question. What do you love about Michael?"

Grace opened her mouth, then made herself pause. The easy answer—the critical one, the list of everything he wasn't—rose immediately. She set it aside.

"He's brilliant at what he does," she said finally. "I've always respected that. He's responsible. The kids feel safe with him." She paused. "When he's present, he's a good father. And a good man." She looked at her hands. "I think he married someone he genuinely cared for. I don't think he ever stopped caring. We just—" She stopped.

"You just what?" Elisa said.

"We just never learned how to show each other that we cared." She looked down at her hands. "That was my failure, too."

Michael looked at her then. She felt it but didn't look back. When he finally spoke, he said, "We've been married seventeen years. We have kids. Sustaining passion isn't realistic."

Elisa wrote something, then set her pad aside. "It sounds like you two have developed parallel lives—busy, overwhelmed, both focused on your own worlds. Somewhere along the way, you stopped turning toward each other, making the other matter."

She let the words settle. "Tell me if this feels accurate. Michael, it seems your response to marital stress is to withdraw and double down on work. Grace, yours is to seek connection elsewhere. And now that's become Ruth."

Neither answered. Grace's eye twitched.

"The question is," Elisa continued, "whether you want to turn toward each other again, whether you're willing to do the work to rebuild this marriage." She paused, her eyes settling on Grace. "But before we get there, I want to stay with something for a moment."

Grace looked up.

"Grace, you've described feeling invisible in this marriage. Unseen, unheard. And I believe that's real." Elisa's voice stayed measured. "But I'm also hearing that your response to that pain has been to build a very rich inner life elsewhere—with Ruth, with work, with late evenings away from home. And I want to ask you something." She paused. Then, in a gentle voice: "Is it possible that some of that—the late nights, the energy you've been pouring into this other relationship—has made it harder for Michael to reach you?"

The room went quiet.

She wanted to deflect, to point back at Michael's long list of absences and failures. But she recognized the question. She'd asked versions of it herself, to clients, in this same careful register. She knew what it meant when a therapist asked it.

"Maybe," she said finally. "I hadn't thought about it that way."

Michael looked at her. She didn't meet his eyes.

"I'm not assigning blame," Elisa said. "I'm suggesting that these patterns tend to feed each other. Withdrawal invites withdrawal. Distance invites distance." She glanced at Michael, then back to Grace. "Which means that rebuilding—if that's what you both want —will require both of you to examine your own part in how you got here. Not just what the other person failed to do."

Elisa looked at Michael first. "What do you want from therapy? If it works, what does that look like?"

Michael didn't hesitate. "I want us to reconnect. To be a team again. To remember why we chose each other."

Elisa turned to her. "And you, Grace?"

Grace opened her mouth and faltered. Did she want to fix this? Prove she'd tried? Get permission to leave? "I want …" Her stomach tightened. "As I said, I want both of us to understand what's happening. I want us to be honest about where we are."

Elisa's eyes bored into her. "Grace, I'm going to ask you something, and I want you to answer honestly, with what's true." She paused, and when she continued, her voice was gentle. "Do you want to stay married?"

Michael's gaze turned to Grace.

Silence.

Her heart hammered.

"I don't think I do," she said.

Elisa's pen stilled. Her eyes met Grace's and held them with something like respect.

She'd said it. Out loud. To Michael. To the therapist, a witness.

Michael's head snapped back, as if she'd physically struck him. His face went white. "Grace!" His voice cracked. "What are you— we can fix this. We're here, we're trying—"

"Michael—" Grace kept her gaze on her hands, twisting in her lap. Her heart was racing, but underneath it, a strange calm. She'd said it.

"No, listen. You can't just—" He turned to Elisa. "She can't just decide it's over. We have kids. We have a life. I'm here. I'm willing to work."

"Michael," Elisa said gently, "let's take a breath."

He sat back, chest heaving.

"Don't you see how far our relationship has fallen?" Grace asked quietly. "We don't have shared moments anymore. There's no real 'we' at all."

"That's ridiculous. You're exaggerating, Grace."

"I'm not."

A blanket of silence returned.

Elisa cleared her throat, attracting their attention. "Here's what I'd like. Between now and next week, think about what you actually want—not what you may think you should want." She paused. "Also, try to have at least one conversation this week, just the two of you, no phones or other distractions. Fifteen minutes. Can you do that?"

Michael nodded. "Yes."

Grace nodded, too, though she couldn't imagine what they'd talk about.

"One last thing," Elisa said, glancing at the clock. "Grace, I hear that you have feelings for Ruth. Between now and next week, I want you to think about what you're hoping to find with her and whether you're running toward something or away from something. Or both."

Grace nodded, her shoulders heavy.

Elisa stood. "We'll stop here for today."

They left the office separately, Michael striding ahead. She called after him—"Michael, wait"—but he didn't slow. By the time she reached the parking lot, his car was already pulling onto the street, taillights disappearing around the corner. That was Michael; when things got uncomfortable, he simply vanished.

She sat in her own car for a long time, staring out the windshield at nothing. November rain had started. Light, persistent, blurring the world beyond the glass. She watched water trickle down and felt numb.

She needed to see Allie. She pulled out her phone and texted her: *Just finished first session. It was hard. Need to see you. OK if I stop by your house tonight?*

Allie's reply came quickly: *Of course. Are you okay?*

Was she? *I don't know,* she typed in reply.

She set the phone down and started the car. She had patients to see, a life to resume. But as she drove back to Cambridge, she thought about the look on Michael's face when she'd said she wasn't sure if she wanted to stay married. The way it had landed.

Something had shifted in that room.

She saw her afternoon patients on autopilot. Michael was in surgery tonight until at least nine. She arranged for Sofie to watch the kids so she could have several hours with Allie. Hours she needed.

The November darkness came early now. By the time she reached Allie's porch, the door closing behind her brought its own relief.

Allie pulled her into an embrace. Grace leaned into her, trembling.

"I've got you," Allie said into her hair. "It's okay. I'm here."

They stood like that for a long moment, Grace's face pressed into Allie's shoulder, breathing in the scent of her, something clean and familiar that made Grace's chest ache.

Allie pulled back first, hands still on Grace's arms. "Come sit."

She led Grace to the living room, warm lamplight drawing Grace's eye to a throw blanket draped over the back of the couch. Grace sank into the corner, and Allie disappeared into the kitchen. A cabinet opened. The clink of glass. The glug of liquid pouring from a bottle.

Allie returned with two wine glasses and handed one to Grace before settling beside her.

Grace took a long sip, then another. The wine burned going down.

"Tell me," Allie said. "What happened?"

Grace turned her glass slowly. Where to start? "Elisa asked

Michael what he loves about me." She paused. "He said I'm reliable. Steady. Keep everything running."

Allie was quiet for a moment. "How did that feel?"

"Like being described by someone who loves you but can only report on your clothes, because they've never asked you to take them off."

Allie winced.

Grace set down her glass. "And then she asked me the same question."

"What did you say?"

"The truth. That he's a good man. That I don't think he ever stopped caring." She looked at her hands. "That we just never learned how to show each other that we did. That that was my failure, too."

Something shifted in Allie's expression. She looked down at her glass. "That was generous of you."

The words were neutral. The tone wasn't quite.

Grace looked at her. "You think I shouldn't have said it."

"I think—" Allie stopped. Started again. "I think you're very fair to him. Consistently." She met Grace's eyes. "I sometimes wonder if you're quite as fair to yourself."

It wasn't an accusation. But it wasn't nothing either. Grace felt the edge in it.

"I'm trying to be honest," Grace said carefully. "In that room, with both of them watching, I wasn't going to perform. I wanted to be as honest and open as I could."

"I know." Allie's voice softened slightly. "I know that." She turned her glass on the table. "I just — I've watched you carry this for months. All the guilt, all the careful management of everyone's feelings. And sometimes I wonder when you're going to let yourself just —" She stopped.

"Just what?"

Allie shook her head. "Nothing. I'm sorry. That wasn't fair."

"No," Grace said. "Say it."

A beat. "When you're going to let yourself want what you want without apologizing for it first."

The room was quiet. Grace felt the complicated truth of it— that Allie wasn't entirely wrong, and wasn't entirely right. And Grace wasn't sure she liked being read that way, even if it was partly correct.

"I said what was true," Grace said finally. "In there, today. That's all."

Allie nodded. Reached over and covered Grace's hand with her own. "I know. I'm sorry. Tell me what happened next."

Allie waited.

Grace's hands shook slightly. She picked up her glass. Wine trembled against the rim. "She asked if I wanted to stay married."

Allie went still beside her.

"I said no." Grace looked up, meeting Allie's eyes. "I said I don't think I do."

Allie's hand found her free one. Squeezed.

"Out loud. In front of him." Grace's voice cracked. "I can't take it back now."

"Do you want to take it back?"

Grace shook her head. "No, I don't." She set her wine down before she spilled it. "I feel terrible. Guilty. But also—" Her breath hitched. "Relieved."

"Hey." Allie shifted closer, one hand cupping Grace's face. "Look at me."

Grace did. Allie's eyes were dark, serious.

"You were honest. That's what matters."

"It felt terrible. The look on his face—" Grace's eyes filled. She pressed the heels of her hands against them. "God."

Allie pulled her close. Grace let herself collapse against her, face buried in Allie's neck. Allie's hand moved in slow circles on her back.

They sat like that for a long time. Grace's breathing gradually steadied. Allie's heartbeat pulsed against her cheek, solid and real.

"I didn't go there planning to say it," Grace said, her voice muffled. "It just came out."

"Maybe it needed to."

Grace pulled back slightly.

Allie's hand came up, thumb wiping away the tears on Grace's cheek. "What happens now?" Allie asked.

"I don't know."

Allie's other hand moved to Grace's knee, a gentle pressure. The air between them was charged. "You don't have to figure it all out tonight."

Grace nodded, but her mind kept circling back. To Michael's face, Elisa's knowing look, the words hanging in that office. "I told her about you. She suggested we give you a fake name. For privacy." Grace managed a small smile. "You're Ruth now."

Allie smiled. "Ruth. Okay."

"I said I had feelings for a woman. That you make me feel seen." Grace's eyes filled again. "That you make me feel like I matter."

Allie leaned forward, forehead touching Grace's. They stayed like that, breathing together.

Grace closed her eyes. Her hand moved to Allie's face, fingertips tracing the curve of her jaw. When she opened her eyes, Allie was watching her.

"Can I—" Grace started.

Allie answered by moving her lips to Grace's.

The kiss was gentle at first. Then Grace's hand tangled in Allie's hair and pulled her closer. Allie's mouth opened under hers and heat spread through her chest, down her spine. When Allie's hands slid under Grace's sweater, palms flat against her back, Grace gasped into her mouth. They kissed until Grace's mind went quiet, until there was nothing in the world but Allie's mouth, Allie's hands, the heat building between them.

The room had gone dark around them except for the lamp in the corner. Outside, a car passed, headlights sweeping across the wall.

When they broke apart, both breathing hard, Grace rested her forehead against Allie's shoulder.

"I wish you could stay," Allie whispered.

"Me, too. But Michael's done at nine. I told the sitter—"

"I know." Allie's fingers traced patterns on Grace's back. "Just wishing."

Grace pulled back to look at her. Allie's face was flushed, her eyes dark.

"Soon," Grace heard herself say. "I'll figure out how."

Allie walked her to the door. At the threshold, Grace turned back.

"Thank you," she said. "For being here when I need you."

"Always." Allie kissed her once more, quick and tender. "Text me when you get home safely."

Grace nodded and stepped into the cold November air. She stood on the sidewalk. Her lips hot. Allie's wine lingering on her tongue. She almost felt calm.

She'd said the words. Michael knew. Elisa knew.

And she was still here. Still breathing. The world hadn't shattered.

The relief unsettled her almost as much as the thought of the silence that would meet her when she walked through her own back door.

27

———————

Tuesday, November 7

At five-thirty, Grace's office glowed amber with the day's waning light. The couple came in mid-argument, settling on opposite ends of the couch, angled away from each other. Carolyn clutched her coat against her chest; Brian's loosened tie hung askew, his smartwatch pulsing with notifications.

Carolyn's shoulders rose toward her ears as she spoke. "Yeah, your career matters. I get that. What I don't get is when I stopped mattering just as much." She paused, fingers twisting the hem of her blouse. "I feel like I've become background noise in your life."

Brian's jaw clenched, then released. He stared at the space between them on the couch. "Every extra hour I put in is for the life we talked about building. The house. The security. I thought we were on the same page about that."

"I'd like to suggest something before we dive in," Grace said, leaning forward a little. "Can we agree that anything said here today comes from a place of care, not harm?" A beat passed. Brian's shoulders dropped slightly. They both nodded.

"Carolyn, would you be willing to start?"

Carolyn's gaze fixed on a spot just past Grace's shoulder. "I've told him a million times what upsets me, many of those times in this room. What happened last Sunday night is a good example. I made his favorite dinner, salmon with dill sauce. I wore a dress he once said he loved." Her throat hitched. "He spent the whole meal scrolling emails under the table."

"Brian," Grace said carefully, "what happens inside you when you hear that Carolyn feels invisible while she's sitting across from you at dinner?"

Brian dragged a palm down his face, stubble rasping against his hand. "I do see her. But there's never enough hours. If I stay later at work three nights, that buys us a weekend together. It's all a calculation. If I walk through the door when she wants me to, then I have to spend the night glued to my laptop—physically present but mentally gone, which she hates more. I can't win. I'm killing myself for that promotion, for the down payment on a house we both want. Somehow that doesn't register."

Color climbed into Carolyn's cheeks, her eyes brightening with tears. "I don't want someone sacrificing himself for some future version of us. I want a partner who's present now. Someone who looks at me when I speak instead of hiding behind a screen."

Grace lifted a hand slightly. "Can I summarize what I'm hearing? Brian, it sounds like you're working to secure the future you both said you wanted. And Carolyn, that future doesn't mean much if the present feels empty. Does that sound right?"

Carolyn exhaled. "Yes. That's exactly it."

Brian looked down at the rug, then at his hands. "I don't know how to fix that."

"Maybe don't go straight to 'fixing' it," Grace said. She held the silence before offering, "What if you start with being curious instead?"

They exchanged glances, doubt written across their faces.

"Think back to your first year together," Grace said. "Those nights you stayed up way too late, just … learning each other. Asking questions, trading stories. That curiosity doesn't vanish. It just gets buried. Under schedules, under the feeling that you already know the important stuff about each other."

They both looked away, uncertain.

"It happens to most couples," Grace added. "They become efficient business partners—managing a household, going through the motions—instead of two people paying attention to who the other is still becoming."

Brian spoke into the quiet, his voice smaller. "Being at work is easier than being at home because it's not personal. If a deal falls apart, I'm disappointed, but it doesn't make me feel like I'm failing as a person. That's not the case at home, where I feel I don't know the rules anymore. I used to know how to make her laugh. I don't now."

Grace nodded, letting his words settle. "Thank you for sharing that, Brian." She turned gently toward the other side of the couch. "Carolyn?"

The office had darkened around them, Grace's lamp the only light. Carolyn exhaled, sinking back slightly. Her voice came out a whisper. "I miss the person I fell in love with. Not the guy who sends me screenshots of his Outlook calendar."

"Here's what I'd like you to try this week," Grace said. "For ten minutes a day, your only job is to be curious about each other. Ask a question you don't know the answer to. Like, *What surprised you today?* And listen to understand, not to reply."

Carolyn's face relaxed, the tension around her eyes easing. "We can do that."

Brian looked up. He cleared his throat. "I don't know if ten minutes is going to …" He trailed off, then nodded slowly. "Yeah. Okay. We can try that."

"Small steps," Grace said. "It's not magic. Won't work miracles. But it can reopen a door that's been quietly closed. And if home feels heavy, change the context—go for a walk, sit in the car. Side by side is sometimes easier than face to face."

They spent the last minutes scripting slip-ups (forgive, reset) and how to signal openness (sit closer than feels natural).

When Carolyn reached across the couch and took Brian's hand, Grace looked down at her pad and made a note.

After they left, Grace sat in the dimming office. The couch still held the impression of their bodies, two dents in the cushions. She picked up her phone and scrolled to Allie's last text. Allie had sent a photo that morning—Noah's pancake attempt, batter on the ceiling. Small things. Ordinary moments. The kind Michael never shared.

She'd asked him weeks ago about the best part of his day. He'd told her about humiliating a colleague, his voice bright with satisfaction. She'd stopped asking. She opened her text thread with Allie and typed: *What surprised you today?*

The response came almost immediately: *You asking me that. Why?*

Grace stared at the question. Because I just spent an hour telling a couple to be curious about each other. Because I realized I do this with you without thinking. Because it matters.

No reason, she typed. *Just thinking about curiosity today.*

Three dots blinked. Grace waited. Then read: *Okay then. A client told me I changed her life. Made me cry in the best way. Your turn— what surprised you?*

Grace's thumb hovered over the screen. What surprised her? That she could sit in her office giving advice about presence and curiosity while her own marriage had neither. That the advice felt true, even as she gave it. That she already practiced it with Allie without conscious effort.

Before she could reconsider, she replied with: *That I'm better at being present with you than I ever was with him.*

The dots appeared, then disappeared. Then appeared again, followed by Allie's text: *That doesn't surprise me at all. You've been present with me from the start.*

Grace set her phone down and gathered her things. Outside her window, the parking lot was nearly empty, streetlights flickering on in the November dusk. She locked her office door and walked to her car, November air sharp against her face.

On the drive home, she thought about Carolyn's hand reaching across the couch. That tentative gesture toward connection. How long had it been since she'd reached for Michael like that? She couldn't remember.

Traffic ground to a halt as she approached the Cambridge Street tunnel by Harvard's Sanders Theatre, red brake lights stretching ahead. She picked up her phone and typed to Allie: *Second couples therapy tomorrow. I know I'll need to see you after.*

The cars in front of her started to move. She tapped SEND and pulled forward.

28

Wednesday, November 8

The night of her second couples-therapy session with Michael, Grace arranged again for Sofie to babysit the kids. Grace arrived at Allie's house at six-thirty, November darkness already complete.

Allie took one look at her face, guided her to the couch, and handed her a glass of red wine. The living room lamp cast warm light across them. "Tell me. How'd it go?"

Grace let out a breath. "Elisa wanted to talk about you, about my feelings. Michael asked if they were mutual, if anything physical had happened. Not sure why. I'd already told him. Maybe he wanted me to say it in front of Elisa. Anyway, I said yes, there had been several times."

Allie stood and crossed the room. "What did Michael do?"

"Just sat there. Completely still. His face went blank."

Grace's voice dropped. "And then Elisa, right in front of him, asked if I could commit to staying away from you while we work on the marriage."

Allie drew in a small breath. "That … I mean, I guess it makes sense."

"I said no." Grace wiped her eyes with the heel of her hand. "I said I couldn't, wouldn't, commit to that." She took Allie's hands. "I told them that I need you—that you're the only thing keeping me together right now."

"How did Michael react to that?"

"Seized on it. Insisted I'm having a breakdown and need psychiatric help."

"Jesus."

"Yeah. And then I kind of … blew up." Grace's hands flew upward for a second, then dropped. I was basically yelling: 'I'm not sick. The fact you think that shows how little you know me.' And then I stopped yelling—and God, I don't know how I got the words out—but I said it straight: 'I can't stay in this marriage any longer. I want out.'"

Her heart had been pounding. Her hands had been shaking. But her voice had been steady.

Allie stared at her. "Grace. … You said that?"

Grace nodded. "Yeah. And he walked out. Just stood up and left. Elisa tried to stop him, but he was gone." Grace brushed tears away. "She looked at me and said, 'Okay. That was even clearer than last week.'"

Allie pulled her close, one hand stroking her hair. "I'm sorry," she murmured against Grace's temple. After a while, she said, "Grace, I need to ask you something. Are you leaving him because of me? I need to know you'd be doing this even if I wasn't here."

Grace pulled back slightly to look at her. "That's not a question I can answer the way you want me to."

Allie's expression tightened.

"I mean— if we'd never met, I'd probably go on being married to Michael. I'm not going to lie to you about that. I'd go on managing. Getting through. Telling myself it was enough." She paused. "You didn't invent what was wrong. I was already disappearing inside that marriage. Maybe I'd have figured it out eventually on my own. I don't know. But you made it impossible to keep not-seeing it."

"That sounds like leaving him because of me."

"It sounds like that. It's not the same thing." Grace held her gaze. "You didn't break my marriage. My marriage was already broken. What you did was make me understand I'd been living inside a life that wasn't mine." She paused a beat. "I can't unknow that. And I wouldn't want to. But that's not the same as you being the reason."

Allie looked at her for a long moment. Then: "Okay. I believe you." She glanced away briefly, then back. "I just need you to keep telling me the truth. Even when it's hard."

"I will."

Allie moved a fingernail back and forth cross Grace's knee, paused, then looked up at her. "And, Grace, one more thing. I don't want to be your experiment. If that's what you need, find someone else. I don't want this—" She moved a hand between them. "—to be something you try and then walk away from. And I know myself. I can't do this halfway. If we come together—"

Grace squeezed her hands. "You're not an experiment. God, no. And I hear you. I won't do halfway. I won't do that to you." She held Allie's gaze. "And if anything changes, I'll tell you. You'll never have to wonder."

Allie smiled and cupped Grace's face, her thumbs brushing tears away. "What happens now?"

"I don't know. Elisa wants to see us again next week. Michael agreed before he left." Grace shook her head. "Maybe she can help us figure out how to tell the kids. But the marriage is over."

"Do they know anything?"

"Not Matthew. Mia knows we're seeing a marriage counselor." A long pause. "Jesus. A divorce."

"Yeah. It's really hard." They stood forehead to forehead. Grace closed her eyes. Allie said, "Lawyers, custody, the house ... I'm worried for you, because I know what you're about to go through. And I can't fix it for you. I can't make it easier."

Grace nodded slowly. "I'm not asking you to."

"I know. But I need you to know I'm here. With you. Through all of it. Whatever comes."

Grace pulled her close. "That's all I need."

Something shifted in Allie's expression: tension releasing, doubt giving way. She kissed Grace slowly, deeply. Her mouth traced the lines of Grace's face, her throat, her ear.

A sofa cushion went skidding to the floor as Allie tugged Grace down beside her. Allie's hair fell forward, brushing Grace's cheek. She kissed along Grace's jaw, pausing to draw her lower lip in, caressing it with her tongue. A hand slid along Grace's side, tracing ribs, settling just beneath her breast.

"Okay if I touch you?"

Grace groaned. "If you don't, I'm going to shred this other cushion."

Allie laughed. Her hand cupped Grace's breast through her sweater, thumb caressing. Grace moaned. Warm breath brushed her ear; her body arched toward it.

Allie shifted her weight to one side, opened Grace's sweater, and kissed down Grace's throat. She unbuttoned it the rest of the way and followed the top edge of Grace's bra with her fingertip, then her tongue. When her mouth closed over Grace's breast through the thin fabric, Grace's head tipped back, a quiet moan slipping out. Allie looked up at her, smiling. Grace pulled her up and kissed her hard.

Allie's hand explored again—breasts, ribs, gentle teasing touches.

"Oh god—" Grace breathed.

Allie moved her hand lower, across Grace's stomach, then slid it toward the waistband.

Grace grabbed her wrist. "Maybe not that. Not yet. Is that okay?"

Allie froze, face falling. "I'm sorry. I—"

They lay tangled but tense on the couch, Grace's sweater still open, Allie propped on one elbow.

"Don't be sorry. I want you to. You know I do." Grace inhaled, steadying herself. "I'm just not ready for that. I don't know why. Maybe because that feels different. More—" She couldn't finish.

Breasts felt like bodies. Below the waist felt like identity. Letting a woman touch her down there would be crossing a line she couldn't uncross.

Allie tucked a strand of hair behind Grace's ear. "I'm glad you stopped me. We go at your pace."

Grace eased back, pulling herself upright, sweater still hanging open. Her breath came uneven. She let out a laugh at her own disarray.

"I don't understand this. I really don't. I'm not into women."

Allie nodded. "I understand. I get it."

Grace laughed again. "Okay then, maybe you can explain why my underwear are soaked."

Allie grinned. "I have theories."

They pressed their foreheads together, laughing. They kept touching—hair, hips, ribs. Gentle, familiar. Whispered confessions of how long they'd wanted this.

Then Grace's stomach growled, loud and insistent, like a living creature. They froze, eyes wide, and then burst into laughter.

"Great timing, body," Grace said, cheeks flushing. "I guess I'm hungry."

Allie tapped her stomach. "When did you last eat?"

"I don't remember. Breakfast? Yogurt?"

Allie kissed her forehead, then her nose, then her mouth. "Come on. Let's feed you before you faint. Bodies need things."

"Yeah, and mine was getting some."

Allie laughed. "I'm talking about fuel. You've been running on adrenaline for hours. We're going to fix that."

"Is this why your clients pay you so much?"

"Exactly. Top dollars flow to the most incisive therapists."

~

When 9:30 rolled around, Grace said, "Shit. I should go."

Allie said, "When can I see you again?"

Grace slapped a hand to her forehead. "I forgot. Michael told me he wants to take the kids to visit old family friends next weekend. Rye, New York. Leaving Friday evening, back late Sunday afternoon."

Allie's eyes widened. "Wow. I don't have the kids until that Saturday morning." She walked her fingers up Grace's thigh. "Would you come over that Friday night?"

Grace's mouth went dry. "I should be able to get here around seven-thirty."

"I'll be waiting," Allie said.

Grace exhaled shakily, eyes falling shut. Her need was immediate, physical.

"How will I make it until then?"

Allie's mouth curved. "You could think of me. When you have some privacy."

Grace's face went hot when she realized what Allie meant. "I haven't done that in years. My libido went kaput after things had been bad with Michael for so long."

Allie's expression melted. "Oh, Grace." She kissed her gently. "We're going to change that."

At the door, she stepped onto the porch and turned back. "Allie?"

"Yeah?"

"Thank you for coming into my life. For helping me see what's possible."

Allie smiled and grabbed Grace's hand. When she spoke, her

breath clouded under the light. "There's no one in the world I'd rather be with." They kissed again.

Grace drove home through quiet streets, hands steady on the wheel despite everything. The dashboard clock read 9:42. Body still alight from Allie's touch, she cracked the window; she needed the cold November air on her face. Michael would be in the guest room. He'd been sleeping there since their first therapy session a week ago. Two rooms, two beds.

She would slide into bed alone but carrying the scent of Allie on her skin, the taste of her mouth, and the sharp, sweet ache of wanting next Friday night to come faster.

She pulled into the driveway and sat for a moment, then slipped her phone from her purse and started a text to Allie: *We're supposed to go to Michael's parents' house in Schenectady for Thanksgiving. I can't do that this year. Not after today.*

Grace's thumb hovered over the screen. She thought about Mia and Matthew trapped at their grandparents' house with the tension thick enough to cut. Thought about making small talk with Michael's family while her marriage dissolved. Thought about Allie and her kids alone, or at her sister's, trying to make it feel festive.

She kept typing: *What if we did Thanksgiving together? Your kids and mine? All six of us? Here or at your place?* She hit SEND.

The three dots appeared immediately, then stopped. Started again. The reply eventually appeared: *Really? That would be fabulous! My kids would love it, and I'd get to spend the whole day with you. Michael's not gonna like it.*

Grace smiled in the dark, her heart beating faster. She replied: *No, but I'm doing it anyway. The six of us. A real Thanksgiving. I'll talk to Michael and the kids tomorrow.*

She got out of the car and walked toward the house, toward whatever tomorrow would bring.

29

Thursday, November 9

The next evening, the kids came home from school and vanished into their rooms. Around six, Grace found Michael in the den, still in his scrubs, reading on his laptop, the room lit only by the screen's glow and the lamp on the side table. November darkness pressed against the windows. They'd barely spoken since he'd walked out of the appointment the day before.

"Do you have a few minutes?" She said from the doorway.

Michael hesitated, then closed the laptop and turned toward her. Grace sat across from him, the old chair creaking under her weight.

"What is it?"

Grace took a breath. "I don't want to go to Schenectady for Thanksgiving."

Michael blinked. "What?"

"We're separated, Michael. It doesn't make sense to go."

"We're not separated."

"I told you yesterday I can't stay in this marriage. You walked out of therapy. We sleep separately, and we're going to get a divorce. What do you call that?"

He sighed. "Can't you just do it this year?"

"Especially not this year." The words gathered speed. "Even in the best of circumstances, going there is exhausting. Four days of performing. The kids are bored, I'm kitchen help for your mom. Your dad interrogates Mia about her grades; your brother's kids run wild. I'm tired of it."

Michael sat back. "So what do you want to do instead?"

"Allie invited us—me and the kids—to spend Thanksgiving with her and her family. I think that would be better. For all of us."

His teeth clenched. "Allie." A silence. "Better how?"

"The kids would actually have fun. They loved being with Emma and Noah that day we went to the Science Museum."

"They love going to Schenectady," he insisted.

Grace snorted and shook her head. "They tolerate Schenectady. There's a difference."

Color crept up Michael's neck. "So you've already decided."

"I'm talking to you about it now."

"Unbelievable, Grace. You want to blow off my family so you can spend the holiday with your girlfriend."

The word hit her like a poke in the chest. "I'm suggesting what's best for the kids," she said.

"Bullshit. You're choosing what's best for you. What'll make you feel good."

Grace stood, the chair scraping against the floor. "Maybe I am. But I can't do Schenectady again this year, especially under these circumstances. And I'd like to enjoy a holiday that doesn't feel like an obligation."

He glared at her. "What about what I want?"

She met his look head-on. The silence stretched.

Grace broke it. "Do you actually want Thanksgiving in Schenectady, Michael? Or are you just clinging to routine because you can't admit everything's changing?"

His face went tight. "Why are you doing this to us, Grace? If everything is so fucking awful for you, why have you stayed? If this isn't just about Allie, why didn't you leave long ago?"

Why had she stayed?

Because she hadn't known the woman whose life she was in. Because familiarity was easier than the truth. Because she didn't want to hurt him, didn't want to upset the kids. Because she kept hoping one more year would make a difference. Because she didn't know what wanting someone actually felt like until Allie showed her.

She looked at him across the space that had grown between them over seventeen years, all of it pressing against the back of her teeth.

"I stayed because I wanted to believe in us," she said. "Even when it was hard. Even when it didn't feel great. I didn't want to give up."

Michael stared at her, breathing hard. "So what changed?"

Grace looked at him directly. "I did. I stopped being willing to settle. I stopped thinking of emptiness as peaceful."

Michael dragged a hand down his face. "Can't you just put me and the kids first for Thanksgiving? Go to Schenectady?"

Heat flared in her. "I've put you and our family first since the very beginning, Michael. I gave up DC so you could take Mass General. I've gone to Schenectady every Thanksgiving for a decade even though your mother makes it clear I'm never good enough."

"That's not—"

"Let me finish. I've made myself smaller and smaller in this family until I almost disappeared." Her voice shook. "And I'm done." She paused and drew a breath. "But I'm going to keep putting the kids first. And the way I'm doing that this Thanksgiving is by not dragging them once again to fucking Schenectady."

"You think you're the only one who's sacrificed? I've worked myself to death for this family. And this is what I get—you running off with your girlfriend for Thanksgiving?" Michael traced the Apple logo on his closed laptop with his thumb, then tapped it. "We'll put it to the kids at dinner. They can decide. Don't be surprised if they choose their grandparents."

"I'd be shocked."

She turned and walked out. Behind her, the thump of Michael sinking back into his chair.

An hour later, dinner proceeded with familiar silence. The chicken she'd roasted sat mostly untouched. Matthew pushed peas around his plate. Mia ate with one hand while scrolling her phone with the other; Grace didn't bother reminding her about screens at the table. Michael's shoulders remained tight, his fork scraping against his plate with more force than necessary. Tension radiated from him.

Grace took a sip of water, then steadied her voice. "So. I wanted to talk about Thanksgiving. Allie has invited us to spend the holiday with her and Emma and Noah."

Matthew's head snapped up. "Really? Can we? Please? Noah got the new Minecraft expansion and—"

"Wait," Michael cut in. "We always go to Grandma and Grandpa's for Thanksgiving. You kids love it: your cousins, Grandma's pies …"

Matthew's face fell into a frown. "But we've done that so many times. This would be different. Better."

Mia didn't look up from her phone. "Grandpa would spend the whole time talking about college and grades, and telling me I need to study harder. And if we go to Schenectady, I wouldn't get to see Chloe for five days." A pause. "Plus, Allie's nice. Her kids are cool."

Michael looked at his children, then at Grace. His jaw worked. "Fine. You all do what you want. I'm going to Schenectady."

He pushed his chair back, carried his dishes to the kitchen. Water started running, plates clattered as Michael slipped back into routine, the shape of their family shifting around him.

Relief washed through Grace.

Matthew's smile faded. "Is Dad mad?"

Mia glanced toward the kitchen where Michael was clattering dishes. "He's always mad lately." She said it matter-of-factly, like stating weather.

"No, honey. Just disappointed," Grace said. "He likes the tradition of Thanksgiving with his family."

"I do too," Mia said. "But doing something different is good, too."

The levelheaded tone steadied Grace.

Matthew brightened again. "Yeah, Mom. This'll be awesome. Way better than New York."

After dinner, the kids cleared their plates and disappeared upstairs. Grace stayed at the table. She looked at the empty chairs, Matthew's crumpled napkin. From upstairs came the kids' voices: Matthew's excited, Mia's measured. The sounds of kids who didn't know their family was coming apart.

She poured herself a little more wine, picked up her phone, and texted Allie: *Done. We'll be with you for Thanksgiving. We're excited.*

Allie's reply came almost immediately: *Wonderful! Something fun to look forward to.*

She waited for the guilt to arrive. For the sadness.

Instead, what arrived was relief. And underneath it, something sharper. Anger at how long she'd waited. Anger at all the Thanksgivings she'd endured, making herself smaller and smaller until she'd forgotten how to take up space.

From the guest room above, she heard the door close. Michael, shutting himself away.

Let him, she thought.

The kids had chosen Allie's house over their grandparents

without hesitation. Had chosen her over Michael, even if they didn't know that's what they were doing.

Grace looked down at her phone. Allie's last message: *Something fun to look forward to.*

30

Wednesday, November 15

The Wednesday of their third couples-therapy appointment, Grace pulled into the lot fifteen minutes early, her stomach tight. Michael's car was already there, parked crookedly, like he'd arrived in a hurry or changed his mind twice before stopping.

She sat, picking at her cuticle until her finger bled.

She went inside. He was hunched in the far corner of the waiting room, still in scrubs, shoulders rounded. The white noise machine hummed. Pale November light filtered through the window. He didn't look up when she said, "Hey."

A nod. Nothing more.

They sat in silence until Elisa opened the door at noon.

"Grace? Michael? Come in."

They followed her down the hall. Michael took the far end of the couch, leaving Grace to perch at the opposite end. She folded her hands tightly in her lap.

Elisa settled into her chair. "Thank you both for coming back. I know last week was painful."

Michael's jaw flexed, but he didn't speak.

"I'd like to start with how things have been for each of you," Elisa said. "Michael, you left abruptly last time. What's been happening for you since then?"

He stared at a fixed point on the wall. When he spoke, his voice was sharp with sarcasm. "Happening? Well, let's see. Grace has corralled the kids into going to her girlfriend's for Thanksgiving instead of spending it as we always do, with my family. And, oh: she underlined her statement of last week by saying she's getting a divorce. So, I guess you'd say a lot's been happening."

Elisa's eyebrows rose. She turned to Grace.

But before Elisa could speak, Michael added, "I realized she must've made that decision long before we ever came here. Therapy is just a performance for her. A box she wanted to check so she could say she tried."

Grace crossed her arms. He wasn't entirely wrong.

Elisa asked gently, "Grace, is that accurate?"

Her instinct was to defend herself. And also cushion the blow—but she wouldn't lie now. "Not a performance," she said quietly. "But yes. I already knew what I needed and wanted."

Michael let out a hoarse, disbelieving laugh. "Jesus." He leaned back, staring at the ceiling.

"I'm sorry," she said. "I should've been honest sooner. I—"

"Don't," he said sharply. "The apologies don't help."

Silence.

Elisa shifted slightly. "Grace, when did you realize you didn't want to repair the marriage?"

Grace searched backward. The night she slept with Michael out of obligation? When she and Allie kissed? No. Earlier. Months.

"I think I've known for a long time. I kept telling myself it was a phase, that I just needed to try harder." She paused. "But I reached a point where I couldn't pretend anymore."

Michael stared at her. "So you were lying. About wanting therapy to help us."

"I wasn't lying," Grace said. "I never said I wanted to fix us. I said I wanted therapy to help us both have clarity about what happened to our marriage."

"Before you left me for a woman," he said bitterly.

"Before I accepted that the marriage was over," she said gently.

Michael turned to Grace. "I need to know if you're going to be with her. After this."

Grace shifted "I don't know. We haven't talked about anything long-term."

"But you want to be with her," he pressed.

"Yes." The word landed simply.

His hands gripped his knees. "You're sure this isn't just some midlife spiral? Infatuation? A crisis?"

Grace shook her head. "It isn't. But even if it were, that's not the point. This isn't about her. The point is: our marriage hasn't been working for a long time. At least not for me. I feel numb with you, Michael. Alone, even when you're right there. I can't live like that anymore."

Michael's face hardened. "I don't understand why you were so unhappy. I wasn't. Not until you were."

Grace stared at him, mouth open with disbelief. "Michael ... I didn't even know who I was in this marriage anymore. We've been living like roommates for years. You think that's happiness?"

"That's marriage," he snapped. "You build a life. You raise kids. The excitement dies down. That's normal."

"Maybe," Grace said. But I don't want to live like that for forty more years. I don't want to look back and realize I spent my whole life settling."

"Settling?" He gave a bitter laugh. "You're getting less than you deserve? What about what I deserve? What about our kids?"

Grace blinked back sudden tears. "I think about them every night. I imagine their faces when we tell them. It kills me." Her voice shook. "But our staying together in a dead marriage isn't good for them either. I don't want to model this for our kids."

Michael was quiet for a long time. His shoulders sagged, and he looked older, tired. When he finally spoke, his voice had lost its edge. "I don't agree with you. About any of it." He looked at his hands. "But I can see you're not coming back from this."

Grace watched his face, the way his eyes wouldn't quite focus, the way his mouth worked like he was trying to swallow something bitter.

Elisa leaned forward, voice gentle. "It sounds like both of you are accepting that the marriage is ending. Is that fair?"

Grace nodded.

Michael hesitated, then nodded, too.

"Then let's talk about what comes next," Elisa said. "Grace, have you thought about how you'll tell the kids?"

Grace pressed her palms together. "Not yet. I know we have to figure out logistics first—what changes for them. Where they'll be. What stays steady. Because that's what they'll care about most."

Michael surprised her. "We tell them after Thanksgiving," he said quietly. "Together. And only after we've worked out the details."

"That sounds right," Grace said.

Michael stood abruptly, face pale, jaw tight. "Are we done?"

Elisa scanned her notes, looked at the clock, then back at them. "Unless either of you has something else you need to bring in."

Grace shook her head. Michael was already halfway to the door.

"Michael," she said, standing. "Wait."

He paused, hand on the knob, but didn't turn.

"I'm sorry," Grace said. "I know I keep saying it. But I am. And just—please don't think this is easy for me. I—"

He turned then, eyes sharp. "Are you sorry you fell for her?"

She thought of Allie's hands, her laugh, the way Grace felt alive when she was near her. "No," she said. "I'm not sorry about that."

His expression flattened. Then he nodded once, curtly. "At least you're honest now." He walked out.

Grace stood frozen, listening to his footsteps fade.

Elisa said, "Grace? Are you alright?"

Grace shook her head, tears slipping down her cheeks. She stood by the couch, not wanting to sit back down. "I just ended my marriage. My kids' lives are about to change forever. And all I can think about is that I need to see her. She's the only person who'd understand how I'm feeling."

"That's normal," Elisa said. "You're grieving. And reaching for comfort."

Grace nodded, unable to speak.

Elisa stood, offering Grace a tissue from the box on her desk. "Take care of yourself, Grace."

"Thank you," Grace murmured. She walked out on unsteady legs, the hallway blurry.

On the building's front porch, she sank into a rocking chair flanked by pumpkins. Seventeen years. Two kids about to be hurt.

She blinked back tears until she could see clearly enough to type a message to Allie: *My marriage is over.*

Allie responded almost instantly: *Oh, Grace. I'm so sorry. Are you okay?*

Grace typed: *No. Can I see you? Your office? After your last appointment?*

When she read Allie's reply—*Done at seven. Come then*—she set her phone down in her lap, her breathing shallow. She had six hours of clients ahead of her, six hours of holding herself together.

Everything ahead was uncertain. Who'd live where, how they'd split time with the kids, what she'd tell her mother, how she'd explain this to friends who thought they had a good marriage.

Michael's words returned, unbidden: *Are you sorry you fell for her?*

No. Not for one second.

31

———————

Friday, November 17

Friday evening, Grace beat the light at Huron and cut down a side street, shaving minutes off the drive home. The saved time did nothing to slow her pulse. Her four o'clock had seemed interminable. She'd nodded, empathized, taken notes, all while silently counting down to escape.

Upstairs, the kids were already packing. Matthew was in his room folding clothes into his weekend bag with a precision that mimicked his father's and made Grace pause in the doorway.

"Need any help?" she asked.

"Nope. I'm good," he said without looking up.

Down the hall, Mia tossed clothes into her bag in loose arcs, singing along to her laptop.

She glanced up when Grace appeared at the door. "Sure you don't want to come?"

"Steph's had a rough week," Grace lied with practiced ease. "And I'm behind on case notes."

Mia gave her a fifteen year-old's side-eye—the kind that said she didn't believe a word, but wasn't invested enough to dig. She turned back to the bag on her bed and started rolling socks.

Downstairs, Michael was loading the car with bags, snacks, jackets. He almost seemed like a stranger, this man she'd built a life with.

She waved as they backed out of the driveway. She stood at the window until the taillights disappeared. Two days since the third couples-therapy session. Two days of clients and case notes and dinners and homework, with Wednesday still lodged somewhere beneath her sternum. *God. I hope I know what I'm doing.*

She poured a glass of wine and climbed the stairs, telling herself she could still back out of the evening. Text Allie, invent an excuse, retreat into Netflix and takeout. Even as she thought it, she knew she wouldn't. Couldn't.

She ran a bath, almost too hot, letting the water pink her skin. She shaved her legs. Twice. Nicked her ankle the second time and didn't notice until she saw the water go pink. Washed her hair, then stood dripping before the mirror. Forty-two, mother of two. What did she even know about pleasuring a woman? What if she was hopeless at it?

She pulled on the black silk underwear she'd bought years ago in a brief surge of optimism about her marriage. Michael hadn't even noticed her in them, so she'd shoved them to the back of a drawer and not looked at them again.

She dressed in roomy jeans and a pale blue sweater—simple, comfortable. Downstairs, she checked her phone repeatedly. Nothing from Allie since a heart emoji. She considered texting. *See you soon* felt trivial; *On my way to change my entire life* felt insane. She sent nothing. They'd said seven-thirty. Grace refused to be early for her own undoing.

At seven-twenty she grabbed her keys and walked out before courage could evaporate.

At Allie's, Grace climbed the steps and paused on the porch, breathing in cold air. Through the window, warm light glowed. She rang the bell.

Footsteps. A familiar silhouette shifting behind frosted glass. The door opened.

Allie. Hair loose, leggings, a white cotton shirt unbuttoned just enough. Grace took her in—the way she was just standing there, like she didn't know that Grace wanted nothing more than to press her lips to that bare throat. Maybe she did know. For a moment, neither of them spoke.

Grace stepped inside. The door clicked shut. The first kiss came immediately. Urgent, then gentle, then urgent again. Allie pushed a thigh between Grace's legs and pulled her tight. Grace gasped. She pressed herself against Allie's thigh.

When they broke apart, Allie smiled, breath catching. "I have wine. Or we could just go up—"

"Wine, please." Grace said, laughing at herself. "I need a minute."

"A minute?" Allie blew out a puff of air, forcing a loose tendril away from her face. Her lips curved into a sly smile. "Sure, Gracie. What the hell. I've only been waiting six months."

Grace laughed and jostled her shoulder.

Allie led Grace into the living room. Candles glowed on the mantle. The usual family clutter had vanished. Music purred low. Grace took it all in: the open bottle, two glasses waiting.

Allie poured, their fingers brushing as she handed over the glass. They perched on the couch, not quite touching.

"You okay?" Allie asked. "We don't have to do anything tonight. We could just watch TV or—"

"I want to," Grace said quickly. "I've just never done this."

"I know." Allie's hand came to her cheek. "And I get it, Gracie."

"Maybe we could just talk first."

Allie nodded and eased back. "Sure."

Grace glanced around. "Thanks for making everything so nice. Is this what you do when you have a woman over?"

Allie laughed. "You make it sound like there's a stream of them through here. No. I've only done all this one other time."

Grace hesitated. "Do you want to tell me?"

A beat. "Her name was Beth. I met her about a year after the divorce was final. She was a teacher—smart, funny, completely at ease with who she was. She'd been out since college." Allie's voice softened. "Being with her felt like finally understanding a language I'd been trying to speak my whole life."

"Tell me more."

"We dated for nine months. Took me six months before I'd even let her meet the kids—I was terrified of screwing it up, of them getting attached and then losing her. Mark kept saying I was 'experimenting,' that I'd come to my senses. That got in my head." She paused. "When I finally introduced her, Emma loved her immediately. Wanted to braid Beth's hair, show her every drawing. Noah barely looked at her. Wouldn't talk to her for weeks."

"What was that about?"

"He was angry I'd left his dad. He didn't understand the gay part yet—he was only five—but he understood that Beth wasn't Daddy, and Beth being there meant Daddy wasn't coming back." Allie's voice tightened. "He'd ask me when I was going to stop 'having sleepovers with that lady.' Like if I just stopped, his dad would move back in."

Grace squeezed her hand. "That must have been awful."

"It was." Allie looked down. "And then about three months after I introduced her to the kids, Beth told me she'd met someone else. A man. Said she'd thought she was gay, but she'd been wrong. Said being with a woman was 'too complicated.'"

Grace's chest tightened. "Oh, Allie."

"I had to tell Emma that Beth wasn't coming back. Emma cried and asked what she'd done wrong—did she talk too much? Was she annoying? I had to explain that it wasn't about her, that grown-ups sometimes make mistakes." Allie's voice cracked slightly. "And Noah — he just looked at me and said, 'I'm glad the lady left.'"

"Jesus."

"Yeah." Allie wiped her eyes. "For months after that, I couldn't even think about dating. I was so confused. To me, Beth hadn't seemed uncertain at all. That left me spinning. And the kids. I felt like I'd dragged them through my mess, and they'd paid a price." She looked at Grace directly. "So, when I say I can't do this halfway with you, when I say I need to know you're sure— that's why. I can't bring someone into their lives again unless I know it's real. They deserve better than that."

Grace's throat tightened. She understood what Allie wasn't saying: *I deserve better than that, too.*

She let the moment settle, then said, "Can I ask something else? About you? What was your first sense you were gay?"

Allie took a breath. "At a sleepover when I was fourteen, I kissed my friend Amber in the basement while we were supposed to be watching a movie. It felt like my whole body woke up. I was so terrified I pretended it had been a joke, that we'd been practicing for boys. Amber went along with it, thank god. Then I buried it for years."

"Until?"

"College. Marilyn. A girl in my dorm. We'd stay up all night talking, and I'd feel this pull toward her that I couldn't name. One night we kissed. Afterward, I told myself we'd been drunk, that it didn't mean anything. Dated a guy two weeks later to prove I was normal." Allie shook her head. "I got really good at explaining things away."

Grace set their glasses on the table. "And coming out— what finally made you face it?"

"Years of relationships with men that felt like I was performing a role. Not awful men, not awful relationships—just never quite right. Always a piece missing." Allie looked at Grace. "When Mark and I split, it was mutual. We were friends, but that's all we'd ever really been. I thought maybe that was just marriage; you settle into comfortable companionship and that's enough."

She paused. "Then I met Beth at a wine bar. She was with friends, I was alone, and she sent over a drink with a note that said, 'You look like you could use some company.' I joined their table and within an hour I knew. Not just that she was flirting with me, but that I wanted her to." Allie's eyes filled. "When she kissed me good night, I finally understood what everyone meant when they talked about desire. I was thirty-six years old and I'd never actually wanted someone before. Not like that."

"How did you tell the kids?"

"I didn't, at first. I told Mark I was dating someone, and he asked if it was serious. I said yes. He asked the name, and I said 'Beth ... a woman named Beth.'" Allie laughed softly. "He just stared at me. Then he said, 'Well. That explains a lot.'"

"How did he react?"

"He said he'd wondered how quickly I'd find someone else, but never imagined it would be a woman. Asked if our whole marriage had been a lie." Allie's voice dropped. "I told him no. That I just didn't understand what I was missing until I found it."

"And telling Emma and Noah?"

"I sat them down and said, 'Mommy is dating someone. Her name is Beth. Some people date men, some people date women. I'm dating a woman.'" Allie smiled slightly. "Emma said, 'Okay, can she come over?' Noah said, 'Does Daddy know?' When I said yes, he just shrugged and asked if he could go play with Lego."

"That simple?"

"At first. The hard part came later—when they realized what it meant at school, with their friends. Emma went through a phase of not wanting me to pick her up because her friends might see. Noah told his teacher we had 'two houses now because Mommy picked a girl over Daddy,' which led to a very awkward parent-teacher conference." Allie exhaled. "I'm not sure that at the time they understood much about my being gay other than how different it made their family seem from everyone else's. That was the hard thing for them to accept."

Grace felt her eyes sting. "I'm terrified of that. Of Mia being embarrassed. Of Matthew not understanding."

"They may surprise you," Allie said gently. "But yes, it'll be hard. There's no way around that." She took Grace's hand. "The question is whether you're strong enough to handle their feelings while you're dealing with your own."

Grace looked at their joined hands. "I don't know if I am."

"I think you are," Allie said. "You're already doing the hardest part—being honest with yourself."

Allie drained her glass, set it aside, and rested a hand on Grace's thigh. "Okay. Tell me if I'm wrong, but I'm guessing somewhere in your past, you had an inkling, too. I can't be the first woman you've been drawn to."

Grace took a long swallow, heat rising in her chest. She turned her glass slowly, watching candlelight ripple through the wine. "High school. My best friend, Hannah. We were inseparable. The night before her family moved to Seattle, we were lying on her floor looking at yearbooks. She said she'd miss me more than anyone. She was looking at me with this unusual intensity. I suddenly wanted her so badly and I was leaning forward to kiss her, when her mom walked in with some packing boxes, and that was that. The chance was gone."

She looked at Allie's hand on her leg. "It probably meant nothing, and I told myself I was just confused. But I've thought about it for twenty-five years."

"You weren't confused."

"No." Grace met her eyes. "I guess not. I just ... couldn't let myself see it." She paused. "Sometimes after that I'd notice someone, appreciate them. But it wasn't until recently with you that I felt something like … a click. An *Oh*.

Allie leaned in and kissed her, and Grace fell into it. They kissed in slow intervals—mouths meeting, pausing, returning. Allie's lips trailed to her throat, collarbone, ear. Grace made low sounds she barely recognized.

When Allie drew back, her breath was unsteady. "Want to … go upstairs now?"

Grace's heart banged against her ribs. She swallowed and nodded.

Allie stood and held out her hand. Grace took it. Halfway up the stairs, her phone dinged from the pocket of her coat, which was slung over the banister's newel post. She almost ignored it, but the sound insisted.

"Sorry," she murmured, backing down three steps to retrieve it. A text from Michael: *Letting you know we've safely arrived in Rye.*

Surreal. Her husband updating her about their children while she stood on the stairs to a woman's bedroom.

"You can still change your mind," Allie said.

Grace looked at her. Allie was offering her a way out. even now.

She texted back: *Thanks for letting me know.* Then silenced her phone.

"I don't want to change my mind," she said.

Allie's bedroom glowed with candlelight. Two sunflowers leaned toward each other on the dresser.

Allie flushed, suddenly shy. "I wanted it to be nice," she said. "Memorable."

Grace touched a petal. "It already is."

Then she saw the framed photos of Emma and Noah. Their bright faces stopped her.

Allie followed her gaze. "I can turn them around if—"

"No," Grace said. "This is real. They're a huge part of your life." It came out steadier than she felt.

The air warmed around them. Allie stepped forward.

"We can just hold each other," she offered. "There's no pressure."

Grace kissed her. "I want this. I'm just scared. I've never ... Allie, I don't know what I'm doing."

Allie touched her cheek. "It's alright. I've got you."

Allie slipped out of her clothes. The shirt, the leggings. Falling fabrics gave off a murmured rustle. Allie wore navy-blue bikini underwear, no bra. A scar ran along her chest, just below the left collarbone—four inches, maybe five, silvered and smooth, the kind that had long finished apologizing for itself.

Grace looked at it without meaning to.

Allie glanced down, then up. Tapped the little white line above her eyebrow with one finger. "Same bike accident."

Grace reached out and lightly touched the chest scar. Raising her eyes to Allie's she said, "You're even lovelier than I imagined." She felt a pinch of desire between her legs. She wanted to touch Allie's breasts.

Allie's smile deepened as she reached for the hem of Grace's sweater and asked, "Okay if I take this off?"

Grace nodded, trembling a bit.

Allie lifted it slowly, grazing Grace's skin. She tossed the sweater onto a chair, then moved her hands to Grace's hips. She paused to kiss her, pulling Grace's lower lip into her mouth. Then she unzipped Grace's jeans and pushed them down.

Grace stepped free, fearing the silk underwear were too revealing. She almost wanted to flee.

But Allie was staring, breathless, her eyes going up and down Grace's body. "Jesus, Grace. You're stunning. How can you be so beautiful?"

The comment bolstered her confidence, but then doubt and confusion crowded back in. This is it. Once I do this, I'm— What? Gay? Bisexual? Queer? I don't know. But not straight.

They moved under the covers. Their legs tangled, knees brushing, ankles catching and releasing. Allie's skin was so soft and silky it almost wasn't there. Nothing like the coarse drag of Michael's legs against hers, the weight of him settling over her. This was different. This was a conversation. Their noses touched, breath mingled. Allie kissed her slowly—eyelids, temples, jaw, throat, shoulders. Grace's body rose to meet every touch.

When Allie's hand moved over her breasts, the silk of the bra made the sensation of each stroke sharper, the ache of desire stronger. Her lips still at Grace's neck and ear, Allie stroked her nipple gently, pinched lightly, then caressed again. Grace arched, a sound escaping her.

Allie paused. "Okay to take your bra off?" Grace nodded. Allie unhooked the bra, slid it away, and returned to Grace's breasts with fingers, lips, and tongue until Grace cried out and gripped the sheet.

Allie's hands moved down, tracing her sides, her hips. Grace's body arched again. Allie's fingers brushed the damp silk of Grace's underwear, drawing slow circles there, occasionally cupping and pressing. Heat spiraled through her.

Then a stillness. Allie's fingers went to the waistband. She caught Grace's eyes, waiting.

Grace nodded, lifted her hips. Allie slid the fabric down Grace's legs and tossed it aside before removing her own underwear and lowering herself onto Grace.

The first press of full skin on skin—breasts, torsos, thighs—stole Grace's breath. She held Allie tightly, stunned at how natural it felt. They stayed like that for a while, just breathing, hot, hands moving slowly over unfamiliar terrain. Grace kept waiting for awkwardness to arrive. It didn't.

Eventually, Allie slid off Grace, pressing the length of herself against Grace's side. She drew a breast into her mouth and moved her fingers down Grace's stomach, below her belly button and down.

Grace opened her legs. Allie slid her fingers between them, gliding in unhurried arcs, up and down, then circling, then sliding again.

"God. You're so wet," Allie said, "Wonderful." Grace watched as Allie drew her hand up to her mouth and licked her fingers. "You taste so good."

The comment sent a spasm through Grace, and when Allie reached below again, Grace's whole body responded. Sensations gathered, pleasure swelled. Allie's touch unimaginably skilled, perceptive. A peak, an edge, a cliff—some finishing point there, on the horizon. Her hips moved without permission, pushing, reaching, chasing it.

Then her mind started churning: I'm having sex with a woman. Michael's with the kids right now. What if they find out? What am I doing? Who am I becoming?

The thoughts crowded in, a disconnect that was its own kind of cruelty. She felt her body slacken, the gathering wave pulling back like a tide reversing. Her hips stilled.

Allie stilled her hand and pressed a kiss to Grace's forehead "Grace," she whispered. "What do you need?"

Grace turned into her shoulder, humiliated, tears starting. "I'm sorry. I want to. God, I want to. But I don't think it's going to happen."

They lay together, breaths syncing, Grace's tears on Allie's skin.

"Hey— what's going on?" Allie kissed her hairline then stroked her hair. "What is it?"

"Everything. Michael. The kids. Who I thought I was. Whether I can be this." A shaky exhale.

Allie pulled her closer.

"And I've never been good at … finishing."

Allie lifted her head. "What do you mean?"

"In seventeen years, I've had an orgasm during sex maybe three times," Grace said. "Only from his hands. And only because I was basically moving his fingers myself."

"That's not you being bad at anything," Allie said, then her tone sharpened. "And that's not on you, Grace. That's him not giving a damn."

Grace let out a bitter sound. "You'd think a surgeon would understand female anatomy. But it was always—press, poke, press—like he was searching for a button."

Allie winced. "Did he ever go—?"

"Down on me? No. He didn't like it. But he wanted that from me."

A muscle in Allie's jaw flexed. "That's not a couple having sex. That's him getting off."

Grace let out a half laugh, half sob. "It was my marriage."

Allie slid an arm around her waist. "You've come before," she murmured. "You can come again. We'll get you there."

"Climaxing isn't all that important to me." Grace said. "I've learned to be okay without that. It's the closeness I want. And what you were doing felt good. Really good."

She traced a line along Allie's collarbone. "I just worry about what it means if I *can't*. Even with you being so good at it and with me wanting you this much." Her voice caught. "It would mean something's just ... wrong with me."

"There's nothing wrong with you."

"But also, I worry it won't be fun for you. You'll try, and I'll fail, and eventually you'll want to be with someone who's more fun, not broken."

"Hey." Allie cupped her cheek. "There's nothing wrong with you. And there's no scorecard here. Just us."

They lay there a long, silent moment, each of them lost in their own thoughts. Allie's hand lazed back and forth across Grace's lower abdomen.

Grace groaned. "Ugh. Are you trying to embarrass me? Why are you concentrating on my mommy pooch?"

Allie propped up on her elbow. "I'm not. And what pooch?" She looked at Grace's lower belly. "You're fabulous!" Then her fingers moved to a scar, about four inches long, angled on the lower right side of Grace's belly. "What's this? Not a cesarian."

Grace glanced down. "Appendix. Twelve years old. They went in big back then." A small shrug. "I forget it's there."

Allie lowered her head and pressed her lips to it.

Grace went very still.

Allie ran her tongue along it.

Grace moaned and pulled Allie's face up to her own. "Would it be okay if I touched you?"

"You don't have to—"

"I want to. I need to," Grace said. "But I know I'll be clumsy. No good at it. Apologies in advance. I feel like I'm learning everything from scratch."

Allie smiled at her. "I remember that feeling. The disorientation. How about if I grade on a curve?"

Grace laughed, then kissed her way down Allie's throat, learning with mouth and hands. She listened for the breath hitch, the little laugh—*there, that.* When her mouth found Allie's breast, the sharp intake confirmed it. She'd done that. She'd made Allie feel that.

"Oh, Gracie," Allie murmured, fingers tangling in Grace's hair.

Grace moved her hand lower, gradually reaching between Allie's legs. The wetness startled her—not the fact of it, but what it meant. *I did that. She wants me.*

"Show me what to do," Grace whispered.

Allie guided her—rhythm, pressure, angle. Grace listened with her fingers the way she listened in session: for the shift, the catch, the thing beneath the thing. Allie's breath changed. Her hips moved.

Grace felt a rush of something she couldn't name—not arousal exactly, though that was there, too. Power wasn't the right word either. Agency. She was making Allie feel good. She wanted to give her every possible kind of pleasure.

When Allie called her name—*her* name—Grace held her through the tremors, through the gentle, ending collapse, and thought: So this is what it's supposed to feel like. Both of you, present. Both of you, there.

Candlelight painted their bare skin. Grace lay on her back, staring at the ceiling, feeling electric. Then she burst out laughing.

"That was … fun!" she shouted. "Oh my God, that was *fun!* Why didn't anyone tell me this was fun?"

Allie laughed. "I'm glad. And we'll get you there too, Gracie. When you're ready."

"I want to," Grace said. "With you, I want to."

Allie kissed her forehead. "I'll be here."

Time blurred. Candles burned low. A glance at the clock—1:20 AM —pulled Grace back to the world waiting outside this room.

"I should go," she said. "You'll be wiped when Mark brings the kids."

Allie didn't argue, but disappointment flickered in her eyes.

Grace dressed slowly, aware of Allie watching from the bed. At the door, they kissed one more time. Unhurried, lingering.

"Text me when you're home safe," Allie whispered.

Grace drove through empty streets, stoplights cycling for no one, her body thrumming with sensation. The feel of Allie's hands, the taste of her still on Grace's lips. She turned onto her street and saw her house, dark except for the porch light.

Inside, she locked the door and stood in the silent foyer. The house felt different. Or she felt different in it.

She climbed the stairs to her bedroom—not their bedroom anymore, just hers—and sat on the edge of the mattress. She pulled off her sweater, still carrying Allie's scent, and held it to her face.

What have I done?

But she knew. And she was glad of it. She pressed the sweater tighter.

32

———

Thursday, November 23 — Thanksgiving

Allie held the front door open for them. She wore skinny jeans and a light blue sweater. A loose strand had slipped free from her ponytail. Grace's hand twitched with the urge to rein it in.

Warm air wrapped around them as they shouldered into the foyer. Grace carried the green beans and foil-tented rolls. Matthew cradled the pie like an organ transplant. Mia held the sweet-potato casserole at arm's length, its foil crimped and listing from sliding in her lap on the ride over.

Noah appeared at Allie's side and zeroed in on Matthew's pie. "Pumpkin?"

"Apple. But there's whipped cream," Matthew said.

"I'll allow it."

They moved into the living room. Emma was curled on the couch in leggings and an oversized sweatshirt, watching the Macy's parade: a giant balloon wobbling over a Manhattan street while a commentator chirped.

"Oh my god, is that SpongeBob?" Matthew dropped his coat on the nearest chair and moved toward the TV like he'd been summoned.

"Shoes off," Allie called, disappearing toward the kitchen with the pie. Grace followed, balancing her dishes.

"Kitchen is triage," Allie said. "I have coffee and exactly two square feet of counter space for your offerings."

"Two feet?" Grace said. "On holidays at my house, that's considered luxury."

They did a quick ballet—pie to the back corner, beans tucked beside it, sweet-potato casserole rehabilitated under fresh foil. Grace glanced toward the doorway, then leaned in and kissed Allie's cheek.

"So good to be here," she said. "Thank you."

Allie's hand found Grace's hip and slid a little lower. "You look so good I could eat you," she murmured. "I know where I'd start."

Grace laughed and squirmed away.

She went back to the kitchen doorway. The kids were sprawled around the couch like cats. Emma and Mia squeezed together on one end, Noah and Matthew on the floor with pillows, all of them heckling a line of underdressed tap dancers trying to smile through cold November wind.

When the parade cut to commercial, Emma tugged Mia upstairs. "Come hear this track I found." The boys migrated to Noah's room, already talking Minecraft strategy.

"Okay," Allie said, clapping once. "Bird time."

Together they wrestled the turkey from the fridge, laughing as it nearly slid free. While Allie worked butter and herbs under the skin, Grace handed her tools and seasoning.

"You're unreasonably good at this," Grace said, brushing Allie's wrist as she reached for the salt.

"I watched three YouTube videos," Allie said. "I could spatchcock this little fucker if you asked."

"Oooh." Grace chortled. "Talk dirty to me."

Allie turned and wiggled her greasy fingers. "I'm all lubed up. Tell me what you want."

Grace yelped and bolted out of the kitchen, laughing, as Allie lunged after her.

❧

By three-thirty the whole house smelled of roasted turkey and caramelized butter. The bird rested on the counter, golden and gleaming.

"Everyone to the table!" Allie called.

The kids thundered downstairs and claimed seats around the dining table—Mia at one end, Emma at the other, Grace and Allie on the side opposite the boys.

"This looks amazing," Emma said, already reaching for the rolls. "Thanks, Mom."

"You're welcome, sweetie." Allie lifted the glass of rosé Grace had poured. "Happy Thanksgiving, everyone. I'm thankful you're here. To new traditions." Her eyes flicked to Grace.

Grace raised her own glass. "Thanks for having us." Looking at Mia and Matthew, she said, "I'm grateful for the two of you. Always."

"Cool," Matthew said. "Can we eat now?"

They dug in. Emma told a story about her chorus teacher insisting they "taste the vowels like soup." Matthew described accidentally submitting the wrong math file and starting his apology email with "Dear Madam." Emma and Mia got into a full-scale debate over whether a certain pop song was good or merely loud.

Halfway through, Noah looked up, curiosity unfiltered. "Why didn't your dad come, Matthew?"

Matthew's eyes shot to Grace.

Oh god. There it was. The question she knew would come.

"He had other plans." Grace kept her tone even. "With his family in New York. His parents and his brother's family."

"But you're his family," Noah said, frowning.

"We all are," Grace said. "Sometimes families split holidays between different places. It just worked out better this way this year."

"Oh." Noah accepted that and went back to engineering a mashed-potato volcano.

"We alternate holidays with our mom and dad," Emma said, glancing at Allie with an easy smile.

"And how is that for you?" Grace asked.

Emma shrugged. "Fine. Our dad lives in Winchester. Eight minutes away. We see him all the time, so it's not a big deal either way."

Mia was watching Grace now, eyes narrowed in a thoughtful way that made Grace focus hard on her plate and start cutting her turkey into tiny pieces.

The moment almost slipped away. Conversation drifted to stuffing preferences: cranberries inside vs. cranberries on the side, a debate fiercer than Grace thought reasonable. Allie's fingers found Grace's forearm beneath the tablecloth's drape and gave a small, grounding squeeze.

Mia didn't miss it. "You two are like ... really good friends," she said, not accusing, just observing.

How long has she been watching us?

Grace blinked. Her face warmed. "We are," Grace said, with as much lightness as she could muster. She laid her free hand over Allie's. "It's nice."

Then she picked up her water glass and drank slowly, giving her face time to rearrange itself.

After dinner, dishes were cleared and leftovers packed into containers that never quite matched their lids. The kids were bribed into helping with the promise of extra pie. When the last pan was soaking in the sink, Allie snapped open a game box.

"Codenames," she announced. "You'll love it. Cooperative mind-reading."

They regrouped at the cleared dining table and divided into teams. Somehow—Grace suspected "somehow" had Allie's fingerprints on it—she and Allie ended up together.

"Harvest, two," Grace tried.

Without hesitation, Allie tapped *corn* and *gourd*.

Allie leaned forward, considering the grid. "Blue, three."

Grace scanned the words. "*Ocean*, *jeans* and ..." She squinted. "*Jazz*."

The kids erupted in protest.

"Jazz isn't blue," Noah protested.

Grace smiled. "Historically, it is."

Allie snorted so hard she nearly choked.

They kept winning. Grace said "kitchen, two" and Allie went straight to *stove* and *knife*. Allie said "music, four" and Grace landed all four in one go. The kids accused them of cheating, of using "secret mom code," of sharing a brain.

"This is weird," Mia said after the third win. "You two are like telepathic or something."

They played two more rounds anyway. Laughter ricocheted off the walls. Noah kept insisting the mothers were whispering clues in some parallel dimension, his voice rising with each round they lost. He wanted a rematch. Then another. When Matthew suggested switching partners to make it fair, Noah vetoed it immediately—if he couldn't beat them, he wanted to be the one to finally crack the code. Grace watched him work through his frustration with focused, narrow-eyed determination.

His mother's son, right down to the bone.

The dining room had gone warm with bodies and leftover cooking heat. Grace's cheeks hurt from smiling. Her stomach ached from laughing. Every time she looked up, Allie was already looking at her.

If they were at Michael's parents', she'd be in the kitchen right now, listening to his mother critique her cooking. Michael would be watching football. The kids would be bored. Nobody would be laughing like this. This was so much better.

By six, the kids had scattered upstairs again, music and chatter already floating through the floorboards.

In the quiet that followed, Grace stood at the sink beside Allie. Their sleeves were pushed up, shoulders nearly touching. Grace scoured the muck off the bottom of the roasting pan, rinsed it with hot water, then scrubbed a serving platter while Allie dried the roaster. The kitchen was warm, the window above the sink steamed from hot water.

Allie set down the dish towel and came up behind Grace, wrapping her arms around her waist, chin resting on Grace's shoulder. "Thank you for being here today."

Grace leaned back into her, letting herself have this moment. "Nowhere else I'd rather be."

"Not in Schenectady listening to Michael's dad interrogate Mia about AP classes?"

Grace laughed quietly. "Mighty tempting alternative."

They stayed like that for a moment, swaying slightly, until footsteps creaked in the hallway.

Allie stepped back just as Emma appeared in the doorway, holding an empty glass.

Emma stopped, eyes moving between them. She looked down quickly. "Oh. Sorry. I just need water."

"No, it's fine, sweetie," Allie said, too quickly. "Just— Grace was helping with dishes."

"Uh-huh." Emma crossed to the sink, filled her glass from the tap. She stood there for a moment, not drinking, not leaving. Finally, she turned to Alllie. "Are you two ... I mean, is Grace ..." She trailed off, face reddening. "Never mind."

"What is it?" Allie asked gently.

Emma glanced at Grace, then back at her mom. "Are you guys girlfriends?"

Allie's face went carefully neutral. "What makes you ask that?"

"Well, it's like Mia said ... you seem really ... I don't know. Close? Like, you keep looking at each other the way you used to look at Beth. Plus her husband isn't here, which is kind of weird, right? For Thanksgiving?"

Grace's pulse jumped. She kept her hands in the soapy water, gripping a platter beneath the suds.

Allie exhaled. "Emma—"

"I'm not mad or whatever. I just want to know if this is, like, a thing. Because we've already met her—" Emma gestured at Grace. "Her kids are upstairs with Noah. So if you two are together, we should probably know. Not like with Beth, where you waited forever to tell us."

Allie looked at Grace, then back at Emma. Grace felt her face burning. She should say something—help Allie navigate this.

She started. "Emma, we're ..." Her throat seized up.

Emma looked again at her mother. "You seem happy, which is good." She looked at Grace briefly, then away. "And you're nice. I like you. Even better than Beth."

Grace managed a small smile. "Thank you."

Emma started toward the door, then stopped. "But, Mom? When you and Beth broke up, you were really sad. For a long time."

Allie's expression softened. "I know. I'm sorry you had to put up with that. Beth leaving was hard on you, too."

"I don't want you to be sad again." Emma's voice got smaller. "That's all."

"Come here," Allie said, and Emma crossed to her. Allie hugged her daughter. "I'm okay. I promise."

Emma pulled back, nodded. She turned to Grace. "Do Mia and Matthew know? About you and Mom?"

"No," Grace looked at her feet, then at Allie. "Not yet."

"You probably should tell them," Emma said. "Mia knows something's up. It was her comment at the table that got me thinking about it."

Grace's heart hammered. "Would you ... could you not say anything to them? About this? I need to be the one to tell them. When the time is right."

Emma shifted her weight, thinking. "Okay. I won't say anything. ... But I'm guessing you shouldn't wait too long."

"Thank you," Grace said quietly.

Emma nodded and left quickly, as if suddenly embarrassed by the whole conversation.

Allie braced both hands on the counter, head bowed. Grace realized she was still gripping the platter so hard her knuckles had gone white. She set it down carefully.

"She's thirteen," Allie said. "How is she already that perceptive?"

"She's worried about you."

"I know." Allie turned to face her. "Are you okay?"

"I don't know." Grace's hands were shaking slightly. She looked toward the stairs where she could hear the kids' voices. "But Emma's right that I have to tell Mia."

"When will you?"

"Soon. After Michael and I tell them about the divorce." Grace exhaled. "One impossible conversation at a time."

Allie took her hand. "We'll figure it out."

Grace nodded, but Emma's question echoed in her mind: *Are you dating her?*

She still didn't know how she'd answer that. Didn't know what they were to each other—only that whatever it was had become the most real thing in her life outside of Mia and Matthew.

Allie rinsed her hands, dried them, then cupped Grace's face and kissed her—slow, sure, lingering. "Two weeks from today," she murmured, "I'll get to do that for hours."

Grace frowned, one brow arching.

"Chicago, dummy," Allie said. "Have you forgotten?"

Grace leaned into Allie and rested her chin on her shoulder. "I've been a little distracted," she said. "But no. I haven't forgotten."

They were both going to an annual counseling conference in Chicago. For weeks, their text thread had been dotted with *Can't wait for Chicago* and *Three whole nights.*

"I was thinking," Allie said. "Why don't we skip the hotel rooms and get an Airbnb together? Given the state of you and Michael, why not?"

Her *yes* was immediate. "Book it," she said.

Allie pulled up her laptop, and within minutes it was done. Three nights in Lincoln Park. They'd just committed to sharing a bed at a professional conference where colleagues might see them. Allie stood and wrapped her arms around Grace, covering her face in small, delighted kisses that drifted down her neck.

Grace started laughing, which gave Allie the excuse to tickle her until she was shrieking and trying to escape.

The noise drew Mia to the top of the stairs. She paused, taking in the scene: her mother and Allie pressed together, laughing, hands on each other.

"What's going on down there?"

Grace tried to catch her breath. "Allie started it," she called back, laughing harder when Allie lunged for her again. "We need to go, you guys! It's getting late."

Within minutes, the kids were downstairs, hunting for shoes and coats. Scarves reappeared. Leftover containers were matched with lids that almost fit. Allie packed bags of food like she was sending them to sea.

"Should we call Dad to say hi?" Mia asked at the door, one hand on the knob, the other clutching a lopsided foil packet of rolls.

"Sure," Grace said. "But let's wait till we're home."

Allie stood in the doorway with them, porch light haloing her hair. "Thank you for coming. For being here," she said.

"Thank you," Grace said. "For today. For all of it."

They hugged, a quick, appropriate squeeze, hands lingering just long enough to say what they couldn't aloud.

"Text when you're home," Allie said.

"I will."

They walked to the car under a clear sky with a first star pricked above the roofs. The kids tumbled in, still arguing about which CODENAMES team had been robbed.

As Grace pulled away from the curb, she glanced back. Allie stood in the doorway, one hand lifted in a small wave, the other tucked into her sweater sleeve against the cold.

"Mom?" Mia said sleepily from the back seat. "Today was perfect."

"I know," Grace blinked hard and watched the road ahead. "It was."

In the rearview mirror, Mia's eyes were open, watching her. Not sleepily at all.

33

Sunday, November 26

When Grace woke Sunday morning, she lay still, listening to the house. Matthew's music leaked indistinctly through the wall—he'd been up for a while. Downstairs, the coffeemaker hissed on the timer she'd set.

Michael was due back from Schenectady by noon. She hadn't missed him in the least. What she'd felt, if she was honest, was relief. Four days of not performing the marriage. Four days of being only herself.

And Thursday. Thursday had been—

She closed her eyes. The CODENAMES game. Mia's narrowed gaze. Allie's fingers under the tablecloth. The kids scattered through Allie's house like they'd always lived there, like the six of them were already a family. She'd replayed the dishwashing moment a dozen times since: their reflections in the window above the sink, Allie kissing her slowly, the absolute certainty in her own body that *this was right.*

She got up, pulled on a sweatshirt. She stopped at Matthew's room and looked in. He was lying on his bed, earbuds in, catching a tennis ball he repeatedly tossed toward the ceiling. "Morning," she said.

"Hey." He didn't look up.

She padded downstairs, poured coffee, and stood at the counter, watching the backyard through the window. The maple had dropped the last of its leaves. The yard looked stripped.

Mia appeared ten minutes later, still in pajamas, hair piled in a messy knot. She poured herself orange juice and leaned against the counter beside Grace.

"When's Dad getting back?"

"Around noon, he said."

Mia nodded and sipped her juice. A long silence. Then: "Thanksgiving was a lot better with Allie and her kids than being in Schenectady."

"It was."

Another silence. Mia examined her glass, tilting it so the pulp slid. "Do you think we'll do it again? Go to Allie's for holidays?"

Grace kept her eyes on the backyard. "Would you want to?"

"Yeah." Mia paused. "Allie's nice. You seem happy when you're around her."

Grace's throat tightened. "She is nice."

"Mom?" Mia said.

Grace looked over. Mia had that particular expression—jaw set, eyes wary—that meant something important was coming.

"What's going on with you and Dad? He's been sleeping in the guest room. You barely talk. You act like strangers. You were apart for Thanksgiving. You already told me you're seeing a marriage counselor. So ... what's happening?"

Grace kept her eyes straight ahead. "Your dad and I are going through a rough patch. We're trying to figure things out."

"By ignoring each other?" Mia asked.

"By giving each other space," Grace said. "Sometimes what worked for years stops working. We're trying to figure out how to move forward."

"What's going to happen?" Mia's voice had gone small again.

"Not sure." That part was still true. "As I say, we're working on it."

Mia stared out the window for a long moment. "Okay," she said. "Just ... it's hard not knowing. So, talk to us about it as soon as you can."

She left before Grace could answer.

Grace set the phone down. *Just breathe.* As if breathing were the hard part. As if the hard part weren't standing in this kitchen, about to greet a husband she was leaving while all she could think about was Allie.

Around eleven-thirty, a car door slammed in the driveway. Then the mudroom door opened and Michael came in carrying his overnight bag, looking tired and slightly rumpled. He set the bag down.

"Hey," he said.

"Hi. How was the drive?"

"Long. Lots of traffic on 90." He stood there, like a guest who wasn't sure of the house rules. Watchful. Two people being careful around something cracked.

"How was your Thanksgiving?" she asked.

"Fine." The way he said it—flat, no details—told her everything about the four days he'd spent with his parents, fielding questions he couldn't answer.

"Did you tell them?"

"No. Didn't seem a good time for that. I told them you and the kids were with your family this year."

Grace nodded. That's what it had felt like. "Well, you're going to have to tell them soon."

"Dad!" Mia appeared and hugged him. Matthew followed with a

wave from the stairs. The kids carried the conversation for a few minutes. Mia talked about Emma, Matthew about Noah's Minecraft setup. Grace watched Michael listen, watched him nod and smile, and felt the ache of seeing a father trying with his children as his marriage was ending.

After the kids drifted away, Michael lingered in the kitchen.

"Grace."

"Yeah?"

"At our last session with Elisa, we said we'd tell the kids after Thanksgiving. But I don't have the heart to do it today. Could we wait until next weekend?"

It hadn't occurred to her that he might've been thinking of doing it today. *God, no. Not today.* "Sure."

He nodded and picked up his bag. "I'm going to unpack."

She listened to his footsteps on the stairs. Steady, familiar, receding.

She stared at the backyard, where Matthew's old basketball hoop still stood at the edge of the driveway, its net swaying in the wind.

That afternoon, Grace closed the door of the den and picked up her phone. She'd been putting this off too long. Five rings before Margaret Brennan answered. "Hello?"

"Hi, Mom. It's Grace."

"I know it's you." A pause. "What's wrong?"

"Nothing's wrong. I just wanted to call and see how your Thanksgiving was at Sean's."

"It was fine. Your brother always does too much. There were three kinds of potatoes."

Grace shifted the phone to her other ear. "How is he? Kathleen and the kids?"

"They're good. And your children?"

"Fine. Matthew made the basketball team. Mia's doing well in school."

"That's nice."

Grace listened to a television murmur in the background, one of those home renovation shows her mother watched but claimed to hate.

"Mom, I wanted to tell you something." Grace pressed the phone harder against her ear. "Michael and I have been going to couples therapy."

The television sound stopped. "You mean like marriage counseling?"

"Yes. We've been having some difficulties. We thought it might help to talk to someone."

"What kind of difficulties?"

"Just—marriage things. We've been talking past each other for a while. You know: communication problems."

"I see." Margaret's voice had gone flat, careful. "Is he having an affair?"

Grace's stomach dropped. "No. Nothing like that."

"Then *what*?"

Grace closed her eyes. "We're just not connecting the way we used to. We thought therapy might help us figure things out."

"People go to counseling when they've already made up their minds."

Grace said nothing.

"Marriage isn't about connection, Grace. It's about commitment. You made vows. So, you work through the difficulties. You don't run to some stranger to complain about your husband."

"We're not complaining. We're trying to—"

"Your father and I had difficulties, too. Everyone does. We didn't need therapy. We just did our duty."

"And were you happy?"

The silence lasted long enough that Grace thought the call had dropped.

"Happiness wasn't the point," she said. Then, sharper, "People quit more easily now." A pause. "I hope you're not considering anything foolish."

"Foolish?"

"Your marriage is seventeen years old, Grace. You have two children. You don't throw that away because you're not 'connecting.'"

Grace said nothing.

"I have to go," Margaret said. "My show is back on. You'll call me next week?"

"Always do."

"All right."

"Bye, Mom."

Grace set down the phone. The call had lasted four minutes.

People go to counseling when they've already made up their minds.

Her mother was right about that, at least. Grace had made up hers weeks ago. What she hadn't done was say it to the people it would hurt most, the ones whose lives would change, too.

34

Tuesday, November 28

Mid-afternoon sunlight cast long shadows across Grace's office as she was finishing a progress note in Nicole Fiori's file. Her phone rang a second time in two minutes with a call from Michael. She decided to pick up.

His voice was tight. "Grace, you need to come home. Now."

Michael never called during the day. Never used that tone.

"What? Why? I have a client in ten minutes, Michael. I can't—"

"Just come home. Please. It's Mia."

"What happened?" Grace's voice came out strangled. "Is she hurt?"

"She's ... okay. Physically."

"Please, Michael. Tell me."

"Just come home."

His voice cracked on the last two words, and that was enough.

"I'll be there as soon as I can."

❦

Grace drove too fast, running a yellow onto their street. The Hendersons' Yorkie started yapping the second she opened the back gate.

She burst into the kitchen.

Michael sat at the table with a Scotch, elbows on his knees, head bowed. He looked up, hollow.

"What happened? Where's Mia? Is she—"

"She's in her room."

Grace's eyes snapped toward the stairs. "What's wrong?"

"I came home early. Surgery got canceled." He swallowed. "I thought the kids would still be at school. But Mia's backpack was in the mudroom. I called up. No response. So I went upstairs. Knocked. No answer. So I ..." He paused, drew a breath. "I opened the door."

"Oh God, Michael." Grace braced herself. "What did you—"

"Mia. And a girl. On her bed." He rubbed his forehead. "They were— It was obvious what was happening. I told them to get dressed. The girl ran out. Mia locked herself in her room. I ... didn't know what to do. That's when I called you."

Grace was already heading for the stairs.

At Mia's door, she knocked gently. "Mia? Honey, it's Mom."

A muffled, tear-raw voice: "Go away. I don't want to talk."

"Mia ... I'm not angry. I just want to make sure you're all right." Grace rested her forehead against the door. A long silence. Then a click.

She waited a few beats, then opened the door slowly.

Mia sat on the bed with her knees pulled to her chest, sleeves over her hands, face blotchy. Her eyes held terror and defiance at the same time.

Grace sat at the edge of the mattress. Not too close. The shades were drawn, afternoon light leaking around the edges. A pile of clothes spilled from the chair in the corner. "Honey, are you okay?"

A small nod.

"Was it Chloe?" Grace asked gently.

Another nod. Mia's fingers dug into the denim at her knees.

Grace kept her voice gentle. "Can you tell me what happened? Just what you feel comfortable saying."

Mia drew a shaky breath. "Model U.N. got canceled. I didn't think anyone would be home. We were going to study. Then we were talking and just fooling around ..." Her face flushed. "And then Dad opened the door."

Grace exhaled. Her daughter looked impossibly young and impossibly grown.

"The look on his face," Mia whispered. "He thinks I'm disgusting."

She reached for Mia's wrist—slowly, giving her the chance to pull away. She didn't. "Honey, he was shocked. That's not the same thing."

Mia blinked hard. "It felt like disgust."

Grace stroked her wrist. "I'm sorry he walked in. He shouldn't have done that."

Silence. Mia twisted the hem of her jeans.

"So, you and Chloe," Grace said. "When did this start with her?"

A pause. "The beginning of the school year. I started feeling ... different around her."

Grace nodded. "Has this happened before? Feeling this way about someone?"

Mia hesitated. Then something in her face eased. "Last year at camp. A girl named Sienna. I couldn't stop thinking about her. I wanted to ..." She trailed off.

"Kiss her?" Grace supplied gently.

Mia nodded.

"Ever felt this way about boys?" Grace asked.

Mia's answer was immediate. "No. Never." She scrubbed her sleeve across her eyes. "I've tried, Mom. I've seriously tried. It's like, my brain gets the idea, but my heart just ... doesn't."

"Not even a little crush?"

Another shake of the head. "Nothing." She looked up, eyes swollen. "Does that mean I'm gay? Like ... officially?"

Grace took a steadying breath. "Only you get to choose the word. But from what you're telling me? It sounds like you might be."

Mia straightened a bit. "I think I am. I think I've known."

Grace tucked a loose strand of hair behind her ear. "Are you afraid I'm mad?"

Mia nodded without lifting her head.

Grace slid an arm around her shoulders. Mia resisted for a second, then folded against her.

"I'm not mad," Grace said. "I'm a little scared, because you're fifteen, and intimacy comes with big feelings and big responsibilities. But I'm not scared of who you are."

Mia's mouth tilted. "You're sounding very therapist right now."

Grace actually laughed. "It's a curse. Sorry."

Mia gave a tiny smile.

Grace kissed her temple. "Thank you for telling me. I'm glad you know this about yourself. I'm proud of you. Really proud, because some people don't figure this out until they're much older. Or they hide from it. You're not doing that."

Mia pressed her face into Grace's shoulder.

After a long while, Grace said gently, "Mia, your dad's going to want to know what's going on. We should probably tell him."

Mia tensed. "About me being gay?"

Grace said, "Yeah. Do you want to tell him yourself? Or would you like me to talk to him first?"

Mia pulled back slightly. "Will he be mad?"

"No, honey. He won't be mad." Grace hoped that was true.

Michael wouldn't be angry, exactly. But shocked? Uncomfortable? Uncertain how to respond? Probably all of those.

"Well, he's going to be weird about it," Mia said.

"Maybe a little weird at first. But he loves you. That won't change."

Mia was quiet, picking at a thread on her comforter. "Can you tell him? I'm not sure I could."

"Of course. I'll talk to him. And I'll do it now, if that's all right with you."

Mia nodded. "Might as well get it over with. Will you tell me what he says?"

"If you want me to."

Mia nodded again.

Grace stood. "I'm going down. Do you want anything? Food? Tea?"

"I'm not hungry."

"Okay. I love you," Grace said.

"You too."

Grace slipped out and closed the door. In the hallway, she pressed her palms to her eyes.

Downstairs, she went straight for the wine.

"Well?" Michael asked from the kitchen doorway.

"Mia and Chloe have been close for a while. And Mia says she's attracted to girls. She's gay."

Michael let out a strained breath. "She's fifteen, Grace. How can she possibly know that at fifteen?"

"She knows." Grace's voice sharpened. "You knew things about yourself at fifteen. Why is this different?"

He rubbed his forehead. "I think we should give her some space. Maybe some distance from this girl."

Grace stared at him. "Her name is Chloe. And, no. We are not separating her from the person she trusts most right now."

He opened his mouth, then closed it. Tried again. "I'm concerned. That's all. Having sex at fifteen—"

"They weren't having sex. They were exploring. It's what teenagers do."

"But with another girl—"

"So what?" Grace said. "So what, Michael? Would you prefer she was experimenting with some boy who doesn't care about her feelings?"

Michael stared at her. "How do you know this girl isn't confused? Or using her?"

"I know Mia," Grace said. "And I know Chloe. They like and respect each other. Chloe's not using her."

Michael stood there, at a loss. "What do we do now?"

"We support her," Grace said. "Go talk to your daughter. Tell her you love her."

He didn't move.

She stared at him until he looked away. "Jesus," she said. Then she walked out of the kitchen, through the mudroom, and out the back door.

In the yard, cold air bit at her bare arms; she hugged her self against the late-November chill. The hypocrisy burned. She'd told her daughter she was proud of her for not hiding. Yet here Grace was, still hiding. But was that hypocritical? Mia seemed to know what she was, who she was. Grace had never really known. Had she?

Standing in the cold, she turned that word over. Hiding. Did you hide from something you hadn't even been sure was there?

Now she was sure. But this wasn't her moment. It was Mia's, and Mia needed it to be hers alone. So Grace would wait. Hold her daughter's truth. Keep her own a while longer.

35

Sunday, December 3

Grace turned off the engine and let her hands rest on the wheel for a beat. She turned to Mia. "Ready?"

Mia nodded and tucked her phone into her pocket. "Guess so."

They fell into step on the path around Fresh Pond, moving clockwise with the small winter crowd—dogs, joggers, a young couple pushing a stroller. The air had a gray, metallic chill that seeped through Grace's coat.

"Thanks for coming," Grace said.

Mia shrugged, tugging her hood tighter. "You didn't give me much choice."

"True." Grace managed a small smile. "But this seemed like a good way for us to be alone. To talk freely."

They crunched through a patch of frozen leaves. A goose skidded onto the dull blue water, wings flapping, and settled with a small splash. Grace watched it for a moment.

"How are you doing?" she asked. "With everything."

"I don't know." Mia's shoulders rose. "It's weird at home. Dad barely looks at me. And when he does, his face says, *who are you?*"

"Has he talked with you? About your being gay?"

Mia huffed out a derisive laugh. "I wouldn't say we 'talked.' You know he can't do that. But he said a few things to me, including apologizing for walking in on us, so at least there was that."

Grace nodded. "That's good. What else?"

"All downhill from there. He unloaded some bullshit about people my age thinking they're gay because of pressure from social media—"

"Mia—"

"Well, it *is* bullshit, Mom. And you know it. That's fucked up. As if the internet made me gay." She kicked at a stone on the path and sent it skittering ahead. "Then he said it was probably just a phase, so I should keep an 'open mind' about all this."

"Jesus."

"Yeah. He doesn't get it. He's the one with the closed mind," Mia said. "Mine is wide open to this. That's literally the point."

They walked in silent for a whole minute, maybe two. Grace pivoted. "How's Chloe? Tuesday afternoon was pretty intense for her, too."

"Yeah, it was." A flicker of tenderness crossed Mia's face. "She was really freaked out at first. But yesterday we were kind of laughing about it. I pointed out it could've been worse."

Grace blinked. "Worse how?"

"Dad could've been ten minutes earlier," Mia said, flushing. "Or it could've been *her* father to walk in on us."

Grace held back a reflexive wince. They avoided a slippery patch of ice that never got any sun.

"Tell me more about you and Chloe," Grace said. "What do you feel when you're with her?"

Mia stopped and looked directly at Grace. "Really? You're going there?"

"I am, honey. I'm not prying. I'm just interested. I want to understand this part of your life."

Mia nodded. "Okay. Well, I feel like I can actually breathe. Like I don't have to fake being someone else." She looked down. "And I'm attracted to her." Mia's cheeks pinked and she started walking again. "But it's not just that. She's my best friend. I want to spend every possible minute with her. It's all of that at once."

"That makes sense," Grace said quietly. "That's how it's supposed to feel." She hesitated. "It's also when things can get intense. I just need to say one thing," Grace said. "If anything ever feels like too much, you get to slow down or say no. Even with someone you trust."

Mia's face flared. "Mom. She doesn't push me. And—"

"I know—"

"—could we please not talk about that part?"

"Yeah. Okay. I just needed to say it."

"Said. Moving on." After a while Mia said, "You think Dad's ever going to be okay with this?"

Grace chose her words. "I do. Eventually. He's just going through an adjustment."

"Yeah, well, I wish he'd get on with it. He's stuck somewhere in the previous century with all that 'going through a phase' shit." She halted and again faced Grace. "Don't some people think you're born gay? Like, it's genetic?"

"The research is complicated," Grace said. "It's probably a mix—biology, environment, experience. There's no single 'gay gene.'"

"But there could still be something inherited, right?" Mia said. "From you or Dad?"

Grace's mouth went dry. She looked down, kicked at a breaking ridge of ice at the path's edge. "Possibly. But what matters most isn't where anyone thinks it came from, but that *you* know what's true for you."

Mia started walking again. Grace fell back into step.

After a few beats, Mia's voice dropped. "Have you ever felt attracted to women?"

Grace looked over quickly. "What makes you ask that?"

Mia shrugged, eyes straight ahead. "Just because you married Dad doesn't mean you've never felt anything else." She glanced sideways. "Right?"

She could feel Mia watching her, trying to fit her mother into the new map she was drawing of the world.

"Your dad and I built a life together," Grace said, her face flushing. "We love you and Matthew more than anything."

Mia shook her head. "Yeah. That's not what I asked."

The path narrowed, forcing them closer together.

Mia had just trusted her with the truth. She owed her more. "The short answer," she said quietly, "is yes. I have felt that attraction."

Mia stopped walking again. Her eyes went wide. "Seriously? When? Who?"

Grace reached for her hand. "Sweetie—"

Mia pivoted, avoiding her reach. "No. You can't just drop that and not—"

Grace let out a low, helpless laugh. "When you asked me to back off talking about you and Chloe, I did." Her mouth twitched. "Would you cut me the same slack?" Grace said. "I promise I'll talk to you about it soon. Just not right this minute. All right?"

Mia held her gaze for a long moment. Her mind was clearly working. Then she nodded slowly. "Okay. But soon."

"Soon," Grace promised.

They started walking again. A hazy strip of winter sun tried to break through the clouds.

"I'm proud of you," Grace said. "For knowing who you are. For saying it out loud."

"It's not like I voluntarily walked downstairs and made some big announcement," Mia said. "Dad barging in was like— my worst nightmare. But ..." She drew in a breath. "In a weird way it's also a relief. I kept thinking if I could just keep it hidden, maybe I could make it not be true." She gave a small, crooked smile. "That secret was taking up all the space inside my brain."

Grace's breath hitched. "So you feel better now that it's out there?"

Mia considered. "Well, I don't like Dad being so weird. And I'm scared about what happens when people at school find out. But ... yeah. It's easier, in some ways. At least I feel like myself."

The parking lot came into view through the trees. Grace remembered standing there in early September, Allie beside her.

"What do we tell Matthew?" Mia asked.

"About you being gay?"

"Yeah. I don't want him to just find out from someone else. But I'm not really ready. I kind of want to wait until things feel less—"

"Raw?" Grace offered.

Mia nodded. "Yeah. That."

"There's no rush," Grace said. "We'll wait until you're ready. Then we can talk to him together."

"What if he's weird about it?"

"He might be at first," Grace said. "But Matthew loves you. That part's not going anywhere."

Mia's shoulders loosened. "Okay. So not yet."

They reached the car and climbed in. Grace started the engine and turned on the heat. The vents coughed cold air for a moment before warming.

On the drive home, Mia texted with Chloe, thumbs moving fast. Grace kept her eyes on the road, hearing their conversation at the pond replay in her head.

∽

Later that day, Michael came in from his run, sweatshirt damp at the collar, breath still uneven. He poured a glass of water and leaned against the kitchen counter, scrolling his phone.

Grace stood in the doorway and waited. He didn't look up.

She cleared her throat. "Hey."

"Oh." He jolted slightly. "Didn't see you."

"The kids are both out," she said. "I thought we could talk."

He set the phone down with exaggerated care. "What's up?"

"We need to talk about when we're telling them," she said. "About us."

His hands gripped the edge of the countertop. For a moment he didn't move. Then he turned, face wary. "Okay."

"We'd said we'd do it after Thanksgiving," Grace went on. "Then this weekend. But everything with Mia and Chloe happened, and now I've got the convention this coming week. I don't want to tell them today and then disappear for four days later this week. I think we should wait until the weekend after I get back."

"That's—" He pulled his phone closer, thumb flicking to the calendar. "The weekend of December fifteenth."

"Right. That Saturday afternoon. When there's time to sit with them. Answer questions. And they'd have all the next day to absorb it without school intruding."

He nodded once. "Fine." His voice had gone flat. "Anything else?"

Grace studied the tension in his shoulders, the way he was halfway turned toward the doorway already. "Yes," she said. "We need to talk about you and Mia."

His face stiffened. "What about us?"

"She and I took a long walk today, and she told me you finally had a chat with her yesterday. Apparently, it didn't go well. Was that your sense?"

"Why? What did she say?"

"That you told her to 'keep an open mind,' like you think this is just something she's experimenting with and she could easily decide it's just not for her."

His chin tilted up. "I don't see anything wrong with saying that. I told you on Tuesday I don't think she can really know this at fifteen. That this is probably a phase."

Grace stepped closer. "I know you think that. But you didn't have to share those thoughts with her. Jesus, why do that? All she needed to hear from you was that you love her and that you're okay with her being gay. What she sees is a father who can't look at her the same way he used to."

He crossed his arms over his chest. "You're reading into everything. I know you deal with feelings all day and you're good at that, but sometimes I think you get so focused on validating emotions that you—"

"Don't," Grace said quietly. "Don't make my work sound small. Or irrelevant. I'm telling you as her mother *and* as a therapist: she needs acceptance. Not a lecture on social contagion."

He flinched.

"She needs you to believe her," Grace went on. "To trust that she knows her own mind."

He stared at her.

Grace went on, lifting her chin. "She asked me today if I thought you'd ever be okay with her being gay. I tried to reassure her. But honestly? I don't know if you will."

Silence.

He looked suddenly older, standing there in his damp running shoes.

"I know you care about her," Grace said. "But all she feels right now is your distance, your disapproval."

Michael picked up his glass and set it in the sink, aligning it neatly. "Okay."

"What does 'okay' mean?" she asked. "Okay you heard me? Okay you agree? Okay you'll actually do something?"

He shrugged slightly. "Okay. I'll ... try to be more accepting."

Grace pressed her palms into the counter to keep from exploding. "Good Lord, Michael. Do you hear yourself?"

"What do you want from me, Grace?" His voice was raw. "I'm trying."

"Try harder," she said. "Talk to her again. Start by asking her how she feels. Tell her you love her and that her being gay hasn't changed that."

He rubbed his jaw, the rasp of stubble audible in the quiet kitchen. He held her gaze for a long moment. "All right. I'll try again."

"But maybe not today. Give her a day or two."

He nodded. "I'm going to shower," he said. Grace watched him leave the kitchen, shoulders hunched, a man trying to love his daughter in the only language he knew and discovering it wasn't enough.

When he was gone, Grace let out a breath she hadn't realized she was holding. The kitchen around her—cutting boards, spice jars, the dent in the table from a dropped skillet—looked suddenly like someone else's life.

December fifteenth. That's when she could stop pretending.

36

———————

Tuesday, December 5

The restaurant in Coolidge Corner was tucked between a bookstore and a vintage clothing shop, the kind of place that attracted BU students and young professionals. Grace and Allie sat in a back booth, set low behind planters, menus open but neither really looking at them.

Grace shook out her napkin and laid it in her lap. "So, Mia asked me point-blank on Sunday whether I've ever been attracted to women."

Allie looked up. "During your walk?"

Grace nodded. "Halfway around the pond. We were talking about whether same-sex attraction is genetic. And I said, the short answer is yes, I have felt that attraction." She laughed, a little unevenly. "And then she wanted to know when and who, and I basically got her to back off by promising I'd tell her soon."

Allie was quiet for a moment. "How did she take that?"

"She said, 'Okay, but soon.'" Grace looked up. "She meant it."

"Of course she meant it." Allie leaned forward slightly. "Grace, we know she's already putting it together."

"I know. And I think about Emma in your kitchen, asking, 'Are you guys girlfriends?'"

Allie sipped her water. "You know, it might be easier than you think, telling her."

"Maybe. But as soon as she knows it's you, she'll want to know what this is. What we are to each other. Where this is going."

Allie held her gaze. "And what will you tell her?"

"I don't know." Grace lifted her menu. "I'm still— I don't know how to talk about this yet."

Something moved across Allie's face—almost like she was consciously having to choose patience. "Of course," she said. "You'll know how when you're ready."

She meant it kindly. Grace heard it that way. And yet, there was a faint outline of distance, between where Allie stood and where she herself was still standing. Allie knew what this was. Had known for years what it meant to be this person, to be sure of this thing. Grace was still learning the feeling, the language.

She almost said something. Then movement near the entrance caught her eye. She went still. David Castellano stood at the hostess stand, coat still on, scanning the room with the distracted air of someone deciding whether to stay or go somewhere else.

Their eyes met.

For a split second, his expression showed surprise, maybe, or recognition. She couldn't tell what. Then he smiled. A small, polite smile. The kind you'd give an acquaintance you weren't sure wanted to be acknowledged.

Grace's face went hot. She managed a slight nod.

David turned back to the hostess, said something Grace couldn't hear, then was led to a small two-top near the windows. Not close or with an easy sightline to their booth. Just a table.

"What is it?" Allie asked, watching Grace's face.

"David Castellano." Grace kept her voice low. "My client. He just walked in."

Allie glanced over carefully. "The widower?"

"Yeah."

"Did he see you?"

"Yes. We made eye contact." Grace's hands tightened around her water glass. "He smiled at me."

"That's ... normal, isn't it? If you see someone you know?"

Grace didn't answer right away. She watched David through the planters as he settled in, shrugged off his coat, accepted a menu. He pulled out his phone, scrolled through it like anyone would while waiting to order.

"Grace?" Allie's voice was gentle. "What are you thinking?"

"I don't know." Grace forced herself to look at Allie instead of tracking David's movements. "This place is in Brookline. He lives in Watertown."

"Brookline's not that far from Watertown. Maybe he had an appointment nearby."

"Maybe." Grace picked up her fork, set it down. "But he was there at Wilson Farm in October, and ... oh, I don't know ..." She trailed off.

"You're not thinking he followed us here?"

Grace heard how it sounded. Paranoid. Dramatic. She shook her head, tried to laugh it off. "No. I don't know. Unlikely. I'm probably being ridiculous."

Allie reached across the table, fingers brushing Grace's wrist. "Hey. Look at me."

Grace met her eyes.

"If you want to leave, we leave," Allie said. "But if we stay, we're going to enjoy our lunch. We're not going to let him take that away from us, whether this is coincidence or not. Okay?"

Grace took a breath. "Okay."

Their food arrived. They ate, and Allie kept the conversation going. Stories about Noah's latest fascination with skateboarding, Emma's drama with her best friend. Normal things.

Grace tried to focus, tried to laugh at the right moments. But part of her attention never left David. She tracked him peripherally through the planter's dusty fronds, the way you track a dog you're not sure is friendly. He ate his sandwich, scrolled his phone, flagged down the server for more water. Once, she was certain his gaze rested on their booth—not a glance but a held look, three seconds, maybe four, before his eyes returned to his phone.

After twenty minutes, David stood, left cash on the table, pulled on his coat. As he headed toward the exit, he passed within fifteen feet of their booth. Close enough that Grace held her breath.

He didn't slow. But he looked her way, smiled and nodded. Then walked past and out the door.

Grace exhaled.

"He's gone," Allie said quietly. "I'm guessing that was nothing."

Grace pressed her hands against the table. "Yeah, probably."

Allie's fingers found hers. "But if your instincts are telling you something, trust them. Document his behavior. And ask him directly next session."

Grace nodded. Her salad sat half-eaten.

Claire appeared at Grace's open office door.

"Grace, do you have a minute?"

"I have about ten minutes before my 3:00. Is that enough?"

"More than needed, thanks." Claire stepped inside, closing the door behind her. "I've been thinking about what you said last week. About Sarah's letters."

"Oh?" Grace set down her mug.

"I'd be willing to let you read them. If you still want to."

Grace felt a flicker of surprise. "I do. Thank you, Claire. I can't stop thinking about her situation."

Claire's eyes took her in, and she smiled with a warmth she rarely showed. "I'll bring them by your office later today, Grace."

"I appreciate that."

After Claire left, Grace pulled out the file of Jessica Caldwell, her 3:00. Their first session since September.

She retrieved the notes.

Recognition, circled twice.

She remembered Jessica's face lighting up when she talked about Cathryn.

A knock. Grace went to the door, the old floorboards creaking under her footsteps.

Jessica stood in the hallway clutching the same backpack Grace remembered from September. MIT sticker peeling on one corner, a recyclable water bottle hanging from a carabiner. Her hair was shorter, and she wore a small rainbow pin on her jacket.

"Hi, Dr. Brennan."

"Jessica. Come in." Grace stepped aside and gestured to the couch. "It's good to see you."

Jessica moved past her, sat on the couch. Less perched than before, more grounded. "Sorry it's been so long. I kept meaning to schedule, but things got ... complicated."

"No apology needed." Grace clicked her pen. "Catch me up. What's been happening?"

Jessica exhaled, a long breath. "I left Nick."

"You did?" Grace kept her voice neutral. "When?"

"Late October." Jessica twisted her hands. "I took your advice, spent more time with Cathryn, paid attention to how I felt. And the more time we spent together, the clearer it got. I wasn't confused. I was in love with her."

"How did Nick take it?"

"Not well." Jessica's face darkened. "He asked if there was

someone else. I told him yes. He asked if it was a guy from the lab, and I said no. It took him a minute to understand." She paused. "He called me a liar. Said I'd wasted three years of his life."

Grace winced. "That must've been painful."

"It was. But also—" Jessica looked up. "I felt relieved. Like I'd been holding my breath for years and finally exhaled."

"And Cathryn?"

Jessica's face transformed. "We've been together since early November. It's been ... God, it's been amazing. But also really hard."

Grace leaned forward slightly. "Tell me about the hard part."

Outside, a car horn blared, and a man's angry voice rang out. Jessica's fingers found the rainbow pin, touched it.

"She wants to be more public. Hand-holding in lab corridors, inviting me to birthday dinners with her friends, meeting her sister and her parents." Jessica rubbed her forehead. "And I thought I was ready for that, but I'm not. I'm still getting used to saying the words *gay* and *girlfriend* without my throat closing."

Grace kept her voice neutral. "Has she been pressuring you?"

"Not intentionally." Jessica bit down on her lower lip. "She just knows who she is. She's been out to everyone for several years—her family, her friends."

"What's it like, being on a different timeline?" She knew the answer before Jessica gave it.

"Like I'm running behind her, trying to catch up. My family doesn't know yet. My mom keeps asking about Nick, and I keep making excuses. My lab partner asked if Cathryn and I are dating, and I said we're just friends. I couldn't help it. Cathryn says she understands, but I can see it hurts her."

Grace made a note. "What makes it hard to be public?"

"I don't know ..." She looked down, then quickly went on. "The thing is: I'm constantly aware of who's watching. Two guys in the lab were staring at us last week, whispering. I wanted to disappear."

"That sounds exhausting."

Jessica nodded, but didn't look comforted by Grace's validation.

"It's not just that. We're realizing we have different rhythms. Different ways of communicating. She's all instinct. I'm all analysis. Sometimes I feel like we're speaking different languages."

"Have you talked to Cathryn about any of this?" Grace asked.

"I've tried," Jessica said. "But then she cries, or I cry, or we both try to fix it and we end up saying things we don't mean."

Grace nodded.

"And sometimes ..." Jessica hesitated. "Sometimes I think about how easy everything was with Nick. Predictable."

Grace let the silence hold. When she spoke, her voice was careful. "Do you regret leaving Nick?"

"No. I mean— yeah, in some ways. It was comfortable to be the girlfriend he expected, everyone expected. I knew that script." Jessica looked up, met Grace's eyes. "But I was hollow inside. Like I was watching my own life happen to someone else."

"And with Cathryn?"

"With Cathryn, I'm terrified half the time. But I'm also more myself than I've ever been."

Jessica looked down at the empty space where Nick's ring used to sit.

"Even if Cathryn and I don't make it—I hope we do, but even if we don't—I don't regret leaving him." She looked up. "Because I finally know who I am. And that's not something I can just put back where I found it."

"That's important," Grace managed. "Really important, Jessica."

"I suppose." Jessica leaned forward. "But sometimes it feels like I've just made everything harder for no reason. Like I should've just stayed comfortable and stopped asking questions."

"What do you think the cost would've been? If you'd stayed?"

Jessica paused. Then: "I would've married him. Had his children. Built a life that looked perfect from the outside." Her voice dropped.

"And I suppose I would've died never knowing ... what it felt like to be loved for who I actually am."

Grace set down her pen. Her hands weren't steady. She pressed them flat against the notebook and took a breath before speaking. "Being loved for who you actually are. That's not a small thing."

"No." Jessica's eyes were searching. "It's everything."

They spent the rest of the session on practical strategies—how Jessica might talk to her family, how to navigate the lab dynamics, how to communicate with Cathryn about timelines and expectations.

When their hour ended, Jessica stood, shouldered her bag. "Thank you. This helped."

"I'm glad." Grace walked her to the door. "Call me when you want to schedule another appointment."

"I will. Actually—" Jessica paused at the threshold. "Can I ask you something? As a therapist, I mean, but also just ... as a person?"

"Of course."

"When you work with people going through big changes, do you ever wish you could just tell them it's going to be okay? That the hard part is worth it?"

Grace felt her breath catch. "Yes. Often."

"But you can't."

"No. They have to find that out for themselves. Because hearing it isn't the same as knowing it."

Jessica nodded. "Right." She shifted her backpack. "Thanks again, Dr. Brennan."

After she left, Grace sat alone in her office. The winter light was fading. She looked at her notes, at the words she'd written: *I finally know who I am. And that's not something I can just put back where I found it.*

Jessica was terrified half the time. But also more herself than she'd ever been.

Grace thought about Chicago next week. Three nights with

Allie. Three nights of not pretending, not compartmentalizing, not rushing home to maintain the fiction of her marriage.

She was terrified too.

But Jessica's words stayed with her: *Even if we don't make it, I don't regret leaving him. Because I finally know who I am.*

Grace picked up her pen and sat with that for a moment. Then she closed the notebook.

37

Thursday, December 7

The Uber pulled away, leaving Grace and Allie standing with their suitcases on a quiet Lincoln Park block. December sunlight slanted between brick buildings, low and golden, warming the cold air. Grace breathed it in. Chicago.

The Airbnb door code worked on the second try. Inside, the apartment wrapped around them. Exposed brick, tall windows, honeyed hardwood floors. A small living room, a neat kitchen, and through a doorway, a wrought-iron bed, crisply made. At the sight of it, Grace's muscles clenched low in her abdomen.

They unpacked in small, wordless motions. In the bathroom mirror, two sets of bottles and jars lined up on the counter. Grace stared at them for a long moment.

Allie's reflection met hers. "This is really happening. We're here for three full days."

Grace exhaled. "We are."

"You okay?"

"I'm ... not sure." She steadied her voice. "Terrified. Excited. Both."

Back in the living room, she drifted toward the windows, an old nervous habit. She needed space when her thoughts got loud.

Behind her, Allie's hands came to her shoulders. Gentle, asking permission. Grace let herself lean back. Eyes closed. Breath slowing.

"Hi," Allie whispered into her hair.

Grace turned. "Hi."

The kiss started gentle. Tentative. Then deeper. Allie's palms cupped her face, her mouth sure and warm, and Grace's body answered before her mind could interfere.

"We could ..." Allie nodded toward the bedroom.

Desire surged, bright and immediate. Then a thought of her body's history flashed: the freezing, the sudden collapse of pleasure into effort, the emptiness afterward.

"Let's take a walk," she said, breath unsteady. "Dinner first." She was stalling. She knew she was stalling. But she needed more time before she had to face— "If we stay here, we won't make it out the door."

Allie kissed her cheek, amused and tender. "Okay. Walk first."

They bundled into coats and scarves and stepped back into the cold afternoon. Lincoln Park spread around them. Tree-lined streets, wreaths on doors, little shops strung with white lights. They pointed out places to return to: a vintage clothing shop, a bookstore with handwritten recommendations taped to the shelves, a café that promised "serious pastries."

It felt like planning a future, even if the future was only three days long.

Grace joked, laughed, nudged Allie with her shoulder. The mental static of her life back home—the kids' schedules, Michael's silences, the invisible chore list—fell away. For the first time in months, she felt unburdened.

They paused at the window of a bath-and-body boutique where

a display of Native products advertised the brand's array of dessert scents.

Allie squinted. "Vanilla Sprinkle deodorant? Boston Kreme shampoo?"

Grace grimaced. "Strawberry Frosted pits. Bold choice."

They found a small Italian restaurant tucked on a side street. Garlic and warm bread in the air. A red candle on the table. They ordered pasta and a bottle of wine.

Conversation came easily. She couldn't stop looking at Allie in the candlelight: her hair catching the glow, the graceful line of her neck, the way she circled her wineglass with one finger. Her mind kept sliding forward. To the apartment, to the bed, to what might happen. Their food arrived. She barely tasted it. She was somewhere else.

"Grace?" Allie's voice broke through the fog.

Grace blinked. "Sorry. What did you say?"

"I asked if you wanted to share a dessert." Concern warmed Allie's expression, the kind of concern that came from knowing her.

"I'm fine without." Grace set down her fork. "Should we go?"

Allie flagged down the server for the check.

Back at the apartment, they shed coats with cold-stiffened fingers. Standing in the dim light, cheeks pink from the wind, they kissed until Grace forgot to think. They moved toward the bedroom, still kissing. They bumped the frame and laughed. Allie's hands found the top button of Grace's blouse.

One button. Then the next. Then another. Each one undone with slow, deliberate intention. Allie's eyes remained on her face, simultaneously watching for permission and for any sign to stop.

The blouse opened. Grace let it fall.

Allie pushed a bra strap aside and kissed the bare place on her shoulder. Once. Then again. Her hands slid around Grace's back, found the clasp. "Okay?"

Grace nodded.

The bra fell away. Allie's gaze dropped, then lifted back to Grace's face. She whispered. "I have to say it again: you're beautiful." Allie bent and kissed the top of her breast. "Really beautiful."

Heat gathered below Grace's belly.

Allie unfastened Grace's slacks and pushed them down. The pale-blue underwear Grace had bought just for this moment suddenly felt too hopeful.

Grace's hands trembled as she unbuttoned Allie's shirt, unhooked the bra. The sight of Allie exposed—smooth skin, breath rising, eyes bright with desire.

They tumbled onto the bed, kissing, laughing breathlessly. Allie moved slowly—mouth on her neck, her collarbone, the curve of her breast. When she took her breast into her mouth, Grace arched immediately.

"Is this the side you like better?" Allie murmured.

Grace nodded helplessly.

Allie kissed lower. Down her stomach. Hands on her thighs. Grace's breath caught when she reached the waistband.

Allie paused. "Okay?"

"Yes," she whispered.

The underwear slid away. She fought the instinct to cover herself. Allie's hands touched her sides, her hips, the tender creases at her thighs. Mapping her like someone learning a coastline. Then Allie touched her.

Grace gasped. Her body opened without thought. A steady rhythm built, pressure looping tight in her abdomen. Everything narrowed to Allie's hand, the breath catching in her throat.

Her hips began to move on their own, matching Allie's rhythm, then outpacing it. Heat gathered and tightened, each stroke pulling her closer to something her body wanted to rise to with Allie. A peak somewhere ahead, now almost within reach.

Then her mind caught up. *It's happening. Stay with it. Don't think.*

But telling herself not to think was itself a thought, and the thought cracked the surface. The pleasure thinned. She tried to pull it back—focused on Allie's hand, on the rhythm, on Allie's breath now in her ear, on the heat between them. But focusing was the problem. She was watching herself from above now, monitoring, assessing.

Her body slackened. The wave reversed.

Allie adjusted pressure, speed—gentle, patient—but Grace felt the shift, felt Allie trying, and the old dread rose: this is what happens. This is what always happens. Even here. Even with her.

And underneath that: If I can't come even with Allie—even wanting her this much, even after everything I've risked to be here—then the problem really is me. And eventually she'll know it, too.

"I'm sorry," she whispered. "I don't think I can ..."

Allie kissed her forehead. "It's okay. We have time."

But time was the problem. The longer it went on, the more she panicked. She tried again, insisted she could, but the harder she tried, the further everything slipped away.

"Let me use my mouth," Allie said gently. "I might be able to help that way."

Grace went rigid.

That was a line.

Hands, she could tell herself, were just touching. Bodies being close. But Allie's mouth on her? Too intimate. Too exposed and vulnerable. Too much.

"No, I don't—

"Grace, I really want to. Let me try—"

"I said no." It came out sharp, jagged.

Allie drew back. Hurt flashed across her face.

Christ. She'd just snapped at Allie for offering the most intimate kind of pleasure. What was wrong with her?

"I'm just trying to help. Why won't you let me?"

"Because I can't!" Grace's voice cracked. She grabbed the sheet, pulled it around herself like armor. Heat flooded her face, tears threatening. "I just ... can't."

Allie sat up, arms tight around her knees. "Can't or won't?"

"Both—" Tears blurred her vision. "What's the difference?"

"The difference," Allie said, voice breaking, "is whether you trust me with your body, with your pleasure."

"That's not fair."

"Then tell me what's happening. Because from here it feels like you want me, but only the parts that don't scare you."

Grace went still. Oh god. That might be true. Might be exactly what was happening. She wanted Allie's love, but feared her mouth on her.

"I'm trying!" Tears spilled now, unstoppable. "I don't know what I'm doing. This is all new and I can't even—"

"Grace," she said gently, "Look at me. This is me. I want to do this with you. I know how. I can make this good for you. If you'd just let me—"

Allie might be able to make it good. But the point was that Grace didn't know if she could relax with a woman's mouth there, even Allie's. And if she couldn't relax, it didn't matter how good Allie was at it.

"Stop," Grace whispered. "Please. Just stop."

She curled onto her side, sheet tight around her, tears sliding into the pillow.

Behind her, Allie lay still, breaths coming in uneven catches.

38

Friday, December 8

Grace woke to gray light and the unmistakable heaviness of dread. For a breathless second she didn't know where she was. Then she turned her head.

Allie lay facing away, shoulders tight beneath the sheet, her whole posture curled inward—as if bracing against something even in sleep.

Grace moved closer, slow and careful, and eased an arm around Allie's waist. Her chest pressed lightly to Allie's back.

Allie stiffened.

"Hi," Grace whispered.

After a beat, Allie rolled toward her. Her sleep-creased eyes were guarded, distant. "Hi."

"I'm so sorry," Grace said, her voice shaking. "I wasn't rejecting you. I was terrified."

Allie's expression gentled a fraction. "It felt like you didn't want me. Like you suddenly changed your mind."

"That's not what happened." Grace cupped Allie's cheek,

thumb brushing the warm skin beneath her eye. "But I hurt you. I snapped at you for offering something intimate and beautiful. I'm sorry."

Allie slid closer, arms circling Grace.

"When you offered, when you wanted to—" She couldn't say it. "I felt exposed. Like if we crossed that line, I couldn't pretend anymore. Couldn't pretend I'm not—"

"Gay?" Allie whispered gently.

Grace swallowed. "Yes. Gay." She shut her eyes as tears slid out. "I just don't know how to be this person yet."

Grace let the sobs come then—shallow at first, then deep, shaking her from the inside out.

Allie pulled her in and stroked her hair.

"I want you," Grace said into Allie's collarbone. "I want everything with you. Even the things that scare me now. I just need time."

"I'm not going anywhere," Allie murmured. "We go at your pace. No rush."

Eventually, Grace lifted her face and kissed her. Slow, trembling, full of apology and longing.

Allie kissed back. Her hands skimmed Grace's sides, her stomach, the curve of her hip. Grace arched into the warmth, her own hands sliding under the sheet to learn the lines of Allie's body, the places that made her inhale sharply.

A blare sliced through the room. Allie's phone alarm. Loud, insistent. 7:30 AM. They froze, foreheads pressed together.

Allie let out a groan. "Oh, fuck!"

Grace laughed, fell back against the pillow, a hand over her eyes. "Shit." It came out half-exasperated, half-wistful. "We actually have to go be therapists."

Dragging herself from Allie's warmth felt like tearing Velcro apart. She forced herself upright. "Tonight," she said quietly. A promise. A vow.

Allie nodded. "Tonight."

At the conference hotel, Grace tried to focus on a morning panel about attachment theory. The presenter's voice became noise. She checked her phone. No messages.

An afternoon session on "cultivating embodied safety" only made it worse.

She thumbed out a text to Allie: *I can't concentrate on any of this.*

A moment later, Allie replied: *Same. How much longer are we supposed to stay?*

Grace glanced at the schedule. Presentations until 4:00. Then a networking reception. No way. Absolutely not. She typed: *Let's get out of here.*

Allie responded: *Yes! Side exit. Ten minutes.*

Grace grabbed her coat and slid out the nearest door like a teenager sneaking out after curfew. By the time she reached the lobby, Allie was already there. Coat on, bag slung over her shoulder, a conspiratorial grin stretching across her face.

"We're terrible professionals," Allie said.

"The worst," Grace agreed.

They pushed out into the cold, laughing as they hurried away from the hotel and the conferees' earnest PowerPoints about emotional presence.

The second the apartment door shut behind them, Grace grabbed Allie by the hips and kissed her hard. Urgent, hungry, certain.

Clothes fell away in a trail across the living room. By the time they reached the bed, Grace's breath came fast.

Skin against skin, everything felt changed—familiar and new at once. When Allie kissed the lower curve of her breast, heat coursed through Grace, immediate and startling. She gasped.

Allie's mouth closed around her right breast. Pleasure shot through her and she arched. Her legs parted without thought when Allie's hand slipped between them—fingers moving with a sure, confident rhythm.

Grace's hips rose to meet her. "That," she moaned. "Just like that."

The sensation climbed—slow at first, then accelerating, a current pulling her toward the edge. Her thighs tensed, her breath came in shallow catches, her whole body drawn taut around Allie's hand.

Fear flickered. What if it collapsed again?

But Allie pressed her forehead to Grace's temple and whispered: "You can. I've got you."

Something shifted in the place where she'd been holding the door shut for years. She stopped trying. Stopped monitoring herself, waiting for it to go wrong.

Allie's breath in her ear. Allie's skilled fingers coaxing her toward climax. She let go.

When it came, it wasn't the sharp, effortful thing she'd produced alone in the dark years ago. Or those rare times with Michael. This one built from somewhere deeper, rolling through her in waves she couldn't control and didn't want to. She cried out. Let it happen.

She held Allie's shoulders, her body shaking. The tremors went on longer than she could imagine, and when they ebbed, she was crying.

"I've never—" She couldn't complete the sentence.

Allie kissed her forehead. "I know."

"I thought I was broken." A shaky laugh. "I actually thought I was broken."

Allie's eyes shone. Grace kissed her—grateful, reverent—and then moved her mouth down Allie's body. Not tentatively this time. She now knew the spot below Allie's collarbone that made her breath stutter. She knew to slow down when Allie's hips started moving, to make her wait.

As Allie came undone beneath her—gasping Grace's name, fingers tangled in her hair—Grace stayed with her through it, watching her face.

When it was over, they lay wrapped together as winter dusk gathered outside the windows. Grace rested her head on Allie's chest, listening to the slowing heartbeat under her ear. Her fingers traced lazy lines across Allie's stomach.

After a long silence, Grace whispered, "When did you know you wanted me?"

Allie exhaled a small laugh. "Several years ago."

Grace lifted her head. "Years?"

"Mm-hmm." Allie brushed a strand of hair behind her ear. "But *crave* you? Probably August. One night you stayed late and we talked in my office. I went home and couldn't stop thinking about you."

Grace remembered that night—the way Allie had watched her, the shift in the air between them. "I think I knew then, too. I just didn't let myself call it what it was."

Allie cupped her cheek. "I love you."

Grace's heart swelled. Allie was saying it.

"I love you, too."

She pressed her forehead to Allie's. "This won't be easy."

"No," Allie murmured. "But we'll find our way."

Saturday morning, Grace woke with her head on Allie's shoulder and sunlight threading through the blinds in pale gold stripes. For a moment she simply lay there, listening to Allie breathe.

Allie's eyes opened slowly. She smiled. Warm, unguarded. "Hi. How long have you been awake?"

"Not long," Grace said. "I was watching you sleep."

Allie smirked. "Creepy."

Grace laughed. Their legs were already tangled, one of Allie's feet hooked behind her calf.

Allie traced the line of Grace's jaw with her fingertips. "What if we skip the conference?" Allie said. "Just ... stay here."

Grace didn't pretend to argue. "Yes. Please."

They drifted—talking, kissing, brushing fingers over skin, letting the morning stretch without edges. It felt like suspended time in an undiscovered pocket of the world where chores and obligations couldn't reach them.

Grace rolled on top of Allie, pinning her wrists above her head. "Well, well," she said, lowering her voice dramatically. "Looks like I have you trapped."

Allie raised an eyebrow. "And what exactly are you going to do with me?"

"Nothing," Grace said. "Until later. Right now I have to pee." She scrambled off the bed, laughing as she hunted for her underwear on the floor.

Allie flopped back with a groan of thwarted desire, then followed her out of the room, tugging on leggings and a T-shirt.

When Grace emerged from the bathroom, Allie was grinding coffee beans—the sound instantly taking Grace to her own kitchen, to Michael doing the same thing Sunday mornings with the little Braun they'd been given as a wedding present. To Matthew padding downstairs in socks, asking what was for breakfast.

Allie looked up. "You okay?"

"Yeah. Maybe just hungry."

"We should get breakfast," Allie said, hair messy, smile easy. "Like normal people. On a normal Saturday morning."

They walked arm in arm through the crisp December air. The neighborhood café they'd noticed on Thursday looked even more inviting today—warm, crowded, full of clinking cutlery and steam from metal pitchers.

Inside, they found a small table by the window. Grace ordered pancakes; Allie chose an omelet. They stole bites off each other's plates with no attempt at subtlety.

"I want this," Grace said quietly, watching Allie's fingers curve around her mug. "Sitting in a café with you back home, holding hands. Introducing you as my partner, not my colleague."

Allie's toes found her ankle under the table. "When?"

The question sat between them. Grace didn't have an answer.

After breakfast they wandered into the neighborhood bookstore. The place smelled like paper and cedar shelves, the air warm from radiators clanking with winter insistence. Grace drifted to fiction; Allie tugged her toward poetry. She plucked a familiar slim volume off the shelf. Adrienne Rich. The same book that lived page-flagged in her Cambridge office. She tucked it under her arm without comment, and her eyes found Grace's.

Twenty minutes later, laden with a small stack of books and two bars of dark chocolate from the register display, they stepped back out into the cold afternoon.

Back at the apartment, Grace closed the door behind them, leaned back against it, and reached for Allie.

"One more time," she whispered. "Before we have to go back."

"Yes," Allie whispered back.

They kissed, slow at first. Grace's hands slipped under Allie's sweater; Allie's fingers traced the curve of her hips, pulling her closer. They drifted toward the bedroom, leaving a trail of clothing behind them, laughing when they bounced lightly on the mattress.

Grace lay back and looked up into Allie's eyes.

"Thursday night I said no." She reached up, touched Allie's lips, and ran her tongue across her own. "I'm saying yes now."

"Really?" Allie smiled, searched her face. "Are you sure?"

"Yes," Grace whispered. "I want to feel that with you."

Allie moved slowly, waiting for a nod, a breath, any sign of hesitation. Grace felt the old fear flicker as Allie kissed lower: the instinct to close, to protect, to stop this before it became something she couldn't take back. But Allie's hands were steady on her hips, and her mouth was warm as it moved down. And when she arrived there, Grace didn't freeze; she trembled. But moved toward, not away.

The orgasm came relatively swiftly. Fierce, consuming. She held Allie's shoulders, body trembling, tears on her face.

Afterward, curled together, Allie ran her fingers up and down Grace's thighs.

Grace pressed her forehead to Allie's shoulder. "I'm going to remember this whole day. When I'm back in Boston, when life gets complicated, I'll remember this. That you and I had this."

Tomorrow they'd catch their flight home. Next Saturday, she'd tell the kids. This was the last perfect day before everything exploded.

"We'll have more days like this," Allie said. "When things settle. We'll have whole weekends. Whole weeks. A whole life."

Grace's breath hitched. "You really believe we can have a life together?"

"Yes," Allie said. "Otherwise what are we doing?"

On the dresser, Grace's phone buzzed. She slipped out of bed and trotted across the cold floor to retrieve it.

A text from Mia. She read it, then read it again: *Chloe asked me to the Winter Dance in January. Dad says I can't say yes until you two have had a chance to talk about it. Will you call him?*

"Oh, Christ. Fuck that man."

Allie sat up, sheet pooling at her waist. "What?"

Grace handed her the phone. Allie read it, jaw tightening.

"I won't let him stand in my way," Grace said. "I refuse to let him stand in hers either."

She texted Mia: *I'll be home tomorrow. I'll talk to him then. It will all be okay. Promise.*

She set the phone down on the nightstand and climbed back into bed. Allie pulled her close. Outside, the light was already going—their last Chicago afternoon fading away.

39

Sunday, December 10

They were mostly quiet on the drive home from the airport. Grace dropped Allie at her house in Arlington, kissing her once more through the open car window. By the time she turned onto her own street in Belmont, the sky had gone dark.

Nothing had changed since Thursday. Wet maple leaves remained glued to the sidewalk. The Hendersons' melting snowman still leaned against the fence, listing to one side. Her own house glowed with its steady porch light next to the red door.

Four days ago she'd driven away from this house. Now she was back, with the same luggage and no idea how to be the person who lived here.

In Chicago, life had been simple: one woman, one bed, one agenda. Now she had to return to being the predictable mom who remembered dentist appointments and kept the refrigerator stocked with everyone's favorite yogurt.

But not predictable for long. Six days from now, she and Michael would sit the kids down and tell them the marriage was ending.

She hauled her suitcase through the back door. "It's me," she called, dropping her luggage in the mudroom with a thud.

The sound of some medical documentary drifted from the living room. Michael's voice cut through the noise. "In here."

Grace stepped into the doorway.

"There's Chinese in the fridge," he said, eyes flicking up from the diagrams of arterial blockage. "Have a good trip?"

Chicago flashed through her: Allie's skin under her mouth, the warmth of waking up tangled together, still present in her body like an afterimage.

She smiled. "Yes. Good."

Grace shrugged off her coat, hung it in the closet, and climbed the stairs to check on the kids. Her phone buzzed. She pulled it out in the hallway between Matthew's and Mia's rooms. A text from Allie: *You okay?*

Grace's thumb hovered over the keyboard. The house around her: familiar photographs lining the hallway, the children's height marks penciled on the doorframe, Michael's documentary droning downstairs. In six days, she would change all of this.

She typed: *I will be.*

She knocked on Matthew's half-open door. He was hunched over his desk, headphones clamped on, lost in whatever digital kingdom he was defending. He only noticed her when the widening band of hallway light hit his screen. He pulled off one side of the headset.

"Mom. You're back!"

"I am." She moved toward him, folding him into her arms. She inhaled his familiar smell. His hug came quick and stiff. But it was there.

"Everything okay while I was gone?"

Matthew grinned, dimples appearing. "Dad totally let us eat garbage. Pizza Thursday and Friday. Chipotle yesterday. Chinese tonight."

"Living the dream."

Matthew's eyes flicked up from his screen. "How was Chicago?"

"Froze my butt off. Terrible coffee, boring panels." She kept her voice level.

"Cool." His fingers twitched toward his headset. "Mind if I get back to this? Just need like five more minutes to reach this checkpoint."

"Go ahead. But lights out by ten, okay?" She backed toward the door and watched him put the headphones back over his ears, disappearing into his world again.

She made her way to Mia's room. Door open. Mia lay sprawled on the bed, thumb flicking upward on her phone screen.

"Hey, Mom."

"Hi, sweetheart." Grace sat on the edge of the bed. "How was the weekend?"

Mia shrugged. "Dad forgot most of the stuff you usually do, but I was at Chloe's a lot."

"How's Chloe?"

"She's good. We're good."

Grace brushed a loose strand of hair from Mia's forehead.

"I'm sorry about your dad's reaction to Chloe's invitation. I'll straighten it out with him tonight. Don't worry."

Mia smiled. "Thanks. Glad you're home."

Grace stood to leave.

Mia stopped her. "Mom, when are you going to tell me? About your attraction to a woman?"

Grace sighed. "Mia—"

Her daughter leaned forward, eyes earnest. "You promised 'soon.' It's been a week. Just so you know, 'soon' has an expiration date."

"I know. And I mean soon. Please trust me."

Mia's eyes narrowed, sharp. "You smell different."

Could she smell Allie on her?

"Just hotel soap. You come home smelling strange when you travel," Grace said lightly, kissing her forehead. "Lights out by ten, okay?"

Later, in her bedroom, Grace unzipped her carry-on. Each article of clothing she pulled out conjured a different image of Allie in Chicago —pulling aside the strap of the pale-blue bra and kissing her shoulder, her toes tugging at her socks under the cafe table.

She put an unused pair of underwear back in her dresser drawer, and her gaze came to rest on the framed photo of the kids sitting on top. Chicago instantly evaporated.

She picked up her phone. Texted Allie: *I'm scared. Saturday's coming and I'm terrified. What if they hate me?*

A reply came back almost immediately: *They won't. You're their mom. All you mean to them doesn't go away.*

Grace stared at the words, wishing she could believe them.

She dropped her phone on the bed. She moved through the remaining motions of unpacking. The clock read 9:35. The house felt huge. Mia's occasional laugh filtered down the hallway. Matthew's video game music pulsed under his door. Downstairs, Michael's documentary droned on. She straightened the bathroom counter even though it was already clean. At 9:50, she heard Michael climb the stairs to the guest room.

A little after ten, a knock.

"Come in," she said.

Michael stepped inside, closing the door gently. He stayed by the doorframe as though keeping an exit close at hand.

"We need to talk logistics," he said. "About the separation."

Grace set her book down, spine-up. "Okay."

"An opportunity has come up that might make this easier." His voice had that detached clinical polish he used at the hospital.

Grace drew her knees up. "Go ahead."

Michael cleared his throat. "Bill Frasure at Hopkins called again Thursday. They want me to train their surgical team on the thoracic technique Jerry and I developed." He paused. "I'd go to Baltimore for two weeks, leaving here on the Thursday before New Year's—I think that's the 28th—and return on January 12th, in time for Mia's birthday."

Two weeks without Michael in the house.

"Grace?" he said.

"That's ... soon. How could you make that work with your schedule?"

"It's actually perfect. I didn't have many electives scheduled those two weeks, and I've already set things up for my team to handle those while I'm gone."

So he'd gone ahead and accepted without even texting her. Arranged it all—Baltimore, his team here—without consulting her. *The nerve.* But then, she supposed she was the last person who should complain about unilateral decisions.

"Well, sounds like a good opportunity." Her voice sounded to her like someone else's. "Everything paid for?"

"Yes," he said with a curt nod. "And I'm thinking we should hold off until I get back to tell the kids about us."

"You want to wait until mid-January?"

"It's better for them," he said. "They get one last normal Christmas. And when I come home, we can present it clearly. No confusion about whether Baltimore is a trial separation." He lifted his eyebrows. "What do you think?"

"Well, it may save Christmas for them, but will pretty much screw up Mia's birthday celebration, don't you think?"

"We could wait a few days after that."

She blinked. Five more weeks of pretending. She needed this charade to end. But she nodded.

Michael exhaled, relieved. "Okay. That's the plan."

He turned toward the door.

"Michael?"

He paused.

"January 15th," she said quietly. "No later than that. We tell them."

A muscle ticked in his jaw. "Understood."

"One more thing," Grace said. "Chloe invited Mia to the Winter Dance. You told Mia she couldn't say yes until we'd talked about it."

He stopped, hand on the frame. "Right. I told her we'd need to discuss it first."

"What's there to discuss? Mia received an invitation to a high-school dance."

"It's not that simple. She's fifteen. We don't know this girl's parents. We don't know—"

"I know Chloe. She's been at this house a dozen times. And if a boy had asked Mia, would you have told her to wait?"

The silence answered for him.

"She's going to the dance, Michael. With Chloe. And you're going to tell her it's fine."

His jaw worked. Then he nodded once and left.

The door clicked shut. Grace stared at the white panel.

She picked up her phone to text Allie: *Change of plans. Michael will be away the first two weeks of January. We'll tell the kids when he gets back.*

She followed it quickly with another: *Not thrilled. But the kids get one last normal Christmas, so…*

The typing bubble appeared, disappeared, reappeared, then: *Five more weeks?*

Grace grimaced, hearing the pain behind Allie's words. She replied: *I know. I'm sorry. But upside is he'll be away a couple weeks!*

A long pause, then: *If that's what you think is best.*

Grace stared at the screen. No emoji. No warmth. Her heart beating harder, she typed: *Allie, I love you. This doesn't change anything. It's just logistics.*

The screen stayed still. Eventually, another message arrived: *I understand.*

She stared at the two words, then set the phone on the nightstand and turned off the light. She could still smell Allie on her skin.

40

Monday, December 18

Slush collected on the Victorian's steps in gray piles. Grace shook off her boots in the entryway and climbed the stairs to her office. She had fifteen minutes before David Castellano's 2:00 PM appointment.

At 1:59, she heard his footsteps in the hallway.

"Come in, David."

He entered, unwinding his scarf, and settled into his usual spot on the couch. "Grace. Good to see you."

"You too." She let the pause stretch. "Before we begin today, I need to talk with you about something important."

His eyes narrowed. "Okay."

"David, I need to revisit something we discussed before. The gifts, the late-night voicemails, the questions about my personal life. I thought we'd reached an understanding about boundaries."

"We did. And I backed off, even though those were just gestures of my appreciation. I thought—"

"Since then, there have been other incidents that concern me. In October, you appeared at my side at Wilson Farm. You mentioned your daughter and grandchildren were with you, but I saw you leave. There was no one with you."

David moved to the edge of his chair. "My daughter had already left with the kids. They were having meltdowns. I stayed to finish my shopping." His voice had gone defensive. He glanced around the room, as if searching for an answer to what was happening.

"There's more. The restaurant last week in Brookline. I—"

He stared at her; recognition dawned on his face, understanding what she was saying. "What are you—? You think I'm— What? Following you?"

"I think you're struggling with appropriate boundaries. And I think the grief has made it harder—"

"No." He shook his head. "Those were coincidences. I can't help if we run into each other. You're making me sound like some kind of stalker."

"I don't think you're dangerous. But I do think you're in pain, and you've been looking for connection in a place where it can't exist the way you need it to. The pattern suggests the boundaries of our work together are unclear for you."

"Unclear for me?" His face flushed. "You're the one making this into something it's not."

Silence dropped between them.

David's hands clenched on his knees. "I thought you understood. I thought—" He stopped, jaw working. "Elena always said you were different. That you actually gave a shit."

"I do care about your wellbeing. That's why we're having this conversation."

"No." He stood abruptly. "You're having this conversation because you want me gone. Because I make you uncomfortable."

"That's not what I said."

"But it's what you mean." He reached for his coat. His voice broke slightly. "This was just a job to you."

"David, that's not true. I'm just concerned about—"

"My 'inappropriate behavior.' My 'boundary violations.'" He pulled on his coat with careful movements. "Yeah, I get it. I understand. You've made it very clear."

"Please sit back down. I think we should—"

"No." The word came out hard. He paused, seemed to struggle with something. When he spoke again, his voice had an edge beneath the hurt. "Maybe you're right. Maybe I can't tell the difference between therapy and—" His jaw clenched. "But I don't need to pay you to make me feel pathetic. We're done."

Grace kept her voice level. "I think it would be helpful if we could have one more session to process—"

"Process this?" A bitter laugh. "So you can explain to me, in therapeutic language, exactly how I've misread everything? No thank you."

He moved toward the door, then stopped, hand on the knob. His shoulders sagged. When he turned back, the anger had drained from his face.

"The worst part is I actually thought you cared. About me, about what I was going through." He looked at her directly. "But I was wrong."

"David—"

"Don't." He held up a hand. "Just send me a final bill. I'll pay it."

He opened the door and walked out, pulling it closed behind him with careful control.

Grace didn't move. His footsteps in the hallway—quick at first, then slower. They stopped at the top of the stairs. Her stomach clamped.

After a long moment, the footsteps continued down. The front door opened and closed. She breathed out.

Through her window, she watched him cross the parking lot to his car. He stood by the driver's door for a moment, hand on the handle, head bowed. Then he got in and drove away.

Grace stared at the spot where his car had been. Had she been fair? The voicemails were real. The gifts were real. The personal questions were documented in her notes. But Wilson Farm? The restaurant? David's explanations were plausible. People did run into each other unexpectedly. Maybe she'd been so on edge about her own boundary violations with Allie that she'd seen stalking where there was only coincidence. Or maybe the pattern was real and she'd been right to address it. She couldn't know for certain. And that uncertainty sat in her chest like a stone.

Grace pulled up David's file and typed her clinical note:

*Client terminated following discussion of boundary concerns.
Strong transference evident throughout treatment. Client
unable to recognize pattern. Termination appropriate outcome.
No follow-up contact unless initiated by client.*

She saved the note and closed the file. Her hands were shaking. She pressed them flat against the desk.

She walked to the window. Fresh snow was falling, small flakes that wouldn't stick.

Her 3:30 was in fifty minutes. She went back to her desk. Her eyes went once more to the window, to the empty parking space where his car had been. Then she pulled up the next file and began to prepare.

41

Saturday, December 24

Grace drifted through the day before Christmas on autopilot: checking off last-minute items from her shopping list, doing some cooking. The house smelled like cinnamon and pine. She'd put up the tree with the kids a week ago, strung lights and balsam sprigs along the mantel. The stockings hung in a neat row, names stitched in red: Michael, Grace, Mia, Matthew.

Grace was wrapping a gift for Matthew when Mia appeared in the doorway of the den.

"Mom?"

Grace looked up. Mia stood with her arms crossed. "You okay? You seem weird today."

Grace took in her daughter—fifteen, nearly sixteen, long past the age when you could wave things away with a quick, *I'm fine, sweetheart.* Mia's gaze was too direct for that now.

She reached for Mia's hand. "Just the holiday rat-race. I'm worn a little thin."

"Yeah. You do everything around here. Dad doesn't do shit."

Grace looked up, surprised that Mia would say that. Notice it. Then again, of course she did. Mia was perceptive. Observant.

"And he's going away for two weeks, leaving everything to you. Typical." Mia said. She gestured to the remaining gifts and wrapping paper. "I can do that for you. I'm pretty good at wrapping."

"You are, and that's sweet of you to offer. But I'm almost done." Grace forced a small smile. "Thanks, honey."

They ate an early Christmas Eve dinner at the dining room table. Grace had pulled out the festive Christmas china, as if formal dishes could somehow elevate everyone's mood.

Matthew talked about the Gsyker telescope he was hoping to get, his enthusiasm filling the silence. Mia pushed food around her plate, stealing glances at her parents like she was tracking invisible currents. Michael ate methodically. Small talk about the apartment near the hospital that Hopkins had arranged for him. About the weather in Baltimore.

"You're going to miss New Year's," Matthew said to his father.

"I know. Sorry about that."

"But you'll be back for my birthday?" Mia asked.

"Yes. It's a Friday. I'll be home that evening." Michael put his fork down. "Look, I'm sorry to be going away, and I know the timing is bad. But this is important for my career."

"Everything's always about your career," Mia muttered.

"Mia—" Grace said.

"It's true. He's never here. And now he's leaving for two weeks and sticking you with everything. As usual."

"Mia, please don't—" Grace tried again.

"But she's pretty used to that." Mia glared at Michael.

Something shifted in Michael's face—the careful mask dropping.

"Don't feel too sorry for your mother. She has a new toy she's having a lot of fun with these days."

"What's that supposed to mean?" Mia's gaze snapped from him to Grace. "Mom?"

"Michael, what the fuck—" Grace was on her feet before she realized she'd moved. Her chair toppled backward with a crack. She flung her napkin onto the table and fled the room.

Upstairs, she slammed the bedroom door hard enough to make the wall shudder. She locked herself in the bathroom, sat on the closed toilet lid and sobbed, hands shaking on her knees.

Mia had heard. She'd heard Michael say Grace had a "new toy." She'd heard Grace swear. She knew something was seriously wrong.

After a while, when her breathing had steadied and the tears had stopped, voices drifted up from the driveway. Car doors slammed, an engine started.

She went to the top of the stairs. Silence. Downstairs, the dining room lay abandoned—food congealing on plates, napkins crumpled.

In the kitchen, a note in Mia's handwriting waited next to a stack of dirty dishes.

Gone for ice cream.

Rancatore's, probably.

Grace moved quickly, almost frantically. Rinsing dishes, stacking plates, wiping counters as if restoring order could fix what had fractured.

Then she grabbed her coat and keys. She didn't care where Michael and the kids were or when they'd be home. She needed to see Allie.

Ten minutes later she was on Allie's porch, heart racing in the cold.

Allie opened the door holding a glass of wine. Her cheeks were pink, eyes slightly glazed.

"Grace?" she asked. "What— what're you doing here?"

"I couldn't stand thinking of you here alone," Grace said. Her voice sounded raw in her own ears.

They looked at each other for a beat.

Then Allie stepped back. "Come in."

Grace shut the door behind her.

"Your family—" Allie started.

"I am so pissed at Michael right now," Grace cut in. "I cannot fucking wait for him to be gone."

Allie's eyebrows rose, but she didn't press. She led Grace into the living room. Two wine bottles sat on the coffee table—one empty, the other on its way. Allie poured her a glass."Want to talk about it?" she asked.

Grace exhaled. "If I start, I'll just get worked up again." She took a long gulp. "I just... needed to be here."

They settled side by side on the couch, their hands finding each other without any ceremony. The silence between them wasn't empty; it was ballast.

After a while, Grace asked, "What time did Mark pick up the kids? Two?"

Allie nodded.

Grace touched her cheek. "I'm so sorry you've been alone all afternoon. What've you been doing for five hours?"

She lifted her glass in a tiny salute. "Mostly this." She said, her voice slightly slurred. "And some shitty Lifetime movie."

"And you'll be alone again tomorrow," Grace said.

"It'll only be the first half of the day. I've decided to go up to my sister's in Portsmouth. Texted her right before you knocked. I'll stay until Friday. Mark's dropping the kids back here that afternoon."

Relief loosened something in Grace's chest. "Good. I'm glad you'll be with them."

Allie squeezed Grace's hand. "Will you and Matt and Mia come over here on New Year's Eve? Celebrate with us?"

Grace squeezed back. "Absolutely. That would be wonderful." She kissed Allie's cheek.

They leaned into each other then—kissing, clinging, tears starting again in both of them. At some point, Grace ended up with Allie in her lap, arms wrapped tight around each other. They stayed like that for a long time, breathing each other in, not saying much at all.

~

Christmas morning came too bright, too loud. Grace woke to Matthew's voice in the hall.

"Mia! Wake up! It's Christmas!" His voice cracked—at twelve years old, a brittle thing. Part boy, part stranger.

Grace dragged herself out of bed, shrugged into her robe, and went downstairs. Michael was already in the living room, coffee in hand, smile set in place like something he'd put on along with his sweater.

Matthew tore through his pile. When he hit the telescope box, his whole face opened. Mia moved slowly, peeling tape, folding paper. The new phone earned a real smile. She spent twenty minutes transferring apps and texting Chloe.

Grace unwrapped a mug from Matthew: WORLD'S BEST MOM in cartoon font. She held it in shaking hands.

Around 9:00, Grace went to make another pot of coffee, forcing herself into each familiar movement. She watched Michael move into his one unshakeable Christmas tradition: his pancakes. Batter, blueberries, flip, repeat.

"Grace?" Michael was looking at her. "I asked if you wanted blueberries."

She realized she'd been staring. "Sure. Blueberries are fine."

He poured batter onto the griddle, added berries, flipped them. They moved around each other, polite and careful.

Around one o'clock, Grace was loading the dishwasher when the doorbell rang.

"Mia, can you grab that?" she called, hands dripping.

She dried them on a dish towel and moved toward the foyer, expecting a neighbor with cookies. Through the sidelight, she saw Allie on the porch, breath puffing white in the cold, collar turned up against the wind, a bouquet of red roses and white lilies in one hand, and in the other, a glass baking dish containing what looked like a coffee cake.

Mia opened the door.

"Hi!" Mia said, surprise warming her voice.

"Merry Christmas," Allie said. "I brought you something." She lifted the flowers and dish. "Your mom home?"

"She's right here," Mia said, stepping aside as Grace came forward.

"Hi," Grace managed, her voice tight. "What a surprise."

"Merry Christmas," Allie said again. "I'm driving up to New Hampshire and wanted to drop these off on my way."

Mia lingered in the doorway, eyes bright. "Come in. It's freezing."

"I don't think—" Grace began.

Before she could finish, Michael appeared at the top of the stairs. He took in the scene—Allie on the porch, Grace and Mia at the door—and his face hardened.

"Jesus Christ," he said. Then he turned and walked back down the hall.

Grace's vision blurred. She could feel Mia watching her.

"Come in for just a second," Mia was insisting. "You're going to freeze."

"Mia, it's okay," Grace said quickly. "Allie can't stay."

"Sorry," Allie said. "Bad timing. I don't know what I was thinking."

Grace stepped past Mia, took the flowers and the coffee cake from Allie and passed the dish to her daughter. "Thank you," she said. "This is thoughtful of you."

They stood there for a beat.

"Come on," Grace said. "I'll walk you out."

On the curb, Allie opened the driver's side door. The air was sharp with cold. They huddled close, using the car as a shield.

"This was a bad idea," Allie said. "I was looking at the gifts the kids gave me before they left for Mark's and I just— I couldn't sit in that house alone anymore. I wasn't thinking. I'm sorry."

"Don't say that." Grace shook her head. "I'm glad you came. I just wish you could stay—but ..."

"Yeah," Allie said.

"As soon as I drop Michael at the airport Thursday morning, I'll drive up to Portsmouth," Grace said. "We'll have lunch. Just us. Text me your sister's address."

"You don't have to—"

"It's only an hour," Grace said quickly. "I want to."

Allie searched her face. Then nodded. "Okay. I'll text it."

"I love you," Grace said.

"I love you, too, Gracie. So much." Allie's voice wavered. "Merry Christmas."

They kissed. A real kiss—three, four seconds. Long enough that if anyone looked out a window at that exact moment there would be no question what they were seeing. She didn't care anymore.

When she came back inside, the house felt quiet. Too quiet. Where was everyone? Where was Mia?

She rounded the corner into the hall.

Mia was waiting for her.

"It's Allie, isn't it?" she said.

"What's Allie?"

"She's what Dad was talking about last night," Mia said. Her voice shook but her gaze didn't. "And who you've been waiting to tell me about."

Grace's stomach knotted. She grabbed Mia's wrist and tugged her into the den.

No more deflecting. No more *someday*. Mia was asking point-blank. Grace had to tell her.

She closed the door behind them, the latch clicking loud in the small room.

42

———————

Thursday, December 28

The drive to the airport Thursday morning was silent except for NPR droning from the radio, something about post-holiday retail sales. Michael sat in the passenger seat with his carry-on at his feet, staring out the window at the gray morning. Grace kept her hands at ten and two, her focus on the road.

They were almost to Logan before Michael spoke. "Take care of the kids," he said.

"I always do."

He looked at her for a long moment. His mouth opened, then closed. He shook his head and climbed out, slammed the door.

What had he been about to say? *I'm sorry? Don't fuck this up while I'm gone?*

She watched him disappear through the sliding doors, then pulled away. Christmas was over. Michael was gone. She turned up the radio and smiled.

Portsmouth's downtown was busy three days after Christmas. But Grace found parking on Market Street and walked two blocks to the restaurant Allie had suggested—a small bistro with an Edith Piaf song drifting from the ceiling speakers.

Allie was at a corner table and stood when she saw Grace. They hugged.

"Hi," Allie said against Grace's hair. "I'm so glad you're here."

They pulled apart and sat down across from each other. The waiter appeared, took their drink orders—hot tea for Grace, wine for Allie—and left them alone.

"You made it," Allie said. "How was the drive?"

"Easy." Grace reached across the table, took Allie's hand. "How are things at your sister's?"

"Chaotic. Her kids are six and eight, so it's constant noise and energy. But it was nice to be around family. To not be alone."

"I'm sorry you had to spend Christmas without Emma and Noah."

"That's divorce. You trade off. We had a lovely Thanksgiving with them, and next year I'll have Christmas." Allie squeezed Grace's hand. "How was your morning? Getting Michael to the airport?"

"Tense. Silent."

The server returned with the wine and tea. They both ordered Salade Niçoise, and then they were alone again.

Grace concentrated on Allie's face. "Mia knows. About us."

"She said something to you?"

Grace nodded. "Christmas Day, after you left. She said, straight out: 'The woman— your attraction. It's Allie, right?' And I had to tell her."

"I'm so sorry. For showing up like that. Impulsive and stupid and—"

"Don't." Grace's voice was firm. "Don't apologize for wanting to see me. But the timing ..." Grace exhaled. "It forced a conversation I wasn't ready for."

"Oh, Grace—"

"Really, don't worry about it. Mia needed to know. And she said she's been putting pieces together for a while. I just wish I'd been the one to choose when."

Allie was quiet for a moment. "How did she take it?"

"Better than I deserved. She wasn't angry. More like ... intrigued at seeing both of us in a different light."

"And you? How are you?"

Grace removed the tea bag from the cup. "Terrified. Relieved. Guilty. The usual cocktail."

"Well, you told me she already knows you and Michael are in couples therapy. She's smart. It won't take her long to land on the obvious conclusion—that I'm the reason your marriage is ending. I don't like the thought of that."

"Allie—"

"Really, Grace. That's a lot of weight to put on any future relationship she and I might have."

"What can I do about it?"

Allie looked into the middle distance. "I don't know. But I wish it weren't the case."

A silence.

Grace laid her napkin on the table. "Excuse me a moment. Ladies' room."

When Grace returned, their food had arrived, and Allie apparently had chosen to change the vibe. "Tell me something good. Nothing about Michael or the kids or any of this."

Grace smiled. "Like what?"

"I don't know." Her eyes scanned around. "How about your favorite Christmas memory from when you were a kid?"

Grace's eyes searched the ceiling. "My grandmother made Irish Christmas pudding—dense, boozy, full of spices. I used to sneak chunks from her fridge. She died when I was in college. I never learned the recipe."

"That's sad."

"It is. But also nice. It'll always be special and perfect because it's gone."

"That's very Proustian of you," Allie said with a smile.

"Minus the seven volumes."

They ate slowly, savoring both the meal and the time together. They talked about Allie's sister's kids, the latest snowfall predictions. Nothing that mattered, but all of it a welcome pressure release.

When they finished eating, Grace paid the check—insisted on it, even when Allie protested—and they walked out into the cold afternoon. The sky was still gray, threatening snow but not quite delivering.

"Do you have to leave right away?" Allie asked.

"I should. I told the kids I'd be home by two or so."

"That gives us a little time."

"Yeah. I don't want to say goodbye yet," Grace said.

"Then don't. Come to my car for a few minutes. Just around the corner."

Grace followed her to where Allie had parked her car on a side street. They climbed in, and immediately Allie reached for Grace's face, pulled her close, kissed her. Grace moaned and kissed her back. They struggled to get closer in the front seat.

"This is ridiculous," Allie said against Grace's mouth.

Forty-two years old and making out in a car.

Grace got out, then into the back seat. Allie laughed and climbed over the center console. She straddled Grace's lap.

Grace's hands went to Allie's hips, steadying her, and then they were kissing again—deep, urgent.

"I've missed you," Grace said between kisses. "God, I missed you."

"I know. Me too."

Grace's hands slid under Allie's sweater, warm against her skin. Allie arched into the touch, her breath catching.

This was insane. Grace didn't care.

"Grace." Allie's voice was rough. "We should—"

"I know. I know." But Grace didn't stop kissing her. Didn't stop moving against her.

"You're going to kill me," Allie said.

"Good."

They kissed long past the point when the windows had fogged up. Allie finally shifted off Grace, and they both released a small, embarrassed laugh.

Back in her own car, Grace sat in the driver's seat for a moment, trying to collect herself, trying to calm her racing heart. She could still feel Allie's hands on her skin, could still taste her.

She pulled out her phone. 2:16. Shit. She'd be over an hour late getting home. The kids would ask where she'd been.

She started the car and headed south, back toward Boston, back home. But for now, she held onto the feeling of Allie's lips on hers, her hands.

She almost missed her exit, swerving at the last second, heart pounding.

Jesus. Distracted. Reckless. *Get it together.*

When she pulled onto their street, it was 3:37. Later than she'd planned. Michael's car was in the driveway. It had been in the garage when they left for the airport. Did he not go? Her stomach dropped.

Grace's knees were weak as she opened the back door and stepped inside. She could hear voices from the living room. The kids. And Michael.

Grace stood in the foyer, coat still on, heart hammering.

Had he told them already?

43

Grace's legs were wooden as she stepped into the mudroom, shrugged off her coat. Maybe his flight was canceled. Maybe he forgot his ID. Maybe—

She turned the corner into the living room. Michael on the couch, Mia and Matthew on either side of him, all three faces turning toward her. Grace froze.

Michael's face was stone.

"Dad's home," Matthew said. "He didn't go."

She stared at Michael, watching the muscles in his face flex, his hands curl into fists on his knees.

"Where've you been?" His voice was low, controlled.

She could lie. Say she'd been running errands, had a client, anything. But what was the point? And she was so tired of lying.

"I drove to Portsmouth," she said, meeting his eyes. "To see Allie."

Michael nodded slowly, as if he'd expected this. "I figured you were with her."

"What are you doing here? You're supposed to have been on a plane to Baltimore."

"I couldn't make myself get on." Michael's voice was tight. "All the way to the gate, I kept thinking you'd bring that woman into this house the minute I left. Into their lives. The thought made me sick. So I turned around and caught an Uber home."

Grace flinched at "made me sick." Her mouth opened.

"What's going on?" Matthew's voice pierced into the tension. "Why are you talking about Allie like that?"

She took a deep breath and crossed to the armchair across from the couch. "Your dad and I need to tell you something. We've been seeing a marriage counselor. Trying to work through some problems."

"We know you have problems," Mia said. "That's obvious."

"Right." Grace swallowed hard. "Well, we've decided we can't fix them. We're going to get a divorce."

Matthew's eyes widened. Mia stared at her, her face unreadable.

"Am I going to have to move?" Matthew asked.

The question cracked something in Grace's chest. She moved to him, dropped to her knees, and took his hands. "No, sweetie. No." She shot a glance at Michael. "We haven't worked out all the details yet. But this will still be your house."

He held on to her tighter than she expected. He finally let go. When he pulled back and looked at her face, he startled a bit, as if remembering something. "Wait. I still don't understand the thing about Allie."

Grace looked at Michael. He looked away. *This is your problem. You explain it.*

She looked at Mia. Nothing.

She turned back to Matt. "Allie and I have been spending a lot of time together for the past few months, and ..." How to say it? What can he hear? "Matty, your dad and I love you and Mia more than anything in the world. And nothing is ever going to change that."

Matt's eyes moved between Grace and Michael, as if by looking hard enough, he might find something understandable.

"But sometimes the feelings that bring grown-ups together ... they change. My feelings for your dad have changed. So we're going to live apart. But we'll still love you and Mia with all our hearts."

Michael's face was icy. "You still haven't told them what Allie has to do with this." He was going to make her do this. Right here. Right now. In front of them.

Matthew agreed. "Yeah, what about—"

Mia erupted. "Jesus, Matty. Don't you get it? Mom's in love with Allie."

Grace's breath left her. Her fifteen-year-old daughter had just outed her, said the thing she couldn't.

Matt's eyebrows knitted tight. "But she's— a woman."

"Duh," Mia said.

Matt's brows shot up. "Wait— so, you're gay?" He stared at her. Then at Michael. Then back at Grace. He looked like someone trying to solve an optical illusion. "I don't get it," he said quietly.

"I know, sweetheart. It's a lot."

His eyes darted around the room, then back to her. He said again, "You're *gay?*"

"I— I'm ..." She paused. "Yes." She looked away, then back at him.

"The important thing for you to know right now is that your dad and I don't work as a married couple anymore. And I can be a better mom if I'm honest with myself about that. With all of you."

Matty's eyes filled with tears. For the first time in this conversation, Mia's were wet, too.

Grace looked at Michael. His face was icy, but something underneath it had cracked—the look of a man who'd pulled the pin and now realized he was still in the room.

She needed to get them out of there. Away from Michael. Where she could talk to them without the shrapnel from his anger cutting them all.

Grace tapped each of them on the leg. "You know what? I think it would be a good idea for the three of us to go somewhere—just us —and talk about this some more. I bet you're hungry. How about we go get pizza?"

To Michael, she said, "We'll be back later."

~

Matt wanted to go to Tony's, the place with the arcade. Grace wanted someplace quieter, where they could talk without having to raise their voices.

Twenty minutes later, they were sliding into a corner booth at Matteo's, the kind of place with checkered tablecloths and, in summer, a chalkboard promising *Local Arugula,* as if that might make people feel more virtuous about scarfing down cheese.

A server appeared almost immediately.

"Two margheritas, one with mushrooms," Mia said.

"Half pepperoni," Matt added. "But like … the good pepperoni."

Mia immediately began shredding her napkin into precise strips while Matt constructed an elaborate fort out of sugar packets and parmesan shakers.

"Mom, watch this," Matt announced, balancing a red-pepper-flake container on top of his structure. "It's the Leaning Tower of Pizza."

Mia groaned. "That doesn't even make sense."

"It makes perfect sense. It's a tower. Made of pizza stuff. In a pizza place."

Grace watched them bicker.

The pizza arrived, and they fell into their usual rhythm. Matt provided running commentary on everything from the cheese-to-sauce ratio to his theory that pepperoni was actually a vegetable since it came from animals that ate grass.

Grace decided not to unpack that logic.

Mia managed two slices—a victory.

As Matt was launching into his third explanation of why pineapple on pizza was "scientifically wrong," Grace said, "I'm sure you two have questions for me, and I thought it might be easier to do this without your dad around. So, what do you want to know?"

Mia said, "Why didn't you tell me? That day we walked Fresh Pond. Why didn't you just say it then?"

"I wasn't ready." She reached over and squeezed Mia's hand. "I think you can understand that, sweetie, if you think about it."

After a while, Mia nodded.

Matt said, "So, can we go back to what's going to happen to us? If you and Dad get divorced? This is really screwed up."

"I know, honey. It's scary. And I'm sorry we don't have all the answers for you right now. Dad and I hadn't expected to deal with it today, so we're a little off balance."

"You don't know anything?"

"One of us will move out. You'll have two homes, like a lot of kids you know. Like Emma and Noah." She paused. "I promise your dad and I will do everything we can to make this as easy on you as possible. I know it hurts. It's going to hurt for a while. But we love you. And we'll get through this."

Matt nodded. He was silent for a long moment, then he looked up at Grace. "Do you kiss? You and Allie?"

He wasn't judging. Just trying to understand.

"Jesus, Matty," Mia said.

He raised his shoulders in defense. "Well …" He trailed off.

Grace took Matt's hand. "Yes. We do. I like kissing her. I love her, Matty. She makes me happy. But Allie isn't why Dad and I are splitting up. That's happening because our marriage stopped working."

"Yeah. Okay, I guess. But, I still don't understand how you can just start loving a woman after being married to Dad for so long. Our science teacher said gays are born that way. But you're old."

Mia snorted.

Grace laughed, too. She squeezed his fingers. "Sorry. Not

laughing at you, kiddo. It's just funny. I am old. ... Well, here's the truth. Some people figure it out when they're young. Some people—like me—take a lot longer. There's no rule about it."

Mia was folding a napkin into triangles, the way she did when trying not to chew her cuticles. She looked up at Grace, shrugged and said, "You know what? Fuck it." She turned to Matthew. "You might as well know: I'm gay."

She was doing it. Right now. Coming out with Grace.

Matt snorted his Pepsi. "What're you talking about? You're not gay."

"I am. Chloe's my girlfriend. We've made out. On my bed. With you in the next room."

"No, you haven't."

"Have so."

Matthew looked to Grace, who raised her eyebrows and pressed her lips into a thin line. She nodded.

He said to Grace, "You knew about this?"

"Only recently," she said.

"Oh, my god. What's going on around here?"

Mia looked at Grace and laughed, then back at Matthew. "There's some bad chemical in our drinking water." She leaned toward Matty, her eyes big, expectant. "So it's only a matter of time before you start having feelings for Jake."

"Eww. No!"

Grace said, "Okay, you two. I'm glad you're laughing. But listen, Matty— I'm happy Mia told you. And I'm proud of her for being honest about who she is."

He shrugged. "Yeah. I guess that's cool."

"And if Mia gets shit from some kids at school for this, that's just a sign that they're ignorant, not that there's anything wrong with her. Your dad and I love her unconditionally; nothing about her could ever change that." She paused, then winked at Matty. "Same with you and Jake."

Matty laughed, but his mind already had moved on to his next thought. "Tyler in my class has two moms. They came to career day. One's a doctor, and one fixes computers. They seemed totally normal."

Mia let out a frustrated groan. "That's because they *are* totally normal, dumbass. Are you even listening to her?"

"Unnecessary, Mia," Grace said.

"Yeah, well ..."

Matt said, "Can we go? I want to play with that new Minecraft module you got me."

They stopped for ice cream on the way home.

When they got to the house, Grace opened the garage door and saw that Michael had moved his car in there.

On the kitchen counter, there was a note from him:

After thinking it through, I decided to go to Baltimore after all. My staying here right now would be harder for all of us. Got a seat on a 7:35 flight.

I'll be back the weekend of Mia's birthday. And will call every day.

Love you all.

Dad / Michael

They all read it. The kids left the room. She read it once more, crumpled it, then dropped it in the trash.

Upstairs, she could hear the kids in their rooms—Matthew's video game music, Mia on the phone with Chloe.

Two weeks. Just her and the kids.

44

Sunday, December 31 - New Year's Eve

Matt pressed the doorbell, and the three of them waited on Allie's porch, their breath visible in the crisp air. Allie swept the door open and hurried them in from the cold.

"Come in, come in. Emma and Noah are in the living room."

Emma popped up from under a throw blanket. "Mia!"

Mia lifted a hand in greeting.

Noah and Matthew exchanged a slight raise of the chin.

The house smelled like popcorn and rosemary; music murmured from the kitchen. Holiday lights were looped across the mantle. Cozy.

Grace handed over the brownies. "Homemade," she said.

"Fancy," Allie teased. "I bought two frozen pizzas, so between the two of us we're hosting like competent adults."

Soon, Mia and Emma were passing Emma's phone back and forth, shrieking with laughter at a TikTok. Noah and Matthew sprawled on the rug, arguing over which Mario Kart track to race.

Grace didn't care what they were discussing; she was just relieved they weren't sulking or fighting.

"What can I do?" Grace said.

"How about slicing these limes?"

As Grace worked, she realized this was the first New Year's Eve she could remember where she wasn't at home, waiting for Michael to get back from the hospital, then asleep by ten-thirty because there was nothing else to do.

The blender roared to life. Grace poured the lime juice in, watched it swirl green and white.

Allie came up behind her and placed her hand on the small of Grace's back. The contact sent a familiar current through Grace's body.

"It's good to have you here. I've missed you." Allie filled two glasses, handed one to Grace. Their fingers brushed. "You've had a rough few days. You deserve to relax."

They clinked glasses. The margarita was perfect—tart and cold, and so strong Grace's eyes watered slightly on the first sip.

Allie leaned her hip against the counter, watching Grace with an open fondness that still caught Grace by surprise.

"I've thought a lot about how this might go. The kids. You and me. I know it won't always be easy, but ..." Allie exhaled. "Seeing them all together like this? It feels possible."

Allie looked so hopeful. Young, almost.

Grace reached for her hand.

"Mom—" Matthew appeared in the doorway.

At the sight of him, Grace dropped Allie's hand. A guilty reflex.

The look on Allie's face—shoulders pulling in, breath catching, smile not reaching her eyes—was worse than any accusation.

She opened her mouth. To say what? There was no explanation that would make it okay.

Allie shook her head slightly.

"Yes?" Grace said to Matthew.

"Noah says Toad and Yoshi are gay. That's not even a thing in the game. Tell him."

"I also said our moms are dating," Noah yelled from the living room. "That actually *is* a thing."

A beat.

"We know, Noah," Mia said flatly, from somewhere Grace couldn't see.

Matthew rolled his eyes. "That's not the point. The point is Toad and Yoshi—"

Grace went to Matthew. "Honey, I have no idea who or what you're talking about."

Matty rolled his eyes again. "How can you not know?"

Allie laughed. "Come on, Matty. I'll settle this. Your mother knows nothing about video games."

"Not true," Grace protested. "I played Pac-Man in college."

"Pac-Man." Allie shook her head, grinning. "Jesus, you're old."

"I'm only two years older than you."

"And yet somehow ancient." Allie said.

The women followed Matthew back to the living room. Allie launched into an interpretation of Mario Kart characters' ambiguous or non-existent genders that soon had both boys tuning out.

When their eyes had glazed over, she pivoted. "Okay, who wants to help me with snacks? We've got—let me see—chips, salsa, those little pigs in blankets from Trader Joe's—"

"I'll help," Mia said, standing up.

Grace blinked. Mia volunteered to help with food prep approximately never.

In the kitchen, Mia pulled plates from the cabinet without being asked, while Allie arranged the pigs in blankets on a baking sheet.

"How's Chloe?" Allie asked, sliding the tray into the oven.

"Fine, I guess." Mia's voice had gone flat.

"You guess?"

Mia shrugged, focusing intently on opening a bag of tortilla chips. "She's been kind of distant lately. I don't know. Whatever."

Grace opened her mouth to ask more, but Allie caught her eye and gave a small shake of her head. *Let it go.*

"Well, if you want to talk about it," Allie said lightly, "I'm around. I know what it's like when someone you care about goes weird on you."

Mia glanced up. "Yeah?"

"Oh yeah. High school relationships are brutal. College ones too, honestly. Pretty much all relationships are brutal." Allie grinned. "But some are worth it."

Something passed between them, some understanding Grace wasn't quite part of.

The timer dinged. Allie pulled out the pigs in blankets, golden and sizzling.

"Don't eat them yet," she warned as Matthew and Noah materialized like hungry bears. "They're molten-lava hot."

"Worth it," Matthew said, reaching for one anyway.

"Kid's gonna burn his mouth," Allie muttered to Grace.

"Yep."

Matthew bit into it. His eyes went wide. He made a strangled sound and bolted for the sink.

"Told you," Allie called after him.

Grace laughed.

The others filled their plates and drifted back to the living room. Emma stayed behind, stacking napkins with unnecessary precision.

Grace picked up the empty baking sheet and carried it to the sink. She kept her voice low. "I know I put you in a difficult position at Thanksgiving, Emma. Asking you not to say anything to Mia and Matthew—about your mom and me.. Thank you for that."

Emma shrugged, the way thirteen-year-olds shrug when they're more moved than they want to let on. "I'm glad they know now. Glad it's in the open."

"Me too," Grace said. "Me too."

Emma grabbed a handful of chips and headed back to the living room.

Later, after pizza and brownies and a failed attempt at charades ("Noah, you can't say the word you're acting out"), the kids drifted upstairs to watch a Marvel superhero movie, leaving Grace and Allie alone on the couch.

It was now nearly 11:20.

"Can I ask you something?" Allie said.

Grace looked up. "Of course."

"I've been wondering what you're going to do when Michael gets back from Baltimore in a couple weeks. What happens then?" She looked down at her hands, then back up to Grace's eyes. "I was thinking you could stay here with me. While you figure things out."

"You know I can't do that."

Allie tilted her head.

"The kids need to see that I can stand on my own," Grace said. "And so do I."

Allie nodded. "Yeah. I knew you'd say that. But I thought I'd try. Anyway, Therese would kill you if you moved straight from your house with Michael into mine."

Grace laughed. "Yep. Therese would kill me."

After a beat, Allie said, "So, what will you do?"

Grace set down her glass. "He and I talked about it. Right after Christmas, before he left. I'm moving out. I'm the one who's changing everything, so I should be the one to go. We'll split time with the kids. At least initially, they'll probably want to stay at home most of the time, keep their rooms, their routines. But I'll get a place big enough to have them."

"That makes sense." Allie was quiet while she swirled the slushy margarita in her glass.

"I think so, yeah." Grace looked up. "Sometimes I wonder if I'm just ... taking on the punishment I think I deserve. Like I'm the bad guy, so I should be the one who has to leave."

"Are you?"

Grace considered this. "Maybe partly. But also, Michael loves the house as much as I do. He shouldn't have to lose it just because I'm the one who couldn't stay in the marriage." She paused. "And honestly? I think I need the clean break. A new space that's just mine. Not the house where we raised the kids, where everything reminds me of who I thought I was."

"Okay," Allie said. "I can understand that."

"You think I'm making a mistake?"

"No. I think you're being thoughtful about it." Allie reached over and took Grace's hand. "I just want to make sure you're not sacrificing yourself because you think that's what you're supposed to do."

"I'm not. Or, at least, I don't think I am." Grace squeezed her fingers. "Getting my own place feels like the right thing."

"When will you start looking?"

"Soon." Grace paused. "I'd like to be out by February 1st. I need to figure out what I can afford, where I want to be. Close enough that the kids can come over easily, but far enough that Michael and I don't feel on top of each other."

"That gives you some time to get through Michael coming back, figure out your budget." They sat in silence for a moment, hands still linked. "I could help you look. If you want company."

"I'd like that."

At about 11:55, the kids hurried downstairs and turned on the TV. Noah bounced on the couch with excitement. Emma had her phone out, probably texting friends. Matthew was eating another dough-wrapped hot dog. Mia sat slightly apart from the others, her face illuminated by her own phone screen.

Grace picked up her margarita from the coffee table.

Allie came to stand beside her, close enough that their shoulders touched.

On TV, the crowd in Times Square was chanting.

Ten. Nine. Eight.

Grace reached for Allie's hand.

Seven. Six. Five.

Allie's fingers laced through hers.

Four. Three. Two.

"New year, new life," Allie murmured.

One.

The TV erupted in cheers. Confetti cannons. Strangers kissing in Times Square.

Grace turned to Allie and kissed her. Brief, warm, real.

"Eww," Matthew said, without looking up from his phone.

"Happy New Year, Mom," Emma said softly, and hugged Allie from behind.

"Happy New Year!" Noah shouted, throwing a handful of tortilla chips in the air.

"Noah, what the hell," Emma said, but she was laughing.

Allie raised her margarita glass. "To 2024," she said. "To new beginnings."

Grace lifted her own glass. Their eyes met over the rims. "To new beginnings," Grace said.

Mia caught Grace's eye and gave her a small, private smile. Grace felt it land somewhere deep.

Around 12:30, Grace gathered up Matthew and Mia. Matthew was half-asleep on the couch, Mia yawning despite her best efforts to seem awake.

Allie kissed her quickly. "Happy New Year, Grace."

"Happy New Year."

As she drove home through empty streets, something in her steadied. She had a plan now. Not vague promises but actual next steps. Find a place. Move out by February. Start the life she'd been building in her head since Chicago.

She didn't turn on the radio. Matthew drowsed beside her. In the rearview mirror, Mia's eyes were closed.

45

Saturday, January 6, 2024

Grace found Matthew and Mia in the living room—Matthew on the couch with his phone, Mia cross-legged on the floor doing homework.

"Hey, guys. I'm driving down to Connecticut this morning. To see Grandma."

Matthew's head came up. Mia's pen stopped moving.

"I'm going to tell her," Grace said. "About your father and me. And about ... me."

The kids exchanged a quick glance.

"Do you want to come?" Grace asked. "We could get pizza in Mystic on the way back."

Matthew looked at Mia. Mia looked at Matthew. Their gazes held this time.

"I'm supposed to be spending the day at Chloe's," Mia said. "But I haven't heard from her. Anyway, I have lots of homework."

Grace almost asked about Chloe, then stopped herself. One crisis at a time.

"Yeah," Matthew added quickly. "And I'm supposed to go to Connor's later."

Grace didn't push it. "Okay. I'll be back by three or four."

"Good luck," Matthew said.

Mia nodded. "Tell her we say hi."

Grace took the exit for Stonington just after eleven. The drive from Belmont had taken two hours, long enough that she'd rehearsed the conversation a dozen different ways. In the best version, her mother said, "I just want you to be happy." In every other version, her mother said nothing at all.

Her mother's house sat three blocks from the water, a tidy Cape Cod with white trim and shutters her father had first painted green thirty-five years ago.

Grace sat in the car for a moment, gathering herself. Through the front window, her mother moved through the living room, straightening things.

She grabbed her purse and walked to the door.

Her mother opened it before Grace could knock. "You're late."

"Traffic on 95." Grace kissed her mother's cheek. The skin was papery, cool. "Hi, Mom."

"I made coffee. And I have that cranberry bread you like." Margaret turned and walked toward the kitchen, not waiting for a response.

Margaret Brennan was seventy-one, thin and angular. Silver hair pulled back in a bun. Cardigan, practical shoes, a small gold cross at her throat.

The house smelled of lemon Pledge and coffee. The furniture

hadn't changed since Grace's father died eight years ago. Still the mauve sectional, the glass-fronted hutch displaying her mother's good china and Hummels, the crucifix above the television. Family photos lined the mantel in matching frames.

In the kitchen, her mother was already pouring coffee into mugs Grace recognized from childhood.

"Sit," her mother said.

Grace sat at the small kitchen table. Accepted the coffee. Watched her mother cut two precise slices of cranberry bread, arrange them on matching plates.

"How are the children?" her mother asked.

"They're good. Matthew's playing basketball. Mia's in the school concert chorale."

"And Michael?"

Grace set down her coffee cup. "That's actually why I'm here."

Her mother's hands stilled on the bread knife. "What's wrong?"

"Nothing's wrong. Well— I told you in November we were in couples therapy." Grace took a breath. "Now we're separated. We're getting a divorce."

The silence stretched. Her mother carefully set down the knife, wiped her hands on a dish towel, and sat down across from Grace.

"I see."

That was all. Just: I see.

Grace waited.

"What happened?" her mother asked.

Grace's throat was dry. "I told him I wanted a divorce."

Her mother's expression shifted—something hardening in her eyes. "I see," she said again. "What did you do?"

Not what went wrong. What did you do.

"It's not about what I did—"

"It's always about what someone did. Or wants to do." Her mother's voice was flat, factual. "Marriages don't just end."

Grace was fourteen again, explaining a bad grade at this same table.

"The marriage was dead, Mom. It's been dead for years."

"Marriage is about commitment. The children."

"The children will be fine—"

"Will they?" Her mother's eyes were hard. "You think children are fine when their mother decides she's done and chooses to blow up the family?"

Grace's nostrils flared. "I'm not blowing up—"

"Michael is a good man. He's provided for you. Been faithful to you." Margaret's voice was steady, certain. "What more do you want?"

Grace almost laughed. *What more did she want? Everything. A life where she could breathe.*

"I want—" Grace stopped. "I don't know how to say it. I want to feel like I fit in my own life."

Her mother's lips pressed thin. "That's selfish, Grace. Marriage isn't about your comfort. It's about stability. It's about making yourself fit in order to raise your children in an intact home. I raised you to honor your commitments," her mother continued. "To put others first. To understand that marriage requires sacrifice."

"I've been sacrificing for seventeen years."

"And that's what wives do. I gave up a teaching position when your father got transferred to Hartford. Did I complain? Did I leave?"

Grace's stomach turned. All those years, watching her mother shrink herself. She remembered her mother crying in the bathroom when Grace was ten, saying she was just tired. Her father's voice from the den: *The answer is no, Margaret.*

"Would it have mattered?" Grace asked quietly. "He never saw you anyway."

Her mother's face went tight. "Your father was a good man."

"I didn't say he wasn't."

"He worked hard. Provided for us. Never raised his voice."

"He didn't have to. You never disagreed with him."

"That's not—" Her mother stopped. Set down her cup with a sharp clink. "You don't know what you're talking about."

"Don't I?" Grace leaned forward. "I watched you, Mom. My whole childhood. I watched you make yourself invisible around him. Smooth off every edge that didn't suit him—and never, ever ask for anything for yourself. And you know what I learned?"

Her mother said nothing.

"I learned that's what good women do. We disappear. We make ourselves small so everyone else can be comfortable. We call it love."

"That's enough—" Her mother stood, reaching for the plates.

"But it's not love ... it's erasure." Grace didn't let her clear the table. "And at the end, we don't even know anymore who we were. I doubt you do."

She stopped. Her mother was staring at her, face pale, mouth a thin line.

"I'm done erasing myself, done living a half-life." Grace leaned back, her hands pressed into her lap. "I'm not asking your permission," she said quietly. "Michael and I are separated and are going to divorce."

Her mother kept her eyes on her untouched cranberry bread. Finally, a small voice: "What will people say?"

"I don't care."

"You should care. This reflects on the whole family."

"Mom—"

"Your father would be ashamed."

Maybe he would be. But she couldn't live for a dead man's approval anymore.

"Is there someone else?" her mother asked suddenly. "Is that what this is about?"

Grace's eyes searched the room.

"There is." Her mother's voice turned bitter. "Of course there is. That's why you're so eager to leave. You've been unfaithful."

"This isn't about infidelity, Mom."

"Then what? You met someone and now you're willing to destroy your family for—for what? Some infatuation?"

Grace couldn't look at her. Her gaze wandered and caught on the crucifix above the TV in the other room.

She could lie. Let her mother think it was another man. Let her be angry about an affair, disappointed about the divorce. But not this. Not the truth that would change everything.

"It's not an infatuation."

"Then what is it?"

The question hung there. Her mother was staring at her, waiting.

She could soften it. Say she had feelings for a woman. Say she was figuring things out. But her mother didn't deal in nuance.

Grace took a breath. "I'm gay."

The words came out raw. Final.

Silence.

Her mother stared at her. The color drained from her face. "What did you say?"

"I'm gay." Grace's voice steadier now. "I'm in love with a woman."

Margaret stood so fast her chair tipped backward. "Get out."

"Mom—"

"What am I supposed to tell people? What do I say to Father Doyle? Her mother's voice quivered. "I will not sit here and listen to this."

Grace stood. "It's the truth."

"You have children, Grace. You can't—" Her mother pressed her hand to her mouth. "How could you do this to them? To Michael? This isn't how I raised you."

Grace picked up her purse.

"You're destroying your family," her mother said. "Your life."

"No." Grace's voice was quiet but firm. "I'm intent on having a real one."

Her mother turned away, gripping the counter.

Grace waited. Part of her wanted to apologize. To take it back. To make her mother feel better.

She didn't.

"I love you, Mom," Grace said. "But I'm not going to keep sacrificing myself to make you comfortable. If you want a relationship with me—with your grandchildren—you're going to have to accept this. Accept me."

Her mother didn't turn around.

Grace walked to the front door. Put her hand on the knob.

"Mom?"

No response.

"I hope you can find a way to be okay with this. I really do. But I'm not waiting for your permission to live my life."

She opened the door and stepped outside.

Behind her, she heard something crash.

Grace didn't look back.

She made it to the car before she started shaking. Sat behind the wheel, hands trembling, breath coming in short gasps.

Her mother's voice was still in her head. *Your father would be ashamed.*

Her phone was in her hand before she realized she'd pulled it out. She texted Allie: *Told my mother. She kicked me out.*

She tried to still her breathing as she waited for Allie's reply: *Jesus. Want to talk? I'm busy, but have a minute.*

Grace stared at the phone. She wanted to say yes. To hear Allie's voice. But she didn't want to impose: *It's alright. I'll call you when I get home.*

Allie replied: *OK. What you just did took courage.*

Grace groaned. With unsteady fingers, she typed: *If causing a shit show is courageous.*

She put the car in drive and pulled away. Through the rearview mirror, she could see her mother's house getting smaller. The white Cape. The green shutters. She turned onto the main road and was halfway to the interstate when her father's voice came out of nowhere: *Feeling like a good girl now?*

Grace gripped the wheel until her knuckles went white and kept driving.

46

Monday, January 8

Mondays often ran late for some reason. Still, Grace had hoped to pull into the driveway earlier than this. Her headlights cut across the darkened garage. Matthew's bike leaned against the house, half-buried in snow. She turned off the engine and sat for a moment, hands on the wheel.

Inside, the house was quiet. She kicked off her shoes in the mudroom and called out.

"Mia? Matt? I'm home."

"In here!" Matty's voice from the den, muffled by video game explosions.

But no sound from upstairs.

She went to the den and kissed Matty on the top of his head. Back in the kitchen, she paused. A muffled cry drifted down from upstairs.

She went up quickly, following the sound to Mia's room. The door was closed. Another muffled sob.

She knocked gently. "Mia? Sweetie."

"No!" A choked voice: "Go away."

Grace's hand was already on the doorknob. "I'm coming in, honey." She waited a beat, then slowly pushed it open.

Mia was curled on her bed, knees pulled to her chest, sweatshirt sleeves soaked with tears. Her face was blotchy, devastated. String lights looped above her desk, casting delicate shadows. Her phone was on the floor in the corner, surrounded by the broken glass of a framed picture that lay beside it.

"Mia—"

"I said go away!"

"Oh, sweetheart." Grace crossed the room, sat on the edge of the bed. "Talk to me."

Mia turned toward the wall, sobbing harder.

Grace waited, one hand resting on Mia's ankle. She didn't speak. Just sat there.

After a long moment, Mia's sobs began to slow. Her breathing hitched, then evened.

Grace shifted closer, reaching for her. "Come here."

Mia resisted for a second—a stubborn, teenage second—then sat up and collapsed against Grace's chest, the dam breaking again.

Grace wrapped both arms around her, held tight.

"Tell me what happened."

Mia shook her head, couldn't speak.

Grace waited. Stroked her hair. Said nothing.

Eventually, between gasps: "Chloe."

"What about Chloe?"

"She—" Mia's breath hitched. "She broke up with me."

"Oh, honey. I'm so sorry."

"She said—" Mia choked on the words. "She said she's in love with someone else. A girl in her math class."

Mia's whole body shuddered. "She replaced me." Her voice broke. "Like I was nothing."

Grace rocked her gently, the way she used to when Mia was small. "You're not nothing. Don't you dare think that."

"She told me she loved me," Mia cried. "She said it. And now—" She couldn't finish.

"I knew she'd get bored of me." Mia's voice had gone hollow. "I shouldn't have told her how much I liked her. I was so stupid."

Grace's arms tightened around her. After a beat, she said, "You are not stupid."

"I am. I should've known—"

"Mia, stop. Listen to me." Grace pulled back enough to see her daughter's face—blotchy, streaming—and used her sleeve to wipe Mia's cheeks. "You're not stupid for loving someone." For a second she was back in her mother's kitchen, saying I'm gay to a face turning white. "Being honest about how you feel is never stupid."

"But she left."

"I know. And that's awful. But it doesn't mean you were wrong to love her. It means she hurt you. And I'm so, so sorry about that. It's really hard, I know."

Mia dissolved into tears again, and Grace pulled her close.

Grace almost asked how Mia was processing this—then stopped herself in time. This wasn't a session. This was her daughter.

After a while, Mia pulled away long enough to grab a tissue from her nightstand, blew her nose, then collapsed against Grace again.

"Does it ever stop hurting?"

Grace kissed the top of her head. "Yeah. It does. I promise it does." She hoped that was true.

"When?"

"I don't know, honey. But it will. Not right away, but you won't feel like this forever."

Mia curled into Grace's side, the way she had when she was little.

Grace held her and stroked her hair. Her phone buzzed in her pocket. Probably Allie, wondering if she wanted to meet for a late dinner. She didn't look at it.

Mia lay down, and Grace pulled the covers over her. She stayed there as Mia's breathing evened out, as her daughter's body went slack with exhaustion.

The string lights above the desk cast shadows across the ceiling. Outside, snow began to fall again, silent against the window.

Grace watched Mia sleep—face still blotchy, eyelashes damp. She looked so young. Too young for this kind of pain.

She slipped out quietly, pulling the door almost closed. In the hallway, she leaned against the wall, suddenly exhausted. Her legs felt weak.

Her phone buzzed again. This time she looked. A text from Allie: *Hey. How was your day? Want to talk?*

She stared at the text. She wanted to call—wanted to hear Allie's voice. But something held her back. Not just Mia. But something harder to name. She was needed here. That was true. But if she was honest, it was also easier—just for tonight—to stay inside the life she knew how to navigate.

She typed: *Long day. Mia's having a rough night. Can I call you tomorrow?*

The response came immediately: *Of course. Give her a hug from me.*

Grace walked to her own room, where the bed was still unmade from this morning.

She thought about Mia, crying herself to sleep. About Matty downstairs, probably hungry. About her mother, angry and scared in Connecticut.

She sat on the unmade bed and stared at the wall.

47

———

Tuesday, January 9

Grace was between sessions, steeping her tea, when her phone rang. The number was local but unfamiliar.

"This is Grace Brennan."

"Ms. Brennan? This is Susan Porter, a guidance counselor at Belmont High. I'm calling about Mia."

Grace's hand tightened on the phone. "Is she okay? Did something happen?"

"She's fine—nothing like that. But I wanted to touch base about some concerning patterns we've been seeing. As you know, Mia is usually a diligent student. But just in the past week, three of her teachers have reported that she's missed assignments and seems disengaged."

Grace closed her eyes. Of course Mia was struggling at school. How could she not be?

"We're going through a family situation right now," Grace said carefully. "A separation. Mia's dad and I are getting a divorce. I'm sure that's affecting her."

"I understand. That's always hard on kids." The counselor's voice was kind but professional. "I just wanted to make sure you were aware, and to see if there's anything we can do to support her through this transition. We have resources available—"

"Thank you. I'll talk to her. And I'll make sure she gets the support she needs." She hung up and set the phone face-down on her desk. *How long had Mia known Chloe was pulling away?*

During a mid-afternoon break, Grace's phone lit up with a text from her brother Sean: *Mom in ER with chest pains. They're running tests. Thought you should know.*

Grace's stomach dropped. She stepped from the hallway into her office and called him immediately.

"Sean? What happened?"

"Hey. Don't panic—she's okay. They already sent her home." Her brother's voice was tired. "Cardiologist said it wasn't her heart. Just stress or anxiety or something. She wouldn't tell me what's bothering her."

Grace closed her eyes.

"When did this happen?"

"This morning. I took her in around ten. She was clutching her chest, said she couldn't breathe. Scared the hell out of me." A pause. "Grace, did something happen? She's been ... I don't know. Different. Won't talk to me."

Grace leaned against the wall. "I told her about the divorce. And some other things. She didn't take it well."

"What other things?"

Not now. Not over the phone with her brother. "I'll explain later. Is she home now?"

"Yeah. I stayed with her for a bit, but she basically kicked me out. Said she wanted to be alone." He sighed.

"Yeah. Okay. Thanks for letting me know."

Grace stared at her phone. She should call. Make sure her mother was okay. She dialed before she could talk herself out of it.

Her mother answered on the second ring. "What do you want?"

Not *hello*. Not even a pretense of civility.

"Sean told me you were in the ER. I wanted to make sure you're all right."

"I'm fine. It was nothing."

"Mom, chest pains aren't nothing. Did the cardiologist—"

"I said I'm fine." Her mother's voice was cold, clipped. "Is there something else?"

Grace's throat constricted. "I was worried about you."

"Were you." It wasn't a question. "How convenient. Worrying now, after you—" She stopped. "I don't need your worry. Or your concern."

"Mom, please—"

"I don't need phone calls from a deviant pretending to care about my health."

Grace stood very still, phone pressed to her ear.

"I don't want to hear from you, Grace," her mother continued. "Don't call here again."

The line went dead.

Grace lowered the phone slowly. Her hands were shaking.

Muffled sounds came from outside her door—Travis's voice from the hallway, someone laughing in the waiting room.

Her next client was in ten minutes. Grace went to the bathroom, splashed cold water on her face, and looked at herself in the mirror.

Her mother had been in the emergency room. With chest pains.

She dried her hands and went back to her office to review her notes.

Michael was due home Friday. Mia's birthday. Three days away.
Grace opened the file and started reading.

48

Friday, January 12th

Grace pulled out the ingredients for birthday pancakes—Mia's favorite birthday tradition, one that had begun when she was four and had insisted that chocolate-chip pancakes were "the only breakfast a princess should eat." Michael was usually the one to make them. Chocolate chips, real maple syrup, whipped cream.

Grace measured flour, cracked eggs, whisked the batter. The tradition dictated that the pancakes this year be shaped like the number sixteen, or at least a reasonable approximation. Sixteen.

The batter sizzled on the griddle. Grace flipped pancakes, arranged them on a plate with a swirl of whipped cream, scattered fresh blueberries on top. She stuck a single candle in the center— ridiculous, maybe, but tradition.

"Happy birthday, sweetheart," Grace said when Mia shuffled into the kitchen, hair tangled from sleep, face closed off.

Mia looked at the plate and managed a small smile. "Thanks,

Mom." Then her expression went flat again. She picked up the plate and turned toward the stairs.

"Mia, wait—we could eat together. Talk about your—"

"I have to finish some math problems before school."

Grace watched her daughter disappear up the stairs, heard her bedroom door click shut.

"Those look amazing!" Matthew bounded in, hair sticking up in every direction. "Can I have some? Even though it's not my birthday?"

Grace managed a smile. "Of course, honey."

He took a closer look at the pancakes. "Those don't look like a sixteen."

"They look like a one and a squiggle. Close enough."

He climbed onto a stool at the counter, attacking his snake-shaped pancakes with enthusiasm. "So what are we doing for Mia's birthday?"

"We'll probably go out to dinner, wherever Mia wants. Your dad's plane gets in around 5:00."

"But we're all going together?"

Grace nodded.

"Okay. Good."

Grace stood at the kitchen counter early Friday evening, staring at her phone. The text from Michael had come through a moment earlier: *Flight canceled. Snowstorm. They can't cope with snow here. Will try to get out tomorrow morning.*

She stared at the message for a while longer, then called up the stairs. "Mia? Matt?"

Matthew appeared first, hoodie half-zipped. "What's wrong?"

"Your dad's flight from Baltimore was canceled because of snow there. Won't be home 'til tomorrow."

Matthew shrugged. "Okay."

Mia appeared behind him, hair in a messy bun, eyes tired. "So he won't be here tonight?"

"No."

"Whatever," she said, turning away.

Twenty minutes later, Mia came into the kitchen. Her eyes were made-up with liner and mascara. Not typical for Mia. She said to Grace, "Can I go over to Emily's?"

"But it's your birthday, sweetie. Don't you want to go out to dinner?"

"Might as well wait for dad. Do that tomorrow night?"

"I guess that makes sense, sure."

"So, can I go to Emily's?"

"What's with the makeup? Unusual."

"Mom—"

Grace hesitated. She didn't know Emily. But Mia had been so miserable all week. "Okay. I'll run you over."

Twenty minutes later, Grace pulled up to a small Dutch colonial near the Watertown line. Lights on inside, car in the driveway. A wooden fence sagging from neglect.

"Emily's mom said she'll bring me home," Mia said, already unbuckling.

"No later than eleven."

"I know." Mia climbed out, paused. "Thanks, Mom."

Grace watched her walk up to the front door. A woman opened it and ushered Mia inside.

Everything looked fine.

She drove home through darkening streets, the radio off, just the sound of the engine and her own breathing.

❧

Grace and Matthew ordered pizza. Matt finished his homework, then played video games while Grace worked on session notes. She sent him up to bed at 10:30.

The curfew time passed. Grace sent Mia texts at 11:15 and 11:30. Both unanswered. At 11:40, she was reaching for her phone again when headlights swept across the living room wall.

A car door slammed. Footsteps on the walkway. Uneven, too careful. Grace opened the door.

Mia stumbled into the entryway, and Grace knew immediately. The way she moved, the careful overcorrection of her steps, the smeared makeup. Her eyes were glassy, unfocused.

"Mia? Are you drunk?"

"M'fine." Mia kicked off her shoes, nearly losing her balance.

"You're not fine. Have you been somewhere other than Emily's?"

"I was at Emily's," Mia's words slurred. "Then Sasha's. There was cake. For me." She swayed slightly. "Everyone wanted to celebrate my birthday."

Grace moved closer, caught the smell of alcohol.

"Mia, how much did you drink?"

"Dunno. Not that much. Just— Emily had vodka and some other—"

"Vodka? Jesus Christ, Mia—"

Outside, the car had finished turning around and was starting to pull away—Emily's mother, apparently unconcerned that she'd just delivered a drunk sixteen-year-old home.

Grace reached for her daughter's arm.

Mia jerked away. "Don't touch me."

"Mia—"

"I said don't!" She backed toward the stairs, misjudged the distance, caught herself on the bannister and sank down onto the bottom stair, head in her hands. Her shoulders shook with sobs.

Grace sat beside her. Not touching or speaking.

For a long time, Mia just cried—messy, ugly crying, the kind that left her snot-nosed and gasping.

"Just go."

Grace said, "I'm not going anywhere, Mia. I'm right here."

Mia's head turned slightly. After another moment, she leaned—just barely—against Grace's shoulder. Grace put her arm around her.

"You're the one person who's never supposed to leave," Mia mumbled, then looked at Grace, as if realizing what she'd said. She hiccuped. Wiped her nose on her sleeve. "Why can't things just—why can't everything be normal again?"

"I know, honey. I know." Grace kept her voice steady. "But right now, you need to get upstairs. Are you going to be sick?"

"I— I don't think so." Mia pulled away, tried to walk on her own. She made it three steps before Grace had to catch her again.

Grace helped her upstairs, got her into bed, put a trashcan beside her nightstand. She brought water, ibuprofen.

"Drink some of this," Grace said. "You'll feel awful tomorrow if you don't."

Mia took the water, drank obediently. She curled on her side, eyes already closing.

Grace sat on the edge of the bed, watching her daughter's face fall into sleep.

Downstairs, Grace sat on the couch in the dark. She started a text to Allie, then stopped.

Tomorrow she'd have to deal with this—figure out who Emily and Sasha were, whether this was a one-time mistake or something worse. Tomorrow she'd talk to Mia about Chloe, about heartbreak, about better ways to handle pain.

Tonight she just sat in the dark, too tired to cry, too upset to sleep. Upstairs, the house was silent. Both her children sleeping. One of them with a trashcan by the bed.

49

Saturday, January 13

Michael's Uber pulled up just after 11:00 AM. Grace watched from the front window as he climbed out, hauled two suitcases from the trunk, looking rumpled and tired. She opened the door before he could knock.

"Hi."

"Hey." He stepped inside, set his bags down. For a moment they stood there, uncertain. Then Michael pulled her into a brief, awkward hug. She patted his back once, stepped away.

"How was the flight?"

"Sat on the runway for an hour." He rubbed his face. "I'm sorry about last night. Missing her birthday."

"I know you are. The snow wasn't your fault."

Matthew pounded down the stairs. "Dad!"

Michael caught him in a proper hug. "Hey, Matty. Good to see you."

"Glad you're home."

"Where's the birthday girl?" Michael asked.

Grace chose her words carefully. "She's still in bed. Not feeling great this morning."

"Is she sick?"

"Something like that." Grace glanced at Matthew, then back to Michael. "Why don't you get settled? I'll make coffee."

"Sounds good." Michael grabbed his bags, but turned back toward her. "Thanks for the help choosing her gift. Did it arrive?"

"It did. I wrapped it and put it in the guest-room closet. Under a pillow case."

Michael smiled. "Thank you. ... Matt, want to help me unpack?"

After they disappeared upstairs, Grace went to the kitchen and started a fresh pot of coffee. Her hands were shaking slightly. She'd been awake most of the night, sitting in the dark, replaying Mia's drunken sobbing on the stairs.

Why can't everything be normal again?

Ten minutes later, Michael came back down alone. "Matt's playing his game. What's going on with Mia?"

Grace poured two mugs of coffee, handed him one. "You might as well sit. We need to talk."

Michael's expression shifted to concern. He sat at the kitchen table. "Okay."

Grace sat across from him. "Mia's been having a rough week. Chloe broke up with her on Monday."

"Oh." Michael set down his mug. "That's— well, that's hard. First breakup."

"She's been devastated all week. Crying. Withdrawn. And yesterday was her sixteenth birthday, and you weren't here."

"The flight was canceled. I couldn't control—"

"I know. It wasn't your fault. But from her perspective, her dad wasn't there on her sixteenth birthday. That happened the same week as her first girlfriend dumped her. Her parents are divorcing. And she doesn't know how to handle any of it." *Might as well get it out there.*

"She came home drunk at 11:40 last night, Michael. So drunk she could barely walk."

"What?" He stood up abruptly, coffee sloshing. "Is she— did something happen? Was she—"

"She'll be okay. She was with Emily and Sasha, friends from school. Emily's mom dropped her off here."

"Jesus Christ." Michael sat back down heavily.

"She could barely stand. Slurring her words. She—" Grace's voice caught. "She sat on the stairs and cried. Said she wanted everything to be normal again."

"Did she mean before Chloe or before the news about us?"

"I don't know. Maybe both." Grace wrapped her hands around her mug. "I got her to bed, made sure she had water, a trash can. She passed out pretty quickly."

"Where did they get alcohol?"

"Emily had vodka. I don't know where from. I haven't talked to Mia about that yet; she was too drunk last night, and she's still sleeping it off."

Michael was quiet for a long moment. When he spoke, his voice was tight. "What do we do?"

"We talk to her. Both of us. We make sure she knows this isn't acceptable, but we also—" Grace paused. "We need to find out what's going on with her."

"She got drunk because her girlfriend broke up with her."

"Yeah, I know, Michael. For god's sake. I've been dealing with it all week." Grace ran her hand through her hair. "But it's also about us divorcing ... and having to come out to us before she was ready." She stopped. "And I'm sure my own— my own stuff is affecting her. It can't not."

Michael looked up at her. "Her getting drunk isn't your fault, Grace."

She stared at her coffee. She wanted to believe that. "I'm saying there are lots of reasons for the pain she's in." Grace sighed. "Poor kid. She made a bad choice because she didn't know what to do with all that pain."

Silence settled between them.

"I should talk to her," Michael said. "When she wakes up."

"Yeah. But Michael—" Grace met his eyes. "Don't try to fix her pain about Chloe. Don't minimize what she's feeling. Just listen. Just be there."

"I've been told I'm not very good at that."

"Well, you haven't been." She didn't cushion it. "But she needs you to try."

Michael nodded slowly.

Around 1:30, Grace heard movement upstairs. She was folding laundry in the living room when Mia soon appeared at the bottom of the stairs, looking like death—hair tangled, face pale, yesterday's mascara smudged under her eyes.

"Hey," Grace said. "How are you feeling?"

"Like I'm dying." Mia said, coming into the living room.

"That would be the hangover." Grace kept her voice neutral. "There's ibuprofen on the counter. And you should drink water."

Mia made her way to the kitchen. Grace heard the tap running, the rattle of the pill bottle.

Michael appeared in the doorway from the den. He and Grace exchanged a look.

Grace said, "Okay. Go ahead. But listen. And be gentle." She moved into the den, so as not to intrude, but she kept the door open as Michael headed to the kitchen.

Matthew came downstairs and asked Grace where they were going for Mia's birthday dinner.

"Don't know yet, Matty. And we may wait until tomorrow."

He went back upstairs, and by the time Grace tuned in to what was being said in the kitchen, the conversation was underway. She couldn't make out every word, but she tracked the rhythm—Michael's steady tone, Mia's shorter responses—and got most of it. Michael must've started by saying he was sorry to hear about Chloe. Grace moved a step closer.

"—not saying you should be over it," Michael said. "I'm just saying, you're young. There'll be other relationships."

"Dad, you don't understand—"

"I do understand. I remember high school. These things feel huge at the time, but in five years you won't even—"

"You're trying to make me feel better by telling me it doesn't matter. But it *does* matter. She matters."

"I didn't say she doesn't matter. I said there will be other—"

"See? That's exactly what I mean!" Mia's voice cracked. "You don't get it. You don't get any of it."

"Mia, I'm on your side here—"

"Then act like it! Stop trying to make me feel better and just—" A sob cut off whatever she'd been about to say.

Silence. Grace held her breath.

Then, quietly, Michael said, "I'm sorry, Mia. You're right. I'm not doing this very well."

More silence. She could picture him standing there, arms crossed.

"Your mom told me about last night. The drinking," Michael said. "We need to talk about that."

"Do we have to do it now?"

"Yes."

Grace wanted to be there for that part of the conversation. She moved to the kitchen doorway. "Hi, sweetie," Grace said, when Mia glanced her way. "Did you get some more ibuprofen and water?"

Mia nodded, then said, "I know I shouldn't have been drinking." Her face flushed. "It was stupid."

"It was more than stupid. It was dangerous." Michael said, his

tone firm. "You could've gotten hurt. Or really sick. Do you understand that?"

"Yes." Mia's voice was small.

"Was it because of Chloe? Is that why you got drunk?" Michael
asked.

"I don't know." Mia's voice cracked. "Everything just—everything is awful. And Emily said vodka would help. But it just made it
worse, and I—" A sob escaped. "I just wanted to feel better for one
night. Just one night where I didn't feel like everything was falling
apart."

Michael looked helpless. Grace could see him struggling, wanting
to fix it and not knowing how.

"Come here," Grace said.

Mia hesitated, then moved to her. Grace pulled her into a hug.
Mia cried. Not the ugly, drunk crying from last night, but quieter,
sadder.

Michael came and stood beside them. "We're sorry about Chloe,
Mia. We know that really hurts. And I'm sorry I wasn't here yesterday," Michael said. "For your birthday."

Grace blinked.

Mia looked up, wiped her nose with her wrist. "It's okay," she
responded. "The snow wasn't your fault."

"Maybe not. But I still wish I'd been here."

They stood like that for a while, Mia crying into her mother's
shoulder while her father patted her back.

Mia pulled away, wiping her face again. "Am I grounded?"

Grace exchanged a look with Michael, then said, "Yes. Two
weeks. No going out except school. And I need to meet Emily's
parents before you can go there again. Got it?"

"Yeah." Mia said quietly.

"And we're going to talk more about the drinking," Michael said.

Grace pushed the hair out of Mia's face and said, "Go take a
shower, sweetie. You'll feel better."

Michael added, "And if you're feeling well enough by evening, we'll go out for your birthday dinner."

After Mia went upstairs, Grace said to Michael. "Thank you."

Savino's was busy on this mid-January Saturday evening—families celebrating, couples on dates. Occasional bursts of laughter came from the bar. Grace sat across from Michael, with Mia and Matthew on the table's other two sides.

"The salmon special looks good," Michael said, studying his menu with intense focus.

"I'm getting pasta," Matthew announced.

Mia said nothing, her thumb scrolling through her phone beneath the table.

"Mia," Michael said gently. "Can you put the phone away? Just during our meal?"

Mia looked up, eyes flat. "Why? So we can all pretend this is a normal family birthday celebration?"

Grace picked up her water glass. "Your father asked you to put it away."

"Fine." Mia let the phone fall to her lap like a mic drop, but without the self-satisfaction. "Happy now?"

The waitress appeared. "Good evening, everyone. Can I start you off with some drinks?"

"Scotch, neat," Michael said. Then he glanced at Mia, caught himself. "Actually—on second thought, just an iced tea."

The waitress left after taking the rest of their orders. Silence settled over the table again.

Matthew filled it with chatter about a science project and Connor's new puppy. Grace watched him trying so hard, and had to look away.

The food arrived. Mia picked at her chicken parm, while

Matthew demolished a plate of spaghetti. Grace poked at her chicken piccata and tried to remember the birthday speech she'd rehearsed. But sitting here, watching Mia's closed-off face, feeling the weight of Michael's careful distance, all the words felt useless.

Michael set down his fork. "Mia, I know yesterday wasn't what you wanted. And I'm sorry I wasn't here."

Mia shrugged. "You already said that."

"I know. But I mean it." He paused. "And I'm sorry about being away for the past two and a half weeks. I shouldn't have gone, when things are so tough for you two." His glance took in both Mia and Matthew. Grace hadn't expected that.

The moment hung there—fragile, imperfect, but real. Grace felt a rare surge of warmth toward him.

Then the server appeared with a small cake, a single candle flickering. "Birthday celebration?"

The restaurant staff gathered around to sing. Mia's face went scarlet, but this time Grace saw something else beneath the embarrassment—gratitude, maybe. Or just relief that the heavy moment had passed.

Matthew joined in enthusiastically. Michael sang in his careful way. Grace's voice caught, but she pushed through.

"Make a wish!" Matthew said.

Mia stared at the candle, her face illuminated in the warm glow. Then she bent forward and blew out the flame.

"What did you wish for?" Matthew asked.

"If I tell you, it won't come true." Mia's voice was warmer now, the edge gone.

Grace watched smoke curl up from the extinguished candle.

Michael produced a small wrapped box. "Happy birthday, Mia."

She opened it carefully—a delicate silver bracelet, simple and pretty.

"It's beautiful," Mia said, and this time the smile reached her eyes. "Thank you, Dad."

"Your mom helped me pick it out," he admitted.

Grace slid her own gift across the table—the new headphones Mia had been wanting.

Mia's face lit up as she pulled off the wrapping. "Oh my god, Mom. These are perfect."

Matthew gave her a gift card to Starbucks, grinning. "I know, I'm super creative."

Mia actually laughed. "Thanks, Matty." She reached over and ruffled his hair. He swatted her hand away, but he was smiling.

50

Thursday, January 18

Grace was forty minutes into a session with a client—a woman navigating her own messy divorce—when her phone vibrated on the table next to her chair. She'd silenced it, as she always did during sessions, but she saw the screen light up with an incoming call.

Then it lit up again. And again.

"I'm so sorry," Grace said, glancing at the phone. Belmont Middle School. Her stomach dropped. "I need to take this. Just one moment."

She stepped into the hallway, her heart already racing. "This is Grace."

"Ms. Brennan? This is Jim Andrews, principal at Belmont Middle. I'm calling about Matthew."

Her mouth went dry. "What's wrong? Is he hurt?"

"He's okay now, but he had an episode during English class. He couldn't catch his breath, said his chest hurt." The principal's voice was calm, measured—the voice of someone who'd dealt with things like this before. "His teacher brought him to the nurse. We called EMTs as a precaution, but by the time they arrived, he'd started to calm down."

"EMTs?" An ambulance. For her twelve-year-old.

"It appears to have been a panic attack, but obviously we wanted to be cautious. He's in the nurse's office now. Physically he's fine, but he's pretty shaken up. Can you come get him?"

"I'll leave now. Be there within a half hour."

Grace went back into her office, apologized to her client, explained there was a family emergency. The woman was understanding. Of course she was. She had kids, too; she knew how these things went. Grace rescheduled, grabbed her coat and bag, and reached her car within five minutes.

The drive to the school took eighteen minutes, seemed like an hour. Grace gripped the steering wheel, imagining Matthew on the floor, unable to breathe. In an ambulance.

She parked crookedly in a visitor spot and half-ran to the main entrance.

The nurse's office smelled like antiseptic and old carpet. Matthew sat on the vinyl examination bed, small and pale, his legs dangling. When he saw Grace, his face crumpled slightly before he caught himself and looked away.

"Hey, honey." Grace went to him, put her hand on his shoulder, then hugged him. He was trembling. Still scared. Still in his body. The panic attack was hours ago, and he was still shaking.

"How are you feeling?"

"Okay." His voice a hush.

The nurse—a woman in her fifties with kind eyes—stepped forward. "He's doing much better now. Heart rate and blood pressure are normal. But I'd recommend following up with his pediatrician, just to rule out any underlying issues."

"Of course. Thank you so much." Grace looked at Matthew. "Ready to go home?"

He nodded, sliding off the bed. His backpack sat on the floor. Grace picked it up—it was heavier than she expected, stuffed with textbooks and binders—and guided him toward the door.

In the hallway, Principal Andrews was waiting. "Matthew, you did a good job telling Ms. Graham you needed help. That was very brave."

Matthew stared at his sneakers.

"We'll follow up with his doctor," Grace said. "Thank you for taking care of him."

They drove in silence. Grace kept glancing at him—his profile against the window, the way he was picking at a loose thread on his jacket. He looked like the little boy who used to crawl into her lap.

"Do you want to talk about what happened?" Grace asked gently.

Matthew shook his head.

"Okay. We don't have to."

More silence. Grace navigated through afternoon traffic, her mind spinning. A panic attack. Matthew had never had anxiety like this before.

They pulled into the driveway. Matthew got out before Grace had turned off the engine, heading straight for the back door.

"Matthew, wait—"

But he was already inside, the door closing behind him.

Grace sat in the car for a moment, trying to breathe normally herself. Then she followed him inside.

❧

Around 5:30, Matthew emerged from his room and was sitting at the kitchen table doing homework, as if nothing had happened. Grace chopped vegetables for dinner—chicken stir-fry, one of Matthew's favorites—and tried to find the right words.

"How's the homework going?" she asked.

"Fine."

"Anything I can help with?"

"No." After a while, he asked, "Will Dad be home for dinner?"

"I don't know, sweetheart. I know he's pretty busy at the hospital after being away. I haven't heard from him."

Matt nodded.

Grace heated oil in the wok, put in the diced chicken, and tried to focus on the rhythm of cooking instead of the fear still thrumming in her chest. The pediatrician's office had squeezed them in for tomorrow morning. She'd canceled her early sessions. She'd figure out what was happening, get him whatever help he needed.

Behind her, she heard a sound—small and choked. She turned. Matthew was still at the table, pencil in hand, shoulders now shaking. A tear dropped onto his math worksheet, spreading across the page.

"Matty?"

He looked up at her, and his face crumpled completely. "Are you really leaving?"

"Oh, sweetie—" She went to him and pulled him into her chest.

"Are you?"

"Matty ... yes, honey. I'm going to move, yes. But I'm—"

"When?" His voice cracked.

"I don't know exactly. Once I find a place."

"I want you here. I want things to stay the same."

"I know, honey. I know you do."

"So why can't you?" The question came out sharp, almost angry. "Why can't you just stay? You and Dad don't even fight that much."

She and Michael had been so civil, so careful. How could she explain to her twelve-year-old that a marriage could die with a whimper?

"It's complicated, Matthew."

"That's what adults always say when they don't want to tell you the truth."

She flinched. "You're right. That's not a fair answer." She took a breath. "Your dad and I— we haven't been right together for a long time. And I couldn't keep pretending we were."

"But I don't care if you're happy!" Matthew's voice rose, desperate. "I just want you here! I want things to be normal."

"I know." Grace pulled him close again. "I know that's what you want. And I'm so sorry I can't give you that."

"Are you leaving because you don't want to live with us anymore?" His voice went small again, muffled against her shoulder.

"What? No. Matthew, no—"

"Then why are you leaving?" The words came out broken. "If you still want to be our mom, why can't you just stay?"

"I told you. Because I can't stay married to your father. But that doesn't mean—"

"But you're choosing to leave us." He said it flat, factual. And somehow that was worse than the crying. "You're choosing to not be here."

He was right. She was leaving. She was choosing this.

Matt went on. "And I know you'll still be our mom or whatever, but it won't be the same. You won't be here when I wake up. You won't be here when I go to bed. Everything's going to be different and I can't—"

"You're right, sweetie. Things will be different. But I'll find a place close by. You'll have your own room there. We'll set the schedule so that you have lots of time with me. And you can come over whenever else you want."

Some of the anger drained out of him, and he collapsed against her again, sobbing.

Grace held him.

After a long moment, Matthew's voice came out small and desperate: "I'll be better. I promise I can be better. I won't complain about chores or fight with Mia or need you for stuff. I can be more independent. Just please don't go."

"Matty, stop. Listen to me." Grace tilted his face up to see his eyes. "You don't need to be better. You don't need to change anything. This isn't about you."

"Then why does it feel like I'm being punished?"

"Because I'm your mom and you feel like I'm choosing to hurt you. I'm not trying to hurt you, Matty. But I can't stay married to your dad. And I know that hurts you, and I'm so, so sorry."

Matthew stared at her for a moment, looking older, like he'd aged years.

Then he buried his face in her shoulder again and just cried. Not the desperate, gulping sobs from before. Quieter now. Exhausted.

Grace held him and let him cry, her own tears falling into his hair.

Eventually his breathing slowed. His body went slack with exhaustion.

"I'm scared," Matthew murmured.

"I know."

"What if it happens again? At school."

"A panic attack?"

He nodded against her.

"We're going to see Dr. Martinez tomorrow. She'll help us figure out what's going on and how to make it better. Okay?"

"Yeah." But he didn't sound convinced.

Grace turned off the stove—the chicken was ruined—and ordered pizza instead.

When Mia came down, they ate on the couch watching a movie Matthew picked—something animated about talking cars or robots; Grace couldn't tell which and didn't care. Matthew sat pressed against her side the whole time.

At nine o'clock, Grace sent him upstairs to get ready for bed. She threw away the burnt stir-fry and wiped the counter twice, because it was something she could do.

Her phone buzzed with a text from Allie: *Miss you. Here if you want to talk.*

Grace stared at the message. She still hadn't responded to Allie's text from two days ago. She missed her, too. But she was so exhausted. And adding to that was a quiet fear: that Allie's patience wasn't infinite. That there were only so many unanswered texts before "miss you" stopped coming.

Grace replied: *Can't right now. Matthew's having a hard time.*

She turned off her phone, started the dishwasher, and went upstairs.

51

Saturday, February 3

The scent of fried bacon hung heavy in the air. Mia picked at the strips, pulling away bits of fat she didn't want. Then she wiped her fingers on a paper towel and started scrolling through her phone. Michael was at the hospital. Matthew was upstairs, ostensibly doing homework, but Grace knew he was just escaping the tension in any room Mia occupied.

At first Grace had chalked Mia's silent distance up to the divorce announcement, to Chloe dumping her, to Mia needing time to process those traumas.

But then, the previous evening, Mia had been on the phone in her room, the door not quite closed. Her voice had stopped Grace cold in the hallway.

"Yeah, my mom's gay too. ... No, like three weeks after I came out. ... I know, right? ... It's like I can't even have my own thing. Everything has to be about her."

Grace had stood in the hallway, stomach turning. The tone in

Mia's voice—like a girl whose best friend had seen her prom dress, then gone out and bought the exact same one.

Through the night, she'd thought about the way Mia wouldn't meet her eyes. The way she'd stiffen when Grace mentioned Allie's name. Maybe Mia's coldness had to do with Grace's own revelation.

"Mia," Grace began, leaning across the counter now. "Can we talk for a minute?"

Mia sighed but lowered the phone to the counter. Her eyes remained fixed on some point above Grace's head.

"I've been thinking a lot about everything," Grace said. "About how hard this must be for you. Finding out I'm gay so soon after you ..." She trailed off.

Mia's lips drew into a line.

"Maybe you feel I took your moment. Unintentionally made it about me instead of—"

"Did you practice this with your therapist?" Mia interrupted, her voice flat.

Grace's hand stilled on her coffee mug. "No. I'm trying to tell you I understand."

"Oh, you understand?" Mia scoffed. "Because you're a therapist, right? So you can just figure out what's wrong with me and fix it?"

"No. It's not about fixing you. It's about acknowledging—"

"Acknowledging what?" Mia pushed her plate away. "That my entire life feels fake? That every time I remember this family being happy—like, actually happy—I wonder if you were just pretending? Because if you were lying about being straight, what else were you lying about? Loving us?"

"Mia, I wasn't lying to you. I didn't *know*. If I was lying to anyone, it was to myself."

"Does that make it better?" Mia's voice rose. "Because it doesn't feel better, Mom. It feels worse. At least if you knew, you were choosing something. But you're telling me you just ... what? Sleep-walked through our whole lives? What am I supposed to do with that?"

Grace's eyes filled. "I don't know. I'm trying to—"

"And before long, I'm going to have to deal with everyone at school knowing my mom left my dad for a woman. I can't imagine what that's going to be like. I'm already dealing with people whispering, 'She's gay.' Now I'll be the queer girl with the gay mom who blew up her family." Mia's voice cracked. "It's too much. I can't— I don't have room for all of this."

"I'm so sorry," Grace whispered. Tears blurred her vision.

Mia stared past her, unblinking, then pushed her chair back with a scrape. "Yeah. Well ..." Mia stood, grabbing her phone. "A lot of fucking good that does me."

Grace struggled to keep the tears at bay as she drove to Newton Center for lunch with Stephanie. They were meeting at Sycamore, a bistro on Beacon Street. Stephanie's choice.

Grace sat across from her at a corner table, the lunch crowd thrumming around them. She'd texted her friend right after the kitchen drama with Mia—*Can you meet today? I need to talk*—and Stephanie had responded within minutes: *Noon. Sycamore. I'll be there.*

Stephanie looked good—a shorter hair cut, new glasses that suited her. She was studying Grace with the frank assessment only an old friend could get away with.

"Jesus, Grace. You look terrible."

Grace let out a startled laugh. "Thanks."

"I'm serious. When's the last time you ate? Actually ate, not just picked at something while standing at the sink?"

"I don't know. I had coffee this morning."

"Coffee isn't food." Stephanie was still looking at her with that worried expression. "You're too thin. I can see your collarbones through your sweater. And you have circles under your eyes that look like bruises."

The server appeared. Stephanie ordered a burger and fries without looking at the menu. Grace started to say she wasn't hungry, then caught Stephanie's glare and ordered a turkey sandwich.

Once the server left, Stephanie leaned forward. "Okay. What happened? You sounded awful in your text."

The tears came immediately. Grace told Stephanie about the overheard phone call the night before and the conversation with Mia that morning—her attempt to acknowledge that her own coming out might be hard for Mia, and her daughter's pushback.

"And then she said that soon everyone at school is going to know her mom left her dad for a woman, and she's already the gay kid, and now she's going to be the gay kid with the gay mom who blew up her family." Grace's voice broke. "She said it's too much. That she doesn't have room for all of it."

Stephanie's expression shifted, the worry lines easing. "Grace, stop." She reached across the table. "Take a breath."

Grace wiped her eyes with her napkin. "I'm sorry. I shouldn't have dumped all of this on you the second we sat down."

"Are you kidding? That's literally what best friends are for." Stephanie squeezed her hand, then let go. "But I need you to hear something. And you're not going to like it."

Grace braced herself.

"Mia is sixteen. She's hurt and angry, and she's going to say things that devastate you. That's what sixteen-year-olds do when they're in pain. They go for the jugular. Christ, I have the scars to prove it." Stephanie paused. "But you can't let a sixteen-year-old's anger convince you that you've ruined her life. Because you haven't."

"But the timing—"

"The timing sucks, yes. She learned your marriage is ending and that you're queer right after she came out. And that's hard for her.

But Grace, if you'd come out a year from now, it would still be hard for her. If you'd come out when she was twelve, it would've been hard. And don't let her pull this 'blow up the family' line on you. Your marriage is ending and your family is reconfiguring. But it's not gone."

Grace stared at her hands. "She said everything feels like a lie. That she can't trust her memories."

"Of course she did. Because she's a sixteen-year-old girl. Everything is high drama and feels like the end of the world. I'll spare you the shit Zoe says to me."

The server arrived with their food. Grace looked at her sandwich.

"Eat," Stephanie said, already biting into her burger. "I'm serious. You look like you're about to blow away."

Grace picked up half the sandwich and took a small bite. It was good—she hadn't realized how hungry she was.

"I just keep thinking," Grace said after a moment, "that if I'd stayed in the closet, if I weren't divorcing Michael, Mia could have had a normal coming out. Her own thing. Without me complicating it."

"You think Mia's coming out would've been easier if you stayed miserable?" Stephanie raised an eyebrow. "Because I promise you, kids know when their parents are unhappy. Even when the parents think they're hiding it. *Especially* when the parents think they're hiding it."

Grace took another bite of sandwich. Chewed slowly.

"Look," Stephanie said. "I'm not going to tell you this isn't hard for Mia. It obviously is. But you know what would be worse? Raising her to believe that it's better for you to stay small and hidden so other people don't have to feel uncomfortable."

"That's what my therapist said."

"Then your therapist is smart." Stephanie set down her burger and wiped her hands. "So, tell me about Allie."

Grace looked up, surprised by the shift. "What about her?"

"I want to hear about her." Stephanie's eyes were warm. "Grace, you're upending your entire life for this woman. Make me understand why. I get that she sees you. And that you can be yourself with her. But give me a specific. Tell me something about how she makes you happy."

Grace set down her sandwich. "She has this way of making boring things feel like adventures. Back in September, we happened to bump into each other at Whole Foods. She talked me into abandoning my cart and walking Fresh Pond with her. But first, she drew me into this crazy competition with each of us searching for the weirdest-looking vegetable in the produce section. We were laughing so hard the produce manager came over to make sure we were okay."

Stephanie laughed. "I like her already. What was the winning vegetable?"

"Romanesco."

"Oh, absolutely. So weird." Stephanie took a bite of burger, pointed at Grace. "Does she know how thin you've gotten? How exhausted you are?"

The smile faded. "I don't know. Maybe. I've been canceling plans. Three times in the last ten days. Twice because Mia couldn't get out of bed. Once because Matthew had another panic attack. So, I haven't been showing up for her the way I should."

"Grace—"

"I know. I know I'm messing this up. I just—" Grace's voice caught. "I don't know how to be what everyone needs right now. The kids need me to be their mother. Michael needs me to be civil. Allie needs me to actually show up. And I feel like I'm failing at all of it."

"You know what I think Allie needs?"

"What?"

"For you to not disappear." Stephanie leaned forward. "You're so busy trying to minimize the damage to everyone else that you're destroying yourself in the process. And nobody wins when you do that. Not the kids, or Allie. Or you."

Grace nodded, not trusting her voice.

"When's the last time you saw her? Actually spent time with her?"

"Outside of the office? Probably two weeks ago."

"That's not good. Call her. Go see her. Not to talk about logistics or timelines or any of that. Just to be with her." Stephanie paused. "She's why you're doing this. Don't lose sight of that while you're trying to manage everyone else's feelings."

"Yeah. But now I'm scared that I've already waited too long. That she's done being patient."

"All the more reason you need to see her soon." Stephanie ate her last fry. "But first, finish your sandwich. Because I'm serious, Grace. You look like you haven't eaten in a week, and I'm not leaving until you finish that food."

Grace picked up the second half of her sandwich. Took a bite.

They sat in companionable silence while Grace ate. When she'd finished, Stephanie ordered them both coffee—decaf for Grace, "because you need to sleep at some point"—and a slice of chocolate cake to split.

"I miss this," Grace said quietly. "Just sitting with you. Talking."

"I miss it, too." Stephanie's voice was affectionate. "I miss my best friend. I feel like I've been talking to the crisis version of you for months. I want the real you back."

"I don't know if I know who that is anymore."

"Well, you'd better figure it out. Because Allie fell in love with her. And your kids need her. And frankly, so do I."

The cake arrived. They both dug into it.

When they'd paid the check, they walked out together into the cold February afternoon. Stephanie pulled Grace into a tight hug.

"You have to let yourself have Allie. Go see her," she said into Grace's ear. "Promise me."

"I promise."

"Good. Love you," Stephanie said.

"Love you, too."

Grace watched her friend walk to her car, then got into her own. She sat for a moment, phone in her hand. Then she opened her texts and found Allie's name. She typed: *Can I come over? I miss you.*

A minute passed, then a reply: *God. Yes. Tomorrow evening? Kids leave at 5:00. Come at 7.*

52

Sunday, February 4

Sunday evening, Grace sat at the curb in front of Allie's house for a full minute before shutting off the engine. She chewed the inside of her lip. Her recent cancellations were trying Allie's patience. She understood that, so she braced herself, uncertain what sort of greeting she was going to get tonight.

When she got to the porch, the front door opened before Grace could knock. Allie looked hopeful, a little nervous.

"Hi. Sorry I'm late. Matthew needed—"

"It's okay." Allie stepped back, brushing a a wave of hair away from her face. "You're here now and I'm glad you made it." She took Grace's coat, and disappeared briefly into the kitchen. When she returned, she carried two glasses of wine—deep red, already poured.

Grace smiled weakly. "Thank you."

They sat on the couch. The lamp beside them threw warm light.

"How are you?" Allie asked, and there was something careful in her tone. "You look exhausted."

"I am. It's been—" Grace rubbed her eyes. "Mia stayed home from school twice this past week. Won't talk to me. The school counselor called again Friday. Her English teacher is concerned about a paper she turned in—something about death and impermanence that was 'unusually dark.'"

Allie's face turned tender. "God, Grace. No wonder you look tired. And you're losing weight."

The screen on Grace's phone lit up: two texts from Matthew.

She read them, then laid it on the cushion beside her.

"Everything all right?" Allie asked.

"Yeah. Matthew, just checking in." Grace reached for her wine. "He's been clingy lately."

Allie was quiet for a moment. "Is Michael helping? With Mia and Matthew?"

"He's trying. He's been talking to Mia more. Still his awkward self, but he's trying. He was there when Matthew came home after his second panic attack. And he helped me find therapists for both of them." Grace set down her wine. "He's showing up more than he used to. But it's still mostly me, dealing with the hard stuff. The nightmares, the not eating, the texts."

Allie was watching her, and Grace could feel the weight of that gaze—loving, but also measuring something.

"I've missed you," Allie said quietly.

"I've missed you too. So much."

"Have you?" Allie's voice stayed gentle, but something sharp edged underneath. "Because you've been here for fifteen minutes, and that's the first time you've really looked at me."

"That's not—"

"You checked your phone twice before we sat down." Allie paused. "You're here, but you're not really here."

"I'm sorry. It's just—" Her phone buzzed against the cushion. She glanced down reflexively.

Allie saw it. Said nothing.

"I'm sorry," Grace said again, more firmly this time. She picked up the phone, set it on the coffee table face-down. "Okay. I'm here. I'm present."

Allie studied her for a long moment, then shifted closer. Her hand went to Grace's cheek, thumb brushing along her jaw. "I've been going crazy without you."

"Me too."

"Then kiss me."

Grace leaned in, met Allie's mouth. The familiar warmth, the taste of wine and something sweeter. Allie's hand slid into her hair, and Grace tried to sink into it, tried to let everything else fall away.

But her mind kept drifting—to Mia's English paper about death, to Matthew's nightmare about the house splitting in half, to—

Allie pulled back. "Where are you right now?"

Grace blinked. "What?"

"You're kissing me, but you're somewhere else." Allie's eyes searched her face. "Where did you go?"

"I'm sorry, I just—" Grace's voice cracked. She pressed her hands to her face. "I don't know how to do this."

"Do what?"

"Be here with you when everything at home is falling apart." The words tumbled out. "Mia won't eat. Matthew checks my room every night to make sure I'm there. And I keep thinking I should be looking for a place, but every time I sit down to search, something happens and I just—" Her breath hitched. "I can't keep up."

Allie pulled her close, one hand stroking her hair. "Hey. It's okay. You're doing your best."

Grace let herself be held for a moment, breathing in Allie's familiar scent. Then she pulled back enough to see Allie's face.

Something in Allie's expression made her stomach drop. A kind of weary sadness.

"What's wrong?" Grace asked.

"Nothing. It's just—" Allie looked away. "I know you're overwhelmed. I can see it. But Grace, I need you too. And lately it feels like—" She stopped herself.

"Like what?"

"Like I only get the parts of you that are left over. After everyone else has taken what they need." Allie's voice was quiet. "And there's not much left."

Grace felt tears burning. "I don't know how to give you more right now. I'm barely holding it together as it is."

"I know." Allie reached for her hand, held it. "And I'm not trying to make it harder. I just—I miss you. I miss us."

"Me too."

They sat there, hands clasped, the weight of everything unsaid pressing down.

"When you're ready," Allie said, "when you have space to actually start looking—I can help. We can look together. That might make it less overwhelming."

"Yeah. Okay." Grace squeezed her hand. "Soon. I promise."

Allie nodded, but something in her eyes suggested she'd heard that promise before.

Grace's phone buzzed on the coffee table. They both looked at it.

It buzzed again.

"Go ahead," Allie said quietly. "Check it."

"No, I—"

"Grace. Just check it."

Grace picked it up with shaking hands. Two texts from Matthew: *can u come home*

and *i dont feel good. think I'm gonna puke.*

She looked at Allie. "I have to—"

"I know." Allie's smile was sad, resigned. "Go."

"Michael's there. I could text him to—"

"Grace. You're already standing. Your coat is already in your hand." Allie's voice was gentle but firm. "Just go."

Grace stood frozen for a moment, torn between the woman on the couch and the child at home who needed her.

"I'll call you tomorrow," Grace said.

"Okay."

Grace leaned down, kissed her forehead. "I love you."

"I love you, too." Allie picked up her wine glass.

Grace stepped out into the cold. Her hands were shaking.

Behind her, through the window, she could see Allie still on the couch, wine glass in hand, not watching her leave.

Grace got in her car and drove home through dark streets, her chest sore like something had broken.

When she went inside the house, Michael was coming down the stairs. "He's okay now. We did the breathing exercises together. Took about fifteen minutes but he settled."

"Oh." Grace felt simultaneously relieved and oddly displaced. "Good. That's— good."

"He still wants to see you, though." Michael's expression was rueful. "I think he texted you because he wanted you home, not because he couldn't manage without you."

Grace went upstairs. Matthew was sitting on his bed, looking guilty.

"Hi, Mom."

"Hey, honey. Dad said you guys did the breathing together."

"Yeah. It helped." He picked at his comforter. "I'm sorry I made you come home."

"You didn't make me do anything. I wanted to come check on you." She sat beside him. "But were you actually feeling sick, or did you just want me here?"

Matthew's face flushed. "I felt bad at first. But then after Dad helped me, I felt better. But I—" He looked up at her. "I still wanted you to come home."

"Why?"

"I don't know. Because you're Mom." His eyes filled with tears. "And when you're not here, I start thinking about— about after. When you move out."

"Oh, Matt." Grace pulled him close. "I know this is scary. But when I move out, you're still going to see me all the time. And Dad— did you notice how he helped you tonight? He knew exactly what to do."

"Yeah."

"And, honey, you have to start trusting that you'll be okay when I'm not here. That's what Dr. Reeves is helping you work on, right?"

Matthew nodded against her shoulder.

Grace stayed with him until he fell asleep. Then she went downstairs to where Michael was at the kitchen table, his laptop open.

"Thank you," she said. "For helping him."

"Of course." Michael looked up. "Though I'm not sure it helped. He still wanted you."

"He'll adjust. We all will." Grace sat down across from him.

Michael closed his laptop. Sat for a moment looking at his hands. Then: "I was thinking about the night of Bryan and Katie's anniversary dinner. Remember? We were supposed to go together, but Mia had that ear infection and you said you'd stay home with her. And I just— I went. Didn't argue or offer to skip it. I told myself you'd offered, so it was fine." He paused. "But you volunteered because you knew I wouldn't. And I let you." He shook his head. "There were a thousand moments like that. Weren't there?"

"There were," Grace said. "And I won't pretend that didn't matter. But Michael—" She paused, choosing her words carefully. "Even if you'd been present for every school play, every dinner, every hard conversation, I don't think it would've changed where we ended up. Because the problem wasn't just us. It was me. I was living a life that wasn't mine. I just didn't know it yet."

Michael was quiet for a moment. "I thought we were fine. I thought that's just what marriage looked like after a while. Comfortable. Separate but together."

Grace nodded slowly. "That's exactly it. We got along. We coexisted. But there wasn't anything underneath. We never built the necessary emotional foundation."

Michael laid his hands flat on the table. "Grace, if you weren't attracted to Allie, would we still be having this conversation?" The question landed between them, honest and direct.

Grace thought about it. "I think so. Eventually. Maybe not this month or this year, but yeah. Because the underlying truth—who I really am—was there, and not going to change."

Michael was quiet for a long moment. Then: "What's it like? Being in love with her?"

Grace hadn't expected that question. "Why are you asking?"

"Because I want to understand. What we didn't have. What I couldn't do for you." He met her eyes. "I'm not trying to make you feel guilty. I just— I want to know."

She thought about how to answer honestly. "It's like I've been partially deaf my whole life and didn't know it. And then suddenly I could hear. Everything's louder, clearer." He picked up his laptop, stood. Paused. "Grace?"

"Yeah?"

"I'm sorry I wasn't what you needed. And whether or not it's with Allie, I hope you find what you're looking for."

"Thank you," she said.

She listened to his footsteps climb the stairs, heard the guest room door close.

Grace turned off the kitchen light and went upstairs. She brushed her teeth, washed her face, got into bed. The sheets were cold.

53

––––––

Monday, February 12

The microwave's turntable clicked, rotating Grace's leftover soup, no doubt heating it to a scald.

A shadow crossed the doorway. Grace looked up. Allie stood there, lunch bag in hand, frozen mid-step. Their eyes met. For a moment, neither moved. Grace opened her mouth to say—what? *Hi? Good timing?*

But Allie's expression was closed, careful. She gave a small, tight smile—the kind you'd give a colleague you barely knew—then turned and walked away. Footsteps climbed the stairs; her office door closed with a click.

Twenty minutes later, Grace's phone lit up on her desk with a text from her: *Can we talk? Today?*

She stared at the three words. Her hands went cold around her coffee mug. Outside her office door, a phone rang and voices murmured greetings. The sounds went muffled and distant.

She started three replies before managing: *Yes. When?*

Allie's response read: *4:30? Brew & Co. on Mass Ave?*

Someplace public. Neutral.

Grace typed: *Okay. I have a 3:30. Should be there by 4:45*

The coffee shop was half-empty when Grace arrived at 4:40, the after-work rush not yet begun. Allie sat at a corner table, staring out the window, hands wrapped around a mug.

Grace ordered a tea she didn't want and crossed to her. "Hi."

Allie looked up. Her eyes were exhausted, grief written in the lines around them. "Hi. Thanks for coming."

Grace sat, cupping her mug for something to do with her hands.

"How was your day?" Allie asked.

"Fine. Busy." Grace's thoughts raced. "Allie, what's going on?"

Allie took a breath, set down her coffee. "I can't keep doing this."

"Doing what?"

"I love you," Allie said. "But I can't survive in this limbo anymore. You're not in your marriage, but you're not out of it either. And we're not together. I'm just waiting. And it's breaking my heart."

"You think I don't know that? You think this isn't killing me, too?"

"I know it is. I can see how much you're struggling." Allie's voice was gentle now. "But Grace, it's been almost two months since you told the kids. Michael's been back for a month. And you still haven't looked at a single rental. You still haven't taken one concrete step toward actually leaving."

"Because every time I try, something happens. Mia can't get out of bed, or Matthew has a nightmare, or—"

"That's what I'm realizing." Allie's voice was sad but firm. "Every week there's a new reason. First it was the holidays. Then Chloe. Then Mia getting drunk. Now Matthew's panic attacks. And those are all real, Grace. But you're using them as reasons to stay stuck."

Grace looked at her. She's been keeping track. Not cruelly—she could hear that. But carefully. The way you keep track of things when you're trying to survive them.

"That's not fair," she said anyway.

Allie leaned forward. "Maybe not. But it's my honest feeling."

Grace started to speak, stopped. Then: "They need me."

"I know they do. You're a wonderful mother. But you need things, too." Allie's voice was tender. "You can't keep running on empty." She paused. "And I can't keep waiting for a moment that never comes."

Allie wiped her eyes. She pressed her lips together for a moment, looked down at the table, then back up. "I need to stop seeing you for a while. No more lunches at the office. No more texts. No more late-night calls when Michael's asleep and the kids are in bed and you finally have a minute to yourself." Her voice broke. "I can't keep getting little pieces of you while you stay in that house. It hurts too much."

"Don't." Grace's hand moved across the table before she'd decided to move it. "Please. Don't do this. I'll start looking this week—"

"Grace." Allie's voice was both resolute and heartbroken. "I love you so much. But I have to protect myself. And right now, that means stepping back." She stood.

"Wait ... are we— is this over?"

"I don't know." Tears slipped down Allie's cheeks. "I hope not. I really hope not. But I can't keep watching you not choose yourself. Not choose us." She took a shaky breath. "If you move out—if you actually leave—call me. I'll be here. But until then, I need space."

"Allie, please—"

But she was already pulling on her coat, already moving between tables toward the door.

Through the window, Grace watched her disappear down the sidewalk.

She sat alone for a long time, her tea cooling in front of her. Around her, the coffee shop filled with the after-work crowd—people laughing, the espresso machine hissing. Normal life, continuing.

She gathered her coat and walked to her car. The sky had gone dark, streetlights flickering on. She pressed her hands to her face. Then she started the engine and drove home—past the Belmont library, past the playground, past all the markers of the life she'd built. The life she needed to leave.

Allie had said: "If you move out, call me."

If. As though Allie didn't believe it would happen.

It couldn't be *if.* It had to be *when.*

Grace pulled into the driveway. Through the windshield, she could see the house—lights on in the kitchen and in Mia's window upstairs.

She got out of the car and walked inside. Matthew was at the table doing homework. He looked up. "Hey, Mom."

"Hey, honey."

She set down her bag, hung up her coat, and started making dinner.

54

———

Friday, February 16

Grace knocked on Claire's open door. Claire looked up from her laptop, reading glasses perched on her nose.

"Got a minute?"

"Always. Come in." Claire gestured to the chair across from her desk. "What's up?"

Grace sat, pulling a folded photocopy from her bag. "I figured it out. Who P was."

Claire raised her eyebrows. "Sarah's letters?"

"Yeah. Paul Becker. Another therapist who used to work in this building." Grace unfolded the paper. "There are references to faculty meetings, shared clients."

"Paul Becker." Claire tested the name. "I don't think I ever met him."

"He left the building just after I arrived. Around 2014. Moved to Oregon. Never married." Grace paused. "He died in 2019."

"Oh." Claire's voice lowered. "That's sad."

"I found his obituary. No family mentioned. Just colleagues and friends." Grace held the photocopy—of Paul's final letter to Sarah, the one Claire had found tucked in the back of the stack. "I know you've already seen this, but can I read part of it to you?"

Claire nodded.

Grace read aloud: "'I can't keep being your secret. I love you, but I deserve more than stolen afternoons. More than hiding what we have. I deserve to be someone's whole life, not their beautiful secret.'"

Silence fell between them.

Claire said, "Jesus. He ended it and she just … kept his letters. Can you imagine?"

Grace set the photocopy on the desk. "I should get back to work."

"Grace." Claire's voice stopped her at the door. "Don't be Sarah."

Grace turned. Held her gaze for a moment.

"Thanks, Claire."

Grace's own therapist, Therese Hansen, had rearranged her afternoon when Grace called that morning asking if Therese had any emergency availability. Grace now sat in the leather chair across from her, the familiar cream walls, Matisse dancers, and potted fern somehow both comforting and exposing.

"Glad you called," Therese said. "What's going on?"

Grace took a breath. Therese already knew most of the story, including details of the holidays. Grace brought her up to date— Mia's breakup and decline, Matthew's panic attacks, Allie's ultimatum. When she finished, Therese was silent for a moment.

"That's a lot," she said.

"Yeah."

"What did that feel like? When Allie confronted you?"

Grace paused. "It hurt. She was right about some of it. But not all of it."

Therese waited.

"The kids do need me. That's not an excuse."

"No," Therese said. "It's not. What's the part that is?"

Grace's hands twisted in her lap. "I keep telling myself it's about them. But if I'm honest—" She stopped. "As long as I stay in that house, I can pretend I'm still the person I was before. Still married, still living the life everyone expected. But if I move out—"

"Then it's real," Therese said.

"Yeah."

"What do you want for yourself?"

Tears came. "I want to stop living a half-life. I want my kids to be okay, but I also want to be okay myself. And I want to be with Allie." The words came out raw. She looked up. "Is it selfish?"

Therese looked at her. "What do you think?"

Grace reached for a tissue. "It feels selfish when my kids are hurting. Every time I think about moving out, I see Matthew's face when he had that panic attack. Or Mia coming home drunk. And I think: how can I leave them right now?"

"Your kids are hurting because their parents' marriage is ending. That would hurt regardless of whether you stayed in the house or moved out tomorrow." Therese paused, let that land. "So what are you actually preventing by staying?"

Grace didn't answer.

"What do you think your kids are learning right now? From watching you stay?"

Grace didn't answer.

"You've told them you're leaving. You've told Michael. You've told me." Therese paused. "And every week you don't, they watch that too."

Grace stared at the tissue in her hands, now torn into strips. "But what if I'm wrong?" Her voice was small. "What if I blow up my family and it turns out I've destroyed everyone for nothing?"

"That's possible," Therese said. "People do get hurt." She let that sit. "But your marriage was already over. What are you actually preventing?"

"So what am I supposed to do? Just leave while they're in pain?"

"Moving out isn't abandoning them," Therese said. "It's changing where you sleep." She paused. "They'll still have you."

Grace looked at her hands.

"And they'll watch you do it. That matters too."

Grace wiped her eyes.

"As for Allie," Therese said, "it sounds like she set a healthy boundary."

"It feels like I'm losing her."

"Maybe you are. You can't control that." Therese's voice was matter-of-fact. "All you can control is whether you actually do what you keep saying you're going to do."

Grace sat with that.

"Why are you here right now, Grace?"

She looked up. Started to answer, stopped.

"You want someone to tell you it's okay." Therese's voice was matter-of-fact. "So I'm telling you: it is. You're not a bad mother. Your kids will survive this."

"What if I can't do it?"

"Then you can't. But I don't think that's true." Therese held her gaze. "You've already done the hard part. Most of it."

Grace wiped her face with the shredded tissue. Took a breath. Let it out slowly. Outside the window, the city carried on—cars, voices, the ordinary machinery of other people's lives.

～

Grace drove home through late afternoon traffic, Therese's words circling in her mind. Michael's car was in the driveway; he was home early. She could see him through the window at the dining table, laptop open. She sat in the car for a moment, hands on the steering wheel.

This was it. She went inside.

He looked up when she came into the dining room. "Hey. How was your day?"

"Long." She set down her bag. "Can we talk?"

He closed the laptop. "Sure."

They moved to the kitchen. Grace poured herself water, took a sip, set it down. Michael waited.

"I need to move out soon. I'm going to start looking for a place tomorrow. And I think we need to tell the kids an actual date. Not, *someday*. A real timeline."

Michael looked away quickly, but he nodded. "When?"

"April first, at the latest. Maybe March 15th if I can find something that works."

"That's—" He stopped, breathed. "That's soon."

"I know."

"The kids— Matthew's barely holding it together as it is."

"I know that, too." Grace's voice gentled. "But staying longer isn't helping him. It's not helping any of us. We're just prolonging the inevitable."

Michael turned his water glass slowly on the counter. "So how does this work? With the kids?"

"They stay here, at least for now. They keep their schools, their friends, their rooms. I find a place nearby. We split time with them."

"Where will you look?"

"Belmont, Arlington. Maybe Watertown or Medford."

"Three bedrooms?"

"Yeah. One for each of them."

He nodded. "I'll keep paying the mortgage here. And we'll figure out what's fair for support. I'm not going to make this difficult."

"Thank you," Grace said.

"What about furniture? You'll need—" He gestured vaguely. "Beds for them. A couch. Kitchen stuff."

"I'll figure it out."

"Take what you need from here. The guest room furniture. Dishes. Whatever makes sense. Just make a list. We'll sort it out."

"We'll need to figure out a schedule. I realize the usual kind of arrangements people reach aren't going to work with your life. So we may have to improvise for a while."

"Thank you," he said. "I appreciate that." Michael looked down.

After a moment, Grace said, "I think despite his panic over my leaving, Matthew is actually going to want to stay here. At least initially. In his room, his familiar surroundings."

"That may be true. And Mia—" Michael paused. "Right now she'd probably rather stay here too."

Grace looked at the counter.

"But she'll come around." He pointed to a piece of chocolate cake, covered in plastic wrap on a small plate. "She saved that for you."

"She did?" The glow inside Grace was small, but there.

Michael smiled and nodded. He was quiet for a moment. "She loves you, Grace. She's just—"

"Having a hard time with everything. I know." Grace set down her glass. "She talked with me for a while the other day. Asked why I didn't just go live with Allie. I told her the only people I'm interested in living with right now are her and Matty."

"What did she say?"

"Nothing. But I got a small smile. The first in a long while."

Silence stretched between them.

"Let me know what you need," Michael said. "For the deposit, first month. Whatever."

"I will. Thank you." She paused. "I can cover a lot of it. But, yeah. That'll help."

He picked up his laptop, stood there for a moment. "Make sure you find something good. Somewhere safe. As close to here as possible."

"I will."

He nodded once, then left. Footsteps on the stairs. Guest room door closing.

Grace stood alone in the kitchen for a moment. Then she went to the living room, found her laptop on the couch where Mia had left it the night before. She opened it. Stared at the blank search bar.

Her fingers hovered over the keys. She typed: *3 bedroom rental houses Belmont Arlington Watertown MA.*

Then she took a breath and clicked search.

Listings filled the screen. The first one had hardwood floors, three bedrooms. $4,800/month. She clicked through the photos—updated kitchen, small backyard, rooms for her kids when they visited.

She pulled up a listing and started filling out the contact form. The cursor blinked. She typed her name into the first field. Then went on to the next.

55

Saturday, March 16

The kitchen cabinets were half-empty, mugs and plates already wrapped in newspaper and packed into boxes. Grace poured her coffee into the mug she'd kept out to use today—the one Matthew had made at camp and always made her smile. She looked at the boxes stacked against the walls. Dishes. Books. Clothes folded into suitcases. Seventeen years, sorted and labeled in black marker.

Around 8:00, Michael left to pick up the U-Haul. Grace found Matthew sitting on the stairs, still in his pajamas, staring at nothing.

"Hey, honey. You're up early."

He looked up at her with red-rimmed eyes. "Couldn't sleep."

Grace sat down next to him, her coffee going cold in her hand. "Me neither."

They sat in silence for a moment, shoulder to shoulder on the stairs.

"Dad should be back by 9:00 with the truck," Grace said.

Matthew nodded. "I know." He picked at a loose thread on his pajama pants. "Did you know that moving trucks use like twenty percent more gas than regular cars? I looked it up."

"I didn't know that."

"Yeah. It's because of the aerodynamics. The box shape creates more drag."

She put her arm around him. He leaned into her slightly, still talking about fuel efficiency.

At 8:55, Michael came through the front door.

"Fresh pot of coffee there," Grace said.

He poured himself a cup. "Kids up?"

"Matthew is." She glanced at the stairs. "Mia's still in her room."

Michael set down his mug. "Okay. Let's do this."

They started with the living room—lamps, the small bookshelf Grace had claimed as hers. Michael and Grace worked in strange synchronicity. He'd lift one end of something; she'd automatically grab the other.

Matthew appeared in the doorway, dressed now, and picked up a box marked *Kitchen-Misc.* He carried it out to the truck without being asked, then came back for another. Small things—pillows, a bag of kitchen towels, her jewelry box. He moved efficiently, one box after the next.

"Matt, you don't have to—" Grace started.

"I know." He grabbed another box and headed back outside.

Around 10:00, Mia came downstairs. Headphones on, oversized hoodie, leggings. She didn't look at Grace or Michael. Just walked into the kitchen, got a granola bar, stood there eating it while staring out the window.

Grace was taping a box shut. "Morning, honey."

Mia pulled one earbud out. "What?"

"I said good morning."

"Yeah." She put the earbud back in.

Michael came in from outside. "Mia, we could use some help."

Heavy sigh. "Fine."

She walked to the pile of boxes, looked them over, and picked up the smallest one she could find—a box marked *Bathroom-Towels*. Light enough that she barely had to try. She carried it outside at a pace that made the trip take twice as long as it needed to.

After an hour, Mia had made maybe a dozen trips, each time carrying something that weighed almost nothing. A bag of scarves. A box of Christmas ornaments. Grace's yoga mat.

Grace was in the hallway when Mia walked past carrying a single decorative pillow. Just one pillow. Making a whole trip for it.

"Honey, you could take a couple more—"

"I got it." She didn't even slow down.

Matthew came from the den, carrying a heavy box of books that had him slightly off-balance. He set it down with a thud. "Mom, did you know that professional movers are allowed to carry up to seventy-five pounds per box? Regular people should only do forty or fifty, tops."

"That's good to know."

"Yeah."

Mia came back in, surveyed the remaining items. She stood there for a moment, then walked into the living room. Mia picked up a small picture frame containing a photo of the four of them at the beach.

"Mia?"

Mia shoved the picture into a box without looking at Grace, picked up the carton, and carried it outside.

By noon, everything was in the truck. Michael was checking the tie-downs. Matthew stood in the driveway, hands in his pockets. Mia sat on the front steps, earbuds in, scrolling her phone.

Grace went to Matthew, laid her hands on his shoulders. "I'll see you tomorrow. We'll look at your room, and you can see how you want it set up."

"Okay." His voice was tight. "Did you know that it takes the average person six months to fully adjust to a new living space?"

"Matthew, I love you so much." She pulled him into a hug. He clung to her, face buried in her shoulder. His whole body was shaking.

"Love you, too." His voice was muffled. She held him for a long moment, then pulled back and wiped his eyes with her thumb. "Tomorrow. Okay?"

He nodded.

Grace walked over to Mia. Sat down next to her on the steps. Mia didn't pull out her earbuds, didn't acknowledge her presence.

"Mia. Honey."

Nothing.

Grace reached over and gently tugged one earbud out. Mia immediately put it back in.

"Mia, please. Just for a minute."

Mia stood, walked inside without a word, and headed upstairs. Grace heard her bedroom door close. The lock clicked.

Grace stayed on the steps, trying to calm her breath. Then she went back inside for one last check. The living room was strange now —a few shapes of missing furniture visible on the rug, rectangles of brighter paint where pictures had hung.

Michael came in. No anger in his expression. Just exhaustion and sadness. "We should go. So I can get the truck back before four."

Grace nodded and walked upstairs one more time. Stopped outside Mia's door. "I love you, Mia," she said. "Always."

No response. Just the muffled sound of music playing.

Grace waited. Then turned and walked downstairs.

Matthew was still standing in the driveway. "Bye, Mom."

"Bye, sweetheart."

～

The drive took eight minutes. Grace followed Michael's truck into a different part of town, down side streets she didn't know yet. When they pulled up in front of the rental house, it looked smaller than she remembered.

They unloaded in silence. Michael helped her set up the bed frame, arrange the couch, stack boxes in the right rooms. By 3:30, everything was inside.

Michael stood by the door, keys in his hand. "I should go."

"Thank you for all your help."

"Yeah." He looked around the house one more time. "Let me know if you need anything."

He kissed her on the cheek. Then he was gone, and Grace was alone with her boxes in her new home.

She stood in the middle of the living room, surrounded by cardboard. Then she sat down on the couch and cried.

She'd texted Allie the address two days ago—just the street and house number, no explanation, letting Allie draw her own conclusions.

At 5:30, Grace called her.

"Hi." Allie's voice was careful, guarded. "You okay?"

"I moved in." A pause. "I'm here."

Silence. Grace could hear Allie breathing.

"You're there? You're actually—" Allie's voice broke. "Grace. I didn't know if that address was just a place you were considering, or what. So you really did it?"

"I did it. I'm at the house. I'm sitting on the floor surrounded by boxes and I'm a complete mess."

"Want company?"

Grace closed her eyes. "Yes. Please."

"I'll bring dinner. Give me an hour."

When Grace opened the door, Allie was standing there with two bags of Indian food. For a moment neither of them moved.

Then Allie set the bags on the floor and pulled Grace into her arms. Grace grabbed the back of Allie's jacket and held on.

"You did it," Allie whispered. "You're here."

Grace nodded against her neck, unable to speak.

Allie pulled back and wiped Grace's face with her thumbs. Her own eyes were wet. "All right. Come on. Let's eat before this gets cold."

They sat on the couch and ate paneer tikka and chicken tandoori out of containers. Grace told her about the morning—about Matthew reciting facts to avoid feeling anything, about Mia's one-pillow protest.

Allie winced at the Mia part. "She'll come around."

"I hope so."

"You're not going anywhere." Allie set down her container. They were quiet for a moment.

Grace looked around at the boxes stacked everywhere, the bare walls, the windows facing a street she didn't know yet. "It doesn't feel like mine."

"It will." Allie reached over and took her hand.

They sat there like that, not talking, while the light faded in the windows and the house grew dark around them.

Later, at the door, Allie hesitated. She started to say something, stopped. Then: "I missed you. I need you to know that. Even when I was angry, I missed you."

Grace touched her face. "I know. Me, too."

Allie kissed her gently, then stepped back. "Call me tomorrow?"

"I will."

After Allie left, Grace made up her bed with new sheets. Then she texted Matthew: *Goodnight, sweetheart. Love you so much. See you tomorrow.*

She sent the same to Mia, then brushed her teeth in the unfamiliar bathroom, changed into pajamas, climbed into bed.

The house made different sounds. Pipes that clanged. Traffic noise from the street.

Her phone buzzed. A text from Matthew—a long one, for him. Formal: *Goodnight mom. Love you. Mia was in here when your text came. She said, See Matty? She's really not going away.*

Grace typed back: *She's right.*

Then she texted Mia: *Thanks for comforting Matty.*

She waited. Almost set the phone down. Then Mia's reply came: *He's just a kid. He needs it.*

Grace lay back in the dark.

56

———————

Saturday, April 20

Grace slid the lasagna into the oven and set the timer for forty minutes. The kitchen still felt unfamiliar—cabinets in the wrong places, oven that ran hot, tile floor that was harder and colder than the old one. But she was trying. Making the family recipe, the one her mother had taught her.

Matthew was at the dining table doing homework. She could hear the scratch of his pencil, the occasional rustle of pages. Mia was in the living room, visible through the doorway, curled in the armchair with her phone and earbuds in.

Grace wiped down the counter, loaded the few prep dishes into the dishwasher. Checked the timer.

She was pulling salad ingredients from the fridge when Matthew called from the dining room. "Mom? When's dinner?"

"About forty minutes. I'm taking the lasagna out in thirty-five, then it has to sit for five."

"Okay. Thanks."

Grace made the salad, set the table with mismatched plates and bowls she'd bought at Target. Nothing matched in this house yet.

The timer beeped. Grace pulled on the oven mitts—new ones, stiffer than her old pair, the grip not quite right. She opened the oven door. The lasagna was perfect—golden brown on top, bubbling at the edges. She lifted it out, the familiar weight settling into her hands. Turned toward the counter.

The dish slipped. She lunged to catch it, but her hands were at the wrong angle, the mitts too stiff. The casserole dish hit the tile floor and shattered. Glass and lasagna exploded across the kitchen—red sauce splattered on the cabinets, shards of Pyrex skidded across the tile.

Grace stood there, oven mitts still on, staring at the mess. Then she sank to the floor—carefully, away from the glass—pulled her knees to her chest, and started crying. Not quiet tears. Heaving sobs.

She heard footsteps. Matthew appeared in the doorway first, then Mia behind him.

"Mom?" Matthew's voice was high, scared. "Are you hurt? Did you cut yourself?"

Grace shook her head but couldn't speak.

Matthew and Mia looked at each other. Neither of them moved.

Grace wiped her face with the oven mitt, which made her cry harder.

"I'm fine. Just— let me clean this up." But she didn't move. Couldn't.

Matthew took a tentative step forward, but stopped. "Mom, you're scaring me."

"I'm okay. I'm sorry." Grace pressed her palms against her eyes. "I'm okay."

But she didn't get up. Just sat there on the floor, surrounded by broken glass and ruined dinner.

Mia grabbed the broom from the pantry and started carefully sweeping glass into a pile, away from where Grace sat. Matthew swung into action, too, grabbing a plate and spatula; he knelt down to scoop up chunks of lasagna, still glancing at Grace every few seconds.

"You don't have to—" Grace started.

"Just sit there," Mia said, not looking at her. "We got it."

They cleaned in silence. Matthew picked up glass piece by piece, checking each one before dropping it in the trash. Mia wiped sauce off the cabinet doors with efficient strokes. Grace sat against the wall.

When the worst of it was cleaned up, Mia stood with the broom in her hand, looking at the empty space where dinner should have been. "Well. That's not happening."

"That's definitely not happening," Grace agreed.

"We could order pizza?" Matthew offered quietly.

Grace nodded, wiped her face with her actual hands this time. "Yeah. Pizza. Good idea."

He ordered—pepperoni and mushroom, the usual—while Mia finished sweeping.

Grace finally pushed herself up off the floor, her back stiff, her face hot and swollen. They moved to the living room. Grace sat on the couch, Matthew in the armchair. Mia took the other end of the couch. Grace's breathing steadied.

"I'm sorry," she said. "That was— I don't know. That—"

"Are you okay?" Mia asked. Her voice was flat, hard to read.

"I'm trying to be." Grace looked at her daughter. "But this is harder than I thought it would be."

"You chose this," Mia said. "So why are you crying about it?"

Grace took a breath. "Because choosing something doesn't mean it doesn't hurt. I know I left. That doesn't mean I don't miss you two every single day."

Matthew's leg bounced—that familiar anxious tic. "You never cried like that before. At home."

"I know."

"Why not?"

Grace thought about how to answer honestly. "Because I was holding everything together. I had to be the one who had all the answers. And I got really good at not falling apart."

Mia pulled her knees up onto the couch. "You didn't even cry like that on Christmas Eve. After what Dad said about Allie."

"Oh, I did. You just didn't see me."

Silence settled around them. Grace could hear the refrigerator humming in the kitchen, a car passing outside.

Then Mia said, "When did you know about Allie?"

The question landed between them like a stone.

"When did I know what?"

"When did you know you had feelings for her? When did it start?"

Grace took a breath. "I had feelings for her for a long time. Probably a couple of years, actually. But the real shift was last spring and summer. I started noticing more things about her—the variety of her laughs, the way she talked about things she cared about. And I tried not to think about what that meant. But I knew."

"Did you ever love Dad?" Mia asked. "Like, actually love him?"

"I cared about him. Respected him. We built a life together. We had you two." Grace paused. "But the kind of love that makes you feel alive? No. I don't think I ever felt that with him."

"So our whole family was based on a lie."

"It wasn't a lie. I've told you before. It was me not knowing the truth." Grace looked at her daughter. "I didn't know I was gay, Mia. I know that sounds impossible, but I didn't."

"How could you not know?"

"Because I didn't let myself. It wasn't something I could imagine for myself, so I just— didn't."

Matthew spoke up, his voice small. "Are you happier now?"

Grace looked at her son. His face was pale, anxious. "Yes," she said. "And no."

"What does that mean?"

"I'm happier because I feel like myself in a way I never have before. But I miss you both every day." She looked around the room—the bare walls, the boxes still unpacked in the corner. "And I hate the nights I come home to this house and you're not here. That's hard."

The doorbell rang. Matthew jumped up. "Pizza."

He came back with the box and set it on the coffee table. Grace got up and came back with paper towels for napkins.

They ate in silence for a few minutes, sitting on the couch and floor, grabbing slices from the box. Mia picked at the cheese on her slice. Then, without looking up, said, "What if I end up like you?"

Grace set down her slice. "What do you mean?"

"What if I marry someone and then twenty years later I wake up and realize I was wrong? That I didn't actually know myself?" Mia's voice was tight. "What if I'm just as confused as you were?"

"Mia. You came out at fifteen. You already know yourself better than I did at forty-two."

"But what if I don't? What if I think I know and I'm wrong?"

Grace let the question sit for a moment. "Then you'll figure it out. And you'll make different choices. But you're already asking questions I spent decades avoiding. That counts for something."

Mia didn't respond. She took a bite of pizza and stared at the wall.

Matthew had been quiet, working his way through his second slice. Now he looked up. "Do you wish you'd figured this out before you had us?" His voice was barely above a whisper.

"No." Grace's response was immediate. "Matty, you and Mia are not the part I got wrong. You're the part I got right."

Matthew nodded, not looking at her. His eyes were wet.

When they finished, Matthew asked, "Can we watch a movie?"

They settled on something mindless—a Marvel movie Matthew had seen three times already. Grace sat on one end of the couch, Mia on the other, Matthew in the armchair. Halfway through, Matthew's breathing evened out—asleep, his face pressed against the wing of the chair.

"He's out," Mia said quietly.

"Yeah."

When the movie ended, Grace gently woke him. He was groggy, disoriented. "Bed for me," he murmured, and headed for the stairs.

Mia stood, too. She paused at the base of the staircase and looked back at Grace. Her hand gripped the bannister. "Thanks for not bull-shitting us tonight."

Grace nodded, not trusting her voice.

Mia turned and headed upstairs.

Grace returned to the kitchen and tidied up, scrubbing at a stain on the grout where the sauce had landed. From the refrigerator, she retrieved a half-full bottle of green tea she'd started at lunch. The whiteboard calendar on the fridge door was as relatively empty as the fridge itself.

She took the cold drink and stood on the small landing at the top of the back steps overlooking the driveway. Her gaze landed on a basketball hoop above the garage, its backboard rotting at the edges. Matthew would love that, fixed up.

57

Thursday, May 9

Grace arrived at the office early, unlocking the front door just after seven. The early-May morning was cool enough for a sweater.

The coffee maker was already gurgling when she reached the kitchen. Leo stood at the counter, spooning sugar into his mug. "Morning. I made a full pot. Figured you'd need it."

"God, yes." Grace grabbed her favorite office mug—the one Mia had given her years ago that said in gold lettering: I'M SILENTLY CORRECTING YOUR GRAMMAR.

"Quite a stormy session you had yesterday afternoon. White noise was no match," Leo said.

"That couple is so exhausting. They're meta: they fight about fighting about fighting."

Leo snorted. "Just what you need. How are things?"

"Good. Matthew's doing well—Dr. Reeves is helping. We shoot hoops in my driveway after his sessions now. It's become a thing." She sat across from him. "And Mia let me take her for ice cream one evening last week when I returned an English binder she'd left at my place. We had a nice time."

"That's real progress."

"Yeah." Grace smiled.

A commotion from down the hall—Travis's voice calling for an emergency meeting. They exchanged glances, then followed.

In Travis's office, the former closet where Sarah's locked box had once sat was now a lit bookshelf displaying his crystal collection—amethyst clusters, rose quartz, selenite wands. Small plants sat between them. A singing bowl rested on the bottom shelf.

"My cousin does custom carpentry," Travis said. "Family rate."

Leo leaned closer, squinting at a purple geode. "Is that supposed to do something?"

"It promotes calm and clarity."

Leo picked up the singing bowl. "What about this one?"

"Sound healing. The vibrations promote deep relaxation." He paused. "You can try it, just be gen—"

Leo struck it with the mallet. The sound was loud, discordant. They all winced.

"*Not* like that." Travis took it back, demonstrated—a pure, resonant tone that hung in the air.

"Okay," Claire said from the doorway. "That's actually kind of soothing."

They filtered back to their offices. Grace had fifteen minutes before her first client.

At her desk, she found yesterday's mail—mostly administrative notices. But one envelope caught her eye. Personal stationery. Her name and the office address in careful, masculine handwriting.

The return address said David Castellano.

Grace set down her coffee. Opened it.

Dear Dr. Brennan,

I've been seeing a new therapist since late February. He's been helping me understand some things about how I behaved with you.

I know I crossed boundaries. The late-night calls, the gifts, the personal questions about your life. I told myself I was just being grateful, but I can see now that I was looking for something from you that you couldn't give me. I'm still working on understanding why I did that. My therapist says it was about trying to replace what I lost when Elena died. That makes sense, I guess.

But Wilson Farm and the restaurant in Brookline? I really was just at those places. People run into each other around town. Maybe those encounters were just bad luck. It makes me sad that my presence scared you.

In any case, I handled our last session badly. I was embarrassed and I got defensive. You were trying to help me, and I made it harder. I'm sorry for making you uncomfortable. I'm sorry for not respecting your boundaries. That wasn't fair to you.

I hope you're doing well. You're a good therapist. Elena would have been glad I kept seeing you after she died, even though I didn't handle it very well.

I don't expect you to respond to this. I just wanted you to know that I understand now—or I'm starting to, anyway.

Thank you for the help you gave us both.

David Castellano

She folded the letter, slipped it back into the envelope, and filed it in her locked desk drawer. Not in David's clinical file—that was closed. Just documentation, in case she ever needed it.

She picked up her coffee and turned to her notes for the day.

That afternoon, Grace pulled into the parking lot of Dr. Reeves's office around 4:00. Through the plate glass window, she could see

Matthew in the therapist's waiting room, backpack at his feet, head down over his phone.

Soon, the door opened and Matthew emerged, but instead of his usual straight line to the car, he paused. Looked at her. Then walked over slowly, got in the passenger seat.

Grace started the engine. "How was it?"

Usually he shrugged. Or said "fine" in a tone that meant *don't ask.* But today he was quiet.

She pulled out of the parking lot, refrained from asking more. Gave him space.

After a few blocks, Matthew spoke. "Dr. Reeves asked me what I'm most afraid of."

"And what did you say?"

"I said I'm scared you won't be there when I need you. Like, I know we see each other and stuff, but I'm scared one day you just ... won't be there." He ducked his head a little.

She swerved into a CVS parking lot, put the car in park, turned to face him.

"What did Dr. Reeves say?"

"He said that's normal. That lots of kids worry about that." Matthew picked at a thread on his jeans, wrapping it around his finger until the fabric puckered. "He asked me to name one time you weren't there for me when I needed you. I couldn't think of any."

"Because I always will be," Grace said quietly.

"That's what he said." Matthew looked up at her. "He said you're still my mom. Even if we don't live together full time."

Grace looked out the windshield for a moment. Took a breath. "He's right. That's exactly right."

"But it feels different."

He swiped at his nose with his sleeve, still looking straight ahead.

"I know it does." She reached over, squeezed his shoulder. "Matthew, I moved out on your father. Not on you. You're stuck with me for life, kid. Whether you like it or not."

Matthew was quiet for a moment. Then: "He also asked if I was mad at you. I said, 'Yeah, sometimes.'" He glanced over at Grace. "He said it's okay to be mad and also be glad you're happier now. That I can feel both things."

"You can," Grace said. "You absolutely can."

Another silence. Then Matthew's mouth curved slightly. "So are we just gonna sit in this parking lot all day, or ..."

Grace smiled, put the car in gear. "Actually, I have a surprise. Want to come see it?"

"What kind of surprise?"

"The basketball kind."

His head snapped toward her. "What?"

"I had a hoop installed. At the house. A top-end one."

Matthew's eyes went wide. "Seriously?"

"Seriously. I was thinking maybe instead of me dropping you at Dad's, you could come see it. We could shoot around for a bit." She paused. "Maybe HORSE?"

"Yes! I should text Dad."

"Already cleared it with him," Grace said, merging back onto the road.

As they drove, Matthew stared out the window. His shoulders relaxed slightly.

"Mom?"

"Yeah?"

"Can we do this every Thursday? After Dr. Reeves?"

"Yeah, kiddo. We absolutely can. And whenever else you want."

At the house, Matthew dumped his backpack by the door and disappeared into his room. His dirty clothes littered the floor, just like at the other house. He spent every other weekend here, some weeknights, too—different nights each week depending on Michael's schedule. They hadn't found a rhythm yet.

He came out dressed in shorts and a t-shirt, found the basketball by the back door. Grace followed him outside. The basketball hoop stood at the end of the driveway, regulation height, professional backboard.

Matthew stopped. Just stood there looking at it. "This is really nice, Mom."

Something in his voice made her turn.

He was still staring at the hoop. "It's not the same as home." Then he dribbled the ball once, twice. "But it's still pretty cool." He took a shot. Sank it.

"First one to five baskets chooses where we order burritos?"

"You're on."

Later, after Matthew had beaten her soundly and they'd demolished most of a bag of chips and two burritos, Grace drove him back to Michael's. He got out of the car, turned back. "See you Saturday?"

"See you Saturday."

He smiled and headed inside. Grace sat in the driveway until the front door closed. Then she backed out and drove home.

58

———

Wednesday, May 15

At nine o'clock, Rachel Martinez arrived—a woman in her mid-fifties, recently divorced after thirty years of marriage. She and Grace had been working together for two months, and Rachel had spent most of that time cataloging her ex-husband's failings.

Today felt different. Rachel sat down heavily, but her face had lost some of its set, her shoulders were less hunched.

"I've been thinking about what you said last week," Rachel began. "About how I might be angry because anger is easier than grief."

Grace waited.

"And I think you're right." Rachel's eyes filled. "I'm not just sad about losing Tom. I'm sad about losing ... me. The person I was with him. Even though I didn't like that person very much."

"Tell me about her," Grace said gently. "The person you were."

"She was accommodating. Sweet. She never made waves. She wanted everyone to be happy." Rachel twisted her wedding ring, still on her finger. "She never took up space. She let him fill every room, every conversation. And she told herself that was generosity."

"And now?"

"Now I don't know who I am. I spent thirty years being Tom's wife, and now I'm just ... nobody."

"You're someone you don't know yet."

Rachel looked up.

"You're mourning her—the person you were with him. That's real grief. And it makes sense that it's terrifying, because at least you knew how to be her."

Rachel cried quietly, tissues crumpling in her hands. "So who am I now?"

"That's what you're working to figure out."

They spent the rest of the session exploring what that meant—sitting with the grief, being gentle with the transition. By the time Rachel left, something had shifted.

Grace made notes, then sat back.

The afternoon filled—a teenager with social anxiety, a couple navigating blended-family dynamics, a man whose depression had lifted just enough to see how much work he still had to do.

At five-thirty, Grace was writing her final notes when she heard Allie closing her office door upstairs. Then she was in Grace's doorway, chambray overshirt draped over one arm.

"Ready?"

Outside, the evening was warm, golden light slanting across Prospect Street.

At Oak Bistro, the hostess smiled as they walked in. "Good evening. Two?"

"Yes." Allie squeezed Grace's hand. "Two for dinner."

The hostess led them to a table with a view of the street. Grace slid in, Allie across from her. Candles flickered. They ordered a bottle of pinot noir. Grace watched Allie scan the list, the small familiar ease with which she chose.

When the server left, Allie reached across the table and took Grace's hand. "Hi," she said.

Grace smiled. "Hi."

They ordered—salmon for Grace, risotto for Allie—and settled into easy conversation. Allie told her about Emma's latest drama, something about a boy who'd asked her to the eighth-grade graduation dance and then asked someone else.

"How's she handling it?" Grace asked.

"Lots of crying. Lots of declarations that all males are dickheads." Allie smiled. "She has her end-of-year band concert next Monday. I'd invite you, but Emma's still working through things about us."

Grace nodded, understanding. "No rush."

"I think Noah likes some girl, but he won't talk about it."

"Of course he won't."

Their food arrived. They ate slowly, talking between bites.

"So," Allie said. "I've been thinking about this summer. I'm taking the kids to the Cape for a week in mid-July. Would you want to come for a long weekend? Friday through Monday?"

"I'd love that. The kids will be with Michael the middle two weeks of July."

"Good. Because Noah wants to teach you to surf."

"I'm almost forty-three."

"Apparently that's not too old." Allie set down her fork. "Also. More pressing question."

"What?"

"Can I please buy you a new duvet?"

Grace laughed. "What's wrong with my duvet?"

"It's like sleeping under a furnace. I wake up drenched. Every time. I love spending the night with you, but I'm suffering."

"Fine. You can buy me a new duvet."

"Thank you. Light cotton. Breathable." Allie grinned. "You have no idea how happy this makes me."

Grace's phone buzzed. She glanced at it—Matthew asking about shooting hoops with her tomorrow—typed a quick response, and set it face-down on the table.

"One more thing," Allie said. "When are we going to have me meet your mother?"

Grace set down her wine. "Margaret Brennan is nowhere close to ready. Trying to introduce the two of you right now would end badly for everyone."

"That bad?"

"She still thinks this is a phase. My brother's working on her, too. But—not yet."

"Fair enough."

The server brought the check. Allie reached for it. "My turn."

They walked out into the spring evening, the air cool and dry. Grace slipped her arm around Allie's waist. Allie's arm settled around her shoulders.

They reached the car but didn't get in yet. Allie turned to face Grace, kissed her—deep and warm and unhurried.

When they pulled apart, Allie said, "I want you. Take me to your bed. But no fucking duvet."

59

Wednesday, May 22

At three o'clock, Grace's last client of the day arrived.

"Hi, Dr. Brennan," Jessica Caldwell said as she settled into her usual chair, dropping her backpack beside it. She sat differently than she used to—legs crossed, shoulders open, none of the careful self-containment from those early sessions.

"Sorry I haven't been in for a while. Things have been really good, actually."

"That's wonderful. Tell me about it."

Jessica smiled. "Cathryn and I are still together. Seven months now. We're actually out as a couple. My parents know. It's just normal now."

"How does that feel?"

"Weird. Good weird." She laughed. "I keep waiting for something bad to happen. Like I'm going to wake up and it's all going to fall apart. But it hasn't. She's just there. Every day. We study together, we go to her little sister's soccer games, we watch terrible reality TV. It's so normal it's almost boring."

"Boring sounds nice."

"It's amazing." Jessica's face lit up. "I never thought I could just be this. Be gay and still go to Sunday dinner at my parents'. I thought I had to choose."

Grace smiled. "How are your parents doing with it?"

"Better than I expected. My mom's still a little weird. She doesn't ask about Cathryn the way she used to ask about Nick. But she's trying. She invited Cathryn and me to go out to the Berkshires with them over Memorial Day." Jessica shook her head, amazed. "A year ago I'd never have been able to imagine that."

"What changed?"

"I did, I think. I stopped waiting for everyone to say it was okay." She met Grace's eyes. "You helped with that. A lot."

"You did the work, Jessica."

"Yeah, but you—" Jessica paused. "You were the first person who didn't try to talk me out of it. Who didn't say 'are you sure?' or 'maybe you're just confused.' You just let me figure it out."

At the end of the session, Jessica stood and shouldered her backpack.

"I don't think I need to keep coming," she said. "I mean, if something comes up, I'll make an appointment. But I think I'm okay now."

"I think you are, too."

Jessica paused at the door. "Thank you, Dr. Brennan. For everything."

After she left, Grace sat in her office for a moment, looking at the empty chair.

She picked up her pen and made a final note in Jessica's file: *Client terminating. Doing well. Prognosis excellent.*

Then she closed the file and gathered her things.

~

The key stuck in the lock. Grace jiggled it—left, then right—and the door opened. She dropped her keys in the bowl by the door, a Mother's Day gift from Matthew. Ceramic, slightly lopsided, painted blue.

Books on the shelves, photos on the walls, Matthew's drawings held to the fridge with magnets. Half the coffee mugs in the cabinet were Allie's, left behind after overnight visits.

Grace was rinsing lettuce when the doorbell rang. She wasn't expecting anyone.

Mia stood on the porch, backpack over one shoulder.

Grace opened the door. "Hi, honey. Everything okay?"

"Yeah. I just—" Mia shifted her weight. "Can I come in?"

"Of course." Grace stepped back. "You know you never have to ask to come in."

Mia dropped her backpack by the door and followed Grace into the kitchen. She hopped up onto the counter and watched Grace work.

"I'm making a salad," Grace said. "You hungry?"

"Not really." Mia swung her legs. "I wanted to say thanks. For last night."

Grace looked up. "Last night?"

"You came. The concert. I hadn't told you about it."

"Well, I know you're in the Chorale. And I know how to read a school calendar."

"You didn't have to come."

"I wanted to."

Mia nodded, dropping her sandals to the floor.

"You sounded incredible, by the way," Grace said. "That solo in the third piece."

Mia's cheeks flushed. "Thanks."

"I would've come up to say hi after. But you looked busy." Grace paused. "Who was the girl?"

"Her name's Kylie. She's— we've been hanging out for a couple months."

Grace shook water off the lettuce, turned to face her daughter. "Tell me about her."

"She's a junior. She plays soccer." A pause. Then, almost reluctantly, more came: "She's really funny. Like, genuinely funny, not trying-too-hard funny. She makes me laugh even when I'm being a total bitch."

"Does Dad know about her?"

"Not yet." Mia looked down. "I wanted to tell you first."

Grace smiled. "I'm glad you did."

They were quiet for a moment. Grace went back to the salad, giving Mia space.

Then Mia said, "I've been talking to Dr. Wilkins about some stuff. About me. Coming out. Figuring out who I am."

Grace set down the colander, moved to her. "I'm glad."

"Don't make it a big thing." But Mia's voice was bright.

"I'm not. But it's good you have someone to talk with about it."

"Yeah. It is." Then Mia asked, "How's Allie?"

Grace's eyes widened. "She's good. Busy with clients and her kids."

"Why haven't we seen her?"

Grace chose her words carefully. "I didn't want you to feel like I was pushing her on you guys. I know this has all been ... a lot."

Mia studied her mother's face. "I liked Allie. But then I was really mad at her. And at you." She paused. Her finger traced the outline of a counter tile. "But I get it now. Dad outing you to us before you were ready—that wasn't okay. And then I made it worse by being such an asshole about it."

"You weren't. You were a girl whose world got turned upside down."

"I was kind of an asshole."

"Okay, maybe a little bit of an asshole." Grace smiled.

Mia laughed—an actual guffaw.

"I'm still mad sometimes," Mia said. "You know that, right?"

"I know."

"But I also get why you had to leave Dad. I've gotten it for a while. I just didn't want to say it."

They talked for another twenty minutes. About Kylie, about school, about Matthew.

Grace glanced at the clock. "It's getting late. You want to stay for dinner? Or I can run you to Dad's."

Mia slid off the counter. "Actually, would you mind running me over to Kylie's?"

"I'd be happy to."

In the car, Mia fiddled with the radio, landing on a station playing something with too much bass.

"Mom?"

"Yeah?"

"Maybe Allie could come to dinner sometime soon when Matt and I are with you?"

"I'd like that."

"Don't make it weird, though."

"I'll try."

They pulled up in front of a tidy craftsman with a porch light already glowing. A girl in a varsity sweatshirt stood on the porch, shifting from foot to foot. Dark hair in a ponytail.

"That's Kylie," Mia said, already unbuckling her seatbelt.

"She's pretty."

"Mom."

"What? She is." Grace paused. "You want me to meet her?"

Mia considered this. "Not tonight. But maybe ... next time?"

"I'd like that."

Mia grabbed her backpack, then paused, her hand on the door handle. "Thanks again for coming last night."

"I wouldn't have missed it."

Mia got out of the car. Halfway up the walk, she turned back and waved. Grace waved back, watching as the two girls disappeared inside.

Even before she pulled away, Grace's phone buzzed. She assumed it was a text from Allie and was surprised to see Mia' name instead: *Kylie wants to meet you. Doesn't know any old gay women. She thinks it's cool.*

Grace laughed and typed: *Well, I'm definitely old. And gay. Guess I qualify.*

Another buzz: *You and Allie want to come to our soccer game Saturday? We play at 2. Maybe we could get pizza after.*

Grace stared at the screen. Then replied: *We'd love to. Both of us.*

Three dots appeared, then: *Love you*

She smiled and typed back: *Love you too, Mia.*

She pulled out onto the street and headed home.

EPILOGUE

A year later —
       Saturday, June 7, 2025

Grace flipped a burger on her grill, watching fat sizzle and smoke rise into the late-afternoon air.

"Mom, can I have a Coke?" Matthew called from the driveway where he and Allie were shooting hoops.

"One," Grace called back. "So, decide if you want it now or with your burger. And drink some water first."

"That's what Dad always says."

"That's because your father and I occasionally agree on things."

Allie caught the ball, grinning at Matt. "She's a tyrant. I'd sneak you two Cokes if she wasn't watching."

"I heard that," Grace said.

"I know. I said it loud so you'd hear." Allie took a shot. It bounced off the rim. Matthew grabbed the rebound and sank it easily.

"Show-off." Allie said, ruffling his hair. "You've got the stuff, kid."

"If you got a hoop at your house, you might be a contender," he said.

"You wouldn't like it if I got better. I'd wipe the floor with you."

At the picnic table, Mia and Kylie sat close together, Kylie's hand resting on Mia's knee. Kylie was talking—animated, her free hand gesturing—about the admitted students' weekend at Brown coming up in two weeks.

"They have this whole LGBTQ resource center," Kylie said. "Like, an actual building. With a library and meeting spaces and everything."

"That's amazing," Mia said, but there was something careful in her voice.

Grace caught it. She met Mia's eyes. Mia looked away.

"Emma, can you grab the cheese from the kitchen?" Grace asked. "Top shelf of the fridge."

Emma didn't look up from her phone. "I'm in the middle of something."

"It'll take thirty seconds."

"Ask Noah."

"I'm asking you."

Emma's eyes lifted from her screen. "You're not my parent."

Grace's hand tightened on the spatula. Emma was right—she wasn't.

From the corner of her eye, she saw Allie's head turn. Their eyes met across the yard, Allie's filled with exasperation. Grace gave a tiny nod.

"I'll get it," Noah said, unfolding from his chair. He kicked Emma's foot as he passed. "Don't be a dick."

"I'm not being a dick. I'm stating a fact."

"You're being a dick."

Grace focused on the burgers. Breathed.

Noah returned with the cheese, set it on the table, then came over to the grill. In a low voice, he said, "It's not about you. She's just pissed."

Grace looked at him. Allie's eyes. Tall for twelve.

"Boyfriend drama?" Grace asked.

Noah smirked. "Probably. Or she's mad at our dad for bailing on us this weekend. Who knows? She's always mad at something."

"Thanks for telling me that."

He shrugged. "She'll apologize later. She usually does."

He grabbed a Coke from the cooler and headed back to his chair.

Grace heard a car door slam and looked up to see Michael walking toward the gathering, holding Matthew's Nintendo Switch.

Matthew's face lit up when he saw him. "Dad! You brought it."

"Wouldn't want you to suffer," Michael said, handing it over.

Allie walked over to him, wiping her hands on her jeans. Michael extended his hand for a shake, but Allie kissed him on the cheek instead. "Good to see you."

Grace watched Michael's spine stiffen. He smiled anyway.

"You too," he said.

"You want a burger and a beer?" Grace asked.

"No, I should—" He glanced at Mia and Matthew. "Actually, yeah. If that's okay."

"Of course it's okay."

She got him a plate. He stood awkwardly by the grill, beer in hand, making small talk about the weather, NBA playoffs. After half an hour, burger eaten, he set down his plate, touched Grace on the shoulder. "I should head out. Thanks for this."

"Anytime."

He hugged the kids, nodded to Allie, and left.

Allie came up beside her again. "That was big of him."

"Yeah."

"You okay?"

"Yeah."

They ate at the picnic table as the light turned golden. The conversation wandered—summer plans, Matthew's basketball camp, Kylie's college prep, whether Noah would ever clean his room. Normal things.

After dinner, Mia and Kylie volunteered to clean up. Emma helped without being asked. Allie challenged Matthew to another game of HORSE.

Grace stood by the grill, watching. The yard was a mess—lawn chairs scattered, paper plates on the table, the cooler tipped on its side. Her house. Her mess. Her people.

Allie came up behind her, slid an arm around her waist. Grace leaned back into her. She turned her head and kissed Allie over her shoulder—gentle, easy.

"You still coming to Connecticut with me tomorrow to see my mom?"

"Think she'll still be frosty?"

"Probably, but I told her to behave." Grace grinned.

"Then maybe," Allie said. After a moment, she glanced up. "Can we stop for pizza at that place in Mystic?"

"Absolutely."

Grace picked up a paper plate and started cleaning up. Behind her, she heard Mia and Kylie talking in the kitchen, and from the driveway, some comment from Noah that made Matthew laugh—a real, full laugh.

Allie's hand found Grace's hip as she passed, headed to join the boys.

Note from the Author

If you enjoyed this book and have a few moments to spare, please consider leaving a brief, honest rating or review on Amazon, Goodreads, or your favorite retailer. It's one of the most powerful ways to help connect this story with more readers.

ACKNOWLEDGMENTS

Writing outside your own experience is an act of borrowing. Grace's story isn't mine to know from the inside. Leaving a marriage, rebuilding a life at forty, having a lesbian relationship—I could imagine these things, but the texture of Grace's experience required perspectives beyond my own.

This novel required that I depend on the generosity of women—some straight, others gay; some therapists themselves—who read drafts and showed me what I'd gotten right, where I'd gotten it wrong. Some of their journeys were almost identical to Grace's. Their willingness to share that with me is something I won't forget.

Wendy Cassens read an early draft and gave me valuable feedback that helped shape the story's architecture.

Maryanne Fuhrmann and Robin Willis provided sensitive, nuanced comments and affirmed that I was on the right track. Thanks also to Karen Egbert, Evelyne Fallows, and Maddie Gioia for their readings and feedback.

Dora Garcia, Kathleen Smith, Marilyn Carroll Wilson, and Claudia Woods were especially generous with their time and attention, engaging with me through multiple revisions of different sections.

Many thanks to Marnye Young and Denise Black—the women behind Audio Sorceress— who guided the audiobook through production with care and professionalism. Their even greater contribution was finding Katie Hagaman, whose narration brings Grace to life with the intimacy and emotional depth I'd hoped for.

My greatest debt is to Sue Tierney, whose multiple readings were close and honest, and who indulged me in conversation about this story and its characters more than any spouse should reasonably have to endure. Thank you.

ABOUT THE AUTHOR

J.T. Tierney writes character-driven fiction about resilient, sharp-witted women navigating the messy, often painful choices that come with starting over after life upends their plans. His fourth novel, *Perfect Plans,* received the 2025 Reedsy Discovery Editor's Choice Award. He lives outside Chicago with his wife and Great Pyrenees, and is hard at work on his next book

9 798999 230652